BARRACUDA

ALSO BY CHRISTOS TSIOLKAS

The Slap

Dead Europe

The Jesus Man

Jump Cuts: An Autobiography
(written with Sasha Soldatow)

Loaded

BARRACUDA

A NOVEL

CHRISTOS TSIOLKAS

LONDON / NEW YORK

Copyright © 2013 by Christos Tsiolkas

All rights reserved.
Published in the United States by Hogarth,
an imprint of the Crown Publishing Group,
a division of Random House LLC,
a Penguin Random House Company, New York.
www.crownpublishing.com

HOGARTH is a trademark of the Random House Group Limited,
and the H colophon is a trademark of Random House LLC.

Originally published in Australia by Allen & Unwin in 2013 and
subsequently published in Great Britain by Tuskar Rock Press,
an imprint of Atlantic Books Ltd., in 2014.

Permission credits can be found on page 435.

Library of Congress Cataloging-in-Publication Data
Tsiolkas, Christos, 1965–
    Barracuda : a novel / Christos Tsiolkas.—First edition.
        pages cm
    1. Swimmers—Fiction. 2. Social Classes—Australia—
Fiction. I. Title.
    PR9619.3.T786B38   2014
    823'.914—dc23   2014005692

ISBN 978-0-8041-3842-0
eBook ISBN 978-0-8041-3843-7

Printed in the United States of America

Jacket design by Elena Giavaldi
Jacket photograph: 4x6/iStock

10 9 8 7 6 5 4 3 2 1

First United States Edition

FOR ANGELA SAVAGE

And now tell it to me
in other words,
says the stuffed owl
to the fly
which, with a buzz,
is trying with its head
to break through the window-pane.

—*The Best Room,* or *Interpretation of a Poem,*
Miroslav Holub

PART ONE

BREATHING IN

When the rain first spills from those egg-white foams of cloud that seem too delicate to have burst forth in such a deluge, I freeze. The heavy drops fizz on the dry grass as they hit; I think this is what a pit of snakes would sound like. And suddenly the rain is falling in sheets, though the sky is still blue, the sun still shining. The Glaswegians on the pebbled shore are yelling and screaming, rushing out of the water, huddling under the trees, running back to their cars. Except for the chubby young man with the St. Andrews tattoo on his bicep, crisscrossed white lines on blue; he is standing in the water up to his knees, grinning, his arms outstretched, welcoming the rain, daring it.

And just as suddenly the rain has stopped and they all slink back to the beach. Two young boys race past me and throw themselves into the lake. A teenage girl throws away the magazine she has been sheltering beneath, takes out a compact and starts to powder her cheeks and nose, to reapply color to her lips till they are the pink of fairy floss. Someone has turned the music back on and the words *when love takes over* roar through the valley. A pale skinny youth with broken teeth and a mop of greasy black hair dives past me; sheets of crystal-clear water splash all over the wading tattooed guy, who grabs his friend, holds him from behind in a bear hug, and ducks him under. He sits on him, laughing. A woman shouts from the shore, "Get off him, Colm, get off him!"

The chubby guy stands up, grinning, and the thin boy scrambles to his feet, coughing water.

The girls and the women are all in bikinis, the boys and the men are all in shorts, and bare-chested or in singlets. Except me: I have jeans on and two layers on top, a T-shirt and an old yellowing shirt. The sun feels weak to me; it can't get any stronger than pleasant, it can't build to fire, it can't manage force.

~~~

"Dan, I can't go back there. I can't. Everything is too far away."

Clyde's words have been going around and around in my head all day. *Too far away.*

In the restaurant the night before, we were eavesdropping on a nearby table: a group of friends—three couples, one Scottish, one English, one German. They were in their late fifties, the men all with beards and bellies, the two British women with newly acquired bobs, the German woman with her gray hair pulled back in a long, untidy ponytail. She had looked up when we first started arguing, when I first raised my voice.

"And I can't live here."

"Why?"

"Because this, for me, is too far away."

We glared at each other across the table. One of us had to submit. One of us had to win. The young waiter arrived with our mains and we attacked them in viscous silence.

The group seemed to be old university friends, their lively conversation and loud laughter an invasion. The sauce on my steak was all salt and thick melted butter. I tore into it, was the first to finish. I pushed back the plate and headed off to the loos. Behind me I could hear the argument from their table. It seemed they got together every two years, in a different city. The German woman was pushing for it to be Barcelona next time, the Scottish man thought it should be Copenhagen, and the English man wanted it to be in London.

When I returned we were both stiff with one another, miming politeness.

"They took a vote, it's a tie between Barcelona and Copenhagen."

"Really? Even the English guy voted against London?"

"Aye, even he realized what a fucken stupid idea that was."

That made us laugh, the lovers' shared complicit laugh, a peace flag. I looked across and the German woman tilted her shoulders, smiling at me and feigning exasperation.

"Barcelona," I called to them, "I'd make it Barcelona—the food will be better."

The Englishman patted his big belly. "We don't need more good food. We've had enough!"

We were all laughing then.

Clyde leaned in to me. "We couldn't do that if we went back to Australia."

I didn't answer. It was true, and my silence confirmed it.

"It's too far away, Dan, I cannot go back."

It was true. I had lost.

And then the words came from deep within me, were said without my forcing them, they just came like curses. I whispered them: "And, mate, I can't stay here."

That night, in bed, he told me he didn't want my skin next to his, that he couldn't bear my touch, and I obediently moved to the edge of the bed. But soon I felt him moving closer, and then his arms wrapped over mine, binding me to him. All night he held me, and all night he couldn't stop his crying.

〜〜〜

The chubby guy's neck and shoulders and face are sunburned. All the Glaswegians, sunbathing, paddling, strolling, kissing, eating, drinking on the shores of Loch Lomond, all of them have pink shoulders and pink faces and pink necks and arms. There is one Indian family eating Tesco sandwiches on the shore, and one black girl I noticed back in the village, she was with her red-haired boyfriend looking into the windows of the Scots R'Us shop or whatever the fuck it is called. And then there is me. Even with this piss-weak sun, I have gone brown. If I stay here, will my coloring eventually fade away from me? Will I go pale, will I too turn pink in the sun?

The chubby guy is still only in water up to his knees. His mates dive in, they put their heads under, they splash and they play and they float. But they don't swim. None of these people swims. No one ventures farther than a few meters from the shore. But there is nothing to fear here, no sharks, no stingers, no rips, no dumping waves that can strike you down like a titan's fist. There is nothing to fear in this water at all. Except the cold. There's always the cold.

I am at the shoreline. The waves can't muster any energy, the waves lap gently across pebble and stone. They push at my sneakers, they kiss the hem of my jeans.

I am taking off my shoes and I am taking off my socks.

Real water punishes you, real water you have to work at to possess, to tame. Real water can kill you.

And I am taking off my shirt, I am taking off my T-shirt.

Men and women *have* died in this loch, men and women *have* frozen in the water, men and women *have* been claimed by this loch. Water can kill you and water can be treacherous. Water can deceive you.

I feel a twitch in my shoulder, I can sense that the muscles there are stirring.

And I unbuckle my belt, I take off my trousers.

The chubby guy is looking at me, puzzled, his expression turning into a grimace. He is thinking, Who is this bawbag, this pervert, stripped to his Y-fronts on the shore? A girl behind me is starting to titter.

I am walking into the water, to my thighs, to my crotch, to my belly. It is cold cold cold and I think my legs will snap with the pain of it. I dive. Breath is stolen from me.

Muscles that haven't moved in years, muscles that have been in abeyance, they are singing now.

And I am swimming.

I can't hear them back on land but I know what they're shouting. *What are ya doin', what are ya doin', ya mad bastard?*

I am in water. It is bending for me, shifting for me. It is welcoming me.

I am swimming.

I belong *here*.

The first piece of advice the Coach ever gave Danny was not about swimming: not about his strokes, not about his breathing, not about how he could improve his dive or his turns. All of that would come later. He would never forget that first piece of advice.

The squad had just finished training and Danny was standing shivering off to one side. The other guys all knew each other; they had been destined to be friends from the time they were embryos in their mothers' wombs, when their fathers had entered their names on the list to attend Cunts College. Danny kept repeating the words over and over in his head: *Cunts College Cunts College Cunts College.* The nickname he and Demet had invented when he first told her he had to change schools. *"Have to* or *want to?"* He'd had to turn away as he answered, "It'll make me a better swimmer." "They'll all be rich," she countered. "You know that, don't you, only the filthy rich go to Cunts College?" But she left it at that. She wasn't going to argue with him, not about the swimming; she knew what the swimming meant to him.

Danny glanced at the other boys. They had hardly said a word to him all morning, just offered grunts, barely nodded to him. It had been like this all week. He felt both invisible and that there was nowhere for him to hide. Only in the water did he feel like himself. Only in the water did he feel that he could escape them.

Taylor, the one they all followed, made toward the change rooms and as he passed Danny, he said in a loud effeminate lisp, "Dino, I like your bathers, mate, they're real cool."

The others cracked up, turning around to look at him, to look down at his loose synthetic bathers, cackling like a pack of cartoon hyenas. They were all wearing shiny new Speedos, the brand name marked in yellow across their arses. Danny's swimmers were from Forges—there was no way his mum was going to spend half a day's pay on a piece of Lycra. And good on her. Good on her, but he still felt like shit. The boys continued sniggering as they passed by him, all following after that pompous dickhead Taylor. Scooter, who was the oldest, the one with the palest skin but the darkest hair, Scooter bumped him. Just a touch, just enough of a nudge so it could seem like an accident. "Sorry," Scooter said abruptly, and then laughed. That set them all off again. The same stupid cackling. Danny knew it was no accident. He stood there, not moving, nothing showing on his face. But inside, inside he was coiled, inside he was boiling.

"Eh, Scooter, you've got nothing to laugh about, mate. You weren't swimming today—that was fucking paddling."

That silenced them. The Coach was the only one who could get away with swearing at them. Even Principal Canning pretended not to hear when Frank Torma let fly with his curses and insults. The school needed Coach Torma. He was one of the best swim coaches in the state, had coached Cunts College to first in every school sports meet of the last seven years. That was power. They immediately shut up and continued to the showers. Danny went to follow them.

"Kelly, you stay behind. I want to talk to you."

The Coach was silent until the other boys had disappeared into the change rooms. He looked Danny in the eyes for the first time. "Why do you take it?"

"What?"

"Why do you take their shit?"

You could hear his accent in the way he pronounced the word, "chit."

Danny shrugged. "Dunno."

"Son, always answer back when you receive an insult. Do it straightaway. Even if there's a chance there was nothing behind it, take back control, answer them back. An insult is an attack. You must counter it. You understand?"

One side of Danny's mouth started to twitch. He thought the Coach must be joking; he sounded like Demet's mother or Sava's *giagia,* as if an insult were the "evil eye," as if he needed to wear a *nazar boncuğu* to ward against it. Danny's jaw slackened, his head slumped back. He was not even aware of it, he had just assumed the pose; that was how you reacted to instruction back at his old school, the real school: you just looked bored when an adult was giving you a lecture.

But Frank Torma's expression remained serious and Danny realized this wasn't a joke.

"Listen, you stupid boy, if there is no spite, no hate or jealousy in what they say, then it does not matter. Nothing is lost." The Coach patted his enormous stomach, the huge gut hard and round like a basketball straining his T-shirt. He was pointing to something beyond his gut, something inside, but Danny didn't know what that could be. "Trust your instincts, son, don't let them poison you. You have to protect yourself." He pointed toward the change rooms. "They're all jealous of you."

"That's bullshit."

For a moment Danny thought the man was going to hit him: the Coach's right hand danced, spun, jerked in the air. Instead his fat finger drilled hard into Danny's chest. "Listen to me, they're jealous of you—of course they are. You have the potential to be the best in the squad. The others can sense it." The Coach's finger was now pushing harder. "They're going to want to get under your skin, and they're right to. You are not friends, you are competitors."

It hurt where the Coach's finger was stabbing Danny's chest. But he didn't care about the pain at all. He was the best, he was the best in the squad. Better than that dropkick Scooter, that chickenshit Morello, that poofter Fraser, that spineless rabbit Wilkinson, that up-himself spoiled-rich-kid Taylor. He was better than all of them. Stronger, faster, better. Strongest, fastest, best.

The Coach followed him into the showers. Danny was relieved; the boys wouldn't have a go at him with Frank Torma there. The others were still showering, making lame jokes about soap and Wilkinson. The silly faggot was taking it all, giving nothing back to them. The Coach was right, Danny realized. You had to give it back. Hurt them before they hurt you.

Torma sat on the bench as Danny slipped off his swimmers and got under the shower. He turned on the hot tap but the first blast of water was freezing. Only when the steam began to rise did he loosen the cold tap. He soaped himself all over, scrubbing vigorously, almost violently, using the friction to warm himself up.

"Having a wank, Dino?" It was Taylor, his tone full of pretend disgust. The rest of the morons brayed again.

Danny looked over his shoulder to the Coach, who was silent, sitting on the bench, looking straight at him. *Always answer back.* He understood now what the man meant. *Take control, always take control.*

Danny turned to the boys, his feet planted apart, hands by his sides: let them look at him. The water falling on him, drilling his back and shoulders, made him feel powerful. "Yeah, Taylor," he said, tugging at his foreskin. "Why ya asking? Did ya want me to come in your mouth?"

He could tell he had struck Taylor; the boy's eyes were immediately averted, he was floundering hopelessly for a comeback. Then Morello laughed. And Frank Torma was grinning, his eyes aglint.

"What are you laughing at?"

Morello shut up instantly at Taylor's words. Danny turned his back on them again but he had a grin on his face as big as the pool, the school, the universe. He was better than all of them. He was the best. He was the strongest.

～～～

What am I doing here?

The Monday of that week had been Valentine's Day, his first day at Cunts College. His mother had taken a day off work and driven him all the way to the school gates. She'd also arranged to pick him up after practice at the new pool. "Only today," she'd warned him. "From tomorrow you catch the bus and the train."

They drove for what seemed like hours, down the spine of the city then across to the east, stuck in gridlocked traffic, inching ever closer, everything getting greener as they went, the houses getting bigger and farther apart. He was sulking all the way, his face pressed against the car window. He didn't want to go to a new school. *It'll make you a better swimmer.* He didn't want to change to a new pool. *It'll make you a better swimmer.* He didn't want a new coach. *It'll make you a better swimmer.* His mother stopped outside the gate that didn't look like it belonged to a school, that should have belonged to a mansion from the movies, a mansion with a thousand rooms and with butlers and maids and ghosts. The walls were solid bluestone, the ironwork of the gate was black and shiny, the school emblem set on a plaque over the bars and covered in gold leaf: a lion rampant with a crown on its head, its paws resting on a crucifix; there was a burning torch and Latin words. Beyond the gate, the drive wound to a massive gray-stone building with two wings and a huge dome. It looked more like a temple, thought Danny, than a school building. Behind it the grounds stretched out endlessly, with no visible fence, no shops or warehouses or homes to be seen.

And then there were the boys. The boys in single file, the boys in pairs, the boys in threes and fours and fives, in the lavender-and-yellow striped jackets and the charcoal, thick long pants that Danny had put on with great discomfort that morning, the striped tie that he didn't know how to knot, that his father had tried to knot for him last night, but hadn't been able to, had kept knotting and unknotting, knotting and unknotting till he was cursing the school for taking his son, cursing the scholarship for making it possible, cursing his wife for wanting Danny to go there, cursing the tie, fucking bloody shit of a tie, and all the time Danny was thinking, He is cursing *me*, he is cursing my swimming. The knot in the tie was now pushing into his Adam's apple, it was the flat of a knife pushing against his throat. The crisp white shirt his mum said he had to wear, that had made his dad curse even more. "Why new shirts, what was wrong with his old shirts, what the fuck's all this shit costing us?" "Nothing!" his mother threw back, raising her voice, the danger there, and Danny had seen his father waver. "It costs us nothing, the boy's on a scholarship," to which his dad had replied, his own voice now lowered: "I still don't see why it all has to be new. I don't know why his old school pants and shirts aren't good enough."

Danny's mother retorted something under her breath, in a tone that indicated the subject was closed. She hadn't wanted Danny to hear it. But he had. "I don't want him to be embarrassed, I don't want him to think he doesn't belong there."

The gold leaf of the lion's crown and the crucifix and the burning flame. Cunts College. It's my first day at Cunts College, thought Danny.

His mother pushed him out of the car and he was trying to hide in the folds of the jacket which seemed heavy on his shoulders and the thick fabric of the trousers was chafing the skin between his thighs and behind his knees. He thought he must stink of chlorine, and that he must be walking like a retard, he was walking slowly up the drive that seemed too long and too wide, too grand for a school, all that bluestone and gravel, all those statues and granite steps, the buildings reeking of the centuries, not looking like a school, no portables, no concrete sheeting, looking more like a cathedral, a cathedral where the Pope would live. Danny walked up one two three four five six seven steps, following the stream of boys through an arch and into an entrance hall as big as a house, taller than a house, lined with stained-glass windows that towered above him, smooth cream walls from which portraits of old men stared down at him, all mustaches and bald pates.

Boys were pushing past him and around him and in front of him and behind him, and they had the clearest skin he had ever seen and the best cut hair and the whitest and most perfect teeth. He felt dirty and ugly and he was conscious of the pimples on his brow, the chain of them on his chin, the ugly red welt of them along his neck. The boys were all shouting to one another, they all knew each other but no one knew him and he was pushed, pummeled, carried through another entrance of granite and bluestone and he was now on a clean cobblestone path that wound through an expanse of immaculately mowed lawn, perfectly level, perfectly green, not a trace of dry yellow in the grass. A gardener was working in a patch of gold and lavender flowers. The boys rushed past, ignoring him, but Danny halted, watching his wrinkled face and sunken cheeks, and Danny smiled. The man didn't return the smile; instead he looked down at the flowers and kept weeding around them. It was then that Danny realized that the flowers were the colors of the school uniform, that even the flowers here had an order. And it *was* beautiful and overwhelming because he had never before seen such turrets nor imagined such opulence and he wondered again where the squat ugly portables were, the ones that were furnace-hot in summer, wondered where the dry piss-yellow ovals were, where the graffiti was. And then a bell rang, not a siren, not a drill in your ear but a real bell, like a church bell, and the boys all suddenly disappeared and it was just Danny there and the gardener who wouldn't look at him, who only looked down at the ground, at the yellow and purple flowers the color of the school uniform and the school crest. The flowers that none of the boys noticed.

And in that moment, Danny thought of how much the girls at his school—his old school, the real school, with the shitty portables, the ear-ripping electronic bell, the tags and graffiti on the ugly stretcher-brick walls—how much the girls would love to walk past a garden filled with such lovely flowers. But of course there were no girls here, no girls were allowed at this school.

That thought was terrifying. That thought made him want to run away.

It'll make you a better swimmer.

That's when he heard: "Hey, you, what are you doing here?"

The first words anyone said to him at Cunts College: What are you doing here?

It wasn't a teacher who was asking the question. It was an older boy, flaxen-haired, clear-skinned except for a dark birthmark the size of a thumbprint on his left cheek. He marched across the yard to Danny.

"What house are you in?"

House? Danny stood there, confused, trying to decipher the question. He wasn't going to live here; there was no way he was going to stay in these grounds a minute longer than he needed to. He knew that boys boarded here, slept here. He wasn't one of them, he would never be one of them.

"You're new, aren't you?"

Danny could answer that. "Yes."

"Name!"

"Danny."

"Surname!"

"Kelly."

"Right, Kelly, I'm Cosgrave. I'm a prefect."

Cosgrave seemed to think this should mean something to Danny. He wasn't sure what it could mean. It meant that somehow this older youth was in charge, that somehow this older youth was perfect. Perfect golden hair, perfect clear skin.

Cosgrave sighed impatiently and pointed across the lawn to steps leading to the main building. "March."

Danny was conscious of Cosgrave in step behind him. He felt like he was in a war movie, that he was a new recruit. He was Private Daniel Kelly, Blue House.

All that first day it was as if he was slipping away from himself and becoming the uniform. He didn't know how to sit still behind the solid, freshly varnished wooden desks in the classroom, he didn't know what to do, what to say, when to look up, when to speak, when not to speak. He didn't trust himself in the large airy classrooms filled with equipment that all seemed to be new, books that seemed to have been opened for the first time, teachers who assumed they would be listened to and not interrupted. And it all smelled different: full of air, full of light, but also of locker rooms—the nitrous nutty smell of boys, mixed with the fetid whiff of sweat and the acrid stink of deodorant. There was no scent of perfume, of hand cream, none of the sweetness and floral odors of girls. There was no sign of girls anywhere in this world.

With his tie so tight, the flat of a knife pressed against his throat so he couldn't breathe freely in those large and airy rooms, Danny was vanishing and all that was left behind was a uniform, an outline to be colored in. He was becoming Kelly.

Kelly, are you following this?

Kelly, are you familiar with this?

Kelly, pay attention!

The day crawled slowly forward, the flat of a knife against his throat, and he feared he was to be trapped in that day forever, that it would be repeated endlessly and there would be no chance of ever finding the real Danny again. He wanted to be back with his old friends, to be with Boz and Shelley and Mia and Yianni and especially Demet; he ached for the chipped desks and mission-brown plastic seats of his old school. He missed the girls gossiping, the boys flicking paper pellets; he missed the noise, the jokes, the insults, the teasing. The day crept. He had disappeared into the day. He had vanished.

"Kelly!"

His name had been called, it had been repeated. He struggled to recognize it. A fat man was at the classroom door, pointing to him, a man in gray track pants, a white shirt too small for his bulging belly, his brick-like chest. All the boys had turned around and were looking at Danny. The teacher was telling him to go.

"Come on!" The fat man was impatient. He had an accent that made syrup of every word. Danny followed him out to the corridor.

~~~~~

"I'm Frank Torma. I'm your swimming coach."

Now he realized this was the man who had seen him swim at the meet in Bendigo, who had said to his mother, *Your son has talent.* This was the man who had said, *I can make your boy a champion.*

The swim center perched on a rise from which there was a sweeping view of the whole city. The other boys, all chatting to each other, grabbed their bags and piled out of the van. As Danny walked behind them through the front doors of this new pool, he felt the waft of warm moist air, the sting of chlorine, and the day suddenly heaved off its sluggishness. The day began to move again. In the cold locker room Danny kicked off his shoes, stripped off the heavy jacket, the silken tie, the stiff new shirt, the itchy trousers, peeled off his underpants and socks. Naked, it felt as if his body could suddenly breathe again, and he was so eager to put on his bathers he almost fell over.

Torma was talking, he was pointing at various boys, but all Danny could see was the unreal blue of the pool, and he knew that any moment now he would be immersed in water, held and buoyed and merged with water.

Torma was saying something and Danny followed as the boys formed a line and he could see the pale skin of the boy in front of him, the spray of red freckles across his shoulder blades, and the first boy in line dived in and the next boy in line dived in and then the next and then the next, and the boy with the freckled shoulders was standing on the block and he seemed to be taking forever; Danny wanted to push him in, he couldn't wait, couldn't wait, and then the boy dived and it was Danny on the block and he looked down at the water being churned by the line of swimmers and then Frank Torma gave the order and Danny dived and broke through the day.

In the water the day splintered and coursed, and he stroked, kicked, breathed to outrun it, to be faster than the day roaring to its conclusion, but the day won. The day always won. He couldn't believe that two hours were up, that he had to get out of the pool, that he had to go back with the others to the cold locker room and put on his clothes.

"How'd I do, Coach?" It was the tall, lean boy, the one whose skin was so white it was almost translucent: you could see the blue of the veins showing through.

"You did well, Taylor."

The boy grinned and raised his arms into a triumphant boxer's stance.

Then Frank Torma pointed to Danny. "But Kelly was faster."

Taylor's arms dropped as if Danny or the Coach had just punched him.

As the boys filed out of the change rooms, showered and dressed, Danny heard his name being called. His mother had been on the benches, watching him. She almost tripped as she ran down the steps, and was out of breath when she got to him. Danny was mortified that she was there. He couldn't bear to look at her. He knew that all the boys were staring, of course they were: at her scalloped jet-black hair in a sixties style; at the beauty spot she accentuated with a black pencil every morning; at her tight low-necked scarlet dress; at the black pumps with the silver buckles. "My wog Marilyn Monroe," his dad called her, as he serenaded her with Hank Williams or Sam Cooke, as he danced with her in their tiny kitchen. It always made Danny and Regan and Theo laugh. But not today. He didn't want her here today, his mother who looked like some vintage movie star. He knew that

Taylor's mother would look nothing like her. Scooter's mum wouldn't, nor would Wilkinson's. Their mums would look *normal*.

The Coach was the first to speak and he introduced her to the other boys. Danny still couldn't look at her. But he knew the boys would be leering. Why wouldn't they, at her fat tits on display like that? He walked away and she had to almost run to catch up with him. He'd been embarrassed by her before, of course he had, who wanted his mum or his dad around, who wasn't embarrassed by their mother or their old man? But he'd never been ashamed, he'd never wanted her to *fuck off* before.

He barely said a word to her all the way home. But she didn't notice; she kept banging on about how nice the boys seemed, how polite they were. "They're real gentlemen, Danny," she said, and he knew she was trying to convince herself as much as reassure him. He couldn't look at her, didn't turn away from the world outside the window. You're so transparent, he wanted to scream at her, You're so transparent and you were trying too hard, they could all see that.

Once he was in his room, he almost tore the uniform from his body. He pulled on a T-shirt and a pair of track pants and stretched out on his bed. He wanted to stay in his room, to be safe in the room he knew, with the shelf of medals, the glow-in-the-dark poster of the solar system, the pictures of Michael Jordan and Kieren Perkins, the model of the Brontosaurus he had built in primary school, the boxed set of the *Back to the Future* trilogy that Demet and Boz had given him last year for his thirteenth birthday. He didn't want to leave the room—it belonged to Danny, not to Kelly. But his mother was frying meatballs, and as the smell drifted down the hallway his stomach lurched. He was famished, he could have eaten it all, left nothing for his brother and sister, nothing for his mum and dad.

He ate dinner in silence.

It'll make you a better swimmer.

He spoke to Demet for an hour on the phone. *How was it?* I fucking hate it.

It'll make you a better swimmer.

He was so exhausted that he didn't even bother to brush his teeth. He fell asleep still in his T-shirt and track pants.

~~~~

Taylor came up to him at the lockers, just as the bell sounded for first period. "Is your mum on TV?"

Danny slammed the locker door. "She's a hairdresser."

Taylor held up his hands in feigned apology. "That's cool, Dino. She's amazing-looking, we thought maybe she was an actress or something." He winked at Danny. "Someone's got to cut hair." Taylor had his hands in his pockets and he was whistling as he walked away.

That day and the day after that, and all the days following, Danny kept telling himself, *It'll make you a better swimmer.* He was not welcomed, and he was not wanted, but he could already tell that the Coach was indeed making him a better swimmer. Teaching him how to recognize his muscles, explaining exactly how to breathe, how to think ahead of the water. And that most precious and unlikely piece of advice: Always give it back. The boys didn't want him there, not just Taylor and the swimmers, but all the boys at that fucking school with their perfect smiles and their perfect skin, none of them wanted him there. But the Coach did. The Coach thought he was the best, and that was all that mattered.

That weekend he swam, he swam in the morning and in the evening, and he caught up with Boz and Sava, he spent every spare moment he could hanging out with Demet. On Sunday evening, as he was leaving her house, she asked, "Will you be all right at that school?"

"Sure," he answered. "I'll be fine." *It will make me a better swimmer.*

~~~~

The next day, back in the heavy uniform, that tie pushing against his throat, he was aware of some of the boys whispering behind him.

He ignored them through the morning assembly, but when he walked down the corridor toward his locker, he could sense the smirks and the titters following him. He saw it as soon as he opened his locker door; it was lying on top of his books: the glossiness of the paper, the flash of pink nipple, of pubes and folds. Danny's breath stopped, his body tensed. He pulled out the folded papers and some pages fell to the ground.

All the boys around him are staring, jeering; a voice calls out, "Dino, that's your mum, isn't it?" The centerfold is lying at his feet, and he can see a full-breasted, dark-skinned model, one hand on her dense black hair, the other at her crotch, a thin strip of dark pubic hair, her fingers spreading the lips of her vagina. He can't bear the lascivious grin on the woman's face, the way she stares up at him. And then there are the words crudely scrawled in a text: DANNY KELLY'S PORN STAR MOTHER. He notices the words last and he notices the words first, all that matters are those words.

Why did she have to come and pick me up? That was his first thought; his second: I hate her. I fucking hate her.

And the tears come, he is aware of them a second too late, how they sting his eyelids.

Taylor has placed a hand on his shoulder, is saying, "It's all right, mate, it's all right." Trying not to break out in laughter.

Danny knows that Taylor has arranged it all.

He knew he should have just turned and decked him. But the boys had formed a half circle around Taylor, staring and smirking. They were watching Danny Kelly crying.

He wanted to slaughter them all. And he promised himself that if he ever cried in front of them again, he would never forgive himself. He would never let himself feel such shame again.

The shame twisted his heart and emptied his lungs. Danny wiped his eyes, picked up the pages, and ripped the paper into pieces.

Give it back, he told himself, give it back to them all.

And he would.

But he didn't say a word. He collected his books and headed off to the first class. One boy teased, "Your mum in the movies, Dino?" Danny didn't say a word.

All that day, teachers spoke and lectured but Danny didn't hear a word. All that day, boys came up to him, behind him, around him; they whispered, they jeered, they catcalled. Danny didn't say a word.

That afternoon, when he dived into the pool, that was when he finally spoke. He asked the water to lift him, to carry him, to avenge him. He made his muscles shape his fury, made every kick and stroke declare his hate. And the water obeyed; the water would give him his revenge. No one could beat him, not one of the pricks came close.

Regaining his breath and balance, he shivered at the end of the pool, listening to the Coach harangue the rest of the squad. Torma's face was flushed red, he lashed them with his insults: "Not one of you is worth shit, the only one worth anything is Danny Kelly, the rest of you are born shit and will die shit, do you understand me?"

Danny made sure to look straight at each of them, at Scooter, at Wilco, at Morello and Fraser. He stared longest and hardest at Taylor. All the boys had to meet his gaze. *I'm the strongest, I'm the fastest, I'm the best.*

The boys skulked toward the change rooms. Danny walked in step with the Coach. He didn't have to say a word.

And he knew that hate was what he would use, what he would remember, what would make him a better swimmer.

After nearly two hours of fruitless searching through the department stores and boutiques off Buchanan Street, I buy my great-aunt Rosemary a scarf. I want to buy her something special as it has been eight months since I arrived in Glasgow and this is the first time I have visited her. But I don't know her at all; all I know of her are my granddad Bill's stories of when she was a little girl. It is only because I am running out of time that I grab the scarf, a royal-blue cashmere scarf. It could be from anywhere, and as I watch the shop girl wrapping it, I am ashamed of what an ordinary, unimpressive gift it is. But walking out into the square, I tell myself scarves are always handy in Scotland.

Just as I have that thought, the parcel jammed under my arm, the rain pours down. There's no shelter to be had anywhere and I head toward Queen Street station, the rain saturating my jacket and soaking through to my skin, cursing the fact that in this city where it rains two hundred and bloody thirty-nine days of the year—Clyde declaims it proudly, as if the number is a selling point, something to be proud of—there are no awnings. Not one. The shopkeepers, the councils, no one has thought of putting up shelter. They prefer it, I curse sourly, gives them one more bloody thing to moan about.

I dash into the station, cold and drenched and pissed off.

The man who sells me my ticket to Edinburgh is tight-lipped. He studiously avoids looking at me; the whole time he's talking to the young woman at the terminal next to him. She too doesn't glance my way; I might as well not be there. They are talking over each other, absentmindedly checking paperwork; a queue is forming behind me and people are beginning to grumble.

I look at the man selling me the ticket and I see a stern, long-chinned Australian face.

I run to catch the train, slip through the turnstile past the elderly man checking the tickets; he too has a ruddy Australian face. I get on board, squeeze into my seat; a young man in a gray sweatshirt scowls at me over the lowered plastic table between us as he pulls in his feet to make room for mine. He turns away to look out the window, deliberately ignoring me. In his round wide eyes and pink snub nose I see the Australian face. Across the aisle from us, a young mother has a toddler on her lap, she is chatting away on her phone. There are four schoolkids in the seats behind me, talking and giggling. The mother, the schoolkids: in them I see the Australian face. Getting off at Waverley station, climbing the ramp to the bridge, passing people looking up at the timetable screens, passing rail workers smoking in groups, crossing with the crowd at Princes Street—all around me, wherever I look, all I seem to see is the Australian face.

I am walking the long high road to Leith, I crest a rise and I can see the Firth of Forth, the water sparkling in the clear winter light. I walk past betting shops and Pakistani grocery stores, past walk-up gymnasiums and pubs, past frowning boys in hoods masking their faces in shadows. And everywhere, the Australian face.

Clyde had said to me the other day, "Pal, do you think you might be seeing the Australian face everywhere because you want to?" He's right, he caught me out.

Homesickness, I am discovering, is not a matter of climate or landscape; it does not descend on you from unfamiliar architecture. Homesickness hits hardest in the middle of a crowd in a large, alien city. Oh, how I miss the Australian face.

I get to the end of the walk and there is a sad collection of shop fronts with grimy windows, a group of young boys sitting on the dirty concrete rim of a dry fountain, an old woman in a red headscarf resolutely pushing a crammed trolley. I have no idea where to go. *Excuse me,* I say to the old woman, *do you know* . . . but she won't let me finish; she just shakes her head, *I don't know, I don't know,* so I let her pass and look across at the young boys, one of them standing, his jaw jutting out, his eyes fierce, looking as though he will growl, just like a dog, the group of them just like a pack of wild dogs. I keep walking, go through a dank concrete tunnel that stinks of urine and garbage, its walls black from the constant stream of water running down them. I am in a square surrounded on three sides by gray towers.

Heading toward me is a giant insect of a man, so thin that his hooded top and polyester track pants flap against his spindly arms and legs. Walking next to him, trying to keep to his pace, is a young woman, short, as thin as he is but with enormous breasts, her long hair falling limply over her shoulders. She's wearing an electric-blue tracksuit and is clutching what looks like a pink toy rabbit to her chest. As if she's trying to hide her tits, as if by holding the toy close to her she can fool the world into thinking she's a girl, not a woman. The couple are arguing, he's calling her names and she keeps saying, "Just fucken shut up, it's all your fault, just fucken shut up." As I near them, I ask if they know the address I am trying to find, and the man stops suddenly, as if I have clouted him. His head goes back and he says something in such a thick angry accent I'm not even sure it is English. The woman hasn't stopped walking, and she turns around and looks at me as if I am dog shit she's just stepped in. She doesn't have to speak, the scowl and the disgust in her eyes are enough. I know to keep on walking.

Then I hear, "Aye, aye, aye," and I turn around, the man is running back to me, though it is hardly a normal run, he is cradling one hand in the other, as if the effort of it all hurts, as if it is killing him. "Aye aye aye," he keeps repeating when he stops in front of me, not able to say another word, bent over, fighting for breath. He has a big smile on his face, he winks and says, "You're an Aussie, eh, nah?" and I nod but he's already calling out to the young woman, who hasn't moved, who is standing with her feet apart, the pink rabbit dangling from her left hand, her other hand a fist on her hip, and he's calling out, "Aye, aye, aye, he's an Aussie." She's still scowling and doesn't respond, and he turns to me and starts giving directions, asking do I want them to walk me over there, and I say no, but thanks, mate, I make sure to say *mate* over and over, *thanks, mate,* and he winks again and goes back to the woman. I can hear her berating him as I walk toward the gray towers and this time it is he who keeps interrupting her onslaught, with "Just shut the fuck up, will ya, just shut the fuck up."

〜〜〜

My great-aunt Rosemary lives on the ground floor, in the shadow of the towers. On her door is a heavy brass knocker in the shape of a terrier's head. I bang it, once, twice, and I can hear a shuffle. A voice asks, solidly Glaswegian, "Is that you, Danny?" and I answer yes and the door swings open. The smells of fried egg and locked-in bodies, confinement and home cooking, burnt toast and eau de cologne, all hit me at once. There, smiling up at me, a solid white-haired woman is holding out her arms, but I can't move; for a moment I think time and space have played a trick on me, I think I am about to be hugged by my granddad Bill. Then she says, "Let me hold you, love, let me hold you," and Granddad Bill is gone and this stranger has wrapped her arms around me and I smell chips and cheap scent but the hug she gives me is warm and trusting.

There is no light in the front room, so we sit in the kitchen, out the back. There are two chairs for the small kitchen table; a clump of folded knitting lies next to a small porcelain statuette of the Virgin and next to Her is a framed black-and-white photograph of Great-Aunt Rosemary on her wedding day. I take a seat and she shuffles painfully to the kettle, and I jump back up to help but she says, "No bother, no bother," and makes me tea and brings out a plate of biscuits. She sits across from me, smiling, her eyes wet. A tea towel printed with images of Melbourne trams is pinned up over the stove; a toy baby koala peers down from a shelf crammed with cups and saucers. Below that are framed photographs of my granddad as a kid, a photo of my mother and father, of Regan and Theo, and then there is the photograph of me; I am skinny and pale with a toothy grin, in my black swimmers, clutching a ribbon, smiling like an idiot, ecstatic at my win. On a white doily next to the kettle is a snow globe on a red plastic base, Flinders Street station in miniature.

"Aye, Danny, aye, Danny," Great-Aunt Rosemary keeps repeating, "I can't believe we have finally met. Tell me," she urges, "tell me everything. Tell me about Bill and Irene, tell me about Neal and Stephanie." She's lived in this Leith flat for over forty-five years, came here as a new bride. But her accent still carries the thick chopping call of Glasgow. "Tell me, Danny," she says. "Tell me everything."

And I do: over another cup of tea, over the biscuits, over the ham and squishy cheese toasts she makes me as the sun moves across the sky and the kitchen begins to darken, I tell her all that I can. She gets up to switch on the light, saying, "Go on, love, go on, I want to hear it all."

So I do, I bring Australia forth in words, and it seems that I must be convincingly tracing the outlines and filling in the shades and colors of home because the tiny room seems warmer. I take off my jumper as the sharp smell of burnt toast seems to retreat, as if my stories carry with them the scent of silver-gum forests, of fish and chips on a stinking hot day. All around me are reminders of my hometown, the Mother of God and the photographs watching me as I talk. And Great-Aunt

Rosemary smiles sadly and nods, and once, twice, takes hold of my hand, squeezes it, even with her arthritis, squeezes it tight and ignores the pain. And again it could be my granddad Bill who is here with me.

I feel as though I've talked for hours, more than I have since coming to Scotland. Suddenly I have no more words. She nods, and takes out a crumpled tissue from her sleeve, blows her nose and dabs at her eyes.

"I wanted to come to Australia," she says quietly. "But then Jimmy got sick. So there you are." She is smiling again. "Another cup of tea, love?"

It has started to rain again; the bits of sky visible between the towers appear heavy and sodden with black cloud. We sit in the quiet as the rain splatters against the window.

She pats my hand. "I'm glad Bill's done so well, I am so glad. He did the right thing, leaving this cold hard place and going to Australia." She shakes her head, as if the word conjures up enchantment. "It gave him opportunity. Ach, I know my brother has worked hard, I know it, but he's raised two wonderful sons, he and Irene are happy together and he has a home he loves." She can't stop nodding, as if in prayer.

And then she surprises me. "You know he wanted to study?"

"No," I say, "I didn't know that."

"He was a marvel at languages. There was a friend of his, in our tenement, he was Russian—oh, I've forgotten the wee one's name— and he and Bill used to play together all the time. Bill would just go on and on in Russian—he picked it up so quickly. He used to tell us that he was going to learn languages, he wanted to speak five or six, he did."

"I had no idea. I haven't heard him speak anything but English."

I say that and her face drops.

"Aye, our dad couldn't bear hearing Bill talk Russian. He'd shout at him, 'Who do you think you are? What are you doing dreaming, lad? Our sort can't dream.'"

My great-aunt again dabs at her eyes. I am silent. "Ach, can you imagine that, Danny, can you imagine saying that to a wee child, that you're not allowed to dream? That was our world then." She looks out the window to the darkness outside. "No wonder Bill wanted to leave, no wonder he wanted to go as far away from here as he could."

She surprises me again as her smile returns. "And I suppose he did—you cannot get farther than Australia, can you, lad?" She smiles at me, nodding; I know she wants me to agree. "Can you, Danny? It must be such a lovely, lovely place."

In all my time here, she's the first one to say that Australia seems like a lovely place. All of Clyde's friends and family, even those few who have traveled that distance, they say, "It's all right," they say, "Of course, there's beauty there," but they hold back; you know they have seen or heard of the ugliness and the insularity there. They have experienced the *farawayness* of it. I have learned to keep silent, not to berate them for their disregard of the Brits' role in the colonial tragedy of my country. I bite my tongue and hide my frustration at their tedious obsession with Scottish independence, as if *that* would make a difference to life in Glasgow, let alone to a single soul anywhere else in the world. I have learned how to nod and pretend that I agree. I am a stranger. It is my duty to be polite.

"Yeah," I answer my great-aunt Rosemary, "I think I miss it."

She snorts, loudly. "'Course you do. It's your home."

〜〜〜

It is pitch-black when I get home. Clyde is on the phone but he interrupts the conversation—"Just a moment, Dan's home"—and kisses me on the lips and tousles the wet hair plastered flat to my brow. I go through our cluttered living room to the kitchen but he calls out, "Hang on, Dad wants to talk to you."

He puts the phone on speaker and Alexander's voice booms, "Hello, mate, how are you?"

"I'm good, thanks, Alexander."

"I'm glad, I'm glad."

The conversation is awkward but not unpleasant: distaste for small talk, along with a general reticence and withdrawal from the world, is something Alexander and I share.

As always when talking to Alexander, I am disconcerted by the careful correctness of his accent. I had mistaken him for English on first meeting him and he had explained diffidently that it was a product of being sent off to an English public school as a young boy. I had expected everyone in the city to sound like my granddad Bill, but in those first few weeks I rarely heard that particular accent. Ruth, Clyde's mother, also has an accent I had never heard before, a soft and musical lilt that she explained came from growing up in the Borders. I have learned now to spot all the variations of the Glasgow accent among Clyde's friends and family and colleagues, but it is still a rare thing to meet anyone who sounds like my granddad Bill.

Except Great-Aunt Rosemary. I walk into the kitchen; a weariness has returned to my step. The landscape of accents has reminded me, once more, that I am a stranger here.

The laptop is on the table; beside it is an envelope from the Home Office, addressed to me, the Royal coat of arms in its top corner. I open the letter. Its language is brusque, officious and unemotional as it details in a few short sentences that my application for an extension to renew my working visa requires yet another interview. There are still concerns regarding my application for residency. I reread the two short paragraphs. The weariness now rises like a tide, I am flooded by it, the taste of it bile in my throat. I shudder at the thought of having to explain myself once again, to convince some suspicious bureaucrat that I am not dangerous, not a risk. I sit and angrily jab buttons on the laptop keyboard to log on to my hotmail. There is just junk and I am about to click off when I notice that one of the messages is from Theo.

It is very Theo, dry and concise. He informs me that Regan is pregnant, that we are going to be uncles but that he doesn't think much of the bloke and doesn't think he's going to be around for the baby. *Hope you are well, Dan, give my best to Clyde.* I hear Clyde saying goodbye to his father, and quickly crumple the Home Office letter into a ball; with the other hand I shut down the computer screen.

Clyde comes up behind me and starts massaging my shoulders, his chin rubbing my hair. I force myself not to move, willing myself not to give away that I don't want his hands near me. I use all the skills I learned from that long-ago otherworld of swimming to be still and tame my breathing. I don't give anything away.

Clyde kisses the top of my head and leans against the windowsill. "What did the letter say?" His voice is cool, but I know he is desperately keen to hear me say that my visa is approved, that it won't be long before I am a resident.

I shrug. "Nah, it was nothing, just some guff warning me to advise them if my details change."

He says nothing, but the slight drop of his chin reveals his disappointment. I breathe, reach for his hand, squeeze it; then I have to let it go.

"Dad wants us to go with him and Wanda to the Greek Islands this summer. I said to him that you weren't into the water—that maybe we should think of somewhere else instead?"

There it is again, I think spitefully, that damn ease with which the Europeans collect the world. "Yeah. I don't think it would be right for me to see Greece before Mum does."

Clyde is surprised. I can see a belligerent set to his mouth. But all he says is, "Okay, we'll go when your mum and dad come over."

I can't control my breathing, I can't settle it. I'm not sure where the fury and meanness are coming from. To bring me back, to stay the anxiety, I repeat silently, again and again, Clyde's too good for me, the man is too good for me.

"Sorry?"

He's said something and I haven't been listening.

"Wanda said that she might have a job for you. It's just for a few months, working with teenagers with acquired brain injuries; she thinks you'll be great." Clyde is rushing through the words, and now I am conscious of *his* nervousness, *his* unease. "She knows the people who run it, she says, she's talked to them about you. They're fine that you've only got a temporary working visa."

All Clyde's friends and family want to make it normal for him and me. They want to find me work, they want me to lead a *real* life.

"Sounds good." I nod. "I'll talk to her." I know Clyde, I can tell there's something more he needs to say.

"There's just the wee matter of a police check. They'll need to do a check as you'll be working with kids."

"Then I'm not going for it."

Clyde tries to hold me. "You'll be all right. Wanda can talk to them, it won't be a problem."

"No." I say it with such force that he steps back. "I don't want Wanda to fucking know, I told you. I'm not doing it."

Now it is Clyde who is slowing his breathing, reining in his words. I turn back to the laptop.

"Okay, Dan. No bother." He touches my shoulder again. I let him. "How was Rosemary?"

I breathe out. "She's a real nice lady. She wants to meet you."

Clyde is smiling again. As he saunters out of the kitchen, he says over his shoulder, "Of course, of course she does, she'll see me so often she'll get tired of me. Linda and Brendan have invited us for dinner, that okay?"

"Sure, that's fine," I answer weakly.

He has turned on the telly in the living room; I can hear the news. I smooth out the paper bunched in my hand, reread the words and then screw it up even tighter than before. I throw it into the bin, and go into the next room to sit on the sofa next to Clyde.

The wind is howling outside, the rain incessant. I sit next to Clyde, who is happy and at rest in Glasgow, and I disappear into watching the television. And I know, of course I know, that it is time to go home.

The start of the day and the end of the day, they were all that mattered. The last thing Danny did every night was to set his alarm for four-thirty the following morning. He did this without fail, even though his body had no need of the alarm; he always woke up before it went off, but setting it was part of the routine. He always set it on buzz: he didn't want snatches of lyrics or insistent rhythms seeping into his brain and clouding his focus.

His mother was always up, with a small breakfast prepared for him. If his father was away driving, she would take him all the way into the city to the pool. "I don't mind doing it," she'd say to him. "This early in the morning there's no traffic, it's a breeze." When his father was at home, she would drive Danny to the station.

From six to eight a.m. he was in the water with the squad, Torma marching up and down the side of the pool, bellowing instructions and dishing out insults. And, very occasionally, words of praise. In those two hours, the water and Danny as one, he was flying.

As he would fly again after school, when training resumed. That was what was real, the substance and worth of the day; the rest was

the in-between, a thicket of wasted time through which he had to
struggle. The in-between was school.

〜〜〜

It was lunchtime and he was enduring the in-between by playing
chess with Luke in the cool dark of the library. Danny's knees were
pushed against the table as he rocked on the back legs of the tilted
chair, one eye on the librarian sitting behind her desk. She kept looking over at him, her expression sour, suspicious. She didn't think
he belonged here, he could tell; she thought he should be out on the
ovals, or in the gym, not in *her* library, not in *her* space. And it was
true: Danny's body jerked and fidgeted, stretched and twisted; his
body could not be contained by the hushed space. The library was for
kids like Luke, the kids who walked through the day from first bell
to last always looking down. Danny never looked down: he made sure
that he always looked every single one of them, students and teachers, straight in the eye. The way he was now returning the librarian's
glare. The woman knew that he didn't belong there, that his rightful
spaces were the ovals and the gym and the change rooms: there with
the other boys who never looked down at the ground but who acted
as if they owned it. He should have been there with them but they
wouldn't allow it; when Danny approached a lunchtime football game
or cricket practice, some silent code was always enacted and the other
boys stopped their play and walked away. They had to put up with
him in the pool, they *needed* him in the pool, but that was the only
place they would tolerate him. Stiff shit if the librarian didn't want
him, there was no other place for him to go.

He held his gaze steady, and so did she; the battle was on. He
forced a yawn, opening his mouth wide. Now she turned away, disgust on her face. He rocked back farther and the chair overbalanced.
He grabbed hold of the desk as the chair flew out from beneath him,
the force of the jolt upsetting the chess pieces. The crash made everyone look up.

The librarian sprang out of her chair and rushed over, her face tight with anger. "Kelly, you do that again and I'm going to ban you from here."

"Sorry, sorry, Mrs. Arnaud." He picked up the chair and sat on it properly, wishing he wasn't blushing, wanting to tell her where to go. She walked back to her desk, shaking her head. *Bitch,* he muttered under his breath, just an expulsion of air, not daring to let the word travel.

Luke had carefully placed the pieces back on the board.

Danny tried to focus on his move. Luke would win—Luke always won—but Danny was trying hard to understand the possibilities of the game. He could see his bishop was in a position to take his opponent's knight, but then his bishop would be taken by one of Luke's pawns. And then? And then? That was what Luke had been trying to teach him over the last fortnight, to think ahead, two, three, or even four moves ahead. But if he did and then Luke did something unexpected, his whole game fell apart.

The other boy was sitting patiently; Danny hadn't moved a piece in minutes. Screw it. He slid his bishop across the board and took the black knight. Not missing a beat, Luke moved his rook across the board and swiped the white queen.

"Fuck!"

The librarian didn't even bother to whisper. She was on her feet and pointing straight at the library doors. "Get out, Kelly. You are not allowed back for the rest of the day."

He banged his chair on the carpet, slammed the chessboard onto the desk as he put the pieces away, then slung his bag over his shoulder and marched toward the door.

"Excuse me." She sounded appalled.

"What?"

Her expression darkened further.

"I mean, what have I done, Mrs. Arnaud?"

"I am waiting for your apology."

She wasn't going to let him go without it. He could refuse to acknowledge her—but then there would be detention, then there would be no swimming. There would be no chance of exhaling, of escaping the in-between.

"I'm sorry for swearing, Mrs. Arnaud."

She sat down without looking at him. He wished that the doors were the kind that could bang shut, but of course they were old-fashioned, expensive, with heavy wooden frames, and a spring attached that did not allow for slamming. He pushed through and was out in the open air.

"If you had moved your bishop in front of your king, then I would have had both my queen and a rook in danger. I was so sure you were going to do that."

Danny turned around, dumbfounded. The freaking chess game—he didn't give a toss about the freaking chess game. But Luke was so serious, so intent on instruction, that Danny had to laugh. He shrugged. "I'm not as smart as you."

But I am faster, stronger, I am better.

"It's not necessarily about who is the smartest when it comes to chess, though of course it does require a certain intelligence." Luke looked across the yard to a group of shouting boys on the football fields. "Those idiots out there, for example. They'd be hopeless." He sat down on one of the stone balustrades. "You're smart but you don't have any patience."

Danny wanted more than anything to be alone. But he couldn't shake Luke off. The smaller boy had attached himself to Danny; it had happened so quickly that he hadn't had time to think. He wasn't even sure when Luke became visible to him, emerged as a person out of the mass of other boys in his class, in his house. Or maybe it was assumed that they would be friends because they were both half and half. No one had said that to them, they hadn't said it to one another, but Luke's mother was Vietnamese and his father was Greek and that was some kind of relief to Danny—it meant he was not alone. Luke wasn't the only Asian boy in their class and Danny wasn't the only wog. But Ju and Leung avoided Luke and discouraged his attempts at friendship; and Tsitsas and De Bosco, like the older boy Morello on the swim squad, seemed to detest Danny. He'd heard Tsitsas sneer once, as Danny was walking past, "That fag isn't even a true wog." Danny had noticed from his first week that Luke was the boy who always sat alone at recess or lunch, who everyone felt free to pick on. It was because he was so small and slight, and because he didn't fit in with anyone. Cunts College made it clear that Luke Kazantsis didn't belong. So one day during his second week, Danny sat next to Luke at lunch. And he was glad he did: Luke was smart and funny and not cruel. But now, every day, Luke was his shadow, convinced that he and Danny were best friends. It wasn't the case; he couldn't say it to the smaller boy, but it would never be the case. Demet was his best friend. You only had one best friend and his was Demet.

"What time is it?"

Luke glanced at his watch. I bet it's expensive, thought Danny. It was one of those things that no one at school talked about, but it was something everyone knew, who did and didn't have money.

"Twelve-thirty."

"Let's go down to the river."

The color drained from Luke's face. "We can't."

"Suit yourself." Danny turned away. No wonder the others teased Luke. He was so gutless. Danny started walking away, but soon he heard Luke's footsteps behind him. Danny turned around to smile, but he was also a little annoyed. There was no place to hide in the new school. There was no place to be alone.

A tall wire fence separated the school grounds from the bushland that led down to the river, but Danny knew exactly where he was going. He had discovered the path to the river during that first week at Cunts College. There were points all along the fence where it had been damaged and then repaired, but in a few spots the rusting wire had not been touched and part of the fencing had come away from the palings. Danny crouched down and effortlessly slipped under the loose wire netting. When he looked back, Luke was staring at him from the other side of the fence.

"You coming?"

Getting caught meant suspension. There were regular patrols of teachers and prefects. Getting caught was serious, and that was why Luke was hesitating. But then gingerly, fearful of catching his uniform on the rusting wire, Luke crawled under the fence. Danny pounded him playfully on the back and Luke beamed up at him. He'll do anything I say, thought Danny. He thinks I'm a hero.

～～～

Danny sat on his haunches, looking out at the river. The treacly brown water was flowing gently, and in the blue-gray canopy of the silver gums he could hear the cackling of magpies; on the opposite bank he spotted the rainbow-colored plumage of two lorikeets in the trees. He could not believe the beauty of the place, how lush and green it was. The parks near his house were not like this; they were dry, parched.

"We should get back." Luke was twitching behind him. Danny knew he would be looking at his watch, counting down the seconds. Danny didn't want to move, didn't want to leave the peace of the water and trees and birdsong.

"I can't hear anything from the ovals," Luke fretted. "The bell will have rung. We have to go, we have to go *now*."

Stop your whinging, stop your bloody whinging. In one swift movement, Danny was on his feet and running through the bushes, through the long grass. He slipped quickly through the loose netting, knowing Luke would be struggling to follow, would be carefully trying to get under the wire fence without damaging his jacket or his trousers, that he would be close to crying because he didn't want to get into trouble, didn't want to smear his spotless record. He was a wimp, a dick and a wimp. Let them give Danny detention, let them take swimming practice away from him: he'd go to the Coburg pool instead, go back to his old pool, he didn't need them. He didn't need them at all.

He could hear Luke panting behind him. Friendless Luke; a boy who had no one but Danny.

Danny stopped and turned around, relenting. "It's OKAY, mate, tell them I was sick and you were looking after me. You're not going to get into trouble."

Luke nodded, the relief clear on his face.

When they cautiously opened the door to their English class, they could immediately tell that something had happened to upset the inflexible rules and rhythm of the day. Mr. Gilbert turned to them, barked, "Why are you late?" but he didn't even wait for their answer. They took their seats and looked around. The boys were obviously agitated. Danny leaned across and whispered to Sullivan, "What's happened?"

"Kurt Cobain shot himself. He's dead." Sullivan's tone was hushed, solemn.

Danny's first thought was, It somehow all makes sense, and his next thought was, I need to speak to Demet.

Mr. Gilbert had thrown out the lesson for the day, and was asking them about Cobain and Nirvana and what their music meant to them. The boys were throwing themselves into the conversation, some responses measured, some showing care and even passion. It was all so civilized, so articulate, that Danny wanted to scream at them to shut up shut up shut up. He didn't want to reveal to them how he felt, how deeply gutted he was, how his breath itself felt stolen—he was not going to give them that, he was not going to let them see into him. He had to be with Demet. She would need him, she would be inconsolable.

Shut up shut up shut up. He didn't want to hear those rich kids babble, he didn't give a toss what they thought. The whole time Mr.

Gilbert was going on about music and art and suicide and death and the importance of talking to someone and not bottling up your feelings and remembering where he was when John Lennon was shot, and all Danny wanted was for the teacher, for the boys, for all of them to shut up shut up shut up, until Mr. Gilbert turned to him and asked, "Danny, how do you feel?"

Mr. Gilbert always used their first names, but today he wished Mr. Gilbert would call him Kelly—he didn't want to like Mr. Gilbert today, he wanted to hate him—and so when he sullenly looked up and saw all the boys waiting, even Luke who didn't know shit about music but looked sad because he knew that Danny loved Nirvana, Danny shrugged and said flatly, "I don't really care."

Behind him Taylor was laughing. Danny didn't turn around.

"He's a homey, sir," he heard Taylor say, and though he couldn't see it he knew Taylor would have thrown a mocking, deliberately clumsy gangsta move. "You only listen to rap and doof-doof, don't you, Dino? Do you even know who Kurt Cobain was?"

"Doof doof doof doof doof doof." Tsitsas started the chant.

"Doof doof doof doof doof doof." The rest of the boys picked it up.

Until Mr. Gilbert snapped, "Quiet!" And because this was not Danny's real school, because of the kind of school it was, all the boys fell instantly silent. Mr. Gilbert was looking straight at him—Mr. Gilbert was kind, he was a good man—and he said, "Of course you know who Kurt Cobain is, don't you, Danny?"

And Danny answered, "Yeah, he was a whinging white cunt."

He could feel the shock of it, the word had power and velocity, a gust hurtling across the room. The teacher just looked at him, and Danny knew that he had wounded him, knew that the singer had meant something to him, just as he did to Demet, just as he did to Danny himself, but he didn't know how to let the man know and still keep it from the other boys. So he didn't say a thing, he didn't let on, couldn't let on. This was how he was better than them, how he was harder than them, how he was stronger.

"If I ever hear you use that word again, you will never be allowed back in my class." Mr. Gilbert's eyes narrowed, his face pinched. His voice was hoarse from reining in his fury. "That is a foul and hateful word. That is a word that only foul and hateful people use."

No one made a sound.

"Do you understand, Kelly?"

"Yeah."

"Excuse *me*?"

"Yes, sir."

"You could be suspended for using such a word. Worse!" Mr. Gilbert bellowed and it made Danny jump. It made them all jump.

"But these are unusual circumstances." The man's voice softened. "Tonight you're back here, after final period. You have detention."

Taylor couldn't help himself, he let out a gleeful whoop.

"And you, quiet!"

No one made a sound.

"Okay, Mr. Kelly here thinks Kurt Cobain was a whinger. Does anyone else agree?"

More noise. He would not listen, he would not care, he would not give them anything. Instead he imagined himself back at the river, with the sounds of the birds, the green of the foliage. He thought of water and found the stillness, and their noise dropped away so it was a shock when the bell rang. He slammed back his chair and was the first out the door.

〰〰

During the afternoon recess he had to find Frank Torma and tell him he had detention, that he wouldn't be able to train that afternoon. The Coach was supervising a footy game being played by the Year Sevens.

"What did you do?"

"I swore."

"To who?"

"Mr. Gilbert."

Torma glared at him. "You're an idiot." The man turned away, ignoring him, watching a small but fearless kid steal the ball and run away from the pack, bouncing it once, twice, three times, kicking it off the left foot. The ball climbed, curved, and just hit the goalpost.

"Why are you still standing here?"

"I know I can't train with the others tonight, but I'm going to the pool near home, I'll go straight after—"

"Go away." The Coach dismissed him with an abrupt gesture. "With me, you are training, on your own you are just paddling like a puppy."

And Danny knew the truth of that: without Torma, without his training, he was stuck in the in-between.

⌇⌇⌇

The class straight after the break was phys ed. And Danny knew that the boys were out to get him, he could sense it. The air was thick, it carried sound and heat, an electric current transmitted from boy to boy, a living, writhing energy. It was there in the smirk on Sullivan's face, in the slow and careful way Taylor undressed next to him, as if preparing for combat: neatly hanging up his shirt, his tie, folding his trousers. Danny didn't dare look at the other boys as he slipped quickly into his sports gear. The challenge was not only in the air: the crowing magpies announced that Danny Kelly was going to get it; the threat was there in the slow measured tread of the boys around him.

Mr. Oldfield ordered them to run around the oval three times, and as Danny set off he found that Sullivan and Tsitsas were keeping pace with him, all the while chanting, making it a beat: "*Doof. Doof. Doof. Doof.*"

When the last boy had finished, Mr. Oldfield chose Taylor to captain one team, and Sullivan the other. The two captains began to alternately choose from the crowd of boys and Danny knew exactly what was coming. He looked straight ahead, straight at Taylor, who even while calling out names kept his cool gray eyes focused on Danny. The crowd thinned until it was just Danny and Luke left.

It was Taylor's turn to choose. His eyes, unwavering, were still locked on Danny. "Kelly, get over here."

Danny walked to the group. His heart was winter. He had been steeling himself, from the change rooms to the run, to the picking of the teams. But he was not prepared for this. Now he knew what the air around him was whispering.

They were going to get Luke.

At a certain moment, as a group of boys were battling in a scrum and all attention was on who would emerge with the ball, Taylor let out a cry and fell to the ground. Mr. Oldfield blew his whistle, the boys stopped their game, and the teacher ran over to Taylor. The smiles exchanged between Tsitsas and Sullivan said it had all been prearranged. The teacher massaged Taylor's right calf, asked the boy if he was all right, and Taylor answered, "I think I've twisted it, sir."

The teacher got to his feet and called out to the boys, "I'm going to take Taylor to the sickbay. The rest of you get on with the game."

"Right," Tsitsas ordered, "I'm captain now." Tsitsas stood a head taller than any other boy, and his frame was muscular and bullish. No one was going to challenge his claim to the captaincy.

Danny didn't care about the game, didn't give a shit about winning. But whatever the play, he wasn't going to move away from Luke.

Sullivan from midfield had the ball, and though it made sense to go forward, to run or kick it to the forward line, he sent the ball straight to the outer, straight to Luke. And the smaller boy, his eyes half closed, ran full pelt toward the ball, afraid of catching it and even more afraid of missing it. Danny followed but the boy was fast, desperate to claim the mark and prove himself to all of them. The call from Tsitsas sounded like a shriek from one of the magpies circling above them, and just as the ball landed in Luke's open arms, four boys were leaping, slamming into him, dropping on him. Danny ran into the tangle of bodies, trying to get to his friend, but all he could see was the boys crushing Luke; he could see that Tsitsas was lying flat over the smaller boy and was pushing down on the back of Luke's head, forcing his face into the damp earth, one elbow anchoring the nape of Luke's neck. Danny was biting and kicking and shoving and scratching, boys were yelling at him, he thought it was Sullivan screaming, "You don't bite, you don't bite, that isn't fair," but Danny was kicking and shoving, biting and scratching, until it was just him and Luke and Tsitsas. He threw himself at Tsitsas, wrenched him off the ground in a headlock with the thought that he could snap his neck, and he could hear Luke coughing and retching, and he raised a fist to smash Tsitsas when he felt arms tight around him and then it was him being lifted off the ground and him in a headlock and Tsitsas had got to his feet and his hands had formed fists and he started pummeling Danny, punching him again and again in his stomach, his flank. Danny convulsed with the pain, unable to breathe, but his first thought was, Please don't let him crack a rib, please don't let him do anything that will stop me swimming, and his second thought was that whatever happened, no matter how much it hurt, he would not cry, he would never let himself cry in front of them again, and so every punch took away his breath but he didn't look down, he looked straight at Tsitsas, he would not cry.

Tsitsas's arms dropped to his sides. His breathing was ragged. Whoever was holding him let go of Danny. He staggered but stayed on his feet.

Tsitsas pointed down at Luke, his face caked in dirt, his tears two white rivulets on his cheeks. "Right, faggot," he said, "why don't you look after your boyfriend?"

Danny watched Tsitsas walk away, flexing his muscles, lifting his arms in a champion's pose. And that was when Danny started running, running so hard he didn't think his feet were touching the ground, and Sullivan yelled, "Tsitsas, watch out!" Tsitsas turned, a bemused sneer on his handsome chubby face, and he put up his hands as if to indicate he was untouchable, and that was when Danny crashed in and headbutted him. There was the sound of bone against bone. And Danny felt no pain, there were no stars or dizziness. So he did it again. Once more the shock of impact, a wet, sharp sound, and Tsitsas stumbled, blood on his shirt, a red mess at his nose. His knees buckled and he fell.

Then Mr. Oldfield came running from the other side of the ground, bearing down on Danny. Behind him, Taylor was surveying the field, his gaze coming to rest on Danny too.

"Kelly," Mr. Oldfield called out, "what happened?"

But it was Sullivan who answered. "They were contesting a mark, sir, and Kelly accidentally headbutted Tsitsas."

The frowning teacher squatted and carefully examined Tsitsas's bleeding nose. "Is that what happened, son?"

The boy's ashamed assent was muffled.

The teacher helped him to his feet and ordered everyone to the change rooms. Danny waited for Luke, who was still distressed, rubbing the dirt off his face and neck and asking anxiously if Danny was okay.

Luke's mouth fell open in shock when his friend started laughing, a rich, crazy cackle as he watched the other boys trudge away, their heads down. Taylor kept turning back to look at him, and Danny wiped his mouth; his fingers were stained with Tsitsas's blood. He couldn't stop laughing, because at his old school he would have been beaten to a pulp by then, he'd have been on the ground, teacher or no teacher, he would have been belted, but this wasn't his old school, this was Cunts College, and he was the strongest and the fastest and the best. The magpies were wheeling above him and he felt as if he was one of them, among the silver gums, gliding over water.

"I'm okay," he said, slapping Luke on the back, forcing his own breathing to slow, wiping more blood from his chin. "I'm not hurt at all."

In the change rooms, no one would look at him. But no one dared to mock him, no one dared say anything to him. He could just hear the murmurings behind him and around him, sensed the whisper first taking shape in Luke's astonished and admiring stare. He could hear the words: "Jesus, that Danny Kelly," they whispered, "that Danny Kelly. He's a psycho."

The day that Kurt Cobain died, that was the day Danny Kelly became a psycho.

〜〜〜

"Where are you?"

"I just got home."

"Come over."

"I have to go swimming first."

Demet groaned, then there was fury and pain in her voice. "Fuck your swimming, I need you now."

But he had to be in water, he needed to be in water. "I'll come straight after training, promise."

Silence. He waited. She would understand, she had to understand.

"Nine-thirty, you arsehole, and don't you dare be late." She slammed down the phone.

It rang again and he grabbed the receiver. "Dem?"

It was his mum. She had taken Regan and Theo to the pub for fish and chips; he could hear orders being called out in the background.

"I'm sorry, Danny," she said over the noise. "You know, about Kurt Cobain."

"Yeah, I know."

"We'll be home in an hour."

"I have to train at Coburg tonight."

"Why?"

He should have lied. But she would catch him out in a lie. She always did.

"I got detention."

She swore in Greek. "You have to be more careful, Danny. There are rules you have to obey to stay on the scholarship."

"It was nothing, I forgot about some maths homework I was meant to hand in."

"What time will you be home? I was going to pick up some Chinese for you."

"I'm going over to Dem's."

"That's good, I'm sure Seda will feed you well."

"Okay."

But his mum wouldn't hang up, his mum wouldn't let him go. "Danny?"

"What?"

"I'm really sorry," she said once more.

~~~~

He was unsettled by how strange it felt to climb the concrete steps to the entrance of the Coburg pool. He had swum there for four years, knew all the staff, had won competitions in that pool. But he had not returned since that first day at Cunts College, and it felt like going back to school after the long summer holidays. The guy at the front counter was new and Danny was pathetically glad about that, didn't want to talk to anyone, just wanted to get in the water. The after-school training squads had finished and it was just him and the older, serious swimmers.

The first dive into the water made his heart leap. Stroke, kick, stroke, breathe, kick, stroke, kick, stroke, breathe, kick. He slammed down the pool, the water slipping past him, cradling him, holding him. Stroke, kick, stroke, breathe, kick. He touched the tiles and effortlessly propelled himself back down the lane. There was a man in front of him and Danny had to slow his pace. He needed a lane to himself. Stroke, kick, stroke, breathe, kick. There was a slight pull on his side every time he raised his left arm, a dull tension, and he guessed that one of Tsitsas's punches must have bruised his ribs. It wasn't painful but he couldn't shake his awareness of it; it kept pace with him and the water, and he wished he was at training—the

Coach would know exactly what he should do. He lessened the force
of his stroke, maintaining the power of his kick and slowing his
breathing, and, minutely, reduced his pace. The man ahead was resting against the tiles, allowing Danny to cut in front. Giving the man
a nod as he entered his turn, Danny kicked off, but in overcompen-
sating for his injury he rolled to his right side and reeled clumsily,
rising for breath off-kilter, all his weight on his left; stroke, kick, he
balanced himself, felt the water holding him. Stroke, kick, stroke,
breathe, kick. He slowed his pace, for one lap, for two, then turned
and belted through the water, thrashing it, and he would not think
about the soreness in his side, and then it came, the sense that he
was no longer conscious of the individual parts of his body, not his
arms or legs or the muscles on his left side, the muscles on his right,
and there it was, that moment: it came, the stillness came, and he
was the water. His thoughts were suspended, floating free, and then
he was thinking of the musician's widow, seeing her face. One day he
would be a famous swimmer and he would meet her at a party and
he would tell her how much it meant to him, the music she wrote and
the music she sang, her music and her husband's, the pain he sang.
Stroke, kick, stroke, breathe, kick; the thoughts were no longer separate from the movements of his body. *All denial. All denial. I've made
my bed I'll lie in it, I've made my bed, I'll die in it.* She would ask him
to sit with her, tell him how she'd watched him win his gold medals
at the Sydney Olympics, when all of Australia and all of the world
was watching him and cheering him and he won the four hundred
meter freestyle and then took the fifteen hundred meter freestyle and
the cheering was so loud that it flooded the arena, flooded the country, flooded the world. And there would be a national holiday and he
would ride through Melbourne with the prime minister and everyone
would be cheering him, except Taylor and Scooter and Wilco and
Morello and Fraser, except Tsitsas and Sullivan—they wouldn't be
there, they wouldn't have dared show their faces, because they knew
he was better and harder and stronger and braver and faster.

Danny's hand touched tile and he set down his feet, came to, looking over the water. There was no one else in the lane, there was only
one other lonely swimmer in the pool, a woman whose dogged strokes
hardly unsettled the surface. There was a tightness in Danny's belly,
a hole there, a monstrous hunger that he needed to feed. He was red
all over, his upper body free of the water; he was shaking uncontrollably, feverishly.

He looked up at the clock. It was eight-forty: he had not stopped
for an hour and a half. *Nine-thirty, you arsehole, and don't you dare
be late.* He jumped out of the pool, the cold now painful, grabbed his
towel, and rushed to the showers. He was the only one in there and
allowed himself just enough water to rinse off the chlorine, enough
soap to try to mask the smell of it. His skin was still damp as he
pulled on his clothes and grabbed his bag and ran.

It was nearly nine o'clock. He pounded the hard cold ground, he
needed to ride the air as he rode the water, and he braved the steady
stream of traffic on Sydney Road, weaving through the cars, ignoring the horns. He was out of breath and in pain, now he could feel the
ache where the punches had landed; tomorrow he would have to ask the
Coach what to do about it. He tried not to hit the asphalt so hard; he
couldn't trip, he couldn't twist or strain a muscle or tendon, but even
more important he couldn't be late, he must not be late for Demet. The
wind whipped around him and behind him but he was ahead of the
wind, he had outrun the wind, and he pounded down Murray Street
and he was at the Celikoglus' house and he was pressing the buzzer,
and when Mr. Celikoglu opened the door Danny couldn't even speak,
the sweat was pouring off him, he was wet and in pain. But he was on
time. The world was spinning but he was on time.

Mr. Celikoglu said, "Danny, are you all right?" but he couldn't
answer, his breathing was rasping and it hurt but that didn't matter because he was there on time, and then Demet came out of her
bedroom and she was rushing down the hall and almost knocked her
father out of the way as she threw her arms around Danny, holding

him so tight that now he really couldn't breathe, but it didn't matter, he was home. Demet's arms were around him, he was home.

She wanted to escape with him straight into her bedroom but her mother wouldn't let her. Mrs. Celikoglu insisted that Danny had to eat, and he was grateful for that; he was famished. He sat at the small round table in their kitchen. There were green beans in a yogurt sauce, grilled lamb chops, toasted pita bread and olives and salad, and within minutes he had cleared the plate. He had a milk of grease on his lips as he wolfed down the last of the pita bread, and after swallowing it, he let out a burp.

"Excuse me," he said, wincing.

"Listen to you," Demet taunted. *"Excuse me."* She made it sound so prissy. She folded her arms and leaned back in her seat. "Do you realize your voice is changing?"

"What are you talking about? Leave the boy alone."

Demet ignored her father. The look she threw Danny was contemptuous. "Your voice is so gay and polite since you started at that new school."

Mrs. Celikoglu spoke sharply in Turkish.

Demet rocked in her chair, looking at Danny. "Mum, it's true. His voice has changed."

It was *not* true. His voice was the same, he was the same; Cunts College would never change him.

Demet got up and grabbed his hand. "Come on, come to my room."

"Demet." Mr. Celikoglu's voice was quiet, he was tapping a cigarette on the table. "Please, no more crying."

"Fuck you!" It horrified Danny how much spite was contained in her words. He saw the flare of anger on the man's craggy thin face, and then it settled into weary disbelief.

"Cry, cry, cry, for some foolish rich rock star. Cry your heart out for the idiot who leaves a widow and a child behind."

"Shh, Ohman," counseled his wife. The man slammed his hand on the table, but he said nothing more.

⌃⌃⌃⌃⌃

Demet did cry. She sat on the floor and began a long steady lamen-
tation. Danny knelt beside her, holding her shaking body, his chin
pressed down on her thick matted hair. But he was aware that part
of her outburst was aimed at defying her father. He wouldn't dare
say it but there was something rehearsed about her bawling. He knew
Dem too well. She was crying to punish her father as much as she
was crying for Kurt Cobain. She pulled away from him. Her eyes
were red, her face blotchy, and a line of snot hung from her nose.
Danny wiped it clean, then rubbed the mucus off his fingers onto his
track pants. That was how they were, he thought, they would never
shrink from doing anything for one another.

Demet's crying had eased but she couldn't yet talk. She tried to
form words but they stalled, fell back into her throat. The two of
them sat there, up close to each other, their backs now against the
bed, feet outstretched, Demet playing with a frayed thread on the
collar of Danny's T-shirt. He laced his arm through hers.

"You smell of chlorine."

Danny exhaled, relieved. Her voice sounded normal, or near
enough. "I had a really quick shower, I didn't want to be late."

"Good," she sniffed, still pulling the thread, loosening it further.

"Do you want me to put some music on?"

"Nah," she said, shaking her head vigorously. "I can't bear any
music today."

Something had changed in her room—she had taken down all her
old posters of the Carlton Football Club. Now there was only a small
photograph of a sullen Kurt Cobain taped to her bedroom mirror, an
advertisement for Hole's *Pretty on the Inside* ripped from a magazine
and glued to the wall; pinned next to it was the sleeve for Nirvana's
Bleach. He could see the dust lines on the wall from where the football posters used to be. He didn't understand it and didn't like it but
he wouldn't mention it. He knew what she would say: "You can't talk

to me about change—you've gone off to Cunts College and left me behind." So he just kept hold of her arm.

Then she wriggled away and sat cross-legged across from him, taking his hand. Her palm was sweaty, it felt soapy and sticky, but he couldn't let go.

"I miss you." She made it a wail.

"I miss you too."

Their parents joked about it, teased them both about it, how Demet and Danny would get married one day. Demet and Danny belonged together. Not that they were boyfriend and girlfriend, nothing as frivolous as that; he couldn't imagine kissing Demet, even if they were old enough to do *that*. But he knew that they were *right*, everyone knew that about them. He would look after Demet forever and she would always look after him. There had to be a word beyond marriage, he thought, there had to be a word that would fit.

"Have you got a new best friend?" Eyeing him suspiciously, she pulled her hand away as she asked the question.

"Nah, course not." He wanted to respond: And you? She'd been at Mia's, after all, when he'd spoken to her earlier. He couldn't believe how ugly and mean and awful the thought felt. But she rested her head on his shoulder again and all the awfulness just went.

"When did you find out? About Cobain . . . offing himself?" She meant to sound nonchalant, but she hesitated and stumbled over the word.

"At school, one of the guys told me." Sullivan: his voice hushed, fearful.

"Like they care."

"They do. Everyone was really upset."

Her eyes rolled. She didn't believe him and he knew that for Demet those boys he was at school with would never be flesh, would never be real—would always be alien.

"So they were upset, were they?" Her eyes narrowed. "You making friends there, are you?"

She was jealous. It was sweet that she was jealous, it warmed him. He would have liked to tell her about Luke, who read books and played chess; he would have liked to tell her about how he had defended him. But he knew not to say anything today.

"Nah," he said, "I've got no friends there."

She was nodding as if to music in her head. He wondered if she was even listening to him.

"I beat the shit out of this arrogant wog today, this total Greek dickhead."

Demet snorted. "You? That proves what pussies they must be at that school. Man, *I* can beat you up." Then she frowned. "So there are other wogs at Cunts College?"

"Yeah, but you know, Templestowe wogs, with trust funds and beach houses in Lorne."

"Yuck," she said dismissively. "They are the *worst* kind of wog."

He giggled at her exaggerated disgust. She was still glowering, but his giggling started her off and then they were both laughing so hard that tears were forming, so hard that it aggravated the pain in his ribs. But they couldn't stop laughing and that was when Demet said, her eyes opening wide, "Can you see it, Danny, can you see it?" She was pointing to the space between them, then drew a line from his stomach to hers. "See, Danny, can you see it? There's this light there, look, it's connecting us! Oh wow, Danny, can you see it?"

He understood it was the exhaustion and the sadness of the day. He had seen her etch the line in the air. But there was no light. "Yes," he lied. "I see it." He wanted to see it. He wanted it to be there.

Demet clapped her hands. "We are soul twins!" Her voice was full of joy. "That means we are soul twins forever. That means we'll be best friends in the next life and the life after that."

~~~~

Mr. Celikoglu knocked on the door before coming in. He asked his daughter if she was all right but Demet just snarled and looked away.

"Danny," the man said, "it's nearly eleven o'clock. It's time to go home."

"Let him stay."

"No." Her father was firm. "The boy has practice in the morning."

Danny was grateful that he understood that swimming came first. Demet shrugged.

"See ya," he said.

"See ya," she answered, not lifting her head. But as he was walking out she added, "I love ya, faggot."

"I love you, ho," he responded.

"Call me tomorrow?"

"Straight after training," he promised.

The man and the boy stood at the front door. Mr. Celikoglu was wearing a white singlet and blue pajama bottoms. "I'll drive you home, wait till I change."

Danny shook his head. "Please, no, it's not far. I'll be fine."

The man reached out and lightly pinched Danny's nose, gently cradling his cheek, as he had done since Danny was a toddler. "Say hello to Neal and Stephanie. And thank you for helping Demet."

〜〜〜

The night was chilly and Danny wished he had brought a jacket. He had to hold himself in tight to ward off the cold.

There was not a soul about. It was just him and the hum of the streetlight above, the sound of traffic off Murray Road. But a song was running insistently through his head. It wasn't Nirvana and it wasn't hip-hop or techno, not a golden oldie or one of his parents' rock 'n' roller songs. He couldn't quite grab at the music, couldn't quite recognize it, but he knew it was there, just above him. He tried to snatch the song out of the air, to recall a lyric, a rhyme, but it was no use. He couldn't remember the words to the song at all.

At the end of the day, at the other end of the in-between, he hummed that song all the way home.

"Have you applied for the fucken visa yet?"

I have to tell him. This is the moment I have to tell him. "I haven't had time."

Clyde looks at me like I am an idiot, as if he is wondering how he could have ever got involved with such a fool. *This is when I have to tell him.*

"Dan, the tickets are booked. We need to get ready. Time's running out, pal."

"I know."

"Then fucken make the appointment, man. I'm sick of this."

He charges off to the bedroom. I can hear his shoes bang against the wall as he kicks them off. This is when I have to tell him. I walk into the room and he is lying on the bed, his eyes closed, his tie unloosened. He senses that I have come in and opens his eyes. They are wary, unwelcoming. I sit down next to him on the bed. He doesn't move.

"How was work?"

He doesn't respond.

I blather on, asking after his colleagues, trying to remember the projects he is working on, what campaign he has just finished, which one he has just begun. I babble and stumble until he groans and says, "Just shut it, just shut it, I don't want to talk about my work."

So I shut it, and I don't move and I don't say a thing.

"How was your day?"

Is he relenting? Is he letting me in?

"I had to clean up the cache on Stanley's computer, had to erase what seemed like a million photos of tits. No wonder there was no speed on the bloody thing. I think all he does all day is look at porn and wank."

"What else is he gonna do? The man will never be well again."

Is he baiting me? I try not to get angry, try to let it go. There is a cruelty buried deep in Clyde. It isn't hot and spiteful, it is rational and cold. He thinks that men like Stanley, the men I work with, are broken and cannot be fixed, that it would have been better if Stanley had died in the car crash. He doesn't want them in our home, he doesn't want to think about them. "I couldn't live with brain damage," is what he claims. "I couldn't be half a man." Somewhere deep inside him, he is cold. I am scared that he is too unforgiving.

This is when I have to tell him.

"I'll make that appointment tomorrow."

"Good." He still won't concede. He wants me to do the work, he wants me to beg. I can't, because if I start to apologize, I won't be able to stop. I am sorry for being lazy, I am sorry for being deceitful, I am sorry for not being good enough brave enough tough enough.

This is when I have to tell him.

"I'm sorry."

His hand moves, I feel his weight shift behind me; he is gently rubbing the small of my back. "I don't think you want to move to Scotland, pal. I think that's why you aren't doing anything about organizing the visa."

This is when I have to tell him.

He stops massaging my back. "Is that it, Dan?"

I don't have to tell him.

He is sitting upright now, our shoulders are touching. I can smell the stale odor of the office on him and traces of the takeaway he had for lunch.

He sighs, a deep unhappy sound, and it comes from somewhere beyond the callousness and the aloofness. It is where the tenderness is, where I will find the staunchness, where he will do anything for me. He's scared I don't want to go and I am scared that I *can't* go. I am so terrified I can't bring myself to say anything.

"I guess that means you don't want to go," he says frostily.

This is when I have to tell him. That I do want to go, that I want to be there when his sister Nina has the baby, that I want to meet his half-brother, meet his mother, his father and stepmother, that I want to see the neighborhoods he grew up in, the schools he went to, the friends he made, walk the grounds of the university he attended, go to the clubs he danced in, the pubs he drank in, that I want to get to know his city, the stink of it and the beauty of it, the poverty of it, and the inspiration of it. And I want to believe that when I am there I will shed my skin, become a new man. I want to go. I have to go.

But I'm scared. I'm scared that I won't be able to.

"Dan?"

I love the whisper of warmth he offers to my name.

This is when I tell him.

It takes an age for the words to come, to take shape, to transform into sound. I am hollowness, my voice is not my own, my body seems drained of everything that makes me human: blood and tissue and muscle and guts. But I don't cry. I can't cry.

"Clyde, there's something I have to tell you."

He is the one afraid now, he senses the vast distance between us. His whole body has tensed, his eyes are wide and frightened.

"I've been to prison."

I haven't really thought of his face for years, not really. I have thought of the moments before and all those millions of moments afterward, but not of the man's face, how it became jelly under my blows, of the blood, the cuts on my fist as I broke his face. How I did this to someone, made him insensible, took him to the edge of life.

"I'm scared they won't let me into the UK, Clyde, and I think they have every right not to let scum like me in."

I can see the face, for the first time, I can see what I did, how I destroyed something. But there is that calmness inside me, it is flowing through me, sedating me. It is as though I am speaking through the narcosis of a dream.

And it is Clyde who is crying.

"I've been to prison, mate. I nearly killed a man. That's what I did. That's who I am."

He was standing in the motel bath, his Speedos on, his arms clasped tight across his chest. His mother was shaving his legs. The lather was pasted thick on his thighs, on his calves, and she guided the razor through it slowly, carefully, not wanting to nick him. She said, "Don't move, Danny, stay still."

He didn't like looking down at the soapy, filthy water around his feet. His mum flicked the razor into the dirty mess. Spools of black hair floated on the surface of the foam. His legs were covered in coarse black hair. He thought it was ugly, he was pleased the hair was being shaved off, that it would be gone. But now the skin on his legs was dotted with pink blotches. "Don't move," she warned him again. He looked up at the bathroom mirror in which he could see his brother and sister sprawled over his bed in the main room. Theo was on his back, his neck and head bent over the end of the mattress, watching the television upside down. Regan was on her belly, her elbows bent, her knuckles pressing against her chin. Her feet were kicking—up down, up down—banging on the mattress. He couldn't see the television in the mirror but he could hear the voice of the race commentator.

"Hurry up, Mum, the race is going to start."

His mother ignored him. He looked down to see the razor scraping away what looked like a wad of thick dark fur, as though he was some sort of animal she was shearing. She flicked the razor in the water again and the clump of hair floated on the surface around his left foot.

"Okay, that's your left leg done." His mother smiled up at him.

He was itching all over where she had just shaved him but she poured some lotion into her hand and then rubbed it up and down his calf and the back of his leg. The cool gel instantly soothed the prickliness.

"I'm going to miss the race," Danny complained. He craned his neck, trying to glimpse a reflection of the television. All he could see was his brother's upside-down head, his sister's legs still kicking the bed.

"Theo," his mother called out, "has the race started yet?"

"No."

"You'll tell us when it does?"

He could see the reflection of his brother nodding. The little boy caught his eye and gave him a smile but because he was the wrong way 'round it looked like a frown. Theo effortlessly propelled his body over the bed, landed on his feet, and ran over to the bathroom door. He watched as the razor scraped down the back of Danny's thigh.

"You're really hairy."

Their mother flicked some suds at him and the little boy shrieked, "Don't!"

"Then get out of here."

Theo scampered back to the bed.

"Should I close the door?" his mother asked.

Danny shook his head. He thought it would feel strange if the door was shut, with his mother shaving his legs—it would feel a little sick. He didn't want that thought in his head. He shivered.

"Stop moving or I'll nick you."

If he was nicked, he would bleed. And if he bled, a scab would form, and he would feel it in the water, he would sense it as he was swimming.

It would be just a small sensation, just a niggle. But it could be enormous. Like a fly landing on his naked shoulder over summer, when it became all he could think of. All you could think of was that small, trivial thing, but before you knew it, it would be the scab he was thinking of in the water the next day, the feel of it as the water rushed past it, an itch that would want to be scratched, that would make him pause, for a third of a third of a third of a second. But that was all it took, the Coach said it all the time, for that third of a third of a third of a second to make you lose concentration and then you would slip back, fumble a stroke, and then you would find yourself a quarter of a body length then half a body length then a whole body length behind. He couldn't be nicked, he couldn't dare be nicked.

He stood absolutely still.

She had shaved both his legs and still the race hadn't started.

As she changed the water he ducked into the next room to check the TV. There were ads, then interviews with former Olympians. All they wanted to talk about was Perkins. Would he, wouldn't he? Did he have it in him? Most of the commentators were dubious. He had barely scraped through the heat, one of them warned; another started listing the swimmer's old injuries. The third disagreed, said proudly that just going for an Olympic medal brought something special out of a true athlete: Perkins could do it. The other commentators couldn't answer that; they hadn't been there, didn't know what it felt like. To be in the pool, to be going for an Olympic medal. To have everyone in the world watching you.

Danny wanted to hear about Kowalski. It would be Kowalski's medal. Danny knew exactly what Kowalski would be thinking: that this time he could get there, step out of the other swimmer's shadow, that this time the race would be his. Why wouldn't they talk about Kowalski?

"I think Daniel Kowalski will win this." The other commentators nodded their heads and one of them was about to answer when Danny's mother called from the bathroom.

He pretended he hadn't heard. He wanted to hear them talk about Kowalski.

"Danny!"

Regan raised her head, looked over at him.

"In here, now!"

There was fresh warm water in the tub. He slipped the towel off his shoulders and stepped into the bath. His mother had fitted a new blade into the razor.

"Lift your arm."

He raised his right arm and she began to lather his armpit.

"Has it started?" he asked.

"Nah," Regan called. "It's boring. Just stupid men talking—can't we change channels?"

"Regan," his mother cautioned, "don't you dare change the channel."

"I won't let her, Danny."

Danny smiled at his brother's reflection in the bathroom mirror and Theo grinned back. Danny knew what his brother was thinking, he could read him as clearly as if there were actual words going from his brother's brain straight to his, like telekinesis might be. Theo was thinking that it would be his brother there one day, where Perkins and Kowalski were. That would be Danny one day.

"Ouch!"

The razor scraped the inside of his armpit. It was tender there.

His mother slid the razor carefully against the thicker hair. "Sorry, Danny, this will hurt more."

"Don't cut me, Mum."

"I won't, but you have to stand still. I know what I'm doing."

Did his mother do this for the women whose hair she cut? She had wanted to use wax on him as she did for her clients. But he had been fearful of the wax, thought it might burn, and if it burned, it might blister. And blisters were worse than nicks. Blisters niggled worse than anything.

His mother was close to him as she shaved him. He could smell her, the perfume that smelled like fruit but also had the hint of something unpleasant, too sweet. It made his nose twitch. His legs were all pink from being shaved. They didn't look like his legs anymore. He turned away, impressed by what the mirror revealed. They were strong legs. Almost imperceptibly he tightened his buttocks and glanced back. He could see the muscles of his thighs, stretching, flexing, clearly defined. His calf muscle was like steel.

"Don't move," his mother scolded. She wiped the black hairs onto a small washcloth. He wanted to scratch; the itchiness stung now. He stood absolutely rigid, looking at his legs again in the mirror. He would not scratch, he would not scratch. He disappeared into the words, spelled them forward and backward. I space W-I-L-L space N-O-T space S-C-R-A-T-C-H space H-C-T-A-R-C-S space T-O- . . .

There was an excited cheer from the TV in the next room.

"Is it starting?"

The letters disappeared, but the sting under his armpit was still there. There was a strong odor, like meat mixed with earth, coming from his mother. He had never been close to such a smell before and he knew, as if by instinct, that it only belonged to women.

"Mum," he whined, "it's starting."

"Kids, are they anywhere near the starting blocks?"

"No," Theo answered. Nevertheless he was excited about something, he could see something that Danny couldn't see, because he was now kneeling on the bed and looking at the screen.

"There," his mother announced, satisfied.

The flesh under his arm was red, inflamed. She rubbed him with lotion but the sting didn't quite go away. He flinched and she gave him a mocking smile and unexpectedly kissed him on the brow. "Now you know what we women go through."

What? He didn't understand. Then he remembered from when he was a small boy a summer picnic in Whittlesea, his mother lying on the grass smoking, a glass of wine in her other hand. She had been wearing a sleeveless dress, and whenever she raised the hand with the cigarette in it he had caught a glimpse of coarse short black hairs growing back in her armpit. It had disgusted him, like seeing stubble on an old woman's chin.

He raised his other arm for his mother to shave him there.

~~~

Danny was saying the names to himself like a kind of prayer: *Kowalski, Perkins, Brembilla; Kowalski, Perkins, Brembilla*. That was what he was hoping for, Kowalski, Perkins, Brembilla. There was a hush in the motel room, and even the television announcers fell silent. The first youth was called to his block; he raised his arms and the South African flag appeared in the bottom right-hand corner of the screen. Ryk Neethling; Danny didn't think anything of Ryk Neethling, for it wasn't possible that he could win. After Neethling was Hoffmann from Germany—he was a chance. Neethling, then Hoffmann, then Akatyev from Russia. Danny leaned forward as the young man approached the block. He hadn't seen Akatyev before. He turned the name around in his mouth, liking the sound of it: A-KA-ty-EV. It was a much better name than Kelly.

And then it was Kowalski. Who tried to smile, who waved at the cluster of Australian supporters waving their flags in the stalls, but Danny could see that all Kowalski was thinking about was the race ahead, the race that was his, that now belonged to him. It is yours, it is yours, Danny whispered deep into himself, because he knew that everyone else, everyone in the world wanted Perkins to win, to shrug off the lack of form, the illness, the bad year, nearly missing out on a place in the finals. Everyone—except Danny—wanted Perkins to win. But it was Kowalski's race. Danny hardly registered Graeme Smith, the man from Great Britain, take to his block; he was still seeing the strain on Kowalski's face as he tried to smile. A feeling of unease crept up from Danny's gut. The strain on Kowalski's face seemed a premonition of bad luck.

Emiliano Brembilla was called and moved to his block, looking relaxed. Danny noticed his strong long legs—Danny's would be that strong one day. One day he too would stand on an Olympic block, not anxious, not strained. Brembilla could win it, he thought, he had been the best swimmer in the heats; Brembilla could steal it from Kowalski. He whispered to himself, *Kowalski, Brembilla, Perkins. Kowalski, Brembilla, Perkins.*

His eyes were on the screen but he didn't see Masato Hirano from Japan. (Hirano can't get it, Hirano can't win it.) He could only see Kowalski and Brembilla. It was the cheers that forced him to make sense of the images in front of him. Theo and Regan were cheering, his mother was smiling; Perkins had his arms in the air and the Australians in the crowd were making a din. It sounded like the whole world was cheering. He thought of Kowalski: what must he be thinking? Was he not worthy of such adulation? The bad feeling grew in Danny's gut. He had a smile on his face; he could have even said to Theo, Perkins can still get it, but that would be a lie. That wasn't his prayer. His prayer was Kowalski, Brembilla, Perkins. *Kowalski, Brembilla, Perkins.*

〰〰

His prayer wasn't answered. Perkins led at the one hundred, at the five hundred, at the one thousand; and even though by the twentieth lap Danny could see that Perkins had slowed, was showing fatigue, the others were not equal to his swim. It was only to be silver for Kowalski, but then Danny started fearing that the swimmer might have started too strongly. Kowalski had been chasing Perkins from the very beginning. It was Perkins and it was Kowalski and then Perkins and Kowalski and Brembilla and for a moment Danny thought, *He's got it in him, he's gonna push through,* but then it was Perkins and Hoffmann and Kowalski and then it was Smith who began to scare Danny, for it was Smith who didn't tire, unlike Brembilla and—Danny knew it as well as if he was there in the pool, as if he himself had become the struggling swimmer—unlike Kowalski. The race was won long before it was over; Perkins was half a body length, then a body length, then two body lengths in front, and then he pulled away to a place where victory seemed to be propelling him forward, where victory seemed to be swimming alongside him, where every doubt and every injury and every failure had been vanquished. And it was half a body length and a body length and two body lengths before it was five meters and then ten meters and finally he was twenty meters in front, and it was the last one hundred meters and Danny's heart was sinking though he was not showing it at all, he was screaming, just like his brother and sister were screaming, both of them jumping up and down on the bed, "Go, Kieren! Go, Kieren!" just like the commentators were screaming, like the crowd in the stadium, like the whole world. It was the last one hundred meters and Smith was coming in second and Kowalski was trailing and Brembilla could not win, and then it was the final fifty meters and Kowalski's turn was beautiful, it put him neck and neck with Smith, and Danny heard an announcer yell, "Fight for the silver, son!" and he didn't know why but he felt that he had to scream so loud that it would tear his throat, "Fight for the silver, Daniel, fight for the silver, son!" It was twenty-five meters and Kowalski and Smith were neck and neck and it was ten meters, Perkins had gold and Kowalski and Smith were neck and neck. And it was the finish, and the first hand to touch the tiles was the hand of the swimmer in lane four and just as it did so the swimmer in lane five also slapped the tiles. It was Perkins, Kowalski, Smith. It was gold for Australia, it was silver for Australia. Theo was jumping so high his mother was calling for him to stop, fearful he might hit his head on the ceiling, Regan was crying, the whole world was shouting and screaming and crying. This was what it felt like, thought Danny, this was what it should feel like. But there was an emptiness at the center of him.

No, there *wasn't*. There *couldn't* be.

It was the best result—Kieren Perkins had made history. But

there was a hole in Danny's stomach. No, no, there *wasn't*. This was one of the great moments in sport.

"Yes, yes, yes," he screamed. "We've got silver, we've got gold. What a hero. What a hero." He didn't look at the screen, not yet, not yet, because he didn't want to see Kowalski's face.

"Look," his mother announced, "look at Perkins going to shake Daniel's hand. That's the first thing he does, that gives you the measure of the man, doesn't it?"

But Danny couldn't look, couldn't look at Kowalski's face, at Brembilla's face, at the face of the man who had come fourth—who wouldn't stand on the dais, who wouldn't hear any cheers. Only one man won. He could hear the Coach: *Only one man comes first.* Perkins won. But Kowalski and Smith, Brembilla, Neethling, Hirano, Hoffmann, Akatyev—they all lost. *Only one man comes first.* "Silver and gold," he screamed, hugging Theo, hugging Regan, hugging his mother, dancing. But it hadn't been Kowalski, Brembilla, Perkins. He knew then that he had learned something, something about not letting it show. Not showing the strain of it, the anxiety of it nor the terror of it. He wouldn't ever let it show. Only losers let it show.

〜〜〜

Later, when they had seen Perkins and Kowalski and Smith be awarded their medals, after hearing "Advance Australia Fair," his mother called him back to the bathroom. "We haven't finished, Danny."

She had filled the bottom of the bath with lukewarm water and this time she lathered his chest, spreading foam down his firm flat stomach to just above the line of his Speedos. Her hands were warm but he didn't like that her hands were on him, didn't want to think about how close they were to his bits. He could see a thin knot of black pubes escaping from the top of his costume and he wanted to push her away. He wanted her hands off him. He closed his eyes, screwing them shut so tight there were streaks of red and white light dancing in the blackness. But within the twists and the twirls of the light, he could see the face of Daniel Kowalski, he could see the tightness of his forced smile as he approached the block. Danny would not give in to fear and anxiety. He would learn from Kowalski; he would be as good a swimmer as Kowalski was, but a better competitor. Like Kowalski, he didn't have the perfect skin, the perfect smile, the perfect pedigree. At the school meets, it was Taylor who got the loudest cheers, whose name was called, who got the other boys stomping their feet in the bleachers. It was Taylor they screamed for—*Tazza! Tazza! Tazza!*—not Danny. He would fight the envy, he would take it on and give it back to them. He would not swim for the adulation. He would swim to win.

He could feel the cold blade scraping down his sternum. It was only when he could feel that she had finished that he opened his eyes. He went to step out of the bath.

"Hey, hey, hey," she chided softly. "We haven't quite finished. Turn around."

"Why?"

"There's just some hair on your back—"

"My *back*!" He was furious at her. He hated her and he hated his dad. Who wouldn't pay for the electrolysis. Who wouldn't pay for fucking anything.

He saw that Theo was looking up, alarmed by his shout.

"It's okay." He knew his mother was stifling a laugh. He wanted to insult her, to call her something that would humiliate her. *Bitch.* You're a *bitch.* "It's normal, just some hair on the small of your back. It's normal, Danny."

It wasn't normal for Taylor or for Perkins. It was normal for wogs. Normal for ugly wogs, like her.

"It's okay, we don't have to do it." His reaction had startled her.

She wasn't ugly, she was beautiful. She was going gray but she still looked younger and more attractive than any of the other mums at school; those women were all hard, sharp lines: the cut of their hair, the jut of their chins and cheeks, the fit of their clothes. His mother was curves and flesh. His mother was beautiful. She would do anything for him. He watched her work the gel into a lather in her hand. He was the one who was ugly.

He turned around, and let her shave him.

~~~~~~

It is your race to win. It was the first thing he told himself that morning when he threw back the blanket and looked down at his new smooth body. *It is your race to win.* He kept whispering it to himself while warming up in the gym. He repeated it to himself as he flexed his muscles in front of the long mirrors, wishing he could strip, wishing it was like the ancient days when athletes competed naked, wishing it were those days so he could stand in front of the mirror loving his new hairless body that allowed him to see every curve and hollow of each muscle. He worked out—nothing too strenuous that could pull a muscle. At one point Danny put down the barbells. He was sweating heavily, it was a shiny casing over his new skin. No one was looking at him, they were all concentrating on their own bodies, their own future. He slowly pulled up the bottom of his singlet to his upper chest. His abdomen glistened, his chest gleamed. He was all muscle and he was clean and smooth. He looked like Kowalski and Perkins and Brembilla.

He would win the two hundred meter freestyle. He would win it because he deserved it, because it was his to win. *It was his race to win.*

He kept telling himself that with every lap he swam in his preparations that morning. The water slid by his new body, caressed it. In the water, he could *feel* his speed and power.

He could feel *this* speed and *this* power standing on his block, awaiting the signal to dive in. He knew Taylor was in the third lane but he didn't think about that again. He thought no more about Taylor, who also wanted to win that race. But Taylor wouldn't win that race because it wasn't his to win. *It is my race to win.* He dived and his body entered the water as if he were in one of his flying dreams. Time once again receded. He knifed into the water and then he was slicing the water that bent and shifted and became his. He breathed more freely than he did in the air. He knew that he was at the twenty-five-meter mark, but time did not exist. He was breathing, swimming, bending and being in the water. He was at one hundred meters and he was breathing and bending and shifting the water. One hundred and twenty-five meters and his muscles, his new body, were doing all that he wanted them to do. With every turn he could feel the muscles in his thighs, in his calves, in his shoulders as his arms lifted and broke and shifted the water. It was one hundred and fifty meters but time did not exist and he was shifting and bending and conquering the water. His hand touched the tiles at the end of the pool and he didn't even need to look up, he didn't need anyone to tell him that he had won.

He had won.

〜〜〜

In the warm-down pool he found that he was shivering and fighting wave upon wave of nausea. Then the pain started, first in his chest, then in his leaden arms which felt as if the muscles were ballooning. They felt as though they would burst through his skin, but he knew that they were in fact constricting, that the pain would come sporadically throughout the day, and would intensify and deepen in the night. The next morning his body would feel far from new, but he would have to get back in the pool and struggle to make his body bend and conquer the water once again. The water would not love him as it had during the race; tomorrow it would once more be a force to battle, to master, to defeat. He exhaled and the pain lessened. Slowly his teeth stopped chattering, his muscles loosened, and his cramps began to subside. He looked around to see Taylor shivering next to him. The other boy was taller, with a bigger chest and longer arms, but his legs weren't as strong as Danny's. Danny suddenly understood that he had won it with his kicks, in the water and at the turns.

He felt down to his smooth new thighs and almost groaned as the pain kicked into him again. He raised his arm in a mock salute.

Taylor nodded quietly, a half smile on his face—a loser's attempt at a smile, thought Danny. Taylor extended his hand. "Congratulations, Danny."

He'd fucked it. He should have been the first to offer the handshake, as Perkins had with Kowalski. That was what a true sportsman did, that was what would be in all the papers that morning, he was sure of it: the handshake. Should he hug Taylor or would that be a loser's thing to do? He should have been the first to extend his hand. He would never make that mistake again. Being gracious was Taylor's attempt to get under his skin, Taylor trying to undermine him. *Give it back, turn it on him.* Danny put an arm around Taylor's shoulders, looser than a hug. Taylor's skin was smooth, he still had a child's skin—he could afford electrolysis but he didn't need it, he would always be smooth. Danny's arm over Taylor's shoulder wasn't drawing him in, it was just an affectionate jokey touch which said, We both did well, we were neck and neck for a while, but I won.

Taylor shrugged off his arm.

"We did well," Danny said, grinning widely.

"No," answered Taylor, his voice giving nothing away. "You won it. I came third."

I was always going to win it, thought Danny. It was always mine to win.

〜〜〜

It was dark when they got home. His dad was waiting up for them and offered Danny his hand. "Congratulations, Danny, I'm proud of you. So's your granddad Bill—he was over the moon when I told him."

Danny glanced at the clock. It was too late to ring, Granddad Bill would be in bed. He'd ring him from school tomorrow, to hear the pride in his voice.

Before he went to bed, Danny asked his mother to wake him at four-thirty as usual.

His father cut in before she could reply. "It's been a big couple of days, Danny. Why don't you take the day off tomorrow, sleep in?"

His dad didn't understand that it was harder not to train—that when he wasn't training he was walking through the sludge of the in-between. "Nah, I'm going to the pool tomorrow."

His father's mouth tightened. "Fine, but your mother isn't taking you. She's driven all the way to Albury and back for you—she's exhausted. You can train if you want to, but she's sleeping in."

Danny breathed in, sensing that he was about to lose it and yell, which would get him nowhere; it would never move his father. He turned to his mother, whose eyes were darting between her son and her husband.

"It's okay, Neal, I can take him in."

The man continued staring at Danny, as if he hadn't heard a word his wife had said. Then he raised his arms, shrugged. "Suit yourself." He beckoned to Theo and Regan, and they ran to his open arms for a hug. "Well, the three of us are sleeping in, aren't we? And I'm going to cook us pancakes with ice cream."

Theo and Regan loudly chorused their delight. But his father wouldn't look at him and Danny couldn't look at his father.

〰〰〰

Danny watched TV as he brushed his teeth, transfixed by the constant replaying of the Perkins triumph. The commentators kept asking: was Kieren Perkins the greatest swimmer ever? But Danny was focused on the footage of the man who'd come second, the man who was forcing a smile but looked as though he wanted to weep—because second wasn't winning, second was losing. A heroic effort by Kowalski, they were saying, a great sporting moment for Australia; they were saying that Kowalski swam an honorable race—but second wasn't winning, second was losing.

The phone rang and his mother answered it. She called out, "It's for you."

"How do you feel, champ?"

He swallowed his toothpaste, coughed, grimaced at the burning in his throat. "Pretty good I think—"

Demet interrupted, "We're all so proud of you. Boz reckons he's going to tag your name all over Keon Park station. You're the champion under-sixteen two-hundred-meter-freestyle king! How does that feel, Mr. Kelly, how does that feel?"

"Good, I guess."

"Good, you guess? Dickbrain, it's fucking excellent. Are you free Saturday night? We want to take you out, kiss your arse, rub your nob for good luck."

"You're gross."

"You're retarded."

The old schoolyard insults made him giggle like a little kid. Then there was a strange awkward silence. Dem's voice rushed in to fill it.

"So Bell Street Macca's on Saturday?"

Macca's on Saturday. Taylor would be in stitches, Scooter would be on the floor. He could hear them: *They're taking you to Macca's? To celebrate? Are you serious, fucking Macca's?* He didn't want that thought, didn't want Demet to ever know that he could have such a thought.

"Yeah, yeah, that's good, Macca's."

"All you can eat, hero."

He put down the phone, caught a glimpse of the TV. They were playing the race again. Over and over and over. The hero and the loser.

〰〰

At Flinders Street he fell in with a group of boys from his school but none of them said a thing about the day before, no one asked him about the championships, no one even mentioned Perkins winning gold in the fifteen hundred, even though it was on the front pages of all the papers. No one asked him about his swim. He shrank into a corner of the carriage. So he'd won a pissy all-Australian under-sixteen swimming contest. So fucking what. That wasn't being Perkins; being Perkins was something a million miles away.

He lagged behind the other boys as they walked from the station to the school. Luke was standing in a crowd and he peeled off and came over to wrap an arm around Danny, but even he didn't say a thing.

He could see Taylor and Fraser, and Scooter and Wilco and Morello all huddled together. Taylor said something and they all laughed, of course they laughed. But didn't they know that Taylor came third? Didn't they care that he was a loser?

Danny went into the Great Hall for assembly. He didn't hear the morning prayers, didn't hear Principal Canning ponce on about *this great school* this and *this great school* that. It didn't matter what medals Danny won. They didn't want him, he didn't belong there.

But then Luke was shaking him, grinning, pointing him toward the podium. And Principal Canning was looking down at Danny, looking straight at him and clapping. Luke pushed Danny into the aisle and then everyone was clapping, the juniors and the seniors, even the teachers; everyone was applauding and then they were starting to cheer, the whole school was shouting out his name, *Danny Kelly, Danny Kelly, Danny Kelly!* His school was shouting out *his* name. He was walking toward the stage and one of the seniors, Cosgrave, held out his hand and Danny shook the older boy's hand, and then another prefect, Radcliff, came forward and Danny shook Radcliff's hand. His name was thundering through the Great Hall and as he climbed the steps to take his place next to Principal Canning he looked down to see Luke jumping up and down, cheering like a maniac, like it was the proudest moment of his life, and all the boys, all the teachers, were standing, stamping their feet, cheering and clapping. Coach was there, looking stern, but he too was standing, he too was clapping. Danny searched the sea of faces, looking for Taylor; he was shaking Principal Canning's hand but all the time he was trying to find Taylor, and when he did spot him, Taylor winked and raised his arms, clapping above his head, and then called out, so clearly and so loudly that he could be heard above all the other cheers, "Good on ya, Danny Kelly. Go, Barracuda!"

Danny froze. Tsitsas took up the call, and so did Wilco, so did Scooter, and now they were all yelling, *Barracuda!* Danny wondered, was this an insult? Had it all been planned? He felt helpless, standing there next to Principal Canning. There was no way possible for him to give it back.

"You *psycho*." Taylor's voice again carried above the din. "You dangerous crazy *psycho*! You *barracuda*!"

And Tsitsas and Wilco, Scooter and Fraser, they took up the chant.

Barracuda. Barracuda.

And the rest of the boys joined in.

Barracuda.

And even Coach, even Frank Torma was calling it out.

Barracuda.

Calling it out, clapping, stamping, cheering. All cheering for him.

"Barracuda!"

"Danny Kelly!"

"Barracuda!"

"Danny Kelly!"

Then he felt it. Then it really meant something.

〰〰

That afternoon, as Danny was getting ready for training, Frank Torma came into the locker room. He walked past the others and went straight up to Danny, who held out his hand, grinning.

Torma just looked at it. "Where were you this morning?"

Danny's hand hung limply, just hung in nothingness.

The Coach didn't give him time to answer. "There are no excuses for missing training. Got it?"

"I got it," mumbled Danny, letting his arm fall.

"And what happened in the relay yesterday? Did you give it your best effort? Did you give your team your all?"

The blood rushed to Danny's face. He'd been feeling so good, he'd been feeling so high, and now his skin was on fire and his body was ice. Coach had made him ashamed.

That shame made him look up, made him stare Frank Torma right in the face. Give it back, send it back a thousand times stronger.

No more ice, then, just the fire, but it no longer burned. "I think I did good," he answered, slipping out of his jocks. "Yeah, I reckon I gave it my all—it was the others who weren't any good."

Come on, hit me.

Hit me.

Come on.

Then Coach made a sound, deep and dirty, right from the very center of his body, the sound of spitting. It was so full of disgust and so repellent that Danny flinched. He hadn't spat, but Frank Torma had made his point.

The Coach snarled at all the boys as though he detested them, "Get in the pool. *Now!*"

∿∿∿

He was kicking. Barracuda. Breathing in. Fury. The water parted for him. Barracuda. Breathing out. Fast. The water shifted for him. He breathed in. Barracuda. The water obeyed him. Dangerous. He breathed out.

I have completed three consecutive night shifts, two I was rostered on for, one that I filled in as a favor to Barry. I am looking forward to the long weekend, or rather my version of a weekend. It is Tuesday morning, dawn has just been overwhelmed by the fierce sun rising in the east, and Hassan, the old Sudanese gentleman who runs the Half Moon Café in the mall, is hosing down the footpath outside. He hasn't opened up yet but he's brewed me a coffee anyway, and I sip it gratefully, huddled under the shop awning, the mug keeping my hands warm. It is the final week of the semester break and I don't have a shift at the halfway house till Saturday afternoon. For the next three days there are no assignments due, no one I have to feed, no one I have to bathe or clean up after. It feels like freedom.

But then my gut plummets. I remember: I am catching up with Luke's friend tomorrow. The cocoon of stillness has gone. My joy evaporates, instantly.

It was an e-mail, out of the blue. The subject heading read: DANNY, IS THAT YOU?

I had to make concessions to the twenty-first century when I started college, when I began the diploma in community services. I still don't have internet at home. If I am honest, I am fearful of what I would do if I had the leisure to roam that still-uncharted territory on my own. If I am honest and accurate, it is the world of pornography and anonymity that compels me and terrifies me. It is just a hunch I have, that, lured into the world of the screen where I don't have to reveal myself, not my voice, not my body, not my truth, I would be engulfed and be lost, roaming that world. When I swam— how strange that phrase sounds to me, as absurd as if I were to say "when I was a woman," so distant and so foreign is that experience to me—no one had to tell me not to masturbate, to insist that it would dissipate and corrupt my will. I just knew. As I think we all did, all of us boys, in the team, in the heats, in the competitions, in those pools and in those change rooms, we all knew what giving ourselves over to another thrill that could equal swimming would do. And now I know it about porn and about the internet. I know how it taints desire, how it poisons memory and corrupts time. I have a second-hand laptop given to me by Regan on which I do my course work. I log on at the TAFE library or the Vietnamese internet café on Main Street. I save my work on a USB stick and I print it off at the library.

I feel a stab of something like pain. It must come from thinking back to the swimming, recalling being back with those boys. A rush of shame sluices right through me, as real as a blade disemboweling me from my groin to my throat. Those boys. The shame: the weight and the cost and the dishonor of what I have done.

I sigh so deeply that Hassan turns around. I'm okay, I say apologetically, and he doesn't answer. He leaves the bucket upturned just outside the café door and goes inside to fetch his broom. But not before he squeezes my right shoulder gently. Again, wordlessly. He's been making me coffee for close to a year and—apart from the most generic of pleasantries—I still don't know if he can speak English at all.

It is the e-mail from Luke that has unsettled me. I thought at first that it must have been Demet who gave him my e-mail—dk03101980@ hotmail.com: my initials, my birthday. His first message was cursory—

DANNY, IS THAT YOU?—but since my equally brief response—YES, MATE, IT IS—he has been e-mailing me every fortnight or so, with news of China, of work, of family, sending me photos of Katie and their child. He had found Regan through Facebook and she had passed on my e-mail address. ARE YOU ON FACEBOOK, DANNY? he asked. NO, I typed back, I HAVEN'T HEARD OF IT. I enjoy his letters, am proud of my friend, the shy fragile Eurasian boy who is now an executive in China, who e-mails me photographs in which he wears expensive suits and has a stylish haircut, and who has mastered both tennis and squash and lives in that exotic-sounding place Shanghai, a city more populous than the whole of my vast country. YOU HAVE TO COME OVER, he wrote, and I replied, DO THEY ACCEPT EX-CONS IN CHINA? A week later I logged on at a computer at Sunshine Library and I read his six-word response: LIE ON YOUR VISA APPLICATION, DICKHEAD. And then three capital letters: LOL. I was puzzled and had to ask Sophie in my class what it meant. "Laugh out loud," she snapped, her eyebrows arching, appalled at my ignorance. "Oh my God, Dan, get with the program!"

Katie has a friend, a classmate from the university she attended in Glasgow. All I have been told about him is that he works in film and television, "in production." He has been living in Sydney for over a year and is only now making his first trip to Melbourne. And Luke couldn't help it; when he asked if I could meet up with this man Clyde, he joked that it was no surprise that Clyde had been in Australia for nearly two years but had not yet bothered to visit Melbourne. ARSE END OF THE WORLD, Luke typed.

I finish my coffee, I walk home, I read one hundred pages of Dostoevsky's *The Devils*, immersing myself in the nineteenth-century novel, in all its digressions, its cul-de-sacs, its world in which fate determines destiny far more ruthlessly than does choice or desire, where youth is cruel in its creativity and righteousness. Increasingly those are the worlds I want to disappear into: I love to lose myself in Dickens, Eliot, Hardy; I devour Dostoevsky and Tolstoy, Zola, Balzac, Hugo and Stendhal. I walk through the parks and the backstreets of the surrounding suburbs and neighborhoods, following the creek or the railway track, and I am Jude Fawley dreaming of Christminster, I am Julien Sorel wishing he could go back to a heroic past and serve in Napoleon's army. I am Silas Marner exiled from the world and from community, his gold stolen and his dreaming gone. This is what I was wanting from the next three days, to read and to walk, to walk and to dream. I don't want to talk, I don't want to struggle to find words and conversation. I don't want to be in this world. But I will do it for Luke. I will meet this Glaswegian, we will have a coffee, I will be polite and answer his questions about my city. The thought of it brings a smile to my face. I am the last person to ask about what to do and where to go in my town; Luke should have asked Demet. I will put this stranger in contact with her. And then I will have peace.

Once again, I will be safeguarded by my solitude.

~~~~

The first thing I notice about Clyde is that his accent reminds me of Granddad Bill. There is a similar bass tone and rumble to his voice, the same lilt to his speech. I want to close my eyes, just listen to that voice, masculine, musical, and resonant, as if someone just notched up the treble in his voice box by a degree. Then I notice the sparse cadmium hair on his wrists, and it is disconcerting how much I want to lay my fingers there. It has been so long since I touched another's skin.

~~~~

It took me an age to decide where to meet, as if it were a date. I paced up and down my bedroom, unable to make up my mind. First I thought it should be the city, of course he would want to see the city, it is his first time here. Then I decided against it, as I didn't know where to go in the city. I wondered if it wouldn't be best to meet just down the road from my flat but I quickly decided against that option. It was a train ride out, it was the suburbs; why would he want to see the suburbs? I finally settled on a small café in Brunswick where Demet took me a few months ago, a small place so nonchalantly trendy that you have to sit on upturned milk crates, so chic that sitting there hurts your arse. Then I spent a fitful night wondering if I could remember exactly where it was, so first thing the next morning I walked to the internet café near my flat and googled a map of Brunswick. I located Demet's house and traced the route we took, where we turned left onto Sydney Road and how far we walked before we took a right. I worked out exactly where the café must be.

I texted Clyde the location of where we would meet.

Ten seconds later I got a text back. COOL, it read. LOOKING FORWARD TO IT X. I stared at that X for an age, astonished. It seemed so audacious. I didn't dare text back, I could never sign off in that way. X.

Clyde has finished his coffee. There is a chilling wind blowing up the street but he wants to sit outside where he can smoke. I wish I had thought of bringing a scarf. It is spring but winter hasn't yet unwrapped itself from around the city, and I am shivering. A young waitress with Islander tattoos on her arms comes out, picks up our empty glasses, and asks, "Another?"

Clyde looks across at me. "Yeah, sure," I say, "I'll have another," and he grins. As she walks back inside I mumble, "Sorry about the shit weather."

His answering laugh is as strong and hoarse as my granddad Bill's. He pretends to look at a nonexistent wristwatch and says, "I cannot believe it. A half hour has passed and it is the first mention of weather." His grin broadens. "I think I'm going to like you, pal."

Pal. I like the word—it is unfamiliar but warm. Pal.

We are surrounded by students, girls in op-shop jackets buttoned to the collar, with seventies tinted sunglasses; guys in tight black jeans and Converse sneakers.

"You're all obsessed," Clyde continues. "It's such an Aussie trait, to always go on about the weather. That's all they can fucken talk about in Sydney. 'Is it going to be sunny? Can we get a swim in?' It drives me mad."

I am taken aback by how free he is in denigrating my country. It has only been half an hour and I know already that he thinks us narcissistic and that he thinks us lazy and that he thinks we always bang on about the bloody weather. *So what are you doing here?* I want to say, but of course I don't. I just nod and look at the blush of ginger hair on his wrists. I can't help it, I'm wondering if he is hairy all over. It shocks me, the excitement I feel wondering what he would look like naked.

What would his chest look like? His nipples?

He tells me how bored he is with Sydney, that it is too white and too stratified and that the brute strength of the ocean scares him. And that it is too full of English people.

What would his legs look like? Would his thighs be solid, would his calves be firm?

And he tells me that he already likes Melbourne, that it is ugly, like Glasgow. He smiles at a young scarfed Turkish woman navigating her pram past the upturned milk crates.

Was his cock thick? Did he still have his foreskin?

And he tells me about going to the Center, to Alice Springs and Uluru, how shocked he was at the apartheid there, he calls it that, how outraged he was that the whites and the Aborigines live in two different worlds, how immediately he comprehended the disgrace of it. "I couldn't look the Aborigines in the eyes, but they didn't want anything to do with me anyway. It's not even different worlds, Danny; it is different universes."

What would his sweat taste like?

"My father would agree with you," I answer. "He's a truckie, he's driven all over this country and he reckons it is apartheid."

"And you, do you agree with him?"

The direct question is disconcerting. I know I am blushing. It is a question that has no adequate answer. Of course I agree and of course I don't, there is no possible answer that can encompass the breadth of the continent.

I'm never going to see him again. Fuck him if he can't take a joke. "You don't get a get-out-of-gaol-free card, mate. You're a European—you pricks caused this mess."

It is the way he abandons himself to his chuckling that makes my mind up: I like this guy. He laughs so much he nearly falls off his crate. I am aware that everyone around us is staring. I look down.

When I look up, he is eyeing me carefully, appraising me, and it is then that he seems to make a decision.

"I was meant to come over with my partner, we'd been planning it for a year. And then the prick goes off with some Polish twink he met at a *disco*." Clyde elongates the word, makes it sound ugly, makes it sound like the most hideous of words. "So I thought, fuck it, I'm going to go anyway, I'll go to the other end of the world and see if I can forget him. And I woke up this morning and it was drizzling and I was freezing and I looked out the window of the hotel and it was gray and miserable and I realized I couldn't remember the cunt's face. That's when I thought, I'm going to like Melbourne."

We are silent for a moment, then the coffee arrives and he says, "So tell me about you."

Slowly, hesitantly, I begin to talk. About study, about working with men with acquired brain injury. He asks more questions, asks about what Luke was like at school, and says something about how my parents must have worked hard to afford to pay for me to study at such a school.

Then I know that Luke has told him nothing about me, about my scholarship, about my swimming, what I was and what I have done. And I am grateful, but I am also hurt: maybe Luke is ashamed of me. So I don't say anything about my past; instead I tell him about now. I hope that the now is enough.

The waitress returns to collect the empty glasses. Clyde looks down and says, "I can't really have another."

"That's okay," I say. "I guess I should go."

Clyde looks right at me, and I notice how gray and certain his eyes are, the rigid line of his nose, the sharp cleft in his chin. He hasn't shaved and there is a smudge of drying coffee at the bottom of his lip. He says, "Do you want to go out for a drink tonight, Danny? I was going to meet some work people but I'd prefer to have a drink with you." He says it straight out, no hesitation.

I clear my throat. "Dan," I say. "I prefer to be called Dan."

"Oh." He's taken aback.

And I am wondering, Do I want to go out for a drink with him? Don't I just want to enjoy my version of a long weekend, walking and reading, lost in my own space, not talking, not seeing, not answering to anyone?

"Luke just keeps talking about Danny, so I thought—"

"It's okay," I interrupt, "I just prefer Dan. Danny was a long time ago."

His cool gray eyes are questioning but he remains silent.

So I continue. "Yeah, yeah, I'd like a drink."

What would it be like to kiss him?

"This used to be the front entrance, but Dad had it all torn down before we moved in."

Danny and Martin were on the balcony of Martin's bedroom. To get there you had to step through the enormous open window, its frame carved from a heavy hardwood painted white, with lead ballasts on either side. There was just enough space on the balcony for four people. Martin pointed to the houses across the street, three- and four-storied with front yards as big as football fields. Houses like Martin's.

"Most of those houses," he said, "are owned by Jews. Dad didn't want us to live on Jew Street so he spent almost as much money as it cost to buy the place knocking down the original walls and putting the entrance on Orrong Road."

Danny nodded as though he understood what Martin had said, though he didn't. He thought that there was something obscene in what Martin had just told him. He also thought there was something very stupid in what Mr. Taylor had done, something wasteful and ignorant. It was more information he would have to keep from his parents; his father would rant and rave, his mother would shake her head and say, *How awful.* And of course he would have to keep it from Demet, who would go spare. *Fucking racists.* He could hear her saying it. He blocked it all out. Demet and his mother and his father were in the other world. It was like his two worlds were parts of different jigsaw puzzles. At first, he'd tried to fit the pieces together but he just couldn't do it; it was impossible. So he kept them separate: some pieces belonged on this side of the river, to the wide tree-lined boulevards and avenues of Toorak and Armadale, and some belonged to the flat uniform suburbs in which he lived.

Martin pointed to a house across the street with what looked like castle turrets on each corner, and with two tall liquidambar trees in the front yard through which Danny could see the Yarra River. "That's Jacob Latter's house," Martin said. "Ugly, isn't it?"

Jacob was a Jew. Sometimes the boys at school would tease him and say, "Hey, Jacob, can you smell gas?" If Demet were to hear them, she would be furious: it was all politics now with Demet, all New World Order and Srebrenica and Arafat selling out the Palestinians on the White House lawn. She'd say that the boys who teased Jacob at school were rich racist scum. But it wasn't like that, he knew, it was just something that happened at a boys school, you just mocked and teased and joked. Like in the showers when Scooter would joke about being careful not to drop the soap around Tsitsas or when they said to Luke, "We'll-have-six-spling-lolls-and-one-sweet-and-sour-pork-and-two-flied-lice." It was no different to Demet and Yianni calling him a skip or a bogan, or calling Boz a blackfella or Shelley a curry muncher or Mia a Leb. It was no different, but he couldn't get the pieces to fit, they wouldn't go together. He couldn't explain it.

There was a knock on Martin's door and a soft voice called, "Where are you?"

"Out here."

Emma, Martin's sister, stepped over the window frame and almost fell on Danny, then steadied herself on the balcony rail. In the cramped space their bodies had to touch. Danny and Martin were shoulder to shoulder. Danny stepped back from the rail, anxious about getting too close to Emma. He was sure he reeked of chlorine. He thought Emma was the most dazzling creature he had ever seen. Her blond hair was cut short, which made her blindingly blue eyes seem enormous. She was wearing a man's oversized white shirt with the top two buttons undone. Her neck was pale, flawless; he tried to avoid looking there, near the second undone button where the plump swell of her breasts began. Emma was two years older than he was, had just started university. She was not only the most beautiful girl he had ever seen but also the smartest. The first time he'd visited the Taylors' house, Martin had showed Danny her bedroom and he couldn't believe how many books she owned—a whole wall of book- cases, books on the floor, a book lying open on the bed, a stack of books on her bureau, on her dressing-room table. It was like a library, her room: everywhere you looked there were books. "Emma reads all the time," Martin had said to him, and the way he said it made it sound shameful, like something wrong. Demet would have loved Emma's room, as would Luke. Emma and Luke and Demet should meet, but the pieces just didn't fit.

Emma smiled at him. "I'm really glad you're coming with us, Danny."

"Me too," Danny blurted out, but it came out as an indecipherable grunt. It felt as though he had something stuck in his throat.

Martin smirked. "She likes you, Dan."

Emma rolled her eyes and said, effortlessly cutting, "Marty, you're so childish. I don't know why you hang around with him, Danny." She sighed and looked out across the skyline of gabled roof- tops and transplanted European trees. "God, I have to get out of Toorak. Living here is like private school continuing all your life."

Martin glowered at her. "What's wrong with Toorak?"

She turned to Danny, smiling. "Go on, tell him what's wrong with Toorak."

Danny didn't know what to say, what was expected of him. Was it a trick question, a challenge, a plea, a joke? Toorak was the most expensive suburb in Melbourne: was that what she wanted him to say? But everyone knew that. The more confused he was around her, the more entranced with her he became. He wondered what her skin would be like to touch, what her breasts would feel like. He thought, I am an astronaut and she is another planet. He thought, Is that childish? Toorak was also another planet. He didn't answer and Emma turned her back on him.

Somehow, he couldn't exactly work it out, but from that dismissive turn, he knew he had failed her.

"Are you packed? Mum wants to head off soon."

"Yeah, we're packed."

We're packed. He liked that Martin included him straightaway, instinctively. Martin and Danny—it was now nearly always Martin and Danny. At school, in the pool, it was now all Kelly and Taylor. All the boys knew, assumed it. Kelly and Taylor, mates. They were going to the beach, to another Taylor house, to celebrate the seventy-fifth birthday of Emma and Martin's grandmother. Martin could have invited Wilco or Fraser—his family had known theirs forever—but Danny was the one to be invited. Wilco hadn't complained, Fraser hadn't said a word. It was Martin and Danny, that was how it was.

Emma pulled a packet of cigarettes out of her jeans pocket. She was about to put one in her mouth when Martin shook his head. "You can't smoke up here, the smoke will go into my room."

"I'll shut the window."

"I don't want your filthy cancerous smoke in my face."

Emma licked a finger and raised it. "The wind's coming from the north," she announced, and gently pushed Danny to one side so she could get to the other end of the balcony. "I'll make sure not to exhale in your faces." She lit her cigarette and Martin shut his window with a bang.

"You're a cow."

Emma blew smoke into his face.

She had perfect skin, thought Danny, they both had skin like the surface of milk. Martin's skin would be rough and Emma's skin would be soft. That would be the only difference.

~~~~

He was in the backseat with Martin and they were joking around and gossiping about school and talking about swimming. Mostly they were talking about swimming. The Australian Championships were on in October in Brisbane, and he was convinced that both he and Taylor would be there. He wanted to go to the Pan Pacs, he wanted to prove himself there, but the Coach said that it wasn't the year, that it wasn't time yet. But he wanted to prove himself against the world, not just Australia. It had to be the world now, it had to be the world if he was to have a chance of getting to Kuala Lumpur next year, to Sydney two years after that. "Be patient," said Coach. "You're not ready yet." How Danny resented that phrase, hated it. Danny didn't think it was a matter of patience, he thought it was all about competition, that it was only in the pool itself, in his control of the water and of his breath, in the being in his body not in his head, that he would prove he was ready, that he could beat them all.

"Be patient," said Coach. "This is not your time."

He would prove him wrong. He knew he was ready. First the Australian Championships, then the Pan Pacific Games, then the Commonwealth Games, and then it would be the Sydney Olympics. He was certain of it, he had it all mapped out. He would be there.

Martin flicked him across the thigh.

"What?" said Danny. Mrs. Taylor was looking at him in the rear-view mirror.

"Mum asked you a question."

"Sorry, Mrs. Taylor." Danny leaned forward. Mrs. Taylor's skin was orange, a color Danny had never seen on humans until he met Martin's mother and Scooter's mother and Fraser's mother. It was a skin cured like smoked meat by the rays of the solarium, then lath-ered with lotions and oils and creams.

"I was wondering if you had been to Portsea before, Danny?"

The house was actually in Sorrento, on the wrong side of Portsea—Emma had told him that. Martin had told her to be quiet. Danny knew from the boys at school that Portsea was better than Sorrento.

"No, Mrs. Taylor, I don't think I have."

"But you've been to Rosebud, haven't you, maaate?"

Danny punched Martin on the shoulder, just hard enough to re-mind him who had the bigger muscles. Martin's attempt at a wog-boy accent was pathetic. Danny had been to Rosebud, and to Dromana and Rye, where all the wogs and bogans went for summer. He had loved Rye as a kid, loved that the water stayed shallow for so far that you could go out from shore until your mother and father and sister and brother had almost disappeared from view, become just dabs of color on the yellow sand, shimmering reflections vanishing in the sun's haze. Danny sat back in the car, ignoring Martin. His smile felt like it could crack his whole face open, that it could explode, like in a science-fiction movie. All that mattered was that he would swim better and faster and stronger than Martin. Better, faster, stronger.

～～～

Sorrento was the most beautiful place he had ever seen. It was noth-ing like Rosebud, nothing like Rye. It was the green of it, the streets shaded by tall, thick-limbed trees. It was the blue of it, on one side the placid waters of the bay, and then, as the car crested the ridge of the peninsula, the roiling ocean came into view. It was the gold of it, the bright sunshine of early autumn, the tanned shoulders and torsos and limbs of the people sitting outside the cafés and the bars and fish-and-chip shops.

The house was the most beautiful house he had ever seen. The length of the dwelling was hidden by ivy and shadowed by a giant red bottlebrush that towered over the front yard. Room after room after room came off the seemingly endless dark corridor and then suddenly they were in a cavernous open space; one entire wall was floor-to-ceiling glass that looked out to the sea, a black leather sofa ran along the length of the room. There was an expensive-looking stereo system, a large-screen television, shelves crammed with games and books and sports equipment, another sofa in front of the television, and four black leather armchairs spread haphazardly across the space. At the far end of the room, double doors opened onto a dining room and beyond was the kitchen. Danny walked up to the window and looked out to a gently sloping yard. There was a tennis lawn, an immaculately neat garden bed, and beyond that, ocean, miles and miles of ocean.

Emma came up beside him. "It's almost an isthmus," she explained. "So from the back garden there are steps down to the ocean beach." She turned and pointed to the other wall. "Behind that is the bay beach, maybe a five- or ten-minute walk."

"It's j-just so incredible," was all that Danny could manage to stutter.

Mrs. Taylor called from the kitchen, "Martin, show Danny where to put his bag."

"Okay. And then we're going swimming."

Mrs. Taylor made a peeved sound.

"We have to train," Martin insisted.

His mother came into the living area, absentmindedly scratching at her white bra strap, just visible beneath the open neck of her light blue linen shirt. She walked over to a cabinet and opened it. "I was going to order us some fish and chips."

"We have to train. We'll all eat after practice."

It couldn't be, but it sounded as though Martin was giving his mother an order. But Mrs. Taylor didn't seem to mind; she was twisting the silver bracelet on her wrist as she examined the shelves of bottles in the cabinet. Danny heard her say, "I told your father to order Bombay Sapphire gin—he knows she only drinks Bombay Sapphire," as he followed Martin out of the room.

"Are we going to swim in the bay or the ocean?" asked Danny, and Martin gave him a what-the-fuck-are-you-talking-about? look.

"In the pool, of course, dickhead," Martin answered.

〰〰

Standing naked in the bathroom, his Speedos in one hand, Danny looked down at his body. His chest was chiseled and strong, his biceps seemed enormous, and so did his calf and thigh muscles. What wasn't changing was his height; while Martin was getting taller, Danny wasn't growing at all. That was all he prayed for, that he would grow taller. That was why Coach said he wasn't ready, why he had to be patient, why the Coach had changed his training, his workout, even his stroke. "The butterfly is your stroke, Danny. Your body dictates your stroke." But he didn't want the butterfly to be his stroke. When he dreamed, when he saw the medal around his neck, the flash of the cameras, heard the anthem playing, it wasn't for the butterfly. "It's your stroke," the Coach insisted. "Take heed of your body. It's your stroke." He didn't want that body, he didn't want that stroke.

〰〰

The Taylors' pool was in-ground and built just below the courtyard; you could sit on the tiled edge and look over the ocean, you could see the sunset from the pool.

Danny said to Martin, "I'm doing freestyle."

"Suit yourself, Shorty."

It was only a twenty-footer, so at first it was more exercise than training and at first Danny wasn't thinking of Martin, wasn't even conscious of the boy at the other end of the pool. All Danny cared about was the commanding and storming of the water, and then, as he found his rhythm, he had no more need to think of moving and breathing and being stable in water than he would walking and breathing and balancing on land. He was thinking of the white of Emma's shirt against the flushed pink of her chest; he was thinking about how lucky Martin was to have such a beach house. He felt at home in it already, felt it was his *and* Martin's. Danny stopped and rested his forehead against the white tiles.

On the other side of the pool, Martin was thrashing through the water. If Frank Torma had been walking the length of the pool, he would have been shouting, "Do not soot your lood too fast, Taylor! Slow it down, slow it down." It was Taylor's weakness: he went too hard too early, exhausted himself. Danny slipped beneath the surface of the water, slowed his stroke till he was in line with Martin, till his left arm punched the water with Martin's left arm, until his right hand touched the tiles at the same time as Martin's right hand. Danny turned and Martin turned and Danny thought, I am going to beat you, bastard.

At first Martin was unaware that they were racing. Danny kept the pace, so they were neck and neck, till Martin suddenly sensed it. Danny kicked, picked up speed. Stroke, kick, stroke, breathe. Martin also increased his speed but his kicks were thrashings, his strokes manic, and though he shot ahead his tumble at the turn was inelegant. Danny maintained his pace, the water turning from liquid to air. He let Martin gain half a length, and then a length—stroke, kick, stroke, breathe—was gliding and then Danny began to kick harder, feeling the pull and surge of his muscles in his arms and across his chest, and then he was half a length in front, a steady half a length, breathe, stroke, kick, breathe, stroke, kick, and the water was speaking to him, whispering to him, the water was a tumult, a spray, a thrash of waves as Martin picked up speed; it would not be enough, he had exhausted himself. Danny felt his legs as part of a machine, kick kick kick kick, and he was a body length in front and the water was whispering to him that Martin was dropping back, that Martin was no longer with the water but fighting the water. Danny was one body length, two body lengths, three lengths in front, and Martin had disappeared, he was a whole lap behind, Martin might as well not be in the water, and Danny glided to the end of his lap and pulled himself up on the tiles and exhaled, long, hard breaths, and he was better and faster and stronger and it didn't matter that it wasn't a race and that Coach said that his body was demanding a new stroke. He had won.

Martin came up for air beside Danny. His face was red, ugly from the exertion; he gasped for breath, spewing water, shivering, his body trying to adjust to being at rest. Danny wasn't spent, he felt the waning sun on his shoulders, saw it spread firelight and ruby rays across the sky and sea. He turned to Martin and said, "You ever call me Shorty again, I'll fucking deck ya."

~~~

By the next evening the house was full of guests. Mr. Taylor had come down from his office in the city. He nodded to Danny but didn't speak to him. It wasn't that Mr. Taylor didn't like him—Martin had assured him that that wasn't the case. But they could not speak to one another, it was as if their shared language did not have the words in it for them to understand one another. So Mr. Taylor nodded and Danny muttered an *aho* for hello and a *té* that would do for a thanks.

The grandmother was yet to arrive—she was being driven down from Melbourne by Martin's youngest uncle—but everyone else was gathered in the enormous living room, waiting for her. Mr. Taylor's eldest sister and her husband were there (she was a car wreck, explained Martin; she was a drunk and he was a loser with no head for money), and their two children, Vincent, who was twenty-one (and a junkie, explained Martin), and Siobhan (who was nineteen and thick as thieves with Emma); another sister and her husband (her second, shrugged Martin, only a schoolteacher, something boring like that); and one more brother and his wife (we call her the gold digger, said Martin) and their three kids who were all under ten and who were quiet and well-behaved and nothing like Regan or Theo. Danny was wearing his white school shirt and his school tie and was sitting between Martin and Vincent, who smelled a little off, like Parmesan cheese, and whose knee kept shaking.

Mr. Taylor came out of the study with a painting and held it up for everyone to see. It was small enough for him to lift with one hand, a white canvas on which thin black brushstrokes had created the outline of a woman's sad face. It was as delicate as a web, thought Danny; as if a rain shower could wash it all away.

"Well," said Mr. Taylor, "what do we think?"

Mrs. Taylor was shaking her head. "I'd much prefer a Streeton or a McCubbin for my seventy-fifth," she sighed.

"So would I, dear, but Mama wouldn't."

Emma and Siobhan both spoke, Emma first but Siobhan's echo following almost simultaneously. "It's perfect! Joy Hester is perfect for Nanna."

"Thirty-five thousand," Martin whispered, his breath warm against Danny's ear. "Can you believe they paid thirty-five thousand for that shit?"

〜〜〜

The arrival of the old lady stopped everyone in their tracks. The adults all looked nervous; even the kids fell quiet. "Turn off the video, please," Mrs. Taylor called out, her voice now sounding high and strained. All the adults, and Martin, Emma and their cousins were standing, and Danny thought, God, it is like we are waiting to see the Queen. He too was on his feet, a little agitated, his eyes darting from Martin to Emma to their father, then their mother; Mrs. Taylor had her hand lightly touching her throat, as if the old lady were an executioner, as if the old lady might announce, *Off with her head.* One of the mothers hissed to the smaller kids, "Get up, get up now," and then the old lady was in the doorway, the youngest uncle behind her. His hair was as fair and neat as Martin's and Mr. Taylor's, but he wasn't wearing a tie; he had on a T-shirt with a picture of some woman Danny thought he should recognize, some singer from the punk era, he was sure of it, knew Demet would love her. The old lady didn't look anything like the Queen. Her youngest son supported her arm but she moved confidently, upright, thin, petite, like a little bird, thought Danny, in a plum-colored short-sleeved dress that fell just above her knees. Her skin was stretched over the bones of her jaw, and her cheekbones were almost level with the plane of her eyes. Her earrings were huge pearls, her bracelets sparkled, one silver, one ruby and another gold. Mr. Taylor approached her and she offered him her cheeks to kiss, one then the other, but apart from lips to skin, their bodies didn't touch at all.

"Happy birthday, Mother."

"Thank you, Simon." Her eyes, unlike the fragile rice paper of her skin, were dark and alive and took everything in; vivid and shining, they rested on Danny for a moment, and then swept across the room. "Go say hello to Nanna," one of the mothers urged, and the children lined up to receive their kisses on the cheek, one, two, one, two; then it was Emma's and Martin's turn, Vincent's and Siobhan's, and then she kissed the adults—except, Danny noticed, she didn't actually kiss the wives of her sons, or the husband of her daughter. In their case, she kissed the air instead, and then pulled back.

Danny was left standing alone in a corner of the room.

"Who is this?" the old lady demanded.

"Nanna, this is my friend, Danny Kelly," said Martin. "We go to school together."

The old woman waved him over. Danny approached and held out his hand. She took it, but dropped it almost immediately.

"Are you Eric Kelly's son?"

"No, I'm Neal Kelly's son."

"Who?" The old woman looked faintly annoyed.

"We don't know them, Mother." Mrs. Taylor stepped in, her voice still avian and tight, as though her windpipe had been elongated. Danny recalled the frog they'd dissected in biology, the intricate raw tubing of the amphibian's intestines being stretched until they tore. "Danny is Martin's swimming companion."

Mr. Taylor's youngest brother was grinning at Danny. "I'm Alex," he said, holding out his hand from behind his mother. Danny took it; the grip this time was firm and it was Danny who let go first. Alex winked at him and then put an arm around his mother's shoulders. "I'm dying for a drink," he announced. "What would you like, Mother?"

"A G and T, of course, Alex." She turned toward Mrs. Taylor but didn't look at her. "I hope you have Bombay Sapphire."

If Mrs. Taylor's face were to freeze at that moment, thought Danny, if the wind were to change, then Mrs. Taylor's face would be forever on the cusp of a pain so extreme that it seemed about to burst and like a plate landing on a hard floor, smashing and splintering and exploding into a million pieces. He looked away, embarrassed by such obvious misery.

In one swift feline drop, the old woman sat on the arm of an armchair; a graceful stretch and her bag was on the floor; another sudden turn and one leg was folded over the other. Danny could not believe how clear and taut and smooth her legs were under the pale silk stockings: no veins, no flab, no scars, they were not old legs at all. He had to look away, the old woman had seen him looking.

"So, are we having a drink or not?"

"Mother, I am so sorry. We only have Beefeater in the house at the moment." Mrs. Taylor's voice was a screech.

"Oh, Samantha, and you know it's my birthday!" The old woman snapped her fingers and Alex was immediately at her side.

"What can I do for you, Mother?"

"Do you mind driving into town, darling?"

"Of course not."

Danny sensed that the youngest brother had just won something, and that every other adult there had lost.

"If you can't manage a gin for me, Samantha, could you manage a nip of whiskey? But something more palatable than your usual Johnnie Walker Black. A single malt, but a *good* one, it has to be a *good* one."

Danny looked up and the old woman was staring straight at him.

It took till the first course for him to understand. She held the money. That was why they were all scared of her, why all the children were on their best behavior, why the siblings didn't bicker. Just before they all sat at the dining table—polished white plates, gleaming silver cutlery, all set and arranged by two women from the peninsula who scurried in and out of the kitchen, preparing, cooking, serving, refusing to look Danny in the eye, to look anyone in the eye— Virginia, a university friend of Emma's, arrived. Virginia was seated next to Danny, but ignored him. She kept asking questions of the grandmother. "Emma tells me you practiced law in London just after World War Two. That must have been extremely fascinating."

The old woman dabbed a spot of soup from the corner of her mouth, took a sip of her wine, and scowled at her niece. Emma was looking down at the napkin across her knees. Swiftly Danny unfolded his own napkin, forgotten at the side of his plate. He draped it over his lap.

"London was devastated by the war. I think that only the obtuse describe the experience as *fascinating*."

Ob-tuse. She said it with a soft breath caressing the second vowel. *Ob-teuse*. Danny's lips silently moved and played with the new word.

Virginia's thick-lensed glasses made her eyes appear bulbous, reminding Danny of the bulging eyes of snapper lying on blocks of ice at the Preston Market; they always made him feel that the last knowledge they had gleaned just before death was of desperate futility. Virginia seemed desperate too, like everybody else at the table, even Martin, who was silent apart from *Yes, please* and *Thank you* and *It's lovely*. Danny didn't feel desperate and he didn't know why

Virginia seemed so eager to please. *She* wasn't going to get any money from the old woman.

"Of course, it must have been so upsetting to see the effects of all that bombing and poverty. Still, how brave of you to go overseas and find work when everything would have been so topsy-turvy."

"I always think carrot soup needs a more full-bodied stock." The old woman put down her spoon, placed her hands together as if in prayer, and rested her chin on them. She peered across the table at Virginia. "There was nothing brave about it. I was recently married, my husband had just been appointed to a senior role at the London branch of the company, and we lived in a mews off the bloody High Street in Kensington. Real courage is leaving your home when you have nothing—no money, no contacts. That is real courage and that is real freedom."

Virginia was floundering for a response when the old woman turned to Danny. "Like your mother. Martin tells me she is from Greece. Which part of Greece is she from, my dear?"

Next to Danny, Virginia slumped back in her seat.

"Crete."

He suddenly had the attention of everyone at the table. He hated it, wanted to escape out to the turquoise-flecked sea just visible through the trees. He spooned some soup into his mouth and the slurp of it sounded gross to his ear. The napkin fell between his legs. There was an ocean seething in his ears.

The old woman chuckled. "You eat like a Cretan."

He wanted to throw the soup in her face, all over her plastic fucking gargoyle face.

〜〜〜

It was exhausting being at the table, having to take note of where everyone was placing their drink, having to follow which piece of cutlery to use for each course, and having to remind himself not to put his elbows on the table. He watched and he followed, but he was always the first to finish his course—it seemed to take an age for the others to lift that final spoonful to their lips, and he had to tell himself not to fidget, to stay still.

By dessert, all the adults were drunk and the grandmother had been forgotten. Even Martin had drunk a glass of red wine with his meal. Danny was shocked. Martin's cheeks were flushed—you could tell just by looking at him that alcohol was a poison. Danny refused a glass. He was finishing the last of his blueberry pie when Emma came up behind him and tapped him on the shoulder. She leaned down to whisper, "My grandmother would like you to sit with her. Let's swap places." He swallowed, stood, and then, remembering how Alex had waited behind his mother until she was seated, held the chair out for Emma. He took his glass of water and sat down next to the old woman.

"Have you been to Crete?"

Danny shook his head. He was pretending to be attentive to whatever the old lady was saying to him, but beneath the table he was slowly raising and dropping his heels, pushing against the toes of his shoes so he could feel the muscle pull, then contract.

The old woman's hands were gnarled and white; the skin wasn't plastic there, the skin was dying. "My dear, you must go. Chania is a fabulous town, truly delightful. Was your mother born on the island?"

"No. She was born here." He heard how the "h" had dropped off the last word. So he mouthed it to himself, *He*-ere.

"Ah, so it is your grandparents who migrated. Do you know which part of Crete they are from?"

Again, he just shook his head. He didn't want to tell her that he hadn't seen his *papou* and *giagia* since he was six, that his mother just got exhausted from the fighting and the screaming. *It just never stops, it never stops*, he remembered her howling, and how scared he had been to hear it. His father had held her and said, *You don't ever have to see them again. We're leaving.* He remembered that his grandfather's hands were enormous and that the old man wouldn't give him a hug. He also recalled his grandmother's hands, could only remember them with a coating of flour, like phantom gloves. He would not say any of that to the old woman sitting next to him. She had no right to any of it, none of it was for sale. You are better, he told himself, you are faster, you are stronger. You are better than all of them.

Her gaze unsettled him and he had to force himself to match it. As soon as his eyes caught hers, she looked slightly away.

"I had the most delightful Orthodox Easter on the south coast of the island." She tapped the table, her lips pursed, and she was, momentarily, shockingly ugly. "Now where was it?" Annoyed, she tapped the table again. "Old age is shit."

He didn't know how it could be; perhaps it was the confident enunciation of each syllable, but it didn't sound like swearing, it didn't sound crude.

"It doesn't matter. We were there for the entirety of Holy Week and I remember the black-clad widows leading the procession along the cliff top on Good Friday. The chanting, the incense, everyone holding candles, the ocean booming below us—it was magical."

The old lady's eyes were moist. He felt that if he looked right into the black of her pupils, he might see the mirror of her memory, a candle flame and the crashing ocean.

"Does your mother observe Orthodox Easter?"

"Mum's a Jehovah's Witness." It just came out because he didn't want to admit that he didn't know what Orthodox Easter was, how it was any different from normal Easter.

The old woman's head jerked back as if she was recoiling from something distasteful.

"I mean she *was*," Danny said desperately. "She's not a Joey anymore—she can't stand them."

The old woman nodded approvingly. "I can quite understand."

Danny couldn't bear how stupidly relieved he felt.

"And your father?"

What? He caught himself just in time. "Excuse me?"

"Was he a Jehovah's Witness as well?"

"God no, he really hates them. Dad doesn't believe in God."

The old woman was unmoved. "And he's not Greek?"

"My nan is Irish and my granddad is Scottish. But Dad's an Aussie, he was born here."

"So it was both sets of grandparents who were the courageous ones, it seems."

Why can't you just leave me alone? Toes on the floor, heels up, heels down.

"And where do you live, Danny?"

"Reservoir."

He wondered if she'd ever heard of it, whether she knew where it was. She sniffed and looked down at the table. For a moment he was outraged, thinking that she wanted nothing more to do with him. The year before, at Scooter's birthday, held in a small park in Hawthorn, Scooter's neighbor, an Indian woman with a necklace of smooth white pearls against the coffee-colored skin of her neck, had sat down next to him and asked, "So you are a friend of Paul's?" and he had said yes, and then she had asked, looking away from him, a little bored, "And yes, you live in Hawthorn as well," not even a question, and he had replied, "No, I live in Reservoir," and she had just stood up, with her plate and her glass, and walked away from him, like he had farted, like he had sworn, like he smelled of dirty-pissy-scummy Reservoir.

But the old woman didn't ignore him. She brought her head in close to his, till he thought their foreheads would touch, and she whispered, "Listen to them."

He brought his heels to the floor.

It was twittering and fluffery and gossiping and nonsense. The ladies were magpies and the men were crows and the children were farmyard animals, and even Emma, even Martin, they were all bleating like sheep. It was empty silly noise, about schools and lawyers and stocks and college and shopping. It was crap, it was shit. Across the table, Alex, who wasn't prattling on, wasn't jibbering and jabbering, winked and raised a near-empty wineglass. His mother laughed softly and raised her own glass. No one else had noticed, they were too busy chattering. Alex mimed having a cigarette and stood up, set down his napkin, and left the table.

The old woman sighed. "He is here under sufferance," she announced, not bothering to lower her voice; no one was listening. "His sisters and his brothers have outdone one another in their race to marry the biggest fool." She cocked her head, trying to make out some of the conversation. All Danny could hear was shopping blah markets blah house prices blah school fees blah shopping blah and more shopping blah and interest rates blah and then more shopping blah. The old woman whispered, "Come closer."

Danny lowered his head.

"I've always admired the working class, my dear, always. Like us, you know exactly who you are. But look at them." She waved a hand dismissively at the others at the table. "They have no idea how abysmal they are. Lord, how I detest the middle class."

Danny looked into her bright shining eyes and knew he had just been given a gift, but he didn't know how to unwrap it, could not figure out how to accept it. The old woman shrugged and rose from her chair, dropping her napkin onto the table.

Mrs. Taylor looked up. "Mother," she blurted out, "you mustn't smoke."

"Oh, fuck off, Samantha," the old woman replied as she followed her son out to the courtyard.

The smile on Mrs. Taylor's face was stretching, a cartoonish elongation, as if her cheeks were attached to some invisible puppeteer who was pulling two sticks as far apart as they could go. She sat there with the smile spreading, a parasite taking over her whole face. She was a balloon about to burst; and if that were to happen, thought

Danny, the table, the room, would be covered by her skin, and it would not be flesh and blood but plastic and rubber and glass.

When one of the silent kitchen ladies started cleaning up and the other one brewed the coffee and the tea, everyone gathered in the lounge room to give the old lady her birthday gift. Everyone was polite and charming to Danny—Mrs. Taylor would smile over at him, asking if he needed anything, and Martin's cousins included him in their conversations—but he found that he had nothing to add. They didn't talk about music or movies or politics—they didn't talk about the world. It was all memories of holidays in Lorne, holidays in Sorrento, people they knew. Only when the subject turned to sport did Danny find the courage to say something, to mention their preparation for the championships in October. But even then, Vincent had to stifle a yawn, with Danny in excited mid-sentence. Vincent apologized, urged him to go on, but Danny knew he had bored him. The conversation moved on and he couldn't find the space to finish what he'd been saying. *I'm going to win, I'm going to master butterfly and I'm going to win*. He hugged that thought close. *And I'm going to prove to Coach that I can win in the freestyle*. He would beat them all, and the next time he saw these people again, they would be asking *him* questions, they would want to know all about *him*.

They were polite and charming but the whole time he felt as though there were secrets eluding him, that he was being excluded from something. It was as if they were looking over his shoulder even when they were looking straight at him. He knew that somehow everything about him had gone around the room, that everyone knew that he lived on the other side of the city, on the north side of the river, that he was on a scholarship to the college, that his father drove trucks and his mother cut hair. Somehow they all knew.

Except for Virginia. She too was uncomfortable, her eyes darting from face to face as she tried to follow a conversation, but as soon as she started to join in, the talk always shifted, she was always a beat behind. "I'm studying law," she began, he could hear the pride in her voice, but already the talk had moved on from university. She slumped back onto the sofa and Danny wanted to tell her not to try so hard. How could she not know that?

"Did you go to school with Emma?" he asked, trying to be polite. "No," she answered sharply, not even offering a name for her school, and he guessed that meant she was ashamed of it. He had learned from his own time at school that it probably meant she hadn't even attended a state school, she couldn't claim that with bogan pride: it had to mean she had gone to a piddling private school, probably Catholic, somewhere out in the suburbs. He wanted to tell her that they didn't like it when you tried so hard. He tried to make conversation, to put her at ease, and she nodded and smiled but he could tell she wasn't listening. He remembered the old woman's words. Virginia didn't know who she was, and so she would always be a step behind. She wasn't like him; she didn't know how to win.

〰〰〰

When the old lady ripped the shiny red paper away from the canvas to reveal the painting, Virginia put her hand to her mouth, her eyes bright, as though the present were being given to her. "It's beautiful," she gasped. The old lady looked up, showing them all the canvas. The thick black lines seemed furious to him then, and he thought that the woman's face was as angry as it was sad.

"What do you think, Danny?" The old lady ignored Virginia. "Do you like it?"

He shuffled through his words, discarded them, let them tumble back into his throat. "It's b-beautiful," he finally stammered.

"Oh Danny," she scolded, taking in the painting, "that's so trite."

Emma spoke up. "It's fierce," she said, and her grandmother nodded approvingly.

"That's right." She smiled at Emma. "That is absolutely right."

Danny wanted to say, *That's what I feel looking at it, that's the word I wanted to use.* He wanted to throw it back at her. If he could have cursed her, he would have. He hated her more than anyone else in this room. He wanted to say to Virginia, coiled tight, humiliated beside him, *Throw it back at her, give it back to her, tell the old bitch she can stuff her new canvas up her wrinkled old vag.* He caught Martin's eye and mouthed, "I'm going to bed." Martin looked coldly at him without responding.

The old lady offered her cheeks for Danny to kiss. He didn't let his lips touch them.

~~~~~~

In a sleeping bag on a mattress next to Martin's bed he let out a series of sharp stinking farts, feeling sluggish, engorged by all the rich food. He wished he was at home, that he could set the alarm for four-thirty and that his mum would drive him to the pool. Swimming in the Taylors' pool wasn't enough, he felt caged in. First thing tomorrow he would go to the ocean and swim. He needed the space, the unrestrained power of it, the relief of being in surging, untamed water.

He awoke when Martin came into the room. In the darkness he could hear the boy kicking off his shoes, unbuckling his belt, throwing off his shirt, peeling off his socks. He could smell the mint from the toothpaste that Martin had used. The sheet and the doona were being pulled back, he heard Martin settling into bed. There was his own breathing and there was Martin's breathing. There were the knocks and shudders and rumblings of an unfamiliar house, the flush of a toilet somewhere down the hall, the groan of pipes. There was his breathing and there was Martin's breathing, and behind that was something else, a vibration, a slow, steady pulse, getting faster. Martin's breathing was no longer in sync with his, it was shallow, quickening, and Danny knew that on the bed above him, Martin was beating off, the faint *putt-putt-putt* of the bedhead knocking the wall, breaths escalating. Danny knew, as Martin must have known, that he shouldn't be doing it, that it was wasted energy; no one had told him that but he knew it because every time he had given in to the urge he had felt his strength and power drain away, spill from his body, felt that weakness at the end of the frenzied tugging, the slackened muscles, the spent, listless body. But sometimes he couldn't help it, sometimes he lost the wrestle with himself, and this was one of those times, this once would be okay, and Martin doing it, them both doing it together, that hoarse and shallow breathing, the squeaking mattress, it had to happen. Danny's hand reached down to his own erect cock and he pushed apart his legs and in the small cavity allowed by the sleeping bag rubbed up and down up and down on his shaft, and there was the *putt-putt-putt* of the bedhead knocking the wall and there was the whistling slide of his fist against the fabric of the sleeping bag and there was his breathing getting faster and there was Martin's breathing getting faster and then Danny heard a constricted groan from above and he answered it by choking on his own relief, swallowing it back, as the warm globs of semen flowed all over his fist. He whimpered and then there was silence. He heard Martin's breathing; he brought his own back in sync with that of his friend.

There was a soft thud and something landed beside him on the carpet. It was a crumpled moist face washer. He unzipped his bag and wiped his hand, his groin, his cock. The wet cloth now smelled of him and it smelled of Martin. He rolled it back into a ball and kicked it to the end of the bag. "Thanks," he whispered, but there was no reply.

〰〰

In the morning he was the first up. He slid out of the bag, the stench of his sweat overpowering. He heard a yawn and saw that Martin was also awake.

Embarrassed, Danny pointed guiltily at the face washer. "We should wash it."

For a moment, Martin looked confused; then he laughed. "Don't be stupid, mate, the cleaners are coming right after we leave, they'll do it. It's their job."

They put on their Speedos and headed for the pool. Danny didn't say anything to Martin about how much he wanted to be in the ocean, how much he needed to be in the turbulent wild sea.

He didn't want Mrs. Taylor to drop him at home. She kept saying it was no problem, that she wanted to do it, but he insisted on being dropped off at Flinders Street. She seemed lighter on the drive back into town, as if relieved that the birthday weekend was over. "No, darling," she said once more, "I'm taking you home."

"Mum!" Martin snapped. "He wants to be dropped off in the city. Just do it."

As Danny got out of the car, as he slung his sports bag over his shoulder, he said to Mrs. Taylor, "Thank you so much, I had a lovely time."

The woman smiled sweetly. "Oh Danny," she said, "you are always welcome at our house, come over whenever you like. Remember that: you are always welcome."

The first thing his mother said to him when he walked through the door was, "Shh, your father's sleeping."

His father had driven across the country, from Melbourne to Perth, then on to Sydney and all the way back to Melbourne, all within a week. Danny couldn't imagine being cooped up for such long hours in that cabin that smelled of takeaway food, of stale sweat and cigarette smoke that clung to the surfaces, seeping into the vinyl of the dashboard, sticking to your clothes, seeping into you. His father wouldn't let his mother come near him when he came back from one of those killer drives, not until he had washed off all the grime and perspiration, the rancid taint of sleeplessness, of greasy food, of too many cigarettes.

Only when he'd had a shower, thrown his stinky TWU T-shirt in the wash, shaved off his coppery stubble, trimmed his sideburns, and put on his cowboy shirt with the silver-tipped collars, his clean black jeans, his silver-toed suede shoes, only then would his father grab his wife, grab his daughter, grab his youngest son, hold them and kiss them and vigorously rub his newly shaved and perfumed chin into Theo's hair until he squealed. Just the way he used to do with Danny. His father would clutch Theo and Regan and their mother and sing, *"No, I'm never gonna let you go, never ever ever ever."* But he never did that with Danny anymore, he hadn't done that with Danny for years.

Danny lowered his voice. "I need to train, Mum. I have to go swimming."

"Can't you wait till your dad's up? I said I'd wake him at four."

He couldn't wait. He needed to be in a proper pool, he needed to do serious training. The long weekend had seemed to stretch forever. He wished that Monday was already over, that it would be Tuesday tomorrow so he could go to training. Coach would be yelling at them not to be pussies, and Martin and Danny would be crushing the other boys. He had to be in the pool.

"Mum, can you drive me in?"

"No, Danny. I want to be here when your dad gets up." She didn't get how important it was.

"Fine. Tell Dad I'll see him when I get home."

~~~~

He dived into the water and all the pieces came together: everything was liquid and it was in being liquid that everything became clear. The water parted for him, the water caressed him, the water obeyed him. He swam, he propelled himself through the water; the muscles that moved as they should, the power of his limbs, his lungs and his heart which breathed and beat in a harmony that was clean and efficient. Only in the water were he and the world unsullied. He swam, far beyond mind, aware of only body; and then, coming up for air, he had left even his body behind, and though the exertion continued, though every muscle kept working as it should have, he was wondering if on those long drives through desert and plain, through morning and night, his father's body didn't also seamlessly forget pain and forget time—that the drive, like the swim, was the only constant, the heart beating and the lungs breathing, and whether the long desert roads were liquid as well, not heat and dust but clear and clean like water. Danny calculated the distance his father had just traveled. He knew that it was nine hundred kilometers to Sydney from Melbourne; he drew a map at the edge of his vision, a palimpsest over the solid black lines and the blue tiles, it was etched out on the floor of the pool. He hurtled across the continent, an Atlantis beneath his torpedo body. It had to be at least three times that distance from Melbourne to Perth, four times that from Perth to Sydney. Melbourne to Perth, he breathed, three thousand, Perth to Sydney, he breathed, four thousand, Sydney to Melbourne, he breathed, one thousand; eight thousand kilometers in just under a week. Danny's body came back to him, he felt a strain in his right deltoid, not pain exactly, but a soreness, a twitch, a paper-thin fault line from favoring his left. That was why Coach said he had to change his stroke. He'd poked Danny in the chest, hard, so Danny had to stumble back: "You are lazy, you are not doing enough work, there, *there*." Coach punched the triceps on his left arm. "*There*, you must do work there." Danny let his left arm separate the water, and the water split and created a space for him, searching his body for other fissures and creases. He exhaled, he kicked, he brought his hand to the wall and touched the cool tile. His body shuddered from the pain, burning as it fed ravenously on itself, consuming the fluids released over the last two hours. He let his forehead touch the wall as he floated in the water, trembling, shuddering. Eight thousand kilometers. He could have swum that, Danny thought. He could have swum forever.

When he got back his father was in the kitchen, Theo on his knee, and he was listening to the boy read. They both looked up when Danny entered and his father said, "How was it?"

"How was what?"

"The beach party."

"It wasn't a beach party."

It was as though they couldn't be in the same room; they had to circle around each other, there was no topic or words or action that was safe.

"Where's Mum?" Danny opened the fridge, took out a Tim Tam and wolfed it down. Theo was looking eagerly at him and the Tim Tam.

"She's just gone down to the supermarket for a minute."

"Is there food?"

"In the stove."

Danny dangled a Tim Tam in front of Theo then pulled it away as the little boy tried to grab it. As Theo clamored to get off his father's lap, the man swiped the Tim Tam from Danny and gave it to Theo, who poked his tongue out at his brother before stuffing the chocolate biscuit into his mouth.

There was half a vegetarian lasagna under foil. He tossed all of it on a plate and hungrily attacked it, spoonful after spoonful, the sweetness of the peppers, onions, and tomatoes; the tartness of the olive oil and the heaviness of the pasta sheets; the slight bitterness of the zucchini. He finished it all, listening as Theo continued reading from *The Happy Prince*.

Once Danny had read this story out loud to his father, and so had Regan. Oscar Wilde was one of the great heroes of Ireland, his father had told him when he first gave Danny the book, and a great injustice had been done to him. Danny had only very recently discovered exactly what they had done to him, and why they had done it to him, in English class, accompanied by a chorus of barking and laughter that kept erupting from the boys. Danny couldn't bear to hear the story of the happy prince anymore—the loneliness of it overwhelmed him. It would make Theo cry, he knew it would, as it made him cry when the sparrow fell dead at the statue's feet, when the statue was melted down to molten lead. He tightened his hands into fists, he swallowed. He was glad to hear a car pulling up outside, his mother's footsteps coming up the path.

"Okay, little man," his father said to Theo. "We'll read more of it tomorrow."

His mother came in carrying a six-pack of beer, Regan following behind her, munching on a Bounty. She was getting fat, thought Danny disapprovingly. He couldn't understand why his mother or his father didn't say something to her. His mother handed his father a beer and opened one for herself. He watched his parents drink. His father's arms were ropy, strong, speckled with fair hair, the tan a varnish over his pale skin. There was gray at his temples. Every year his paunch got bigger—the constant driving, the cheap and greasy food. His mother was also going gray but she hid it by sometimes dyeing her hair blond, sometimes red, mostly jet-black. As she lifted the beer to her mouth, her upper arms wobbled, they were getting flabby. Danny sat still in his body, feeling the straight lines of it, the tautness of it. There was no flab there, no paunch, nothing ugly.

"Did you eat all the lasagna?"

"There was only half of it left."

She came over, wrapped her arms around him. "I just don't know where it goes."

He smelled the sour yeast of the beer, felt the loose flesh of her forearms squashing his own firm skin. *It is energy*, he wanted to say, *I convert it all to energy*. It was simple, it was basic physics. Danny pulled away from his mother's embrace and got up from the table. "You're still gunna drive me to training tomorrow, aren't ya?" He was looking at his mother, but he could sense his father's body tensing, a sudden snap of air.

"Your mother is sleeping in tomorrow."

There was no space, no possible space between himself and his father that was safe.

"Fine, then." Danny opened the fridge to get another Tim Tam. "I'll just have to catch public transport." He slammed the door. "Again."

Regan's eyes were darting from the fridge, to the Tim Tam, to Danny, to her father, back to Danny. They found her mother, who smiled at her reassuringly.

"It's a holiday, son," his father said. "You can swim in the afternoon."

No, he will swim in the morning *and* he will swim in the afternoon. He was already behind from spending the last two nights at the Taylors' beach house.

"It's all right, Neal, I'll take him in the morning."

"No!" His father almost shouted the word. Theo dropped his book and Regan rushed to Danny's side. "You and I are sleeping in tomorrow. If he needs to swim, he can fucking walk there."

I do need to swim, you dumbfuck arsehole, I *have* to swim. Danny wished that his father wasn't there at all, that he was lost somewhere in the desert. Regan put her hand in the crook of his arm. The small tender gesture calmed him. Why couldn't it be just him and Theo and Mum and Regan? Just them.

"Okay, okay, Mum can sleep in. I said I'll take public transport." But he couldn't resist it, he wanted to get one dig in, just one small dig. He said it quietly, not quite under his breath: "That cool with you, Mr. Shitkicker Truck Driver?"

But his father heard, his father exploded. "Fuck you, you're not going swimming at all. You're going to stay here and we're going to spend the day as a family."

Danny wouldn't look at his father. "I've got more important things to do."

"Like swanning around with your Portsea mates at their beach parties. That's what you'd prefer to do, isn't it?"

His father made it sound dirty, made them sound dirty, made Danny feel dirty. Couldn't he be four thousand kilometers away, couldn't he be forever and ever and ever away?

Danny couldn't look at him, the contempt would choke him. Put it back on him, throw it back at him.

"It wasn't a frigging beach party. It was Martin's grandmother's birthday."

She said I know myself, she said I'm not like the middle class. He wanted to find a way to express it to his father, to make it all right. His father also hated the middle class; he said it all the time, that the country was so bloody unrelentingly middle class. But Danny couldn't connect the spaces between where he'd been with the old woman and where he was now with his father.

His father slammed his beer bottle down on the table. "Do you know the old dame whose birthday you were celebrating yesterday, Danny? Do you know anything about her? Do you know who she really is?"

She's like you. I can't explain it, but she is exactly like you.

"Do you have a clue who her husband was?"

Danny could sense the danger, he knew he should just get out and go to his room. But his dad's scornful eyes, his dad's disdainful tone, they had trapped him, they wouldn't let him go.

"Her husband was one of the biggest donors to the Liberal Party, one of their key benefactors. His money was behind every strike they tried to break, his money put the bloody premier where he is now. His money helped make Howard prime minister!" His father's voice was shaking. "That's the kind of filth you're associating with, son. Do you really think that kind of shit doesn't stick to you?"

Danny looked around the small kitchen, at the cramped cupboards, the cups with broken handles, the burnt pots, the stove with the one element that didn't work. It was all too small, too mean here. There was no space at all.

"So what? You're just jealous."

They were right, the boys at school were right when they said that people envied the rich. His old man envied him, couldn't stand the idea that his son was going to be better than him. That was why he was punishing Danny. He had to throw it back at his father. Humiliate *him*.

"Anyway, what do you know? All you do is drive from bloody Melbourne to bloody Perth and back again. One day they'll train monkeys to do your job." Danny said it coldly, keeping the emotion out of his voice. He had learned that from Martin. You didn't give your words any heat, you didn't show yourself through them at all.

His father hung his head. Regan started silently to cry. Danny didn't care, he couldn't care. His mother's outraged curse, in Greek so he didn't understand, pounded in his ears as he went to his room. "Throw it back," he whispered to himself, "give it back to them so they are the ones who are hurt."

In his room, he sat on the end of his bed, starting to shake. He thought if he got up, he would faint. The shame was splitting him open, cracking him apart. No one could ever put him back together, there was no way to do that.

He took a deep breath, flexing his triceps, then moving his arms and shifting the energy to his biceps. He straightened his back—the strength there, the power there. He breathed out and looked up, across to the posters and photographs and medals above his desk. There was the photo torn from the *Herald Sun*, in color, Perkins on the dais, kissing his medal, Kowalski in second place, looking straight ahead. Danny would be first, everything would be all right when he came first, all would be put back in place. When he thought of being the best, only then did he feel calm.

〰〰〰

As soon as the race starts, he knows he is going to win. It is an open-air pool and the sun is brilliant and the sky is clear and all around the stadium the crowd is shouting out his name. What astounds him is how effortless it all is, he can't feel his arms, he can't feel his legs, not only is he *in* the water but he has *become* water. The strokes, the kicks, they are exactly like breathing. This is what it must feel like to be a bird, he is rushing through sky. He is in water but he can feel the sun, is reaching the sun. The race finishes and he is first, of course he is first. He has won. He narrows his eyes to slits. He can hardly see the other swimmers, they are trying to reach him but they are miles away, flecks in the far distance. He raises his arm, he salutes the crowd. He looks up and his father's hand is reaching out to him, to hoist him out of the water. Danny shakes his head. No, he wants to stay here, he wants to stay in the sky and in the water. He looks around. The cheers have fallen silent, the benches are empty. Frightened, he turns back and now Martin and Emma are standing either side of his father. And they are laughing, laughing and point-ing at him. Danny looks down. His Speedos have gone, he is naked, and he's pissing. The stream is a vile acrylic blue, it clouds the water around him. "You've pissed yourself," Martin is laughing. Emma stuffs her hand in her mouth, shaking uncontrollably. And his father, his father too, he can't stop laughing.

Danny jolted upright. His room was in darkness. He'd pissed his bed, he was sure of it, he'd pissed his bloody bed. His hands searched the sheets and he fell back in relief. His sheets were dry. He peered at the alarm clock: it was not yet two o'clock.

He needed desperately to piss.

The hall was illuminated, the lounge room lit; someone was still up in the kitchen. Trying to ignore the fullness in his bladder, he stood in the doorway. There were record sleeves strewn across the floor, an LP still spinning on the turntable, the needle clicking and crackling as it ran over and over the same soundless groove.

From the kitchen he heard his mother say, "I think that school is good for him."

And he heard his father snort. "Yeah? By making him despise his father?"

"He doesn't despise you, Neal. He's just angry. You and I can't understand the focus he needs, the obsession he has with swimming."

"Jesus, Steph, the swimming isn't the problem. His selfishness is the fucking problem."

Danny heard a match strike, wrinkled his nose as the acrid smell of the cigarette hit. He was holding his breath, so they wouldn't hear him, so he could hear his mother's answer. Defend me, please defend me.

"Going to that school is a huge opportunity, a really special opportunity, and I am not going to deny him that."

Another match struck, another cigarette lit.

"He's got a chance to be great, Neal. How can you deny your son the chance to achieve that?"

"I just don't think it's fair. Regan is starting high school next year. What about her opportunities? Should we be sending all the kids to those kinds of schools? We couldn't afford that, baby. How is that fair on Regan, how's that fair on Theo?"

"Danny will look after his sister and his brother. I have no doubt about that. He's a good boy, Neal—you know he'll do right by us, don't you?"

Danny slowly exhaled. His mother understood.

He was waiting for his father's answer.

"That's a pretty big burden to place on a young man's shoulders."

"He's going to be an Olympic champion. Don't you get it? He's going to be one of the greats."

Danny held in his breath again. He had forgotten his full bladder; he was waiting for his father to agree.

"Steph, baby, what if he isn't good enough? What if he doesn't make it?"

Danny crept back down the hall. He couldn't go to the toilet now, they would hear him. He couldn't bear for them to know that he had heard them. He softly shut the door to his room.

Danny gently pulled at the window. He winced as it gave with a thud. He was motionless, waiting. But the sound hadn't carried, they hadn't heard. A cold gust of wind struck his face. He stood on tiptoes, pulled down his jocks, and let go. The stream of urine rattled the side fence, but he didn't care anymore whether anyone heard. Steam rose from where the urine splashed on the fence palings. Finally, his bladder was empty and Danny carefully shut the window again.

It took an age for him to fall asleep. He had to count through the muscles in his body, tensing and relaxing, the way he'd been taught. He was supposed to clear his mind, but all he could think was how he was going to prove his father wrong. I am going to be the fastest and the strongest and the best and I am going to look after Mum and Regan and Theo, and I'm even going to look after you, you prick. Even you, you prick.

He breathed out.

He relaxed his shoulders, sank into the bed, pretending he was sinking into water. He was determined now, he was going to bring all the worlds together now. He breathed in. They were doing the right thing sending him to that school, they were doing the right thing supporting him. He owed them, he knew that. He owed them but it would be all right. He breathed out.

He fell asleep, knowing it would all be all right.

"I dunn wanna, I dunn wanna, I dunn wanna."

He repeats it over and over, so many times I am no longer aware of the words; what I am listening to is the rhythm, as if the real meaning is in the fall and tumble and shape of the words. Maybe it is. Four years ago, after shooting up a gram of speed and drinking fifteen beers, Kevin tore his car up Burnley Street, Richmond, and lost control of the wheel when he tried to turn the corner into Highett Street. The car slammed into one of the thick-trunked elm trees that shroud that avenue. Kevin, who wasn't wearing his seat belt, was thrown through the windscreen, his body flung onto the red-brick front fence of a house. It was on the fence that he cracked his head open. He was nineteen and he was lucky. When I first started working with him I was told that if he'd been wearing the seat belt he would have been concertinaed with the car, reality becoming animation as it collapsed from three to two to one dimension. For the neighbor whose brick wall Kevin's head smashed onto, it must have sounded like an explosion.

"I dunn wanna, I dunn wanna, I dunn wanna." Kevin is standing in his shower recess, while I am trying to pull down his pants.

He's shat and pissed himself. "I dunn wanna, I dunn wanna, I dunn wanna." I try to get his pants out from underneath his feet, and the shit and the piss smear on my hands, my arms, my shirt. "I dunn wanna, I dunn wanna, I dunn wanna."

"For fuck's sake, Kevin, stand still!"

The shouting works. I don't like doing it but yelling at him is the only thing that quiets him down. I know why he shouts, why he chants over and over and over, *I dunn wanna, I dunn wanna, I dunn wanna,* I know all about that. You repeat, you repeat, you repeat to block out the shame, to block out the voice screaming at you, *What a mess, what a monster, what a no-hoper, what a disgrace, what an idiot, what a fuckup, what an animal, what a douche bag, what a freak, what a loser, loser, loser, loser,* the voice that won't stop, can't stop, that mocks and taunts and jeers and fills your head till you just repeat the words over and over and over to make them music, to make them rhythm, to make them just sound, *bam bam bam bam bam bam bam bam.* The shame, like a piston ramming right into me; the memory of it flaying me, stripping the skin off me. The shame still cuts me in two, in four, in eight. I am hung and quartered and skewered on it.

"It's all right, Kevin, it's fine, mate, it's fine—I understand."

"I dunn wanna, I dunn wanna, I dunn wanna." But the voice is getting quieter. I carefully guide his feet over the trousers, and he is naked, cupping his dick and balls in his hands.

"It's okay, Kevin, it's fine, mate. I'm just going to turn on the shower."

The pipes knock, scream, and then the water cascades all over him. I grab the yellow sponge and scrub his body. I don't mind getting wet, it washes my shame away, as I rub his belly, his groin, and his thighs. The shit turns runny as it swirls around the plug hole, turning liquid, disappearing till it is just clear water.

Kevin is silent now, Kevin is calm now. His cock is half-erect and he points at it.

"Okay, mate, that's enough." I turn off the water and start to rub him down. His cock is fully hard now and he can't stop chortling.

"I'm sor-ry, Dan."

"That's okay."

He sniffs, his face contorts. "You . . . you . . . you smell, Da-Da-Dan."

I finish drying him and then point to the door. "Out. I have to shower too."

I shower, quickly, scrub my skin. The rush of hot water on my back, it finally relaxes me.

My pants are fine, but my shirt is soiled. I find a plastic bag and place the soggy mess in it. I then search under the sink, find some disinfectant, a Chux, and finish cleaning up the bathroom.

When I go back to the living room, Kevin's sitting on the end of the sofa, drinking a beer and watching porn.

"Is it cool if I borrow one of your T-shirts?"

He is ignoring me, he's fascinated by the athletic contortions of the two women and the man on the screen.

I take a plain blue T-shirt from his room and put it on. I should be scolding him: *You shouldn't drink, you know that. If you drink too much, you'll lose control of your bladder and your bowels, you know that, Kevin.* And he does know that. And he knows that it has taken three years to learn to walk again, three years to learn to slowly put words together again, three years to be able to live away from nurses and doctors and hospital wards. He knows. I don't say anything.

There's no washing machine in Kevin's flat, so I put the bag of soiled clothes in the car boot for us to do later at the Laundromat. I lock up and we begin the slow shuffle to the Sunshine Pool. Sometimes I have to remind him: this foot, I point, bring it forward; that foot, I point to the other, now move that one. This foot, that foot, we shuffle, we crawl, I catch his arm when he stumbles, we reach the pool.

He doesn't want me to undress him, he wants to do it himself.

The smell of chlorine, of toilet soap, the humid air, the stripping bodies. *I dunn wanna, I dunn wanna, I dunn wanna.*

At the pool a cheerful young man in Speedos takes Kevin's hand and starts pulling him away, trying to lead him to the shallow end.

"No. I-I-I wunn wunna, Dan."

"Come on, Kevin. You know Sean is going to swim with you."

"No." Kevin pulls at my T-shirt, trying to get me to go with him. I don't budge. The chlorine is thick in my nose and in my mouth, the heat and the steam is seeping into me. *I dunn wanna, I dunn wanna, I dunn wanna.*

"Ca-cum inn, Da-nee."

"No!" The force of my vehemence hurts him as much as if I have smacked him. He looks down, distressed and ashamed.

I apologize, hug him. "Come on, Kevin, you know, mate, you know I can't swim."

I watch Sean lead Kevin down the slow lane, watch Sean try to teach Kevin how to tread water again. I sit as far away from the water as I can.

I don't swim.

I dunn wanna, I dunn wanna, I dunn wanna.

I won't swim.

I dunn wanna, I dunn wanna, I dunn wanna.

I can't swim.

"You look very handsome, Danny. Don't you agree, Regan? Doesn't your brother look handsome?"

Danny's top lip curled wryly at his sister. She didn't answer their mother, slouching deeper into the sofa, her canary-yellow hoodie stretched over her knees. She was intent on the TV screen, watching actors who just seemed to be shouting at each other. The yelling was interrupted every ten seconds or so by a crack of gunfire which was the laugh track. From time to time Regan sniggered. Danny knew the show was called *Friends,* of course he knew, everyone knew that, but all that shouting and yelling was giving him a headache.

His mother was down on one knee before him. She had pins in her mouth and was turning up the ends of his suit pants. He was impatient to get the thing off him, the new metallic-blue suit that his mum had bought for him from one of the seconds warehouses on Albert Street. It was a good suit, a top Aussie label, and it did look good on him. But the collar of his shirt prickled and the jacket was heavy around his shoulders and he was sick of modeling it.

His mother wanted him to look just right for the opening ceremony. He just wanted to be back in his shorts and sweatshirt. He was packed, ready. Why did she always have to find something else to do?

"Done," said his mum, satisfied. "You can take it off."

Danny carefully laid the jacket on the arm of the sofa, undid the tie, started unbuttoning the shirt.

"Don't!" Regan was scowling. "Don't strip off in here."

"Sorry."

He kept forgetting that Regan was turning into a teenager; unlike him she wasn't used to bodies in various stages of undress. He never thought of those things. He bundled his sweater and shorts under his arms and went into his room to change. When he came back his mother was sitting in front of the sewing machine on the kitchen table. She had earphones on, connected to the Walkman that sat next to the machine. She didn't like the shouting either, thought Danny. He knew she would be lost in rock and roll, something old and in mono. He plonked down on the sofa. "Move," he said, pushing back Regan's feet.

"No, you move," and she kicked him. "Go sit on the chair."

He snickered. She was becoming an adolescent, a mean surly bitch of a teenage girl.

He heard a noise, his ears cocked, it must be *him*, and Danny bolted from the sofa and was running down the hall. But when he threw open the door it was an old woman standing there, beaming at him, a young woman standing next to her, unsmiling, with a lazy left eye and her arms full of magazines.

"Good morning, young man," the old woman said cheerfully, in a thick accent but very precise English. "Do you have a moment for us to talk to you about the coming of the Lord?"

They were God-botherers. The cheap acrylic cardigans and the determined defensive politeness were a dead giveaway. Probably Joeys. The Mormons were always men in white shirts and thin black ties. Jehovah's Witnesses were usually women.

Danny looked past them. Why wasn't he here yet? They were going to be late.

He would have liked to slam the door in their faces. But he knew he couldn't, his mother wouldn't allow it. "Don't let them in," she had counseled all her children since they were toddlers. "Don't let them in, don't listen to their God-bothering, but be polite to them. You must always ask them if they'd like a drink."

He was surly as he asked, "Would you like some water?"

The young woman nodded gratefully. "Thank you, that's very kind."

The old woman started to walk inside but he raised a hand in warning. "Please stay here."

His mother stopped her sewing and took off her earphones.

"They're Joeys," he said. "I think they're your lot."

His mother attempted to flick his behind with her measuring tape. But she was laughing. "I am *not* a Joey anymore," she said. "I haven't been one for a long time, mister."

Danny had two glasses of water. "I didn't mean that," he called. "I think they're Greeks."

The old woman took three small sips and handed back the glass. The young woman gulped down all of hers.

"Have you heard about the Lord?" the old woman began. "Have you heard about Jesus Christ?"

"Yes," answered Danny shortly, "I have and I'm not interested."

He kicked shut the door behind him and fell back onto the couch, trying to concentrate on the sitcom.

He couldn't sit still. He heard a car, he was sure he could hear a car parking outside. This time it *had* to be him.

"Mum, he's here."

She couldn't hear him. He rushed into the kitchen, pressed the stop button on the Walkman.

"He's here."

"Well, go and invite him in."

It was the first time Frank Torma had been to Danny's house, the first time the Coach had seen where Danny lived.

Danny was speechless when he opened the door. The Coach was wearing a shirt, a red one that was too snug for his balloon belly; patches of white singlet were visible where the shirt was gaping between the buttons. He was wearing a red shirt and black trousers and held a small box wrapped in white paper. Danny had never seen the Coach in civvies, never out of track pants. All he could think to do was reach out to accept the gift.

Coach wouldn't let him have it. "It's not for you," he said, but there was a lightness to his voice showing he wasn't annoyed. "Well, Mr. Kelly," he continued, "are you going to let me in?"

Regan was sitting up straight now, and she nodded to the Coach as Danny introduced them. His mother stepped forward, holding out her hand in greeting, and Coach took it but he also leaned in and kissed her, first on one cheek, then the other. Danny could see that his mother was surprised by the first kiss but that she readily accepted the second.

The Coach handed her the wrapped parcel. "These are some *piskóta* and some *krémes,*" he said diffidently, a little embarrassed. "They are Hungarian sweets."

Danny's mother was delighted. She gave the Coach another two quick pecks on his cheeks and he blushed. He seemed taller somehow, larger now that he was in Danny's house. He seemed too big for their small living room.

"Are you ready, Danny?"

"I've just got to pack his suit and we're done. Please take a seat," insisted Danny's mother. "And can I please get you a drink?"

Can I *please* get you a drink? She was trying too hard, being fake.

Coach shook his head. "Thank you but no. The other boy will be arriving at my house in just under an hour. We must be off as soon as we can."

Wilco. The other boy was Wilco. Now it was Wilco and Kelly, they were the only ones left. Scooter had started VCE and made the decision he would never be a champion. He was no longer training. And Fraser was at the Australian Institute of Sport, and Morello, well, he had always been useless, he hadn't come close to qualifying. Nor had Taylor. It was Wilco and Kelly going to Brisbane.

Oh, how he wished it could still be Taylor and Kelly. That was what it should be.

His mother returned with the small black suitcase she had bought especially for the occasion. She was about to hand it to her son but Frank Torma took it from her.

"Thank you so much for coming and picking up Danny. I know it is very much out of your way."

"It is not a problem at all, Mrs. Kelly."

"Please call me Stephanie. Mrs. Kelly makes me sound very old."

Now she sounded like his mum again. There was an uncomfortable moment of silence, and then the Coach said quickly, "And yes, please, please call me Frank."

His mother came up to Danny, rested her head on his shoulder. "Oh baby, I wish I could be there." She smiled up at the Coach. "He looks so handsome in his suit—he's going to be the most handsome boy in that opening ceremony."

Danny pulled away from her, mortified. "Just shut up, Mum, don't say a word."

Then the Coach did something unexpected. The Coach winked at him and smiled back at his mother. "Yes, I am sure he will be."

Danny had to get out of the house right *now*. He swiftly kissed his mother goodbye and then leaned down to give Regan an awkward squeeze, told her to tell Theo that there would be another medal for his collection when he got back from camp.

The strength of Regan's responding hug took him by surprise. "Good luck, mate," she whispered.

She felt lumpy, she was getting fat.

As they walked to the car, he turned to the Coach and said, politely, carefully, "Thank you, Mr. Torma, for picking me up."

Did he sound fake?

"It's okay," said Frank. "As I said to your mother, I am happy to do so."

～～～

As soon as the Coach opened the door, Danny rushed past him and straight into the front bedroom—straight to his room. It was really the Coach's bedroom, but when the squad were staying over it was always Danny's room. He placed his suitcase on the bed and looked around to make sure nothing had changed since the last time. There was the double bed, the wardrobe with the thin mirrored panel down one side, and the white chest of drawers next to the bed, on top of which sat the one photograph in the room, the one of Coach's elderly parents, the stern, sad-looking couple. As always, the Coach had vacuumed and dusted the room, had changed the bedding, in preparation for the boy's visit; it was tidy and immaculately clean. Danny pushed his suitcase aside and lay down on the bed, dangling his feet over the edge so his sneakers wouldn't dirty the blanket. He stared up at the high ceiling, a sea of pressed iron panels painted white, except for the central plaster rosette in the middle of which hung the red cubed lamp. Danny couldn't touch the ceiling, even standing on the bed; he tried every time: it was *that* high. There was space in Frank Torma's house; he wouldn't ever feel trapped in that house.

It wasn't huge or ostentatious like the Taylors' house, the other boys' houses. There was space but it wasn't extravagant, you didn't get lost in it.

He heard his name being called. Danny smoothed the creased blanket and rushed down to the kitchen.

The Coach had ordered pizzas and told Danny to wait for Wilco while he went to pick them up. As soon as Coach was gone, Danny opened the fridge and found a salami. He cut five thick slices off it and gobbled them up hungrily. He wandered into the lounge room, flicked through the scattering of CDs. He was sure that the last time he was there Beethoven's Fifth Symphony was the disk in the player. He turned on the stereo, pressed a button, and the CD holder slid out. He read the black lettering on the silver face of the disk. Again, it was Beethoven's Fifth Symphony. Danny didn't know if this meant the Coach listened to it all the time or that the Coach hadn't listened to music since the last time Danny was there. They'd watched television, movies, eaten pizza, and played cards at Coach's house. But they'd never listened to music.

A sharp drilling sound ripped through his reverie. He switched off the stereo, tore down the corridor, and opened the door. Wilco was standing there, looking sheepish, holding a full sports bag in one hand, his mother standing behind him.

"Hi, Danny," he muttered. He'd had his head shaved, with a number one razor, just like Danny had. It made him look older.

"Hi, mate. Hi, Mrs. Wilkinson." He returned the kiss Wilco's mum planted on his cheek. He liked Mrs. Wilkinson. She had a lean, narrow face with deep furrows in her cheeks and forehead. Her hair was thinning, gray and messy, and her teeth protruded a little. But she looked like a real mum and was always kind.

She peered down the corridor. "Is Mr. Torma here?"

"He's picking up pizza." Danny stood to one side to let Wilco and his mother in. He was enjoying pretending it was his house, that he was welcoming guests to his home. He led them through to the kitchen.

"Oooh," said Mrs. Wilkinson, rubbing her hands, "these old houses are so cold. Where's the heating?"

Danny was put out, he didn't want to hear the house criticized. He switched on the small white radiator on the wall behind the kitchen table.

"Good God," Mrs. Wilkinson exclaimed, going over to examine the heater. "I haven't seen one of these since I was a girl." She pulled her coat tighter around her body. "That will take ages to heat up." She smiled at Danny. "Sweetheart, you'll freeze. Go and grab a jumper."

"I'm all right." And he was, he was fine in this house.

Mrs. Wilkinson pulled out one of the chairs and sat down. "I don't think anything has been done to this house for over thirty years. But it is a gorgeous little terrace, and in wonderful condition. It would cost a fortune to buy now."

Danny warmed to her again. "Would you like a glass of water?"

"You're right at home here, aren't you, darling?"

Danny blushed. Wilco gave him a sly grin, then turned to his mother. "You can go."

"I'm going to wait till Mr. Torma returns, John, and then I'll go. And don't use that tone of voice with me. I always think you're bloody channeling your father when you speak like that." She turned back to Danny. "And yes, darling, I will have some water. Thank you."

Danny poured water for her and another glass for Wilco. He didn't look at the boy as he handed him the glass. He knew Wilco's parents had recently divorced. He could bet that Wilco was furious at his mother, that he just wanted her to get the hell out of there. Then they heard the front door opening, and Coach's steps coming up the corridor. Danny looked over at Wilco and saw the boy's relief.

～～～

Every time Coach returned with pizzas from the Macedonian shop at the end of the street, he would roar proudly, Boys, these are the best pizzas you will ever have! He said it every time. *Every* time.

There were four large pizzas, one with a base of roasted eggplant topped with a layer of wafer-thin slices of potato: that was Danny's favorite. Another was covered with yogurt and mint-flavored mince. There was a hot salami pizza, and a vegetarian one with anchovies. The boys and the man ate them ravenously. They were the best pizzas Danny had ever had.

After they'd finished eating, Danny and Wilco listened to Frank. Of course, it was all about swimming, all about the Australian Championships; of course it was, that was all that mattered, all that any of them could think about.

"You have to listen to everything I say," he kept repeating, and they both nodded emphatically that they would.

He pointed to Danny. "You can do it, you can win the two hundred meter butterfly, if you stay focused. If you work, it is yours." He then pointed to Wilco. "And the two hundred freestyle is yours if you want it. You want it?"

"Yes!" Wilco almost shouted it, pumping his fist.

"Good," said Frank. "Then it's yours."

Danny wanted Coach to say something to him about the one hundred freestyle. They were his, the one hundred freestyle and the two hundred butterfly—they were both his. But Frank didn't say it.

"I'm going to win the one hundred freestyle as well," Danny exploded. "I'm going to win them both."

"Yeah." Wilco punched the air again. "Go, Barracuda!"

But Frank was sour. "What did I say?"

Danny didn't know what he meant.

"You promised me that you would listen to exactly everything I said. Focus on the two hundred butterfly, Kelly. That's your race."

Danny opened his mouth then took one look at Frank's face and shut it. But he said to himself, I am going to win them both, I'm going to prove to you that I can win them both. He settled back on the sofa. He didn't hear the other boy and the man talking, he was thinking of returning home the hero, thinking of the two medals, and qualifying for the Pan Pacific Games. He was going to prove to the Coach that he could win them both.

They played a few quick rounds of gin rummy—not poker, insisted Coach, I don't want you getting overexcited—and then he announced that it was time for bed.

"One more game?" implored Danny.

"No. We wake at four-thirty for training and then it is straight to the airport. No. It is time for bed."

That was when Wilco asked, "Can I sleep in the front bedroom tonight?"

Frank pointed to Danny. "Kelly is in the front room and you have the spare room. I will sleep here on the sofa."

Wilco bit his lip. "Why does Danny always get the front room? I'm a year older, I'm in Year Twelve. I think I should have it."

Danny was frantically trying to think of what to say. That he was there first, that it was his room, that it would always be his room—because he deserved it: he was the strongest, the fastest, the best. He tried to form words, but before he could speak, Wilco got nonchalantly to his feet and said, "I'm just messing with you, Shorty. I don't care where I sleep."

The two boys stood side by side at the small bathroom sink, brushing their teeth. The room was freezing and it took an age for the tap to run warm. Wilco spat out the toothpaste, then washed his face and behind his ears. He rinsed one more time, spat, then looked at himself in the mirror. "Mum reckons this haircut makes me look like a hooligan."

Danny spat into the sink, ran the tap to wash it away. "I think your mum is really nice." He didn't know why he said that, except that it was true, Mrs. Wilkinson was nice.

Wilco turned and leaned against the sink. His right eyebrow was half-cocked, as if he was sizing Danny up. "You know, Kelly, that shit we used to say about your mum?" His next words came out in a rush. "It was just dumb stupid kid shit—you know that, don't you? We all reckon your mum is tops, she's beautiful and really really cool. You know that? It was just dumb shit we were going on with."

Danny pushed Wilco out of the way to rinse his toothbrush. He didn't want to be reminded of that time, of that lewd, ugly centerfold. It was a shock how the thought of it still scalded him.

He splashed water on his face, turned off the tap. "Yeah, I know," he answered.

Wilco surprised Danny again, tapping him on the forehead, not hard, just three soft taps. "Goodnight, Shorty."

This time Danny didn't mind the nickname. He knew that Wilco didn't mean any harm by it at all.

But how he wished it could be Martin and Danny, Taylor and Kelly.

On his way to bed he popped his head round the living room door to say goodnight to the Coach. There was a blanket spread on the sofa and he wondered how Frank was going to fit.

"You know, I can sleep here, Coach," he said. "It's sweet."

"No." The man's voice was firm but then it softened. "In two days, Danny, you have two heats to swim. You take the bed."

Coach was right, of course he was. The only thing that mattered was the competition. Not only for Danny, not only for Wilco, but for Coach as well. That was the only thing that mattered.

∿∿∿

Danny was freezing in his shorts and T-shirt. He and Wilco were in the backseat of the taxi on the way to the airport. Coach was in front, too big for the cab. But then so too were Wilco and Danny. Wilco's shaved scalp made him look adult, gave strength to his jaw. He was no longer a boy, he was getting to be a man. Danny hoped that his own shaved head made him look older too. He pushed back his shoulders, held his back straight.

Wilco was examining the face of his mobile phone. It was new and he was obsessed with it, tapping the buttons constantly, seemingly astonished by what it could do. But then, with a glance at the Coach who was staring resolutely at the road ahead, Wilco pocketed the gadget and leaned closer to Danny. "Mate," he whispered, "my dad says he can get you an upgrade to business class with me. Want me to organize it?"

It was no longer Martin and Danny. It was now Wilco and Danny.

The driver had the radio on, the car was speeding down the freeway—Danny was sure that Coach couldn't hear them. This would be his first flight. It would be so cool to fly business class. It would impress Martin, Luke would be so envious. But then he thought of his father, of Demet. They'd find something wrong with Mr. Wilkinson's money, something about how he got it or what he did or what he didn't do with it. And what about Coach?

Danny mouthed that question.

Wilco whispered, "No, I can only get one of you upgraded."

"Then no, thanks."

"Suit yourself." Wilco took out his phone again, he couldn't stop playing with it.

Danny was going to get one, he'd save up and buy one as soon as he could. He wanted a phone like Wilco's, exactly that brand of mobile phone.

~~~

When the plane started to slowly move along the tarmac, he got scared. That huge and heavy machine of steel and metal—how would it be able to stay up in the air? The Coach was next to him, and there was a woman doing the crossword on his other side. As always the Coach seemed like a giant, too big for the plane. But it made Danny feel safe. He was glad he hadn't gone up front with Wilco. Next to Coach he was safe.

The plane had been moving sluggishly but it began to pick up speed as it taxied down the runway. There was a moment when the cabin was shaking and gravity was being betrayed, when Danny felt that his whole body was going to be flung forward, and then there was the rush of flight, of leaving earth, of reaching height. There was no fear, that was what was flung off.

His face bright, his eyes gleaming, his eyes wide, Danny turned to Coach and cried out, "It feels like swimming! It feels exactly like swimming."

The Coach smiled, a rare moment, and he nodded and said, "You are right, Danny. It is exactly like swimming."

Danny wanted to keep on rising, going higher and higher and faster and faster until the roof of the sky met the halo of the sun. He told himself to remember the ferocious joy, the inexplicable rightness—it was exactly like swimming—and take it with him all the way to Brisbane, take the experience into the pool. He had to remember that water was the same substance as sky. He would take that feeling into his swim and he would be flying as much as swimming.

~~~~

When they landed in Brisbane, they were no longer special. There were competitors from all over the country, from places with names like Esperance and Geraldton, Maroochydore and Tuggeranong. They were met by a harried young woman wearing a gray tracksuit, a Swimming Australia nametag stating her name was Ellen. She carried a clipboard under her arm, and on greeting them, she immediately ticked off their names and gave rushed instructions on how to get to the bus. Coach explained that the boys still needed to get their bags, and for some reason that annoyed her. She ripped out a printed sheet and handed it to the Coach. "Make sure you follow the registration instructions to the letter," she announced, and then abruptly turned and was gone. Danny was incensed. He'd never heard anyone talk to the Coach like that before.

Once the humid slush of Brisbane air hit them, Danny was glad he was in shorts. The air was thick here, he could sense that it would slow you down. Coach had told them they would have to adjust to that. They would need to slow down the pace of everything they did: walking, talking, eating, and especially their exercises. "Conserve your energy," he had said. "Only push yourselves hard when you are in the pool."

And then they were on the bus and it was crowded and noisy—it felt strange to be sitting on a bus with girls, he'd forgotten how talkative girls could be, how they whispered close to one another, how they chatted in low voices, as if everything they said to each other was a secret. And there was chattering and shrieking and laughing too—it was deafening.

And then they were at the convention center and there were huge crowds and what seemed to be hundreds of adults wearing Swimming Australia nametags, and there were queues and more instructions and coaches and trainers and medical staff and more officials. They were signed in and given a booklet to read and one man said impatiently to him, "Okay, you can go now," and turned around to sign in the next boy and all of this made Coach and Wilco and Danny seem smaller. And then there were the golden boys and the golden girls, the swimmers that Danny had watched on TV winning gold and silver and bronze and breaking world records. Everyone was looking at the golden boys and girls and no one was looking at him or Wilco, no one cared about him or Wilco and no one cared about the Coach. And all of that made them feel small.

They were assigned their rooms. They were assigned their heats. They were given instructions and then they were dismissed.

Except for the golden boys and the golden girls. Everyone smiled and was polite and tried to make jokes and conversation with the golden boys and the golden girls.

Danny couldn't wait to come back next time, to the next Australian Championships, when he would be one of them. When he would be a golden boy.

They passed a huddle of men in crisp white shirts sporting the Australian Institute of Sport logo and one of them looked up and nodded at Coach. The man was beanpole tall, with tanned spotless skin and a clipped salt-and-pepper beard. He peeled away from the others and called Frank's name. The other men looked up, one or two nodding at Coach, but they didn't come over. They went back to their conversation.

"This is Ben Whitter," Coach said to the boys as he shook the man's hand. "Ben is a coach at the AIS."

Ben smiled down at both Danny *and* Wilco—he was *that* tall—then immediately turned back to Frank. "I want to say thanks for sending us young Michael Fraser. He's good, he's very, very good." He slapped Coach on the back. Danny couldn't believe that someone had done that to the Coach.

"He is good," agreed Frank. "But keep pushing him. He has a problem with discipline."

"Mate, they all have problems with discipline when they come to us. Don't worry, I'm riding him hard." Ben winked at Coach and again Danny was surprised at such familiarity. "He just might be your first Olympian, Frank. He just might get there."

Danny knew that Wilco was thinking the same thing as he was: Frank Torma had never coached an Olympian before.

"He won't be my first," said Coach, and there was a growl in his voice; Danny could sense the anger there. Coach pointed at him and Wilco. "One of these boys will be my first." He was gesturing at the two of them but he was looking straight at Danny.

Ben's laugh was cynical. He said goodbye without looking at Wilco or Danny.

Danny wanted the Coach to give it back. He didn't know exactly how but he sensed that Frank Torma had been slighted. Give it back, he said under his breath, Give it back.

But Frank Torma said nothing at all.

〜〜〜

There was a dinner and a small procession through the stadium adjacent to the swimming complex. There were photographers and television cameras and a speech by the Queensland Minister for Sport and another speech by the CEO of the main sponsor and another by another CEO and then a final speech by someone from Swimming Australia. All the men and boys were wearing suits, and all the women and girls were wearing their best dresses, and Danny knew it was far from true what his mother had said, that he would be the handsomest boy there tonight. There were many more handsome boys in much better suits, and the ones who were the handsomest were the golden boys, and they were the ones the photographers were crowding around and they were the ones being asked questions by the reporters and being introduced to the CEOs and the Minister for Sport. When the group photograph was taken, with Danny somewhere in the second row, Wilco in the fourth, Danny knew that he would look small, insignificant. Danny knew he would disappear.

The next time he was here, he told himself, after he had won his races, he would be a golden boy.

~~~~

All of that was gone as soon as he dived into the pool the following morning. It was the best feeling in the world. The water took his burdens away from him.

But when he was returning to the change rooms, a young official ran up to him and blocked his way. Danny was about to protest but the man hissed, "Shh, you're in the frame. There's an interview going on!"

One of the golden boys was being interviewed on camera. There were wires and cables and men holding microphone booms. Danny tugged his hand free and made his escape.

He hated them, he absolutely hated them, the golden boys. He hated their blondness, their insincere smiles, their designer sunglasses, their designer swimmers and their designer sports gear. They made him feel dark and short and dirty. He detested them and he couldn't wait till he was wearing those sunglasses, till he had those brand names across his sweatshirt, impatient for when those microphones and those cameras were going to be in his face.

He found Wilco and they headed back to the bus that would return them to the dorms. The humidity made it feel as though they were walking through steam. Danny had made sure not to exert himself too much in the day's training; he knew that he had to learn to manage the air, the humid damp screen that clung to his face, to his skin, that seeped in under his armpits, slipped into the creases between his legs. He told himself that it was not making him itch, he forced his hands to be still. He and Wilco found a seat together in the middle of the bus. The golden boys were all sitting up the back. Danny could smell the chlorine and the bland floury tang of the locker-room soap. He could smell Wilco's sweat, the pong of rotting fruit, they all smelled of it. They all stank of chlorine and rotting fruit and floury soap. The official ticked off the list and the bus rumbled and began to move. Danny's body was bathed in perspiration, his shirt was sticking to the seat. He shifted, he breathed, he told himself that he knew that air, that he did not feel the heat, that there was no itch. He sat still, staring straight ahead. Wilco was saying something and Danny was nodding, but not listening, trying not to think of anyone or anything. He was concentrating on breathing, on the air coming in and the air going out. He was hearing but not listening. There was nothing, no heat, no humidity, no itch, no golden boys, no golden girls, no bodies, no flesh. It was just him. There was no one else but Danny Kelly.

⌒⌒⌒

When they filed off the bus, Coach was standing there. He wanted Danny to wait. Wilco kept looking back, wondering what Torma had to tell Danny. He was jealous, Danny was sure of it. The last people got off the bus just as the women's coach rumbled to a stop. Coach stayed silent while the girls left the bus, talking and swinging their sports bags over their shoulders. Danny had his head lowered while they walked past. He could look at them clinically, critically, when they were in or around the pool, when they were stripped to their togs, being swimmers. But he wasn't sure how to be around them when they were away from the pool, when they were in their civvies. There was no breeze, the air was heavy as a curtain, his shirt was plastered to his back and under his arms, he could feel sweat trickling down his arse crack. He breathed in, transformed it into air that he could control.

The Coach held out his hand and touched Danny's chest, as though he was testing his breathing, reading his heart rate.

The Coach dropped his hand. "Are you ready?"

The words took the boy by surprise. He wanted to snap back, "Of course I am," but something in the Coach's earnest inquiry stopped him. The man was not suited to the Queensland climate. His face was flushed, his shirt drenched, there was sweat on his brow, on the ridge of his chin, under his eyes. There was a small wet patch on Danny's T-shirt, where the Coach's hand had made contact.

"Of course," Danny said quietly.

"You are a young man, Kelly," Coach said. "Still a boy, but you are strong."

Danny had followed all the Coach's instructions, he had worked at the gym, strengthening the muscles in his chest, his back, his arms, his legs. He had strength and power.

"The other competitors will be older boys, but you have the strength to qualify tomorrow afternoon." The Coach clipped and rolled the final word, making it two distinct words: *aftAH noorn.*

And the morning? Danny wanted the Coach to say something about the morning's heat, the one hundred meter freestyle. There wasn't really any advice to be given now—it was all up to him. Still, he wanted to hear something, some encouragement. But the man had already started walking away; he turned in surprise that the boy wasn't following.

Danny didn't know how to ask the question. He thought it was unfair that he had to find the words for it. His mouth drooped, in a sulk.

"Use your strength," the Coach said, turning back again. "Use it in the morning and use it in the afternoon."

Danny could smile then; he wanted to run after the Coach and hug him. He wanted to hear him say those words again and again.

Use your strength. He was the strongest. He could use his strength for both races. He knew the Coach only wanted him to work at the butterfly, wanted Danny to concentrate on the new stroke. He'd been doing that, he'd been mastering it. But he could do both, he knew he could. He wasn't going to fuck it up, he'd show the Coach that he could do it. The freestyle was Danny's stroke—it belonged to him.

∼∼∼

Danny was shaking, his body was folding in on itself. He felt as though someone had reached into his gut and squeezed out his entrails, that there was nothing left inside him. He was quivering and hollow, his teeth chattering, his balls had shriveled and been punched up to his gut and he cradled his shaking frame, telling himself not to throw up, not to shit, not to piss, not to vomit as he limped from the pool. But the air was fighting him and he panicked, struggling for breath, so he forced his lungs to work, commanded his body to work, and he expelled a breath and water streamed down from his nose, spilled from his mouth, he was all snot and all water, a creature more marine than human. But at last he was breathing and he could force his muscles to work and his limbs to move and he was walking and breathing, slowly coming back to himself. As he walked past the tiers of seats he was aware that there were lights flashing and people rushing and that photographs were being taken and swimmers were coming out into the pool area and then he was in the shower and the cold water was raining down on his head and shoulders and he was no longer trembling, no longer thinking that his belly would split, that his bowels would explode. He could think again, he could think and see and hear. A low roar rumbled around the auditorium and all he could think of was that he was third, that he had not qualified in the heat, that the stroke no longer belonged to him, that he wasn't good enough or strong enough. There were two swimmers better than him, a golden boy, a golden boy of course, but also a young swimmer, a swimmer even younger than he was, with a lanky clumsy frame and massive feet and hands, and that boy had come first and the golden boy had come second and he had come third.

Third. A fucking lousy insignificant useless bloody *third*.

He had not qualified. He had lost. He was a loser.

Coach was standing there, a towel in his hand, telling him that it had been a good effort, that he had nothing to be ashamed of, that he had to focus on the next race, that the next race was *his* race, and Danny was listening and nodding and convincing himself that, yes, the next race was *his* race, but there was a thought forming at the corner of his consciousness; he could almost grab it but he knew he must not, he could not. He shook his head, he flicked the thought to the back of his mind. But he knew it would be there; afterward, after he won his next heat, once he came up on top, then he could reach for it. But not now. He knew that Coach trusted him to place in the next race and he wanted to hear that trust from Coach's lips, he needed to hear it, so he could believe it, that he was the best, the strongest, the fastest. Now he had to place all his trust in Coach. That was all that mattered.

~~~~

Danny sat in the back row of the stadium to watch Wilco come first in his heat for the two hundred meter freestyle. He beat one of the golden boys. No, that's not right, thought Danny sourly, Wilco *was* a golden boy. Afterward, Danny waited till Wilco finally emerged from the change rooms and then he bounced down the steps and went up to shake Wilco's hand. The older boy punched the air, raised his fist in triumph. He thinks he's such a hero, thought Danny, the spite so intense it left a foul taste in his mouth. But he knew not to show it, he knew exactly what he had to do.

"You legend," he said, pumping Wilco's hand. "You absolute fucking legend."

Wilco couldn't stand still, his delight had spread across his face, animating his limbs, his whole body. It made him look like a boy again. Danny dropped Wilco's hand but continued to say

congratulations. It was the only word he could think to say. He would
show nothing of what was inside him, that some deadly serrated knife
was carving right through him. He knew that he would not be able to
bear it if he didn't qualify with his next swim. He couldn't stand it
if Wilco was a champion and not him. If it didn't happen for Danny,
he was sure that it would kill him. The knife would cut right through
him, would carve him in half. Would destroy him.

~~~

He knew at his final turn that the race was his. That didn't make him
punish the water less. The butterfly was never effortless, the butterfly was always work: one lapse of exertion led to failure. The stroke
wasn't about being part of the water, it wasn't becoming one with the
substance and matter and DNA of water. The stroke was a machine,
the stroke was about making his body into a craft that razed a path
through the water. It was fighting and twisting and transforming the
element. On the second turn, his chest and lungs and sternum had
morphed into one distinct muscle; his arms a wheel and his hips and
legs and feet a threshing machine that kicked in one unified motion.
By the last turn he was a perfect mechanism and the water had disappeared, bowed to his will, and it was flight now, the water was defeated,
and he was energy working in a cyclical precise motion and the race
was his. There was no water and there were no other swimmers and
there were no black lines and there was not even the pool. All there
was, all that existed, was Danny. He could feel the power of his chest
and the strength of his back and the hardness of his abdomen and the
potency of his arms—the capabilities of a flawless body—and that was
how it was no surprise when he touched the tiles: he knew he had won.
He was exhausted, he was breathless, his chest felt as though it would
explode, but he was not spent. If he had to, he knew, he could have done
it again. He had become the stroke, the stroke was now his. Coach had
been right. And even as he punched the air, even as he heard his name
called, as he shook the hands of the other swimmers who dived under

the ropes to congratulate him, he was pushing a thought to the back of his mind. Not yet, not yet. He was the strongest, the fastest, the best. He was in the finals. He would prove it in the finals.

~~~~~

And he did. At the 1997 Australian Swimming Championships, Danny Kelly placed first in the two hundred meter men's butterfly.

It was in the showers that he had time to think. He thought through every moment of the race. It was mind. He understood for the first time exactly what Coach meant, what the great athletes and swimmers meant when they said it was all in the mind. It couldn't have been done without the strength and power of his body, but that strength and power was also inside of him. He was as strong and as powerful *inside*: the body and the mind were one, and so they could not break, they could not fail.

A stocky unshaven man came up to him after his shower, congratulated him and explained that he was a journalist for one of the Brisbane papers. He wanted to ask Danny a few questions. The man reeked, a sour odor, of too many cigarettes and curdled milk, but Danny eagerly answered the man's questions.

"And your name is Danny Kelly, that right?"

"Daniel Kelly," he corrected him.

As the man scribbled in his notebook, Danny looked around for the photographers. There were none. But next time—next time he knew there would be photographers.

~~~~~

He was prepared this time on the plane for when the craft had to prove its strength, when the machine had to convince gravity that it was the more powerful. Again, as the plane rose he experienced the sensation of being dislodged, thrown away from his own body. Then he was one again, and again it was like swimming and there was a tingle in his belly and a tingle in his crotch.

This time, when the plane had climbed above the clouds and was floating in the canopy of sun and sky, Danny didn't look out the window. He was thinking of Wilco up in business class, thinking of when he, Danny, would be flying first class. But it would be his own money, he wouldn't be dependent on anyone. He would fly his parents first class to exotic places for their anniversaries, he would shout Regan trips to Europe and Theo trips to South America and the Poles.

It was then, with the snow of cloud beneath him, the sharpest, purest light in the universe on his face, that he let himself travel to the corners of thought and allowed himself to give shape to the heresy he had been holding back for days. He knew that he was strong, that he was fast, that he was the best. Body *and* mind. Inside *and* out. It was that he was convinced that one hundred meters was too short for him. He was strength, he was power; he laid a palm across his chest, where the muscles could unfurl at will, where they twitched, hungry and alive. The Coach had not let him swim that extra one hundred meters, because he thought that it would sap his energy, deplete him for his other race. *Concentrate on the butterfly, that is your stroke.* But he knew now that with that extra one hundred meters, he would have found the pace, he would have found the power. He could fly as high as he wanted to, he could touch the sun. He knew it. He looked out at the infinite cloud. Frank Torma had never coached an Olympian. That was why he couldn't give it back, that was why he had let Ben Whitter get away with it. Coach did not know what Danny was capable of.

Danny Kelly could be the best in the world. He knew he could conquer both strokes, it was inside him, it was a revelation written inside him, inked over his muscles, imprinted in his brain, etched into his soul. The butterfly was a given; the freestyle had *always* been *his* stroke. The thought brought a shot of guilt, a shock of illicit danger: the best coach would have known this, a better coach would have made it happen.

He shut his eyes. He was flying and he was swimming and it felt as one. He was swimming and he was flying into his future.

"I am so sorry. I just can't forgive myself for not coming to see you."

She has no idea how relieved I am to hear her say those words. We are in the courtyard of a bar off Lygon Street, it is a dark winter evening and she is shivering, but she wants to sit outside to smoke. It is the kind of place where there isn't a house wine and the beer is all imported. I am warming my hands between my thighs. The wind bites, the cold is close to painful, but I don't mind. It is the smoking that reminds me of the old Demet; it is the tight scissor grip that she has on her cigarette, the fierceness with which she drags on it, the way her fingers play with the packet between each smoke that brings her back to me.

"I don't care," I reply, smiling. "It doesn't matter. In that place visitors make you feel your isolation more keenly. I always felt worse when Mum came, I always felt like shit afterward."

My words tumble into each other in my rush to convince her that there is no hurt, that I bear no grudge. That's what I learned in there, that was the most important lesson: that I did something wrong and that I had to pay for what I did. You construct a ladder and you climb that ladder, out of the hell you have created for your-self and back into the real world. That is atonement, a word I dis-covered in there; it is in such places that the word resides and makes sense. And I am not there yet, Dem, I want to tell her, I haven't got there yet. I have enough of my own guilt, I still have nights when sleep won't come because I am reliving the piercing shame. I have enough guilt. I don't need hers. I don't want hers.

She takes out another cigarette, lights it, looking at me out of the corner of one eye. I want her to be sarcastic, to be sneering and opinionated and strong. I want the old Dem, I don't want this polite stranger.

"Luke visited, didn't he?"

That's more like it. There's the old rivalry. *He's your best friend,* she'd always say, *but* we're *soul mates.*

"Yeah, Luke visited."

The first change I noticed is that she's lost weight. She's some-thing I never thought she'd be: she's fit. I'd place a bet that she's working out, going to the gym. And *that* makes me want to laugh, that's something I could never have imagined, after all the shit she used to give me about my training.

"You're working out, aren't you?"

A resonant laugh comes from deep in her gut. It is so good to hear.

"Yeah, I'm working out." She ruefully eyes the cigarette in her fingers. "But I'm still fucking fagging."

I have to restrain myself from saying, Don't stop, it is part of you—that fervent passion she has for the cigarette. It is a mark of her character and of her personality. I can't imagine Demet without the fags. Something would be missing. The smoking centers her.

She's cut her hair. It is a buzz cut, so short you can see her scalp. The explosion of raven curls, the mad mop, have all gone. The new cut suits her. Demet will never be pretty; now *that's* an inadequate word for how she looks. The new hairstyle accentuates the blockish severity of her face, the strong ridge of her brow, the heavy hooded eyes, the sharp line of her nose, the prominent mouth, that mouth that dominates when you look at her. I haven't seen her for years and I am struck by how none of the components of her face should fit together: everything—eyes, brow, cheeks, nose, mouth—seems over-sized, too much. But that's Dem, she is too much. And that's what I love about her.

It feels good, I let that thought sink in, and I take hold of her free hand. "It's really good to see you. I've missed you."

I'm the one who should be apologizing. For not once getting up the courage to call her to find out where she had moved to, for not once writing a letter to tell her that I hadn't disappeared, that she hadn't vanished from my thoughts. But I didn't know if she ever wanted to see me again. No, that's not true. I believed that there was no way she would ever want to see me again.

She squeezes my hand. "Missed you too, fucker."

The third thing I noticed is how finely cut her clothes are, how fash-ionable she is. Not that Dem didn't always have style: she always stood out in high school. But back then her fashion was a jumble of shapeless long op-shop coats, Che Guevara badges, and thick-soled workman's boots. Her appearance is still masculine—it's there in the severity of her haircut, in the pragmatic cut of her long pants, the flat-heeled shoes—but the red coat she has buttoned up to her neck is made of a thin fine textured leather; the fabric of the shirt that peeks from under the cuffs of her coat is delicate, her trousers tailored and stylish.

She lets go of my hand and sips her wine. "Have you heard from Luke?"

I shake my head. "Not lately. I got a card from Beijing a few months ago, but nothing since. I imagine he's busy."

"I think he's riding the Asian tiger for all it's worth. I guess that's our future. I got an e-mail the other day from him, a group one, telling us all about the money to be made in totalitarian capital-ist China. Blah blah blah. You sure you didn't get it?"

"I'm not on e-mail."

"What?" She is incredulous. I'm used to that response. Not having a computer places me outside the world, renders me invisible. But I also know my time of concealment is coming to an end.

"I do have to get a computer. I'm starting a course next year and as much as I can't stand the bloody things I'm going to need to be on e-mail."

"What's the course?"

"Human services. Or 'community services,' they're calling it. It's a certificate course, nothing fancy. I'm working as a volunteer at the moment, working with adults who have acquired brain damage—you know, through injury or accident. I thought doing the course might make it easier to get a job."

I find that I am blushing, that in revealing something of myself to another person I am awkward and embarrassed; I almost fear that I don't know how to stop. I haven't talked intimately with someone for a long time. It strikes me, speaking to Demet beneath the gaunt naked elm trees in this freezing courtyard, that I have almost forgotten what it is to reveal oneself to another.

"Anyway," I mumble to a close, "that's the plan."

She is looking at me intently, squarely in the eyes. It is disconcerting. "Good for you, Danny. I am so proud of you."

Because I am not fucking up? Because I am not embarrassing you? Because I am not a loser?

～～～

I had literally crashed into her in Lygon Street. I'd been rushing to catch a movie, something I had been doing for a few months, catching a film, any film, on half-price Monday. Attending weekly gave me both the pleasure of routine—and routine is still everything to me—and at the same time forced me into the world. I only saw movies on my own, and conversation was limited to the dry transaction with the cinema staff over tickets. But it was still a forward step into the world. I was running late because when I got home from the night shift at the supermarket I'd started reading Philip Roth's *The Human Stain* and found myself still engrossed in it by mid-morning: *here* was shame, *here* was rage, *here* was indignity, and *here* was retiring from the world. I'd set the alarm but slept through it and had only forty-five minutes from waking to get to Carlton. I'd jumped off the tram in Swanston Street, had run blindly down Cardigan Street, frantically weaving through the crowds of students, and as I was careering down Lygon Street I bumped the shoulder of a woman coming out of Readings. Hey, she had complained, and I, puffing, was drawing in my breath to prepare an apology when I noticed—no longer overweight, her hair short, her clothes stylish—that it was Demet. Her face turned from a scowl into shocked recognition. Danny? Yeah, I answered, yeah, it's me.

At first I thought that she didn't want to talk to me, assumed that she wanted nothing to do with me. She wouldn't look me in the eye, it seemed as if she wanted to draw away.

"What are you doing?" It was a stupid question but all I could think to ask.

"Just browsing," she'd replied, and then added, "I'm working at the uni, just up the road. And you?"

"I'm heading off to a film," and I pointed across the street to the cinema. I had quickly glanced at my phone; if I didn't cross the street now, I would be late for the movie. I had to say goodbye. She hadn't even kissed me or hugged me—she wanted nothing to do with me.

"Are you running late?" she'd asked and I'd nodded, and then, even though it terrified me and broke the pattern of my day, I blurted out, "I can see a film anytime. How about we go for a drink?"

It was clear that the final word had alarmed her: she'd almost recoiled from it. Of course, of course, she was remembering the last night we'd seen each other. Shame beat pitilessly around my ears at that moment, shame was the earth splitting beneath my feet, shame was mortification and fire. She's scared I'll get drunk and become a violent ugly fool; maybe she thinks I'll hit *her*. Of course she can never trust me again.

Shame. I am trying not to be overwhelmed by it, I am trying not to be beholden to it, to find a place for it where I can survive it, where I am not broken by it. I don't know if it will ever happen, or if it can ever happen. I can't bear the weight of all the apologies I need to make. That morning I had underlined a passage in the book where the woman working as a cleaner is asked what it is like to bear the memory of being molested as a young girl by her stepfather and she replies, *Like carrying a house on your back*. I'd underlined it so hard with my ballpoint pen that I ripped the page. That is shame, that is the cost and the burden and the irredeemable fact of it.

There were too many people in the street, there was too much brightness, too much noise. I wanted to be home, the door locked, just myself, my mattress, my books, and my four walls. She didn't want a drink with me, it was obvious that she wanted nothing to do with me. I was poison, I was contamination. I should just walk away, I thought, I should cross the street and go into a film, any film. I should just disappear from her world. So before she could reply, before she could lie and say she was running late or that she had work she needed to finish or a dinner that she had to prepare, I said the words for her. "Nah, of course you're busy. We'll make it another time." She had looked so sad then. Once again, I had misjudged words, I had made them into something despondent and crushing.

"Danny," she said, finally reaching out to me, stroking my cheek tenderly. "Of course I have the time for you, mate. For you I have all the time in the world."

∼∼∼

"It's really nothing," I say. "I like helping them out. It's certainly not heroic."

And it isn't. I feel resentment stirring in my belly, I can sense it in my sudden urge to draw away from her.

She is looking at me as if I am a child who has performed well on an exam, has brought home a prize. "Good for you, Danny," she says again. "You're doing something really good, you're looking after society's dispossessed." But I bet she's thinking, What a perfect thing for a loser like him to do, to look after other losers.

I want to tell her that I like the work, that I don't feel judged or assessed or criticized by the guys I look after. The old German man whose brain has been fried from too much alcohol; the youth who had his skull squashed, driving high, driving fast without a seat belt; the middle-aged carpenter who'd shot too much heroin into his body and had died for a minute. Rolf and Kevin and Jeremy. I do Rolf's washing; he pisses himself all the time. I am teaching Kevin how to dress himself, teaching Jeremy how to wash himself; I help him sit on the toilet when he needs a shit—I do all this and I am immersed and lost in it. I know about bodies, how they need to be sculpted and molded and twisted and made to work. There's not a lot I know, but I know this, that the body can be trained, that the body can be changed, that the body is in motion, is never static. And I know that sometimes the body will roar out its limits, will tell you there is no further to go, that some possibilities will never be realized, despite desire and hope and will. I know this better than I know anything else. The body also fails. Rolf and Kevin and Jeremy know this, too. Rolf and Kevin and Jeremy and I *are* losers, we also know this; but not in the way the world thinks. We don't need the world to pity us, we don't need the encouraging word or the pat on the back. We carry our home on our back.

Demet is saying something else, going on about my altruism or my fortitude, or, for fuck's sake no, my *courage*.

"Really, it's nothing," I interrupt. "It's just a job."

She laughs again and my resentment is gone. "Okay, Danny Kelly, okay. It's a job." She has lit another cigarette, has finished her wine. "I bet it's better than my job."

"You don't like tutoring?"

"I don't like the hours, I don't like that I've been doing it two years and I'm still a fucking casual, I don't like the whinging students at Melbourne Uni, and I especially don't like their sense of entitlement." She groans. "Listen to me—and I call the students whingers!"

She takes a deep breath. "I'm exhausted, Danny, I think that's what it is. I'm working on my PhD and I think I'm never going to finish it and I know that every bloody fool out there doing a PhD is saying and thinking the same thing. I'm boring myself, Danny. I'm not good when I'm bored, you know that, I'm terrible. I'm a bitch to my girlfriend, I'm a bitch to my students, I'm a bitch to myself." She looks again at her empty glass. "I'm going to have another. You want one?"

I have chugged down the wine the way a baby sucks on a teat. Desperately. But then so has Demet. We can't settle, can't find our way back to the easy freedom of our past friendship. Since we sat down she has not referred to prison. It is as if the apology on the street was all that was needed, and she thinks she is now forgiven. But sitting here opposite her, being reminded of what we had, my shame has been banished by resentment. It *did* hurt that she didn't visit, it had crushed me that she had made no effort to find out how I was, hadn't even written a letter. I'll never tell her but every visitors' day it was her I expected to see. She had promised it to me: that we were soul mates. And she had betrayed that. I look down at my empty glass. Do I want another drink with her?

"Yes," I answer, and when she is at the bar I am thinking of how loyalty is more often compromised by carelessness than spite; and I am thinking of how good it is to hear the laughter of a good friend, and I am thinking that I also took our friendship for granted—I assumed she would follow me wherever Cunts College and swimming took me. I had been careless as well. We had both been negligent.

There is music in the courtyard, the untamed noodlings of jazz; light and sprightly, the notes whistle down from the speakers, the melody is purling, it is plashing and rustling through the spindled arms of the naked elm trees. It is hush and it is rhapsody.

Demet returns and I raise my glass. "It's good to see you, mate," and Demet says, "You too." Then she says, "Cheers," and I answer with, "*Şerefe.*" That makes both of us laugh. And so it is through our shared outburst of glee in my customary mangling of that Turkish word that I know we have returned to one another. In the relief of the laughter our bodies uncoil and we are released. We are finally returned to our friendship. And like that leaping, skipping, joyous music above us, we do not need words. I can't see it but I am sure there is a light dancing between us, touching her, touching me. That light, it sings our shared history, and that we are forgiven.

If you want it, it's yours, Coach said. *You can do it.* Coach demanded of him: *Do you want it?*

Yes, sir! I want it, sir.

He barked it out silently, coughed it up from deep within him, spat it out, phlegm and blood, as though he was a recruit in an American war movie, like he was Bruce Willis or Tom Cruise. But he did it silently, so as not to wake Wilco in the next bed. He barked it silently from deep in his gut and from the back of his throat: *Yes, sir! I want it, sir.* But there was that nagging doubt that he tried to ignore, that rising chortle that was itching to get out: You sound like a wanker, who are you kidding, who speaks like that, only frigging Yanks speak like that. He could hear his father: Why are you speaking like a frigging Nike ad? You can't mean it, seriously, you can't *mean* it?

Yes, sir! I want it, sir.

This time he said it out loud. As though Coach were there, in front of him, right in his face, demanding, challenging him: *Do you really fucking want it?*

Yes, sir! I want it, sir.

This time he shouted it and there was a groan from the next bed. Wilco turned, twisted, doubled over his pillow. "Kelly, you okay?"

"Yeah, yeah, mate, sorry. It was just a dream."

Danny lay still in his bed. Wilco's breathing was constant, alert. Danny lay still and waited for him to fall asleep again. He closed his eyes, blotting out the room, the bed, the boy in the next bed. He imagined the pool, the sound of the water slapping the tiles, the heat and the steam, the chill of the change rooms, tried to bring back the image of Coach. He was back in Melbourne, about to hit the water. He was telling Coach how much he wanted it, how it was going to be his.

There was a snigger from the next bed. "You want a wank, do you, Kelly?" It was followed by a disgusted snort. "Not here, mate, that's filthy. Go do it in the dunny if you have to."

Danny forced himself not to think about the room, the moonlight, Japan, bloody Wilco. He wished it were Taylor sharing the room with him, not bloody Wilco.

Forget him, he told himself, don't let him get to you. Concentrate. Stay focused. That was the golden rule, they all knew it—swimmers, athletes, sportspeople; anyone who knew the thrill of competition. Concentrate, reject anything that would be a distraction.

He breathed in slowly, a rattling shiver going down his spine, and a spasm rolled down his back in a wave from the nape of his neck. It took all his will not to move. He breathed out, palms flat against the cool sheets. But Melbourne was gone, Coach was gone, the pool was gone, and he couldn't bring any of it back; bloody Wilco had fucked that up. Danny breathed in. He lay in the bed, palms flat on the cold sheets, legs apart, wishing Taylor was there with him. There was a rustle from across the room and then the light wheeze of Wilco's snore. Danny tried to bring back the pool, retrieve the Coach, the race, the solid slew through water and time. But his cock was full, the blood rushing there, it was now his center of gravity.

You want a wank, do you, Kelly?

He flung back the sheet, got up and searched for his T-shirt and track pants. There was a fumbling from the other bed and the room was filled with blinding light.

"What the fuck are you doing?"

Wilco had half risen from his bed and the sheet fell down to his hips. Danny looked away but not before he saw the boy's moon-pale body, a color whiter than light, white as the cotton of the sheets. So white that Wilco's stubby pink nipples and perfectly round aureoles were almost obscene, so white that the spray of freckles on the boy's shoulders and neck flashed like specks of gold. You look like a skinned rabbit, Danny thought, recalling going hunting with his granddad Bill in Mernda, the sound of the shotgun, the animal leaping, twisting, fitting in the air, his grandfather taking the knife and stripping the fur and skin from the meat, the flesh raw and pink and dead beneath. Danny turned, so quickly that he knew the other boy hadn't seen the outline of his erection under his white briefs, hadn't glimpsed the ugly shock of black pubes showing through the material. Wilco got waxed from top to bottom, every single bit of him, every month. His bloody daddy paid for him to look like an ugly skinned rabbit.

Danny stepped into his track pants, slipped on his T-shirt, sat on the bed and pulled up his socks. "I can't sleep. I'm going for a walk."

Wilco looked at the clock on the sideboard. It was just past eleven o'clock. "You fucking idiot, mate, your swim is tomorrow."

Danny could tell that Wilco was about to lecture him. That was how it was between them; only a year's difference in age, but Wilco thought that made him superior. Wilco opened his mouth but Danny rushed to speak first.

"I won't get to sleep. I need some air."

Wilco switched off the light and pulled up the sheet. "If they catch you, you're dead."

〜〜〜

He was tempted to take the stairs, race down them all the way to the ground floor, then saunter through the lobby. He was confident he could say casually to the concierge at the front desk, *Konbanwa*—that would be the right word, not *konichiwa*; everyone knew *konichiwa* but that was hello; he wanted to be more formal. He would say good evening and he would pronounce it correctly, clipped, with the slightest inflection on the last syllable—those were the instructions that Mr. D'Angelo had given him at school. *Konbanwa,* then push through the revolving doors; he'd be breathing in foreign air, he'd be looking up at a new night sky, with unfamiliar constellations; he'd be stepping into a different world. The buzz began in his belly and spread in sharp bursts of electric energy to every part of his body. He was in another world. He didn't want to be locked up like the other swimmers, he didn't want to be trapped behind the windows of the bus that ferried them from airport to hotel to *shinkansen* to swimming center to hotel. He didn't want to be looked after, checked off, observed. He wanted to step off, to fly into that other world.

If they catch you, you're dead.

The buzz was gone. And he knew Wilco was right. He couldn't give them an excuse to punish him, or a reason to drop him from the team. They didn't want him. He'd come out of nowhere and he wasn't one of theirs. He'd beaten a golden boy, and was taking a golden boy's rightful place at the Pan Pacific competition, and that was why they threw him resentful looks, made him repeat every question and every request. *What did you say, Kelly? Speak clearly, kid. Do you always have to mumble, Kelly?* They didn't believe he belonged there. They didn't want him there.

Danny hesitated in the narrow, white-walled corridor. A pulse thumped, a dull tattoo from the air conditioner vents. At the end of the passageway was a door with a black kanji and next to it a small diagram of a stick figure descending a staircase. Danny made up his mind and headed for the fire exit.

It was just a hunch, it might not have led anywhere, but he would try it. He needed to be in the open air, he felt as though he was choking in the artificial mechanical atmosphere; he wanted to escape the suffocating *in-betweenness* of the accommodation. He ran up three flights of concrete steps and pushed hard on the door at the top of the stairwell. The frame groaned, shuddered, but the heavy door swung open.

He felt the humidity in the air as he walked over to the railing at the edge of the rooftop. The view was surprisingly dark. He had expected Japan to be all neon bursts of light at night, holograms and screens everywhere. But below and across from him most of the buildings were shrouded in shadow. He could hear the rolling of the surf, he could smell the sea, the fish and salt from the port, and the fetid stench of seaweed rotting on the beach.

Arigato gozaimasu, he whispered to the city. He inhaled, taking it all into his lungs, wanting the city to be inside him.

Danny was the only one on the Australian swimming team who had bothered to learn any Japanese. Mr. D'Angelo had printed out a list of words and phrases and Danny had memorized them on the plane trip over, how to say please, thank you and you're welcome, hello and goodbye. That was all he had committed to memory—but they were five phrases more than anyone else had bothered to learn. And not only the swimmers. The coaches and their assistants, the doctors and the physios, the administrators and the child protection officers assigned to look after the under-eighteens: none of them had bothered to learn one Japanese word.

He looked out over the unknown dark. I'm in Japan, he said to himself, an elated grin on his face. China was just across the sea, Russia up to the north. He'd started to see the world. His parents had never got farther than Phuket; they'd made it to Bali twice. He would not be them, he had already seen more than they had. He had beat Demet to the world. Most of the boys at school had got to the world before him. Martin had been to Europe twice; Wilco had been to Los Angeles, the Grand Canyon, and Disneyland; Luke had been to Vietnam and Cambodia, Greece and Rome. They had traveled but they had not *seen,* not like him. Wilco didn't want to eat Japanese food, complained loudly that he thought more people would speak English there. He had looked startled during a walk through the fish markets of Fukuoka when Danny had pointed excitedly to an old yellow-toothed woman packaging a tray of tiny shoal fish. "So? What about it?" It was then that Danny had realized that Wilco couldn't *see,* was walking blindly through it all and not taking in a thing. He couldn't see the thin translucent beauty of the rice paper, the neat symmetry in the way the old woman laid out the fish, the fine lines of emerald script etched on the thin paper wrapping. Danny hadn't bothered explaining it; Wilco and the golden boys would never get it. Demet should have been there with him, she'd have got it. The golden boys and the golden girls had no interest in experiencing the world— they wore goggles in the pool and blinkers out of it. Not him. He was going to take in, possess the whole of the world. *Aussie Aussie Aussie, Oi Oi Oi?* Fuck off. He wanted more.

He breathed in, savoring the unfamiliar scent of the humid air. There was a blinking red light on the horizon where the black ocean met the night sky.

Alone, high above Fukuoka, Danny allowed himself to speak the words: *Yes, sir! I want it, sir.* He would beat the golden boys. He was stronger, faster, better.

On the way to the airport his father had said, "Good on you, Danny, I'm proud of you." But then he'd had to add, "I hope you don't ever forget how fortunate you are, mate."

That was why his father had never been farther than bloody Phuket and bloody Bali. Coach knew, it was Coach who said it: "There is no such thing as luck. There is only work and discipline and talent and courage." Danny was here in Japan because he was the strongest and the fastest. He was the best.

Danny exhaled.

Wilco's bed was empty when Danny crept into the room. There was a light under the bathroom door and he heard a blast of farting and the sound of turds splashing into the toilet bowl. It set him off giggling. He stripped to his jocks and flung himself under the sheets. The toilet flushed and when Wilco returned Danny was holding his nose with one hand.

"Jesus, Wilco, it pongs!"

"Fuck off, Kelly." But Wilco too started a fit of giggling. He leapt into bed. "Can you sleep?"

Danny knew that he shouldn't answer, that he should pretend to snore. He needed to sleep, and mentally he started coaxing his body to unbend, first the muscles in his feet, then moving up to his calves. He was thinking himself toward drowsiness.

"What time do you think it is back home?"

Danny groaned. The prick was not going to let him sleep. "Melbourne is one hour ahead, mate." How could Wilco not know that? How could he be so uninterested in the world?

There was a rustling from the next bed; there was the slow trickle of water into the cistern in the bathroom. Danny couldn't help it, he shifted around to look across. Wilco was on his side, the sheet only covering him from the waist down, and in the faint beam of moonlight coming through the window the boy's skin gleamed silver; his eyes were pinpricks of light.

"I hope we both get gold, Danny," Wilco whispered. "I really want both of us to get gold."

Danny held his breath. Did he trust him?

"Dad says that if I win a medal here, I'm sorted for a place at the AIS next year. No fees, everything paid for, the best coaches in the world."

Danny didn't need to think about uni for another year at least—of course he'd be going to uni and of course the Australian Institute of Sports would want him. He didn't need to think about that shit, he needed to sleep. Bloody Wilco, putting it in his head.

He couldn't help it, it burned him that Mr. Wilkinson was encouraging his son to go to the AIS. It made Danny think of his own father. "This fucking country," Neal Kelly would say, with a laugh undercut by sourness. "There's no money for health and education, nothing for the arts, but we shovel a shitload to sports."

Danny couldn't help it; it needled him that Mr. Wilkinson, unlike his own father, was encouraging his son. He made his voice sound nonchalant, spoke somewhere between a yawn and a whine. "Jesus, bloody Australia, all that money poured into sports. I'm not sure I want to go to the AIS—I don't think it's fair that sportspeople get a free education when every other student has to pay." He'd made himself sound exactly like Neal Kelly.

"Yeah, you reckon?" Wilco sounded unconvinced. "You got a point, Kelly, but come on, you know sports is the only area where Australia punches above its weight. If we didn't fund sports, we'd be shit at everything." Wilco rolled over. "You'll get there, Kelly, you're a shoo-in. You got a scholarship to school and you're going to get a scholarship to uni." Wilco let out a long tired yawn. "Psycho Kelly, you're one lucky bastard. We all think that, mate, you're the luckiest bastard we know. Everything falls into your lap."

Danny had been right about Wilco. He should never have trusted him. Wilco was a golden boy, he didn't believe Danny belonged there. He was outraged to hear a light snore coming from the next bed. He'd got there—Wilco had got under his skin. Danny's body was rigid, his breathing was out, he had to chase air, otherwise he thought he might choke. The bile was bitter and chemical on his tongue. He had to sleep. He had to sleep.

He began again at his feet, tensed and relaxed them to rest, then his calves, cajoling the muscles there to yield. From his calves to his thighs, and then he traced a line up the center of his body, to his buttocks, made a command in the form of a prayer: Let me sleep. Let me sleep. *You're one lucky bastard.* Those words ricocheted through him, his body clenched; he had to begin again. He concentrated on his toes, his feet, his calves. *Everything falls into your lap.* How could that be true? He wasn't a golden boy, he'd never had what they had. It was envy, a poison, that had made Wilco say those words, it was the poison of jealousy. Why couldn't it have been Taylor with him? He would never have said any of that, he knew what Danny was. He began again at his feet.

Danny's eyes flicked open. The moonlight sliced the room in two. He'd been fighting against acknowledging it, but the force of his hard-on beneath the sheets strained the cotton of his jocks, made concentration impossible, sleep unattainable. He tried again.

He began at his feet. *You're one lucky bastard.* He moved to his calves, his thighs. The head of his penis had come out of his underpants and rubbed against the sheet. Danny had to force himself to ignore it, not to move; he had to call back sleep, to catch it and ensnare it. He could do it, he had control over his body. He tried again.

He began at his feet. But almost immediately there was another rush of words around his head, a burst of blood to his ears. *You're the luckiest bastard we know.*

Danny breathed in and tried again.

He began again at his feet, rushing through the meditation this time, moving quickly from calves to thighs to buttocks to stomach to lungs, calling for sleep. He was at his hands, his forearms, and it was beginning—his arms felt like lead, still against the cool cotton sheets. *I hope you don't ever forget how fortunate you are, mate.* The blood surged, his ears burned and his head pounded. He breathed out. He'd have to start again.

His spine was stretched, he had to move. He shifted in the bed. And as he did, as he twisted, the sheets crawled up his body and the cotton rubbed at his crotch, caressed the shaft of his penis, the glans. Danny's body shuddered as the wave of pleasure rushed, as the semen squirted. But immediately he felt overwhelming panic, shame, as the sticky warm fluid seeped over his thigh and belly and onto the white sheets.

He was wilted, spent. He forced himself to breathe slowly. And this time he didn't call on sleep, he called on rage. He spat it out, a loud coarse whisper, and he didn't care if Wilco heard. Let him hear, let him wake; he hoped that at the very least the words terrorized the older boy's dreams, that they were carried by the wave of his fury all the way back home: *It is not luck, it has never been luck, it is because I am the best and I am going to get gold and what you can't stand is that I am better than you.*

Why couldn't it be Taylor with him? He was nauseated: his body had betrayed him. The sensation was strange, terrifying; he had never experienced it before, his body and himself not being one.

Danny realized that the world was rushing in again, that he was listening to the mechanical vibrations of the cooling system; he could hear the boy's snores from the next bed. His body had betrayed him but Danny was spent. It had worked. He went to sleep.

~~~

He sits on a plastic chair in front of the third-lane block, his legs sprawled out in front of him, his arms dangling behind the orange chair back. Danny knows he is in the Fukuoka Swimming Center, he knows there are five other swimmers, he knows that a small crowd is sitting in the decks. They are all waiting for the race to begin. There are Australian flags, Japanese flags, US and Canadian flags fluttering above him, red and blue and white festoons garlanded all around him. He knows all this but he sees none of it. Danny is looking straight ahead, down the barrel of lane number three, fifty meters of clean water, a mirror of blue, a highway of black line ahead of him. He sees the water, he sees the lane, he sees the race. He sees himself dive, he sees himself swim, he sees himself win. That is all he needs to see.

And it is his, he knows it, as soon as the starting pistol cracks, as soon as he dives from the block, as his body enters and dolphins and is accepted by the water. As he breaks the surface of the water, his chest, his arms, his legs, his feet, his whole body is an indomitable threshing machine, but even so, in the foam arms of the water, he is cocooned by a tender calm. He doesn't have to think. His mind and his body and the water are one. All his work, all his effort, all his talent, they are being vindicated. He has won. The water is the future and he has always belonged to it.

It is at the final turn that the water betrays him. His execution is perfect, he feels what it is to be divine. But as he momentarily glimpses the world reflected in the underside of the water's surface he finds that one of the other swimmers has completed the turn before him. That other swimmer is already racing toward the end. Which can't be, for that end is *his*.

And then it is like vertigo when the water drops away and it is only a flicker of time, a second within a second within a second, but Danny is scrambling, struggling in the water. He and the water are no longer one. He can't understand why his arms are arcing so slowly, as if they have lead weights on them, or why his legs kick so sluggishly, why his chest is tight with every breath out of the water, why the end of the lane seems an impossible horizon. The race isn't finished but the exhaustion is a flood. He is depleted. He roars his denial into the water itself and it is then that the water answers. Danny kicks, finds confidence again, reasserts the power and drive of his body. He must not think, he can only trust in his body and in the water. It is *his* race. He pushes forward, he charges, he punches and he owns the water once again; the water has parted to create space for him. He is not thinking of the other swimmers. His body has not failed him, and his mind has not failed him. Of course he will win. Of course he must win. There is no hesitation, no doubt, as his body hurtles through the water, his muscles pumping to his command, his will driving him to swim faster than he has ever swum before, to chase the other swimmer. But the water knows what his body knows. This is his race. His body, the water, they will not betray him. He lunges toward the finish, his hand smacks the tile. He cocks his head out of the water and the sound and the lights and the colors of the outside world explode all around him.

Of course he has won. He has given it all that he has. He has no more to give.

～～～

In the two hundred meter men's butterfly at the Pan Pacific Games in Fukuoka, Japan, an Australian golden boy comes first, an American second and a Japanese swimmer third. Danny Kelly comes fifth.

Danny Kelly has lost.

Danny Kelly is heaving, bawling, crying like a baby, his body shaking and convulsing. His body has so deceived him that he is scared he's going to piss himself in the pool. Spit is foaming at his lips; he won't remove his goggles even though they have fogged up, even though he can only see the world through a mist of cloud and tears. He doesn't want to see the world, he can't imagine how to be in this new world. He senses a swimmer glide under the rope next to him, he feels a hand on his shoulder. He jumps back, alarmed, rips off his goggles and sees the golden boy in his lane; the golden boy's grin seems pasted on, enormous, all teeth and gums; his eyes are sparks and fire and heat, and he is trying to shake Danny's hand but Danny doesn't take it. Danny turns to face the cool surface of the tiles. Danny won't look at the golden boy, he won't face the world. Come on, mate, he hears, Come on, shake. Danny refuses.

The other swimmers have leapt out of the water, will be extending congratulations or commiserations, facing cameras or enduring the lonely walk of the defeated back to the warm-down pool, but Danny won't leave the water. The only thing he wants is to go back in time and begin again. If he can just do it again, he knows that he will win. He can prove them wrong rather than right.

He gave it his best. Strongest, fastest, best. Fifth? It is impossible. His best cannot be *fifth*.

"Come on, kid, get out of the water."

It's a young man, one of the Australian coaches, kneeling on the tiles, looking down at him, holding out his hands. He sees the pity in the man's eyes but he also sees something else—relief, embarrassment. Danny is shivering, his body is beginning to cramp, all his muscles are seizing. He feels hands reach for him, hands grab him and pull him up and he is screaming, he doesn't want to keep it all inside, he doesn't want to forgive them all their envy and jealousy, all their anger that he had taken the place of one of their golden boys; they didn't want him here, they didn't think he belonged here. Arms are pulling him out of the water and Danny is thrashing and twisting and Danny is shouting, "It's all your fucking fault! You didn't want me here. I fucking hate you, I hate all of you cunts. You cunts. You cunts. You cunts, I hate you more than you could ever hate me." But then the sobs come so strongly that all words and motions are stilled. He is being supported by two men, who lift him, almost carry him past other swimmers who can't look at him, who turn away from him, past a man with a camera on his shoulder, past the Japanese volunteers who can only look down at the ground, past the splash pool, into a corridor, into the locker room, where he is pushed onto a bench and someone is holding him and he is racked with sobbing and one of the medics on the squad is holding a syringe and someone has gripped his arm. Danny is still sobbing and trying to find the energy to push them away but he is as weak as if he had swum a thousand miles not two hundred meters, and he is so exhausted that he is as light as a leaf and as heavy as a boulder and he lets them pat his arm and he watches the needle enter his vein and bile slips from his lips as the plunger fills with his blood and then he is quiet. He looks straight ahead and the world too has gone silent. He can't hear a sound, not the doctor talking to him, no noises from the pool outside, nothing. He tries to rise; he is thinking, I have to get up, I have to move. But his muscles no longer belong to him, his body is not his own. I can't fly, thinks Danny, and his chin slumps to his chest, I'm stuck to earth. And out of the corner of his eye he can just see the young coach who pulled him from the water, he is saying something to the doctor, and he realizes that this coach is not so young because there are flecks of gray in his short beard. And though he can't hear any sounds he knows exactly what this man is saying to the doctor. He can't hear but it is as if the words enter through Danny's heart not through his ears, and what he hears are the words: *He's going to be ashamed of this moment for the rest of his life.*

Luke has become a striking-looking man. He has some heft to him now, a solidity that suits him. When we were young I used to think that physically the Vietnamese and Greek genes were ill-matched. Back then he was so tiny that there was an almost simian look to him. I never said it to him, I was too ashamed of even thinking it. But in adulthood his face has acquired symmetry. He is a handsome man.

He is talking nervously, scratching at one elbow, unable to stop himself looking anxiously at the guard, starting at loud noises. His nervousness doesn't worry me. I used to jump at every clanging gate, every heavy footfall, any raised voice. But he has nothing to fear. We have been allowed to sit together on a bench in an anterior courtyard, watched over by Jackson, the youngest guard, who is stupid but well-meaning. There is no meanness in him. I wish Luke would stop shuffling and radiating anxiety, but I am not annoyed. I am grateful that he is visiting me.

I am trying not to think about my shirt chafing the tender welts below both of my shoulder blades. I sit as still as I can because every time I shift my body the thick fibers of my work shirt scrape against the wounds of the new tattoos and a violent pain jolts my body. It is three days since Angus finished the last tattoo; and for the past three nights every time I have taken off my shirt it tears away the skin trying to heal there, and the blood keeps flowing. But I am marked—the scar of who I was and who I am is permanently part of me now.

I sit still and smile at Luke, who is going on about study and work, about life outside. He doesn't say it but every word reveals his concern that I am missing that life, that I am waiting for the day when that life will return to me. I just keep smiling, not really listening to his words. What I notice is the fine line of his nose, the dimples in his cheeks, the dark hairs on his pale arms. He talks to me about study and work, about life outside, and I sit there imagining the shape and color of his nipples—they are dark, small, his chest hair is sparse, I imagine it a swirl around each nipple—and I think of the fine hair forming a line down from his chest to his belly to his crotch. I imagine his cock, long and thin, the pubes thick and soft. I keep smiling, and with every pump of my heart the blood bursts against the tender markings on my back. I lean over with my elbows on my knees to hide my erection.

~~~~

It is just before we are sent to our cells. Carlo is sitting on the chair next to me, his knee touching mine—that's all the contact we have but it is enough to send a charge through me, a pulse that repeatedly pounds through my body. He leans into me and whispers, "That mate of yours who visited you today: tell him he can't have you." The words slip into me and through me, I have to control myself not to react to them. I am careful not to reveal anything, that no expression disturbs the look of feigned boredom on my face. It was one of the first lessons I received here, the importance of appearing oblivious and unmoved.

So my eyes don't move from the television screen, my body is still, my legs outstretched, my arms folded, all insouciant carelessness; but

I feel his warm breath on my face, a light spray of his spit against my cheek. Later tonight, in bed, I will trace my finger along that cheek, then bring my finger to my mouth, and taste him. That is all I need to bring me to orgasm. I will come into a tissue and that tissue I will hand to him in the morning, and he will hand me the one he spilled himself into. I will tear tiny strips from it during the day, in the kitchen, in the library, in the yard. I will chew on them, and I will taste his semen and through his semen I will taste his cock and through his cock I will taste all of him. Sometimes he will shake the last drops of piss into a tissue, sometimes he will have wiped his arse with one; I ask him to keep one in his armpit throughout the long night. In the morning, as I take the still-damp tissue he will wink at me, daring me to guess what secretion I am to imbibe. *You jerked off into this one,* I say. Or I might whisper, *I am tasting your piss, aren't I?* Or, *I am licking your arse.* Or, *I am drinking your sweat.* His thrill is so acute that his words are hoarse. *You're a dirty bastard, Danny Boy, you're filthy.* He loves that word, it is an endearment and a come-on and a plea. *I so want to fuck you.*

And we do fuck. But it is rare. We are always seeking the opportunity. Seeking *that* opportunity, and reading: these are what get me through the hours, get me through the days. I could not choose between the two of them, I would be rendered immobile if the gun was at my head and I was ordered to make the decision. The joy and freedom that I find now in words, and the safety and the bliss that I experience when Carlo's prick has pierced and entered me are both experiences that in this place have become as essential to me as oxygen, as water. I need them to breathe, to live. They both allow me to escape. The first activity frees my imagination and lets me soar up and beyond walls and concrete and steel. The other liberates me from my will, and as Carlo pounds fiercely into my body, I pass through both humiliation and agony and become insensible to both. That is no small gift in prison. That is no small gift *anywhere.*

"An eye more bright than theirs," I whisper back, *"less false in*

rolling, gilding the object whereupon it gazeth." My lips just hover over his rough skin, my breath just moistens the coarse bristles of one sideburn. Like me, he doesn't move, his eyes don't stray from the screen. He doesn't know Shakespeare, he wouldn't give a rat's arse for what I am quoting. But his knee presses more firmly against mine. I fumble in my pocket and tear another fine strip off the tissue. I have to ration these strips, I have to make them last through the night and into the morning, when I will see him again.

What if I told Luke that I finally got Shakespeare in here? All of poor Mr. Gilbert's attempts to make me comprehend *Julius Caesar,* all the resources of our privileged rich school, and it is gaol that finally reveals to me the beauty of Shakespeare, the spirit in his words, the jaw-dropping audacity of his language. What if I said, "Luke, I discovered Shakespeare in here and I also discovered getting fucked up the arse. And they are both beautiful and they are both bliss." I wish I could explain to him that I discovered Shakespeare through getting fucked up the arse and I allowed myself to get fucked up the arse because of Shakespeare.

～～～

"You're looking good, Danny, you really are."

I have to stop myself blurting out, "Of course. It's because I'm content here." But I don't. Such words would dismay him, make him doubt my sanity. But though I am locked in prison, I have once more found routine. Luke has known me since I was a boy. He knows what routine means to me.

"I'm at the gym twice a day," I say, "any chance I get. They've got me working in the kitchen so I'm learning some skills there." Then, so excited that I almost forget myself and go to grab his hand, before the shift in the guard's stance reminds me of my place, I tell him how much I am reading. This pleases Luke more than anything and it makes me smile. Even now, so very handsome, so confident and self-assured, Luke remains a bookworm. I tell him about the books

I am reading, the ancient dialogues, the novels of Hemingway, the sonnets of Shakespeare, the histories of revolution, the biographies of Bonaparte, of Tolstoy and Keating, and he laughs good-naturedly and says that they sound like an eclectic bunch. The remark stings like a rebuke and I press back into my chair but he doesn't notice. University has given him something more than a confidence in his own skin, it has also made him arrogant. Whatever I say, whatever I read, he will always believe he knows more than I do. He assumes we have a full library here, he doesn't know I am eager for anything on those damn shelves that I can open and read. Those of us in the library, we are magpies, picking at the secondhand scraps.

"*A Farewell to Arms* is the best book I've ever read," I tell him.

"I don't really get into Hemingway. The writing is a bit too utilitarian for me."

I can't help it, this further censure makes me twist in my chair.

He notices my shift in mood. "You okay?"

"I'm fine." I have to process his words, to try to make sense of his critique. I know the word "utilitarian," it is a philosophical concept, I know I've come across it. Something about the greater good; I have no idea why he would apply it to Hemingway. I will have to ask Alec in the library how it is possible for fiction writing to be about the best outcome for the greater good. I feel stupid. Luke has made me feel stupid.

On the way to the cells I will tell Carlo that Luke is half-Chink, that his mother is Vietnamese. Carlo's top lip will curl in distaste. He can't stand Asians. He can't stand Asians or Aborigines or blacks or Arabs. For Carlo there are Italians and there are Aussies. Anyone else doesn't matter, anyone else shouldn't be. "I fucking hate Slopes," he hisses back at me. "I can't fucking stand them." Luke doesn't need to know that this is how I will get my revenge.

I thought I knew all about hate but until I got to prison I had no idea how much hate there was in the world. But then, until I came to prison I didn't know how many colors there were to skin. For years I stripped and showered next to only white flesh, only pale and luminous flesh, with slight variations in shade. But here there is flesh as black as the darkest ink, flesh that is as white as freshly pressed paper, mottled jaundiced flesh, skin the hue of black coffee when a few drops of milk are added to it, skin in all shades of yellow and red. There is flesh so black it shines blue; there is flesh that is gray and ashen, the flesh of the meth heads and the heroin users, the flesh that is dying.

Carlo's skin is the tint of the last days of a leaf in late autumn, the dark of ground just touched by rain. Carlo has skin the color of the earth.

〰〰

Luke doesn't know how to say goodbye to me, he doesn't know how to sit in silence. This is something I can teach him.

"Mate, I'm really glad you came."

I am shocked to see that his eyes are moist, stunned that he is trying to fight back tears. This is how my mother's eyes are when she comes to visit me. My father has come once and his eyes were dry. My mum talked, she talked and talked, and my father remained silent. I won't let them bring Regan or Theo here.

"Danny, it's nothing. It was great to see you. I'm going to come again."

"It won't be long till I'm out."

And it won't be, just a few months. Luke nods at this as if it is the best news in all the world. But I am terrified at the thought of it. There are no libraries for me in the world he knows, no bells to announce morning or lunch or supper or bed. There is no Carlo in Luke's world.

Carlo won't be eligible for parole for another five years. I could bash someone, I could hit a screw, I could *kill* a screw, and then I could stay here. But I won't, and neither will I wait for him. I'm the kind of man he would despise, he would hate me with a delirious fury in the world outside of here. And I won't hit or maim or kill, because I have promised myself never to hit or strike or hurt anyone again. But to do that

I have to remain outside of the world. This is what terrifies me most about stepping out into the sun again. I have to find the subterranean world once I am out. I have to find the world without sun.

"There's no sun here."

Of course Luke is startled, he doesn't understand.

I try to explain. "Even in the yard, when it's day, when the sun is shining and the sky's blue, I don't believe it is the real sun. It's another sun altogether." These words only make Luke sadder but I am glad that I have worked them through, that I have revealed the truth to myself. I am in another solar system, another galaxy. That is where I am.

Luke doesn't know what to do as he takes leave of me. He doesn't know whether he is allowed to shake my hand, to hug me, to give me a high-five—what is it we do now we are adults? Should he kiss me on both cheeks? I mumble something again about being glad he came and he mumbles something back about it being the least he can do. The formality of our words makes both of us chuckle, and I am reminded suddenly of the nerdy shy boy back in school. We don't hug, we don't kiss. We shake hands. We bid farewell chastely.

⌇⌇⌇

That night, in my cell, I listen to Kyle wank, his tugs so frenetic that the bunk bashes and shakes against the brick wall. He gulps as he comes; I hear the brush of his wet hand against the blanket and in seconds he is snoring. Only then do I start to bring myself off. I am lying on my front; it is still far too painful to be on my back. I am pushing into the mattress, I am thinking of Luke but it is Carlo's cock I am imagining inside me. It is always painful, it will always be excruciating for me the moment I am opened up, torn into. I wonder if it is the same for women, whether women always feel this pain when they are fucked? Or is it only in sodomy that pain and pleasure are so linked, so inextricable?

I have the last piece of tissue in my mouth. I am tasting Carlo, he is fucking me, and I am seeing Luke, his legs around me, coiled around me, I am fucking *him*. I shiver as I ejaculate, the warm fluid spreads across my thighs, dampens the sheet. I swallow the tissue. I lie on my front and as the pleasure drains away I am conscious only of the throbbing from both shoulder blades. The pain keeps me awake, and as I adjust to it, it also leads me to sleep.

〰〰

It cost me a week's pay from the money I make working in the kitchens. It cost me that and nothing more. Angus the tattooist is awed and nervous around Carlo: he is respected and feared, my lover, my protector.

Angus broke open a biro and carefully dripped the ink into a cup. "So what am I doing for ya?"

"I want two scars, one on each of my shoulder blades."

He shrugged in confusion. "What do you mean?"

"Two scars," I repeated, "for where my wings used to be, where my wings were torn away from me."

"Ah." He nodded, getting it now, flicking his lighter and caressing the needle with the blue flame. I didn't have to tell him anything else, he understood. We share the same false sun.

There was no light, only black night, no moon, no sound except for the burr from the alarm. Dan abandoned his dreams, willed himself awake, pressing the off button and fighting the warm inertia trying to drag him back to sleep. *Feet on the carpet,* he ordered himself, and with that he slipped off his underpants, drowsily searched the drawer for a new pair, and put them on with yesterday's track pants and long-sleeved shirt. Except for the illuminated red numerals of the digital clock, all was black night. He opened his bedroom door.

In the corridor he could hear Theo's short, sharp snores; a floorboard cracked and shuddered under his soft step. He was holding his sneakers and stuffed his socks in his track pants pocket. He crept through the lounge room and into the kitchen, drank a glass of water and munched a banana, all still in black night. In the bathroom he squeezed paste onto his toothbrush, then up and down three times on the left, up and down three times on the right, up and down three times on the bottom left, and up and down three times on the bottom right, scrubbed the bristles to the back of his mouth once twice thrice, and gargled, rinsed, and spat.

He was nearly at the door when his mother called from the front bedroom, "Danny, is that you?"

Dan was still, one hand clutching his sneakers, the other hand at the door. "Yeah, Mum," he whispered. "I'm just going for a run." Don't get up, please don't get up.

There was only comforting silence and he opened the door and was out into the night. The birds were just starting their song and dawn was about to break.

He had an hour till six-fifteen, when Boon would be waiting for him in the car park at Keon Park station, where they always met. Dan put on his socks and sneakers, tied the laces tight. He breathed in, he breathed out, and started to run.

In five minutes he'd crossed Cheddar Road, and in ten minutes he was at the creek and the night was fading and the chorus of birds was getting louder. Dan wasn't thinking, he was only motion. The sweat had banished the cold and he could smell the pungent yeasty tang of himself as he increased his pace and followed the path, which was overgrown with thistles and weeds, but he didn't falter or break step as he coursed up a hill past warehouses and factories, running past people on their way to work. The morning didn't smell of himself anymore, nor of the rotting world of the creek; now it was the acrid and sour human-made stink of chemicals. Breathing and running, he could almost pretend he was flying, that he could fly past the smells and the shadows, but just as he thought that, his steps faltered and his pace slowed, for he was thinking: this is not flying.

And then thoughts came, and would not stop, and the pain returned; he could feel it in the heel of his left foot, in the right side of his body; it tightened around his heart and his lungs. He gritted his teeth and forced himself to keep running, but the thoughts wouldn't stop, of how this was not flying and how it was her birthday tomorrow. Martin had told him it was her birthday and he couldn't think of a present—it had to be something special but he did not know what she had and he did not know what she would want and he could not bear the thought that she might think his gift ugly or silly or stupid, but she probably would. The pain was now cutting into him, his breath was catching and Keon Park station was still fifteen minutes away. Should he get her music? But he didn't know music. Should he get her a book? But he was sure she had read everything. The ache was now ever-present, in his toes and at his heels, in his belly and in his head, and Keon Park station was ten minutes away and he could ask Martin what she might want and what she didn't have but he knew that Taylor would just laugh.

He wouldn't ask Martin. Dan forced himself to run faster, he dared the coming day, and fate, and sped across a street without looking, he dared and he won and he thought that was an omen: he could get her something and she would cherish it, she had to cherish it. Taylor would tease him, Taylor would wrap his arm around him, pretend to punch him; these days Taylor didn't only smell of citrus and fresh soap, he sometimes smelled of the illicit cigarettes he smoked, one before and one after school. Dan could almost sense the boy's arm around his neck, their skin touching, and then he was at the car park and he stopped. He bent over, taking in breath after racking breath. He could almost feel their skin touching.

There were already people on the platform, looking up and down the tracks. The toilets were shut so he went behind a rubbish skip and stripped off his shirt and wiped under his arms. Taylor never ponged like that—how was it that other boys always seemed to smell so sweet? Not in the change rooms, of course; there the chlorine dulled the sting, there the smell didn't belong to anyone, it belonged to all of them. But he hadn't been in a change room for months.

He had forgotten that smell; he didn't remember anymore what change rooms smelled like.

He put his shirt back on, feeling the cold again. A car horn tooted; Boon was waiting. Another toot, and people on the platform turned to stare. The sky behind them now was magenta, the sliver of moon was a vanishing translucent dash. The car looked like a cab, with the solid cube across the top, with the words in English *Boon Tan's Driving School,* and what he assumed was Mandarin on the other side.

"All right, all right, I'm here."

"You are late."

The clock on the dashboard read 6:17. But he wouldn't argue. Boon never listened to argument, just shook his head, saying, "I am the teacher and if I say you are wrong, you are wrong."

"Sorry."

Boon nodded, satisfied. He stepped out of the car and Dan got in front of the wheel. Boon was overweight and always dressed in a beige suit one size too small for him. He waddled around to the passenger side and maneuvered himself into the seat. Then he tapped the dashboard impatiently. "Okay, okay, what you waiting for?" he hissed. "Start the fucking car."

No one could know that Dan was taking driving lessons. His driving test was only a month away now, just over a month till he turned eighteen and could sit the test and get his license. He would be the only boy at school with a license. But he couldn't tell anyone, not Luke, not Taylor, not his family. They couldn't know till he'd passed the test. Because he could fail. He could stall, he could forget to wait the requisite three seconds at a stop sign; something simple like that could mean a fail and he must not fail. All his money from working at the newsagent on High Street was going toward driving lessons.

Most of all, he couldn't wait to tell Theo. He just wanted Theo to be proud of him again; he was tempted to tell Theo just so he could see pride on the boy's face. But he wouldn't say anything until he had passed the test. He could not fail.

〜〜〜

Everyone was up and in the kitchen when he got home. Everyone except his dad, who was on the road. The past year his father had been promising their mother, "Wait till Regan finishes high school, let's just wait till then and then I'm off that frigging road for good.

I'll be a removalist, a courier, I'll do anything to get off that fucking road." Their mother, Regan, Theo, they had all been thrilled when they'd heard this. But not Dan. He enjoyed the space around him when his father was away. It was too small, Dan told himself, the house was too small for the both of them.

The black night had gone but the morning was all gray; low slate clouds drew a curtain across the sun and the lights were on in the corridor and the kitchen.

Dan walked in and they all looked up. Everything stopped: Theo's hand that had been raising a spoon to his mouth, Regan waiting for her toast to pop, his mother filling the bottom chamber of the espresso maker with coffee. Dan didn't know what to say, so he mumbled a good morning and mumbled again when his mum asked if he'd had a good run.

It was a relief to walk into the bathroom, to shut the door.

It was a pleasure to turn on the taps, to peel off his sweaty clothes, and to feel the warm water on him. He scrubbed hard, under his arms, scrubbed between his thighs to get rid of the stink. He soaped and he rubbed at his face and behind his ears and his neck and his nose where all the pimples were, red and ugly.

It was a pleasure to stand there, being cleansed by the clean, warm water. But what was not a pleasure was to stand there, after having dried himself, to stand there and to look.

Dan straightened his back, flattened the upright hair that had been messed by the towel. He forced his gaze to his reflection in the mirror. His skin was blotchy and red. The pimples on his brow were cracked and pink, there was a faint mustache, black bristles on his upper lip, and black down forming on his chin. He would have to shave tomorrow and probably again on Sunday night. The hair wouldn't stop growing.

He had to look, he had to look down.

He had to keep a firm watch on it, Dan's new body, he had to examine it every day, to be on guard. That was never the case with that other body, Danny's body. *That* body was fit, that body stayed lean; he didn't have to think about it and he didn't have to worry about it. But this new body resisted, it felt as though it was not his own. That was why he had to run every morning, why he now went to the gym three or four times a week after school, to keep the new body in order, to keep it in check. This was why he had to watch what he ate, no more sugar and no more fat. That other Danny hadn't known how lucky he'd been, scoffing down Macca's and pizza and Toblerones. The new body bloated, the new body sagged. That useless prick had had no idea how lucky he'd been.

He forced his eyes back to his reflection in the mirror. What repelled him instantly was all that hair. It disgusted him. He had heard that shaving made the hair grow back even thicker, and it had to be true. There were ugly clumps of it across his chest, down his belly, dense black thatches of it under his arms. He hated how it was crawling up to his shoulder blades, he saw it as a virus invading his body, the explosion of it from his crotch, how it crept up his legs and grew thicker and blacker on his thighs. One day he would get it all waxed, have an operation to get rid of it, the whole filthy mess of it. It sickened him.

He pinched at the flab on either side of him, lying deadened above his hips. He could see that it was receding—all that running and ab work was paying off. He pinched the fat between his fingers. The other Danny never had to worry about fucking *fat*.

Dan dropped his hands to his sides. He was done. He turned his back on the mirror.

〜〜〜

At the kitchen table, dressed in his white shirt and striped tie, his fine woolen jumper and thick woolen trousers, his shoes polished, his blazer hanging neatly from the back of the chair, he ate carefully: he didn't want to stain his shirt or his tie. His mother was in her bedroom getting ready for work and Theo was watching cartoons in the next room, but Regan was still finishing her Vegemite and toast. Dan and his sister didn't talk, they just chewed their food. She was wearing black jeans, and the ugly sweatshirt that was part of her school uniform, pea-green, with the name of the school stitched in yellow thread. Both the jeans and the sweatshirt were too small for her—her breasts seemed enormous and her thighs looked fat. He wondered if she was jealous of the crispness and neatness and expense of his own uniform. It sickened him, sometimes, to see what she was turning into; someone should say something. He should say something. His mother didn't dare to, Regan would flare up immediately. It should be him, he should tell her that there was a word for what she was becoming; it was a word he had heard Mrs. Taylor use, about girls who didn't know how to dress well, girls who went to public schools, and that word was *slovenly*.

Dan looked up from his plate and smiled at his sister. It made Regan beam; she was grateful for his smile. She didn't ask anything of him, she didn't quiz him like his mum, didn't demand answers like his father; unlike Theo she didn't dream of him returning to swimming. If it were just him and Regan, there would be space, there would be all the space he needed.

Dan returned his attention to his plate. He had to eat carefully. The school had paid him a uniform allowance as part of his scholarship. But not anymore, not since he dropped out of the swim team. That was another reason he had to watch and maintain his body. His family literally couldn't afford for him to get fat.

The school had paid for the other Danny, they had supported the other Danny, because that other Danny was water. He was water and he was air. He flew. This new Dan, he was solid earth. He wasn't a swimmer, he didn't fly. The shame whipped him; he didn't believe that shame would ever go away. How the very word—*swimmer*—could lacerate, could remind him of how far he had fallen.

Dan waited for the train at the very end of the platform, as far as he could possibly get from those other schoolkids, those girls in jeans or short slutty skirts, the boys who didn't have to wear ties. The other Danny, he used to stand tall, knew he looked good; that other Danny belonged to his uniform. Dan pulled his shirttails out of his pants and loosened the knot of his tie. *Slovenly.* He nursed the word, he loved the shape of it on the roof of his mouth. He could never look as slovenly as those other schoolboys, those regular schoolgirls. Even in the middle of winter, they all showed skin, the boys in short sleeves, the girls in skirts hitched high up above their knees. As they all boarded the city-bound train, Dan tried to resist peeking, to ignore the flesh, the hair, the skin. The other Danny had never noticed such things. Now, all Dan could see was skin.

It was a relief to get off at Flinders Street, to leave the crammed carriage, to jump on the train to school. He easily found a seat; there were only a few people heading out of the city. At the other end of the carriage he spotted three boys from his school, three juniors in colored blazers, not a crease in their jackets, not a spot on their ties. One of the boys looked up and noticed him. Dan glared back and the young boy hung his head. Dan's scowl shifted to a smile. The pip-squeak was scared of him, they were all frightened of Psycho Kelly.

The train rumbled slowly into the station. He waited till the three juniors were out of the carriage, then he stepped out onto the plat-form. The three boys merged with other students. Dan knelt down, loosened his shoelaces then retied them again, to give himself some distance from the other boys. He waited till they'd all left the station and then he began the slow walk up the hill to school.

Luke was at the tram stop, his hands behind his back, neat in his blazer, his tie perfectly knotted. Luke was a prefect now, and had to stand at the tram stop to inspect the boys on their way to school, making sure their shirts were neatly tucked in, their hair wasn't too long, that they weren't doing anything to damage the reputation of the school. Dan smiled, waiting for Luke to notice him. He pulled at his shirttails, further loosened his tie.

As he approached he could hear Luke bawling out some Year Eight or Nine. The little kid was blushing, nodding like a spaz, trying not to cry; his two friends were standing back. No one dared say anything to the prefect. They were lucky they'd got Luke, who knew all the school regulations but was not unkind, not like some of the others, who were bullies who got off on giving shit to the younger kids. But that wasn't Luke. He just wanted them to follow the rules and the regulations. The kid was still nodding his head up and down like one of those bobbing wooden birds, and then Luke let him go and the kid ran off to his mates. Luke was looking up the road for the next tram as the kid raised his middle finger behind Luke's back and his friends burst out laughing.

Dan rushed past Luke, who turned around, surprised, just in time to see Dan grab the kid in a headlock. The boy was squawking like a chicken. Dan smacked the top of the boy's head with the back of his hand. The boy made one last squeak.

"You little wanker, you give my mate the finger again and I'll wallop you." He let the boy go and he ran off. Dan grinned at Luke. "They're all scared of Psycho Kelly."

Luke looked at him but didn't say anything.

Dan knew they didn't respect him but they were scared of him; even Luke, even his best mate was scared of him. Because this new Dan was harder, tougher; he was the toughest and hardest boy in the school.

"If that little cunt gives you any lip again, you just tell me, I'll sort it."

Luke recoiled. From the obscenity, from the blatant try-on of the unkempt uniform. There were words forming on his lips. Dan waited, daring Luke to say something.

Luke turned on his heel, and walked through idling traffic to the other side of the street. Dan hoisted his bag over his shoulder and followed him. A car that had just started to move braked suddenly to avoid hitting him, the furious driver blaring the horn. The boys walking up to the school gate all turned to look.

"Fuck off, wanker." Dan was laughing as he said it, and gave the driver the finger.

Luke hadn't stopped for Dan, was walking as fast as he could.

"Hey, mate," Dan yelled. "Slow down."

Luke spun around, furious. "Do up your tie, will you? You look like a bum."

A tremor whipped up Dan's spine like a slithering grass snake. He scowled, tensing. Luke stepped back, one hand protectively raised.

He thinks I'm going to hit him. Dan smiled, then re-knotted his tie and tucked in his shirt. "That better?"

Luke didn't understand—he never had. Luke thought the worst thing that could happen was getting into trouble at school. If he got detention, Luke's whole world would cave in. Luke just didn't get it, didn't get that the very worst thing had already happened to that other Danny, that they tore apart and fucked up that other Danny. Luke just didn't get that there wasn't anything more they could do to Dan. If Dan were to stick to the rules, to obey every teacher's command, to nod attentively in every class, read every book they wanted him to read, attend their sports meets and cheer along; if he was the perfect student, obedient and meek and respectful, then they would hate him, they would never stop laughing at him. They would never stop reminding him how he had failed them and how he had never belonged there.

Luke just didn't get it.

When they were scared of him they couldn't touch him. They couldn't hurt him.

The boys were streaming past them. Dan wanted to reach out to his mate, he knew he should, he so wanted to touch Luke, but he was scared that Luke would shrug him off, that he wouldn't want someone tainted like Dan to come anywhere near him.

"Hey, Kazantsis," said Dan, the grin still playing at his lips, "I'm sorry, mate."

And that was the moment, when they didn't have to touch, when Luke looked straight at Dan and right through Dan and saw beyond and back and through that grin on his face and he could tell how much his friend was suffering. It was as Demet had said all those years ago—there was a light that went from his heart to his friend's heart and back to him, and that was all the touch they needed. Dan was about to repeat his apology, this time without a stupid smart-arse grin on his face, but at that very moment a voice called out, "Kelly!"

It was Martin.

The grin was back on Dan's face; his arms outstretched, he yelled back to Martin, "How's it hanging, you big faggot?"

Dan fell into stride with Martin, sauntering up the drive, knowing all the boys were watching them. They were both aware of it, the power of it, the way the river of boys parted to let them through. It wasn't till they reached the school buildings, Martin going on about the Hawks, what a great team they were, that Dan realized that Luke wasn't by his side, Luke wasn't waiting for him.

They were heading for assembly in the Great Hall when Martin said, just dropping it from the side of his mouth, "You know there's going to be a special presentation this morning? For John Wilkinson. Did you hear that? They've invited that fag back as a special guest." Martin was shaking his head with disdain. "They want Wilco to inspire us. How are you going to stand for that?"

Not how are *we* going to stand for that, but how are *you*, Kelly, how are *you* going to stand for that.

Dan didn't let anything show but his stomach crashed down to his feet. He swallowed, maintained his composure. Martin had his eyes fixed on him. Dan had to turn away.

Wilco was in the swim team for the Commonwealth Games. It didn't matter how tough Dan was, how much the other boys feared him, none of that mattered. Wilco was the returning hero, Wilco was the hero of the whole school. There was no way Dan was going to stand in that hall and cheer for that cunt. No way.

He stuffed his bag into his locker. "You go on ahead. I'm just going off to the dunny."

Martin's eyes were narrowed, focusing on him, as if Dan were something pinned to a slide under a microscope, something small and dirty on the other side of a lens. "I'll wait for you." Martin's eyes had him trapped.

Dan's smile got wider. He looked straight back at Martin, gave it right back to him. "You want me to hold your hand, do ya?"

Martin's gaze faltered. It started as a grin and then his face screwed up and he was cacking himself. He punched Dan on the shoulder. "Danny Kelly, you crack me up."

Dan punched him back, but harder, so that Martin knew who was the toughest. He'd told Martin to call him Dan, but Martin refused to do that, Martin always pretended that he'd forgotten. Now he was rubbing his shoulder: the punch had hurt. Good.

Dan was whistling as he walked off toward the toilets. A Year Seven, sleek black hair, alabaster skin that had blossomed in hideous acne all over his cheeks, brow, and chin, was rushing down the corridor. He tried to dodge Dan but the older boy stepped sideways, just a small movement but enough to make the younger boy crash into him. Dan's shoulder sent the boy spinning against the lockers. Everyone looked up at the sound of the boy slamming into the metal, at his howl of pain. Dan didn't look back, he was still whistling, his hands in his pockets as he made his way down the stairs.

He was no hero but they were scared of him. He was Psycho Kelly. None of them dared to take him on.

He was the only one in the toilets and as soon as he got in there he made his hand into a fist and smashed it hard against the hand dryer, enjoying the sound of the metal buckling. He punched the machine again. And again. And again. He'd scraped away skin from his knuckles, and drops of blood were forming along the mounds. Delighted at the damage done, at the sharp stinging pain, he brought his fist to his mouth, sucked at the blood. He imagined Wilco's face, imagined what it would be like to punch the boy, hard, like he'd punched the dryer. How good would that feel? To kick him, to get behind him and swing Wilco's arm right up and then to wrench it back, to hear the sound of bone cracking, so that Wilco would never swim again.

Dan slammed the cubicle door, which ricocheted and pounded three times. He pulled it shut and locked it, sitting on the toilet seat, breathing in and breathing out, trying not to imagine the adulation for Wilco, on the stage in his Australian team jacket, his shoes shiny, his tie neatly knotted. As he got to his feet with that smirk on his face, he'd be looking up and down the hall for Dan, searching for Dan's face amid the ceaseless cheering, the wild applause, looking for Danny Kelly, wanting to show him that it was he, Wilco, who was the strongest, the fastest, the best. It was he, Wilco, who was going to stand up on a podium, in Kuala Lumpur, to louder cheers, to more furious applause, when it should have been Dan up there. But he wasn't good enough, he wasn't fast enough or strong enough. He wasn't the best. Dan smacked his fist into the cubicle wall with such force that his head snapped back.

Coach Torma would be there, applauding Wilco, who might just be his first Olympian.

Don't you dare cry, you fucker, don't you dare cry. It would be better to kill himself than cry.

～～～

He didn't want to go out into that world in which Wilco was a hero. He'd rather stay in the toilets all day than face those boys who'd roared for Wilco. But soon he heard the approaching wave of boys as they flooded through the quadrangle, heard their shouts and laughter through the slatted panes of the toilet window, heard the clomping and scuffing of their feet in the corridor, the toilet door opening and boys pissing and shitting next to him, and the sound of water

running. Dan opened the cubicle, washed his hands, making the congealed blood over his knuckles run again. He wet his hair, slicked
it back, noticing the blur of bristle at his chin. Luke should have
pointed that out, some teacher would call him on it, say he couldn't
come to school unshaven, if it happened again there would be demerit
points, again, and there would be detention. Dan sauntered out of the
toilets, kicked open the door, slid his hands into his pockets, slowed
his pace to look like he had all the time in the world. He had practiced this walk in front of the mirror at home, had trained his body
to walk in new ways, to move differently from that other body that
belonged to Danny, that no longer belonged to him.

The prefects were walking together back to the school building. Martin should have been with them but he'd been caught with
a cigarette last week, and that had got him demoted. But next week
he would be back; the Taylors were always prefects, according to
Martin—it was a family tradition. The school wouldn't dare punish a
Taylor for too long.

He wished it were Martin he could have spoken to; Martin would
have been thrilled to help him out, he'd have got off on the dare of it.
But with Martin not there, it had to be Luke. Dan motioned to his
friend and Luke waited for him.

"Hey, mate," Dan whispered, "I need a favor."

The other prefects were watching. Dan glowered at them, wishing
he could mouth an obscenity at them. But he couldn't afford to get
into trouble, not at that moment. The look he gave them was enough.
They turned away.

"What?" asked Luke.

"I'm going to wag today."

"You can't."

"I can. If you tell them at roll call that you've approved my doing
VCE revision in the library. I'll be back at lunchtime. Promise."

Luke shook his head.

"Mate, it won't be a problem."

"And what if you get caught?" Luke's voice sounded younger, uncertain.

"Come on, mate, I won't get caught and you won't get into trouble." Dan winked. "Anyway, they won't expel you, you're their top student. Getting rid of you will fuck up their entrance scores."

The uncertainty vanished from Luke's face. "Piss off, Kelly." He walked off, his arms crossed, striding down the quadrangle.

Dan glanced around quickly, looking out for a teacher, making sure there was no one there to see him. There was only a gardener, some new bloke. Dan had been at school long enough to know that the gardener didn't matter. He ran to the lockers.

Luke would do it for him, Luke would cover. He knew he could count on Luke.

He kept old T-shirts in his locker, with track pants and sneakers, for when he used the gym at lunch or after school. He grabbed the clothes and shoes, bundled them in his arms, walking quietly down the corridor, then more purposefully toward the ovals. Once he got there he started to run.

There was a copse near the river, a circle of oak trees planted a century ago. It was where some of the boys went to smoke, where Dan went to escape. It was safer there than the banks of the river, which were patrolled by prefects and teachers.

Quickly Dan took off his school clothes and shoes, put on the gym gear, wrapped the bundle of his school uniform in a second T-shirt, and stuffed it into a hollow tree trunk. He breathed in and he breathed out.

Finally he was free. Wagging was the best feeling in the world.

Dan followed a path that kept to the river but was shielded by scrub and trees. It reached a bend and then climbed a small hill that rose to the railway tracks. There was an untidy gravel path that ran parallel to the track on one side and the imposing back walls of mansions on the other. One of the walls had broken glass cemented along its top. It was tempting—one day he wanted to scale it, just to prove he could do it. Even Martin would be impressed by that.

A small bridge crossed the railway lines and then he was in the suburbs. He walked up a narrow leafy street, crossed Malvern Road, and was at Toorak station. There wouldn't be any teachers there, no one patrolled that far. He made his way to the end of the platform, hands in the pockets of his track pants, the cold slicing into him. But he didn't let it bother him. The train arrived, he slipped into the last carriage, and he was on his way to town.

～～～

He loved being in the city, the way you could disappear in the middle of the metropolis, the way no one bothered to look at him, how the traffic and crowds and noise had no distinct edges, how everything blended into itself so it was impossible to know where something began and where it ended.

Dan sauntered through arcades and alleys, in and out of shops. Time fell away. He wouldn't check his watch, he wouldn't let himself look up at the Town Hall clock, he'd trust his instincts, savor every moment. He didn't have to be anyone here, he could just move through the city, disappear.

He wished then that Martin was with him, that they could just walk and talk, disappearing together. And if not Martin, then Luke. But they would never wag, they wouldn't have the guts. He was braver and tougher than them. He could call Demet, she could wag, they were slack at her school. But now even Demet probably wouldn't wag, not in their final year; she'd become a swot, always studying, wanting to get into uni. Like Martin and Luke. It was just him, alone and disappearing, conquering the city.

If only Martin could have wagged; it would have been so good to be free in the city with Martin, just the two of them, walking side by side.

Thinking of Martin reminded him that he had to get that present for Emma's birthday.

For the longest time it pierced him right through his gut and into the heart to think of Emma. That was the price of failure, he told himself, having to let go of someone like Emma. Of course it was foolish—she was older than him, had already nearly finished university—but the four years wouldn't have mattered if he had won the gold, if he had been the best and the strongest. But he had failed her. So it would never be. He had nothing to offer, he knew that. She was perfect and he knew that he didn't deserve her. She belonged to the other Danny. She was a bird, flying high above him, while he was fixed, stuck to the ground. She belonged to the sky, not to the earth.

The city broke into sound and color and smell: the heavy pulsing beat of techno blaring from a two-dollar shop; the dull gray of the asphalt; the sharp smell of spice and grease from the noodle shops. Dan wasn't walking aimlessly anymore. Now he had a purpose.

He found the perfect gift for her in David Jones. It was a simple white porcelain plate with a blue finch etched on it. It was delicate, it was brittleness itself; he would be scared to hold it in his hands. Dan didn't even look at the price tag, he already knew he couldn't afford it. He didn't even look around to see whether anyone was watching him; he couldn't hesitate or show caution. Breathing in, his hand darted, and breathing out, the small plate was in his pocket. He walked slowly, confidently to the doors, past the shoppers, past the shop girls at the perfume counters, even stopping to let a woman in a wheelchair have right of way, a young woman with a silver stud in her bottom lip, who nodded curtly at his gesture, as if she hated it but had to acknowledge it, and he was past her and he was at the doors and his pace had not quickened and his breath stayed steady and he was out on the street, the noise and color and smell and light of the city all around him, and it was only his heart that was beating so fast that he could have just completed his morning run. No one called after him, no one ran to stop him. He crossed the tram tracks and headed into an arcade, his heart still pounding. The thrill of it was intoxicating. For a moment, one brief, blissful moment, he felt like the other Danny again.

He didn't take the train this time: in a rush to return, still elated from the theft, he risked the trams. He was running to catch a connecting tram when he bumped into two boys. They were not from his school, they were from another private school, with different stripes across their blazers. They were from the school that his school was always trying to beat, the school his school hated. Dan knew it was a Catholic school, and that for some reason part of hating them was because they were Catholic, though it didn't make much sense because there were Catholic boys at his own school, who were always getting teased about priests fucking them. As he ran past, Dan accidentally knocked his elbow into the hip of one of the boys, who stumbled, then turned and called out something that Dan couldn't quite catch. The tram had stopped but Dan ignored it. He knew what he had to do.

"What did you say?" he demanded.

"I said, watch where you're going, dickhead."

The other boy nudged his mate, whispered something.

"I know you," said the first boy. Then he grinned, mean and sly. "You're that crybaby, aren't you? That loser swimmer. But then you're all crybabies at that faggot school you go to."

Dan had to tell himself, *Not now,* had to quiet the scream in his head. He couldn't do it now, out in the open. But it was a screaming in his head: *I am going to kill you, cunt, I am going to tear you apart.*

All he said was the name of the park and the time to meet there after school. The other boy was nervous now, both the other boys were, but Dan knew that neither of them could back down. Another tram pulled up and Dan went to catch it. "Five o'clock," he yelled again. "I'll be there." And he added, ecstatic, the word a thrill on his lips, *"Cunt."*

A woman threw him a look of hatred and contempt. He didn't care. He wasn't in uniform.

Except that, sitting in the tram, catching his breath, the word repeated endlessly in his head: *crybaby*. That was what he was, and the punch of his failure floored him so violently that he could barely breathe. His skin was flame and his hands trembled and the blood throbbed so hard in his head that he couldn't see and the wretched memories came back; they would never leave him alone. He sat, burning, the shame so intense he thought he could burst into flames.

~~~~

He thought he had got away with it but as he was about to sneak back into the school he heard his name barked out. He instantly recognized the hard consonants and chopped vowels.

He forced his face to go blank. He didn't want the man to know how much he hated him.

"Where have you been?" Coach was running across the road toward him. Dan couldn't help marveling at how his enormous belly was so tight that it didn't shake. Was it possible for it all to be muscle?

The man was in his face, repeating the question. "Where have you been?"

Nothing came to Dan. "I was wagging."

The man's shoulders slumped. "Boy, this is your final year, your grades are not good. What are you doing?"

Dan's first thought was, What business is it of yours? Then, immediately following it: How do you know and why would you care?

"Danny, I want to talk to you."

"Am I in trouble?"

"I said I want to talk to you."

"Am I in trouble?" You failed me. I didn't fail, *you* failed me.

"You stupid boy, don't you know they are looking for any excuse to let you go?"

That's because I'm a failure, that's because I'm no good.

"Am I in trouble?" He was enjoying repeating the question, enjoying seeing how much it was annoying Coach. The man's face was purple now, he was showing teeth. That's what we are, thought Dan, two dogs who want to tear each other to pieces.

Then the man's face slackened, suddenly devoid of expression. "Go. Go back."

Does he want me to *thank* him for not reporting me? Dan wondered. I'm not going to fucking thank him. Dan put his hands in his pockets, felt the smooth cold surface of the saucer. "Okay, I'm going."

"Danny." The man stopped him. His words were all effort, as if he was ashamed of them. "My offer stands. If you want me to train you again, I will. If you want to come around and talk to me, about anything, I am happy to help. You are always welcome in my home."

The man was waiting. Eagerly. Like a dog hanging out for a bone.

Dan said quietly, purposefully, "Mr. Torma, you know those pizzas you always ordered for us? The ones you reckoned were so fantastic, the best in the world? They're no good, sir, they stink, sir, all us boys thought so. We lied to you. We really hated those pizzas."

It had just come out of nowhere, from deep inside him, and it was exactly the right thing. How had he not thought of it before? The fat fool was gutted, as though Dan had kinghit him; he was blinking, speechless. Dan had wanted to yell at him, but this was better. Smarter. No swearing, no losing his temper. Just putting the fat fool in his place. The shame he'd felt on the tram, the disgrace of who he was, all of it disappeared; he wanted to roar with laughter as he ran along the side of the school grounds, scaled the fence into the ovals, ran down to the river, and changed his clothes. He just made the bell for the start of English. Martin winked at him as he took his seat. Luke's face was pure relief.

~~~

It was a double period, two hours of English, and Dan was concentrating. Mr. Gilbert was his teacher, and he had always liked the man; he sometimes thought Mr. Gilbert was the only teacher who liked him in turn, who forgave Dan for constantly fucking up. They

were studying *Life of Galileo* and though Dan didn't raise his hand
or ask any questions, he enjoyed following the reading of the play.
He found that the words calmed him. He knew that it was strange to
get such stillness from the words—he should have been feeling outrage for what they did to a man who was the best and the smartest man of his time. What they did was unconscionable. It was the
word that Mr. Gilbert had used and it was exactly the right word.
The play steeled Dan's nerves; he slipped into its strange syntax and
unfamiliar speech patterns, where there didn't seem to be a discon-
nect between what was said and what was meant, and though Mr.
Gilbert kept saying that they had to read between the lines and look
beyond the text to the subtext, what Dan liked about the play was
that the words spoke truth. They didn't dissemble or disguise, they
didn't deceive. He thought that it was all fantasy, he knew that was
not how words worked in the real world. He felt pity for poor Galileo, speaking the truth and then being forced to speak lies. Accepting
ignominy—another one of Mr. Gilbert's words. That was what happened to the best and the wisest. The world hated them and forced
them into cowardice, forced them to lie.

He disappeared into the words until the final bell rang and the
chairs scraped back on the wooden floor and Dan remembered he had
to fight. He had to fight and he had to win.

He told Martin but didn't dare tell Luke.

Martin said, "Okay, got ya," and whispered to some other boys.

At the lockers Dan carefully took out the blue finch plate and
showed it to Martin. "This is for Emma, for her birthday."

Martin was surprised. "You remembered her birthday?"

"Yeah, of course."

Martin looked at the plate, then raised an eyebrow. "Where did
you get it from?"

Dan had to stop himself from blurting out that he'd taken it.
It would have impressed Taylor, but Emma couldn't know; he'd be
ashamed if she were to find out.

Martin put out his hand. "I'll give it to her."

Dan held the plate tight against his chest. "Nah, I'll give it to her myself. I thought I might come home with you tonight, after the fight."

Martin stiffened. "She won't be there." His tone was surly, annoyed. "She doesn't even live with us anymore, she's got her own place." He reached out again for the plate. "I'll give it to her when she comes for lunch on Sunday. Okay?"

Dan didn't want to let go of it. It was his gift to her, he wanted to hand it to her and see her face when she opened the wrapping; he'd get some at the newsagent tomorrow, some gold paper—that was what the present deserved.

"I'll come by on Sunday then. What time?"

"Jesus!"

Dan didn't understand why Martin was so exasperated, why he slammed his locker shut.

"Don't you get it?" Martin said, almost mumbling, not looking at Dan. "Don't you get it, even after all these years, that you can't just come around? That's not how it's done." Taylor made a joke of the last five words, squeezed them out so they sounded like a joke. "You haven't been invited."

Dan thought, So invite me. Then he remembered Mrs. Taylor dropping him off after their weekend at the beach. "Your mum said that I was always welcome at your house." He could remember her very words: *Danny, you are always welcome at our house.*

Now Martin wasn't annoyed, he just rolled his eyes. "She was just being polite, you dickhead. Don't you get it?" And this time he snatched the plate away. "I'll give it to Emma on Sunday. I'll even wrap it for you, how's that?"

Dan wanted to grab the plate, to raise it high and drop it so that it smashed into a million pieces.

〰〰

The boy he was to fight had his gym gear on. Dan was going to fight bare-chested; he couldn't afford to tear his shirt. He turned away from the two groups of waiting boys, boys from both schools, and stripped off his uniform, embarrassed about all the filthy hair.

The boys started clapping and the other side started one of their sports chants, and Tsitsas and Martin answered with one of their own. They kept it down, in case someone heard.

I'm the toughest, Dan told himself, I'm the strongest. He *had* to win. He reminded himself: no biting, no kicking, nothing shameful. He couldn't win by being dishonorable. He planted his feet, raised his fists.

The other boy punched him, fast. It took him by surprise; he didn't feel the pain of it but it made him stumble and fall. The chanting had stopped. He scrambled to his feet, grateful that the other boy hadn't come flying, that he'd given him the chance to get up. So Dan ran toward the boy, slammed into him and put him on the ground, but Dan didn't wait, Dan just crashed onto him so his weight was fully on the boy's chest. The boy was calling out, "Off me! Off me!" but all Dan did was push his knee harder into the boy's chest. He raised his fist and then jabbed, quickly, three times. He wanted to punch hard, oh how he would have liked to break the boy's jaw and nose and teeth, and he knew he could have—one for Torma and one for Wilco and one for Mrs. Taylor—but he held himself back. He stayed on top of the boy, but told himself to stay cool, it was all over.

And it was. The boy was saying, "Just get off me, okay? You win, just get off me."

Martin came up and helped Dan to his feet, lifting one of his hands high in the air. And then his friends were singing the other school's song while the defeated boys slunk off; they sang at the top of their lungs, not caring who heard them now, but instead of the verses being about pride and honor and history they were singing of pervert homo priests and nympho nuns. Martin was still holding Dan's hand high and he started to chant, "Barracuda, Barracuda," but Dan tore away from his grip and faced his friend.

"Don't. Fucking don't."

"Sure," smiled Martin, watching Dan get dressed. "Whatever you want, you fucking psycho."

As they walked out of the park, Martin had his arm around Dan's shoulder. It felt both heavy and light. He didn't understand how he could want Martin's arm to stay there and how he would also just love to punch it off. Dan was smiling as the boys praised him, but he wasn't satisfied. He'd won but it didn't feel like anything. He'd won but it wasn't worth anything.

~~~~~

Next morning, at the newsagent, getting ticked off by the owner for being five minutes late, Dan couldn't stop asking himself why Coach would have made the offer he did, why he would even bother with him. And then it came to him. Coach no longer believed in him, Coach knew that the other Danny was gone. What Coach was feeling was pity, that's what it was.

That was all Dan was worth. Pity.

Dan hated the man for his pity, and wished him dead; and just for the tiniest of seconds, that childish and malevolent thought warmed him. Then the shame returned in an icy rush.

At the end of his shift he balanced the till and locked up. He thought back to saying to Martin, *I'll come around,* and Martin answering, *You don't get it, that's not how it's done.* He meant that he and Dan came from different worlds, he meant that Dan was ignorant and impolite. He meant, thought Dan, that I am *slovenly*.

The word was ugly. But that was what he was. Shame ran through him again, as sharp and searing as boiling water. Then the cold came back, and wrapped around and froze his heart. That cold too was searing.

"You're getting to be a good driver."

It feels good to hear Dad say that, as he punches on the car stereo buttons, trying to find a song he likes. The AM/FM radio on Mum's Datsun works but the CD player is stuffed, it hasn't worked for a year. Whenever we get into the car, Mum says, "I don't know what happened to it. One day it was fine and the next it just stopped working. Stupid shitbox."

If Regan and I are in the car with her when she says that we don't dare look at one another in case we lose it and crack up. What Mum doesn't know is that last summer Regan and two of her mates were in the car, not even driving, too young for their Ls. They were bored, just hanging out in the car, playing music, and Regan stuck a two-dollar coin in the CD slot, just for a laugh, for something to do. It got stuck and the CD player has never worked again.

Dad finally settles on a song on one of the golden oldies stations. I recognize it, one of those songs that comes up at the barbers or in the supermarket. Something about a man in a rocket.

Dad rests back in his seat. His window is down, and he's humming along to the song. "He used to be good once, Elton John."

"Uh-huh." I kind of know Elton John. Bald, crazy glasses, a big poof.

"*Madman Across the Water.* I had that album when I was a teen-ager, played it to death. That one was all right and *Tumbleweed Connection* was good too. Then they all turned to shit in the eight-ies." My dad is sneering as he says this. That's what he always says: everything turned to shit in the eighties.

I can't relax with Dad in the car. I know he's watching me out of the corner of his eye, even now, pretending he's just listening to the music, looking out of the window. My father has been driving since he was twelve, he knows how to drive any car, any truck, how to pull them apart and put them back together, how to drive in the fog and in the wet, in a tropical storm, how to navigate the sea of the Hume Highway and the ocean of the Nullarbor Plain. Mum says Dad doesn't drive, he flies.

So his compliment glows for me, a spark from the center of my stomach, but it doesn't make me less anxious. It makes me more conscious of every gear shift, every use of the brake and clutch and accelerator. I wish we were out of the city on the open road, where I could really show him how I am learning to control this machine. Except I'd want to be on the open road on my own.

It is a week before Christmas and I can't speed or fly in the bumper-to-bumper traffic cluttering up Glenferrie Road. It takes an age to get from one traffic light to the next.

"Steady, mate," says Dad. "We've got plenty of time. We're not going to be late."

I realize he's dreading this as much as I am.

When we finally cross Riversdale Road and are gliding down toward school he switches off the radio. I turn left into the small street that runs along the bottom of the college. Dad lets out a long whistle.

"Jesus Christ," he splutters. "It's fucking enormous."

This is the first time Dad has even seen my school.

"Wait till we get inside," I say, carefully inching into a parallel park between a new Mercedes and a black Pajero. I want to make it in one effortless glide, the perfect park. Dad can't help it, his hand is pressed flat to the dashboard. I turn the wheel in one smooth motion and the Datsun finds its place. Trust me, I want to say to him. Can't you just trust me?

He doesn't speak as we walk up the long cobblestone drive and enter the quadrangle. The flowers have lost their spring bloom. Emptied of students, the grounds look even bigger, and the sense of space overwhelms me. My father remains silent as we pass the imposing bluestone walls of the chapel.

"What's this?"

On the far side of the quadrangle, the redbrick sports center is lined by scaffolding along its length; there are ladders, ropes, and sheets of blue tarp. A group of workmen in fluoro orange vests are sitting on their haunches, having a break. They take no notice of us.

"It's the sports center—they're extending it," I explain, sensing my father's disapproval. He opens his mouth to say something, then decides against it. But he does snort, a loud derisive sound from the back of his throat. Not for the first time this morning, I wish that it was Mum who was with me, that my old man hadn't come anywhere near this place.

"How can I help you?" Mrs. Marchant is behind the reception desk of the administration building. She is old, nervy, with a wrinkled neck, her thin-rimmed spectacles sitting precariously on the bridge of her nose. Her fingers keep flying over her keyboard as she awaits our answer.

"We're here to see Mr. Canning." My father's voice sounds loud, rough. Aussie.

The old lady keeps typing as she asks, "And do you have an appointment?"

"Yes. I'm Neal Kelly."

She stops typing, takes off her glasses, squints at us, then smiles warmly. "Hello, Danny," she says. "It's nice to meet you, Mr. Kelly."

I am astonished that she knows my name. I've done my best to disappear over the last two years at this school. But then it dawns on me that she knows me from back when I was winning medals for the school, when I was someone. I don't reply. I cross my arms and wait.

∿∿∿

Principal Canning appears distracted as he ushers us into his office. His desk is massive, the size of a billiard table, carved from stained wood. One wall is full of bookcases, made of the same wood, right up to the ceiling. But I don't take in the titles of the leather-bound volumes. I am too conscious of my father, who seems as nervous and ill at ease as I feel. We stand silently in front of the desk, both of us with our hands clasped behind our backs, as if awaiting punishment. It is almost comical, my father's diffident anxious stance: as if he's expecting detention.

"Please, sit."

Dad sits heavily in the leather chair and it squeaks, just like a fart.

"Mr. Kelly, thank you for coming." Principal Canning turns to me. "And I'm glad you could make it too, Dan."

I take a seat. But I don't answer, I know this isn't true.

∿∿∿

It was my mother who took the call, that first week of the holidays. She had agreed, said of course she would come to the school, she was only too happy to discuss my future. But when she told Dad about the phone call, he said that he would be the one going, and that I'd be going with him.

Mum had replied, "No, they just want us—they want to talk to the parents. They haven't asked Danny to come along."

Dad had been firm. "It's about his future, isn't it? If it's about his future he should be there. He's coming."

Mum told me all this yesterday, when I was whinging about

having to go back to school, whining that school was over, kaput for me, that I never ever had to set foot in that place again. In a tone that brooked no argument, a rare reproach in her voice, Mum said, "You are going along, Danny. Your father insists. It's about your future—both of us think you should be there."

"Mr. Kelly," Principal Canning begins.

"Please," my father interrupts, "call me Neal."

I wait for Canning to offer his first name, but he doesn't.

"Very well, Neal. I know this situation is a little out of the ordinary as the VCE results are not released for another few weeks but I wanted to canvass the possibilities for young Dan's future." Principal Canning is looking straight at my father as he speaks; he doesn't once look in my direction. "Of course, the results could surprise us all, but I spoke to Dan after he sat his exams, and I have spoken with his teachers, and I'm afraid that the likelihood is that he has performed below standard in his examinations. Even if Dan passes, it will be a bare scraping through at best."

For the first time he turns to me, his eyes steady and clear, boring right through me. "We are not being unfair, are we, Kelly?"

My father stiffens. He doesn't like that I am being called by my surname.

"No," I answer gruffly, my arms slipping behind the chair. I can't keep my hands still.

"So is that why we're here, is it to be told to fuck off, thanks very much, we don't want Danny anymore?"

I have to give it to him, I have to give it to Canning. He doesn't cringe, or even seem affronted by Dad's obscenity. But he does sigh and lean forward on the desk.

"Mr. Kelly—Neal. There are many teachers here who are supporters of Dan, who want the very best for him. Colin Gilbert, Frank Torma, they have all offered to work hard with Dan next year. They believe with effort and discipline he can do very well if he repeats Year Twelve." Again his eyes drill into me. "They believe in you, son, and I do too. But I need to know that you will commit to your studies, that you will give us the very best of yourself."

"My son has already given this school his very best."

Dad's words stun me. I can't look at him, can't look at Canning. Outside the window a cluster of rosebushes have fallen into wretched bareness. I can't look at anyone; that would release the lump in my throat. I think of Coach, believing in me. That helps; fury overcomes shame and I almost blurt out, *I don't want his help, I don't want anything from any of you. I don't want your fucking pity.*

"And you are prepared to have Danny come back?"

"Yes."

I know my father is taken aback by Canning's answer. This was not what he expected and he is lost for words. I know my old man, the argument he would have been rehearsing all the way over in the car, about how this college was all about the money, how it was going to dump me now that there was nothing more to gain from me, now that I was no longer part of the swim team, no longer winning medals. And I am shocked too. I thought they'd be glad to see the back of me. I expected it and I deserve it. No one wants a failure.

"It will have to be Danny's decision."

"I agree," says Principal Canning. "It has to be his decision, made in consultation with you and your wife as his parents. As I said, I realize these are exceptional circumstances, but I wanted you all to know that we are prepared to have Dan back."

It is almost whispered, it sounds puny as it tumbles from Dad's mouth. "Thank you." He wants to say something else, goes to form the words, but he's shifting uncomfortably, like he doesn't know how to say it.

Principal Canning clears his throat. "Of course, repeating Year Twelve is not covered by the terms of the scholarship. He will have to return as a full fee-paying student." Canning knows what is making my father shift uncomfortably in his seat. Canning can sense that now it is all about the money.

"How much are we talking about?" Now that it is out, Dad's voice is calm, his tone gruff and somehow indifferent.

"You can talk to Mrs. Marchant about those details outside. She'll be happy to take you through the fee structure."

My father is sitting up straight, still, his hands on his knees. His voice is steel. "I asked how much."

Principal Canning blinks and clears his throat again. "It is seven thousand, five hundred dollars a term. Twenty-two and a half thousand dollars for the year."

My father rises and I stumble as I follow, catching my shoe on a corner of the carpet. My cheeks burn. I am doing the maths, I am working out the cost of their investment: twenty-two thousand, five hundred for each of the five years I have been here. Over one hundred grand—I've cost the school over one hundred grand. My cheeks are ablaze and I can't look up. It is not that I despise myself—I know that feeling well and I know how to carry it. And it isn't the shame, though that is part of it, part of me: my shame is always there, and so is hate, they are one with my blood and with my lungs. What is new, what sears through me now, is a clear understanding of my worthlessness. I am the debt that can never be paid off.

My father does now what he would not do before. He offers Principal Canning his hand. "Thank you."

Principal Canning looks my way once more. I don't hear his words, I have to turn away from that sympathy, from that lacerating pity.

～～～

My father and I don't say a word until we walk through the school gates. And then I say, "Dad, you don't have to worry. I'm not going to repeat. Even if I fail, I won't repeat."

My father has stopped. He won't hold me, he can't; he and I live in that physical distance. But he is shaking his head. "Don't worry, son. We'll find the money, don't worry about that. We'll get the money."

"No," I insist. I won't let that word go. "No. I don't want to repeat,

I want to start my life." And as I say the words, I drink in the air: I'm finished with school, I'm out of this place. A cold, shivering sweat breaks out, but I know I am right. I am terrified and thrilled. I want to start my life.

And then it goes, the euphoria vanishes. I realize I can't see it. I have no vision of a life.

"You don't have to make a decision now," says my father gently, as we walk toward the car. We fall back into silence. I know that both of us are thinking about the money.

~~~~~

On Denmark Street, a small lime-green Hyundai brakes suddenly in front of me. My eyes leap to my rearview mirror, to my side mirror. There is no one to my left; I swerve, I overtake the stalled car and straighten. My father turns to me. "I was right. You're getting to be a good driver."

I am heading forward, the future is waiting. School has finished but there is no clear path ahead, nothing solid beneath my feet. I will just have to drive through. I accelerate, and speed into those shadows.

His first beer, that tasted of earth and light, the touch of the first summer sun on wet ground.

His first bourbon, that was the taste of sugar and sulfur, the sting to the nose of toffee burning.

His first vodka, that was licorice; his first wine, fruit juice left out too long in the sun; his first rum, all he could taste was the Coke in it; and his first whiskey, that was fire. That was fire and heat.

"You better watch it, mate, you're getting a belly." Bennie leaned across the table and patted Dan's shirtfront.

Omar snorted and that made Dylan and Herc laugh as well. Dan grabbed Bennie's arm, and twisted it. Not too hard, but hard enough for Bennie to grimace a little.

It was true, he was getting a belly. He had to run in the morning, he hadn't run for three days. It was either run tomorrow or not drink beer for a week.

They were sitting outside the chicken shop at the South Preston Shopping Center, in their white supermarket shirts and gray cotton pants. The remains of their lunch were scattered over the table. Omar tapped the end of his cigarette over an empty container, the ash mingling with the gelatinous dregs of soy sauce and oil. Dan was the only one who didn't smoke, he still couldn't bring himself to do it. He'd tried cigarettes and joints, he'd even sucked on a bong, but with every inhalation he could feel the poison coursing through his lungs and into his blood. He felt its pollution instantaneously. That wasn't the case with alcohol. With alcohol you didn't experience the corrosive effects of the toxins till the day after. That was the seduction of drink. It enticed you, it was deceptive. Even the fire of whiskey seemed medicinal, the shock of it, the jump start to the body.

Elena walked toward them, munching on a pie from the Vietnamese bakery. She stopped at their table. "Are you watching the opening ceremony tonight?"

Elena, she just blurted out statements or questions, as if she resented having to speak. Even now she wasn't looking at anyone, was asking questions of the car park.

"Yeah," said Bennie. "We're watching it at my place. You wanna come?"

Dan looked down at his hands, examining the paper cut he'd got that morning, slicing open cardboard boxes. He hadn't told the guys that he wasn't going. There was no way he was going to watch that fucking opening ceremony.

Elena still hadn't answered, she was munching on her pie, looking out at the car park.

"What time should we rock over?"

Bennie shrugged at Omar's question. "Seven, I guess. That's when it starts. Yeah, nah, come at six-thirty."

Dan's finger throbbed, the pain insidious but relentless. He knew he'd be feeling the subtle pain for days.

"Okay," said Elena.

Bennie made a face, making Omar snicker.

"Okay what?" Herc asked.

"Okay, I'll come." Elena wiped pastry crumbs off her work shirt and walked away.

When she was just out of earshot, Bennie leaned into the table and whispered, "Lard arse." That made Omar snort again.

Dylan lit a cigarette. "I like a bit of flesh on a girl's arse," he said, not bothering to whisper. "Fat arses and fat tits, that's what I like."

"No way." Bennie looked disgusted. "I like my bitches slim, I don't want any fat on them."

Dylan blew smoke in his direction. "That's not a bitch, Bennie, mate. That's called a guy."

Omar nearly fell off his chair from laughing.

Dan got up, checked the time on his phone. "I'm going back."

Bennie had lit another cigarette, and he held it up. "I'm going to finish this."

Dan heard them laughing as he walked across the car park to the Safeway entrance. He knew it couldn't be true, but it always felt as though they had to be laughing at him.

∼∼∼

Everyone asked Dan, *So what are you going to do?* They meant after working at Safeway; they were really asking, *When will you get a real job?* He usually answered that he was taking a year or two off to save some money and that he'd start studying in the new year. If they persisted and asked him what he was going to study, he just made it up. *I'm thinking electrical engineering.* Or, *I'm considering health sciences.* Or, *Maybe communications.* Usually they didn't ask anything more after that; it seemed to be enough that he was thinking about a future.

What he would have really liked to answer was the following: *I like working at the supermarket, I like packing shelves and I like being in the stockroom.* He didn't much like working the registers, and he hated stocktake, but that was only twice a year. Overall, he enjoyed his job.

Dan knew he could never say that to Demet, or Martin, or Luke. They were all at uni, Luke and Martin at Melbourne, Demet at La

Trobe. To them, working at a supermarket was something tangential to life: for it to ever be at the center of life was unfathomable. But for Dan it was their worlds that were unreal.

He liked his job, he liked the people he worked with, he liked that he could disappear into what he was doing, that sometimes hours could pass and he'd been lost in a task, stripping tape off boxes, checking off items on stocklists, stacking and neatening up the shelves. *A job is a job,* said Demet. *At least you can save money,* encouraged Luke. *Are they all brain-dead there?* asked Martin.

His mother found course information for him. His father asked whether he'd thought about what he'd like to do in the long term. Dan knew that they were ashamed of him. From time to time, when some manager was telling him off for getting an order wrong or some impatient rude customer was abusing him because the yogurt was past its use-by date, he realized that if his friends or family had seen it, they would have been ashamed for him.

What's new? he thought. What difference does it make?

〰〰

He was in aisle eight, stacking tins of soup on the shelf. Each tin carried the Olympic logo and the words SYDNEY OLYMPICS 2000.

"Aussie Aussie Aussie," muttered Dan, "Oi Oi Oi."

They were the real brain-dead. The ones who kept screaming, *Aussie Aussie Aussie, Oi Oi Oi.*

He'd asked for a double shift, he wanted to work tonight. But Jim, the floor manager, had smiled at him and said, "Nah, mate, it's the opening ceremony tonight. You don't have to work—there's enough part-timers to carry the load, don't worry about it." Then, all gray hair and sour smoker's breath, Jim had winked and said, "Aussie Aussie Aussie, Oi Oi Oi."

He should have insisted, he should be working tonight.

At the end of the shift, Bennie called out from behind the tobacco counter, "See you tonight, Dan."

"Yeah," said Dan. "See you then." There was no way he'd be going.

As he left work he felt the phone vibrate in his pocket. It was Demet.

"Howya doin'?" he answered.

"All good. How was work?" Demet's voice had changed. She didn't run her words together anymore. She didn't call people cunts anymore. Now she said she had problems with the word *cunt*. She said it was sexist. She said many words were sexist—and if not sexist, they were racist, and if not racist, they were het-er-o-NORM-a-tive, a word he always had to spell out in his head to remember. He could never remember what it meant but he assumed it had to be bad.

Demet didn't want to know about work.

"What's up?" he asked.

He knew her well enough to catch the hesitation. "Luke and I were wondering if you wanted to meet up tonight? We'll be at a pub near his place, the Curry Hotel in Collingwood, in Wellington Street. You know it?"

It kicked. It was irrational and foolish but it hurt that she had spoken to Luke before him. Luke and Demet were always speaking now, seeing bands together, arguing about politics and books and films and music. It stung too that they knew all those pubs and bars and cafés, all over town. He hadn't known there were so many of them.

"Okay. I'll find it."

He knew that they had been discussing him, that they were concerned for him. He should have been grateful that they wanted to be with him, that they wanted to take care of him tonight. But he could hear it in her hesitation. All of that was out of pity.

"Cool, we're getting there at seven."

She'd hung up before he could ask who *we* were. He hoped it meant just Demet and Luke.

Dan checked the screen. There was a missed call from Luke, a message from Regan. He texted Luke that he'd organized tonight with Demet.

He looked at the message from his sister. THEO IS WETTING HIS PANTS ABOUT 2NITE. RU HOME? It was a question but it wasn't. He put the phone back in his pocket. He didn't text back, he didn't call.

The wind had ice in it, and it whipped across his neck and his exposed forearms. If he were to walk faster, he would have warmed up. But Dan loved the walk home, the forty-five minutes it took to leave the Safeway, to walk past the Catholic cathedral on Bell Street and cross into the market through the Chinese grocery on High Street. He never wanted to rush it. He loved squeezing past the cluttered aisles of tinned food, the wall of refrigerators full of cuts of meat he couldn't identify and trays of misshapen frozen dumplings. He walked to the back, passed through the orange plastic strips hanging over the door to keep the flies away; and though he did it three or four times a week no one in the store paid him the slightest attention. The orange strips of plastic slid over his shoulders and Dan waited for a forklift to pick up two large crates of Japanese aubergines before he crossed into the hangar-like space of the market itself. He could smell oranges, the sharp aroma of ripening fruit, and a rich bouquet of parsley and coriander, the Vietnamese mint and the basil. He dodged the shoppers who were picking through the fruit, inspecting the herbs for deficiencies, a skill Dan was convinced he would never learn—he thought it must be a talent that had come from migration; he didn't know anyone Aussie born who had that skill. He shifted sideways to avoid a veiled African woman bearing down on the shop counter with a bag of okra. He walked past a vendor selling potato cakes, chips, and bratwurst hot dogs, and was tempted to stop, the smells igniting hunger. *Better watch it, mate, you're getting a belly.* He wouldn't stop. It had been three days since he'd gone running.

He never changed out of his work shirt for the walk home. The other guys rushed to change their gear as soon as the shift was over, or put on a sweatshirt, embarrassed by their uniform and the job it represented. They didn't want to be known as supermarket workers. But Dan was glad for the uniform, that it defined a station and gave him a role. He liked work and the routine of it, how his days and the week were shaped by the spread of his supermarket shifts.

Every time his dad came back from an interstate haul, he'd ask whether Dan had given a thought to his future. What was he going to do? A few months before, Dan had mentioned something about becoming a manager, thinking that might allay his father's concerns, get the prick off his back. His father had tried to remain impassive, but there was a moment, just a flash; like the ghost of an image under an old spent videotape there was a flicker in his eyes, just for a moment, of something like contempt. Dan had been mortified. "Well," his old man had said finally, after a long pause, "just remember that a lot of those manager positions nowadays don't mean shit, Dan. They're just ways of making people believe they're something but in reality they don't pay you more, you're not learning any skills; it can be a dead end—you know that, don't you, son?"

Dan crossed over the railway track, his chest tight. *Given a thought to your future, Dan?*

He flexed his right hand, opening and closing it, stretching his fingers till he could feel them tingle, then clenching them in tight. Sometimes in the garden he came across dried-up plum kernels from fallen fruit that had been buried all winter and then resurfaced. He'd pick up a kernel, it would be shriveled, the color of the soil, and it would disintegrate into dust in his hand. That was the future, that's what had become of it.

His hand opened and closed.

He'd *had* a future. It had been as hard and as strong as the stony heart of an unripened plum, so strong it would have taken a hammer blow to crack it. He'd had that future for years but it too had crumbled into dust. His theory was that you only got one future to dream. He'd fucked it up. He'd failed and now it was gone.

He was walking through the suburbs. The sun had almost disappeared and the purple and gray half-light made everything seem colder. He concentrated on slowing his steps. He was nearly home.

〜〜〜

Theo had a friend over from school, Joel, a sweet-faced shy boy, all elbows and legs, whom Regan called Spider behind his back; the boys were sitting on the couch, watching the television.

Theo was jumpy. "An hour to go," he said, the excitement making his voice rise. "You're gonna watch, aren't ya?"

The TV commentary was already hysterical: would the ceremony be any good, would the world like it, would the world give it their approval? One of the commentators couldn't stop talking about Sydney, saying the word over and over with the subtlety of a race caller, making it three syllables. And underneath that sound he could hear *that* chant, that ugly stupid chant from the crowd: *Aussie Aussie Aussie, Oi Oi Oi.*

Let it be a failure. Please let it be a disaster.

He shook his head at Theo. "Nah, mate, I'm going out."

Theo drew his legs up to his chest, hugging his knees and looking deliberately in the opposite direction.

His mum appeared in the doorway. "I'll heat up dinner for you, honey. How was work?"

He followed her into the kitchen, where she put a laden plate into the microwave, the aromatic sourness of chilies and ginger hanging in the air.

Dan got out his wallet, took out three notes, and gave them to his father. Behind him, he sensed that his mother had tensed. His father took the board money and pocketed it, muttered a quiet "Thanks."

"No problem."

Dan opened the fridge. There was a six-pack of Cascade on the top shelf.

∿∿∿

His first beer, that tasted of earth and light, the touch of the first summer sun on wet ground.

He pulled a bottle from the carton. "Mind if I have a beer, Dad?"

His father nodded and Dan sipped his beer as his mother placed the plate of chicken stir-fry in front of him.

He ate slowly, knowing that if he let himself eat too quickly he would wolf it all down, and that would mean he'd overeat. He remembered Bennie's sly remark about his belly, how it had got under his skin and made everyone laugh.

Dan put down his fork, wiped his mouth with the back of his hand, then drank from the bottle.

"Is that all you're having?"

Dan and his father traded glances. Stop fussing, said his father's look, just sit down and leave the kid alone. As if he had spoken it aloud, his mum grabbed the plate and threw what was left in the bin. It was Dan giving his father the money for board that had upset his mother. It always did. She and his father had argued about it for years. His father thought that at eighteen a youth should take on adult responsibilities, but his mother would shoot back, "No, I'm a wog and we don't do that to our children—we look after them."

His father would groan and respond, "That's what I am doing. Teaching children about responsibility *is* looking after them—it's preparing them for the real world." His mother wouldn't listen, saying she'd never allow it. "What about when they turn twenty-one?"

his father would counter. "Can we ask it of them then?" and his mother would spit angry words back at him.

Then his father would lose his temper. "And what if he's here when he's forty-fucking-one? Are we still not allowed to ask for fucking board?"

"No!" his mother would scream. "Not even when he's forty-fucking-one!"

It had all stopped the year before on his nineteenth birthday when Dan had come home from work and given his father three notes, a fifty, a twenty, and a ten. "Will that do, Dad?" he'd asked. "Is eighty a week fair for board?"

His father had smiled, a real, full smile, and Dan could still remember the pleasure on his father's face and the relief in his father's words. "Yeah, Danny, thanks, mate. I reckon that's fair."

"Can I have another?" Dan pointed to his empty bottle.

His father nodded but he wasn't looking at Dan, he was looking at his wife, who had her back to them at the sink. He began to sing, *"Something told me it was over when I saw you and her talkin'."*

Dan could see that his mother's stance had relaxed, her hands were no longer gripping the bench.

His dad's voice was low and resonant, there was a croak to it, but it suddenly lifted. *"Something deep in my soul said, Cry, girl, when I saw you and that girl walkin' by."*

Dan's mother had turned and was smiling, and singing along. His dad kicked away the chair, and took her into his arms, and they swayed together, her hand draped around his shoulders and the other hand resting in the small of his back.

"I would rather, rather go blind, boy, Than see you walk away from me, child."

Regan had slipped into the kitchen and leaned on a chair watching their parents dance. Dan thought they looked so good, dressed up to go out dancing at their favorite club. They would dance all night, to Motown and to rock and roll. His mum was wearing a strapless black-and-white-checked dress, finely patterned red lace stockings, and her best shoes, shiny black pumps. His dad was wearing his favorite cowboy shirt, black with white piping, and his black suede oxford dancing shoes. His hair was gelled and quiffed and made him look youthful, even though there were flickers of white in his once sandy-blond hair. They looked beautiful together. Dan stole a glance at his sister. Regan was scowling. She hadn't cut her hair in months, it hung lank and greasy; her clothes were all cheap, sweatshirts and jeans from the Northland mall. She isn't trying, thought Dan, she doesn't dare compete with Mum. He swigged his beer, looking down at his own crumpled work shirt, the shapeless gray trousers and non-descript white sneakers. His mother and father looked good, their children looked ordinary.

Regan sat in a chair beside him. Their parents were still dancing, not singing now, but swaying to the song in their heads. Regan leaned across to whisper to him, "Theo's upset—he wants you to stay and watch the opening ceremony with him. Do you have to go out?"

He couldn't hear anything in her tone, no anger or reprimand. But still her words made him furious. He took another sip of the beer.

"Just go and talk to him, okay?"

He was ready to dismiss her. She couldn't make him stay. He watched his parents, who were still lost in themselves, far away from their children.

Regan whispered again. "I'll stay home, Dan, don't worry about it. But go and say something to him, tell him you'll watch the replay tomorrow. You know what it means to him."

There was no anger in her voice, but there was urgency. She couldn't bear conflict, couldn't stand an argument. He feared for his sister, how she would cope when she found out that the world just happened: you couldn't take something wrong and make it right.

"Okay," he answered, winking at her. "Okay." He picked up his beer and headed into the lounge room.

Dan fell onto the couch, in between Theo and Joel. The boys slid farther apart, grabbing an arm each of the sofa, still entirely focused on the TV, even though an ad was running. Dan noticed that Theo was wearing a Sydney 2000 baseball cap, he was wearing it backward.

Let it be a failure.

"Mate, I'm sorry I have to go out."

Theo didn't respond.

Dan turned to Joel. "You into sport, mate?"

The boy nodded timidly and moved farther into the corner of the sofa. Though spring had yet to beat back winter, both of the boys had on baggy shorts. Dan's knee was touching Joel's, the boy's leg hair long and fine. In contrast, Theo's legs were plump and almost smooth; he might not have even grown pubes yet but his mate was hairy, his mate would have a bush down there. Dan concentrated on the screen. He had to stop thinking about skin; that was what came of still being a virgin: thoughts got perverted and you couldn't shake images out of your mind. The ferocious tide of such thoughts stunned him, the way they couldn't be dislodged. All those years of swimming, all that time surrounded by near-naked boys and girls, and he had never once been aroused by all that skin. He had only ever thought of them as machines, judged them by their ability to command the water. They were not faces, they were not skin, not hair, not arms, not hands, not chests, not breasts, not cocks, not vaginas—they were engineering. But now bodies were skin, they were skin and smell, they were hair and touch. Dan forced himself to watch the screen.

The shot cut back to the sea of people in the stands in Sydney. There were a million lights flashing from cameras, but the crowd was hushed, expectant. *Let it be a failure, let it be a disaster.*

"You think it will be any good?"

Theo had his thumb in his mouth. He nodded emphatically. He wouldn't countenance the possibility of a disaster, would never listen to his father's complaints about all the money spent, about the marketing bonanza that was the Olympic Games. Dan knew that his brother had been waiting for this night as keenly and as hopefully as he himself once had.

Regan flung herself into the armchair across from them. Dan could tell from Joel's sudden stir that the boy was checking out her tits.

"Are you sure you can't stay, Danny?" Theo was pleading. The crowd in the arena had started to cheer and roar.

Dan got to his feet. "Sorry, mate, I can't. I've got to catch up with Luke and Demet. How about we watch the repeat tomorrow?"

"Okay, Danny." Theo was nodding reluctantly but started to grin. "That will be good. Yeah, we'll watch it together tomorrow."

"And I'll stay till it's over tonight," said Regan, smiling at Theo but it was a smile for Dan as well. Theo shrugged and Regan shifted in her chair and crossed her arms. She'd spotted how Joel was watching her.

Their mother called out, "Danny, if you want a lift into town we have to head off in twenty minutes."

Dan checked the time. Good, twenty minutes was just before the opening ceremony started. Twenty minutes meant not having to be there for the *Aussie Aussie Aussie, Oi Oi Oi*. Dan rushed to the bathroom, showered, brushed his teeth. In minutes he had on his jeans and shirt, a thin woolen V-neck jumper and his best shoes.

"See you," he said to Regan, and squeezed his brother's shoulder, reminding him they'd be watching the replay tomorrow. Then he was out in the cold, dark night. Looking down the street, he could see through the gaps in the curtains that everyone had their televisions on. And that it was the same image, the expectant waiting crowd: *Aussie Aussie Aussie, Oi Oi Oi.*

Please let it be a disaster, please let it fail.

He didn't know if it was because his parents were conscious of him there in the back of the car, but they didn't play music on the way into the city. His mother just hummed, a ghost of a melody, and from time to time turned to smile at him. He wished she wouldn't look at him. He could read the love in her smile, he saw that, of course. But also, always, there was the pity.

Between being dropped off and going into the pub, he experienced a warm delicious relief. He could have quite gladly stayed there, in the cold, in the darkness, in the in-between. A drunk couple were sauntering up the street, the man with his arm around the thin girl, and Dan had to step aside so they could pass. The man called back over his shoulder, "Sorry, mate," and then, jokingly, "Happy Olympics, man," and the girl sniffed, "It'll be shit."

The feeling of comfort didn't last long once he was inside. It was an old-school pub, the kind that was fast disappearing; there were no pokies in the intimate, cramped space, and there were fading beer and whiskey posters on the wall, and a signed poster of the 1990 Collingwood Premiers took pride of place behind the bar. And it was crowded. But the first thing Dan noticed was the television sitting at the end of the bar. It was plain that the TV didn't ordinarily sit there—it was a squat domestic model casually put there for the night. Everyone was watching it. Dan's eyes were drawn to the screen, he was seeing the stadium in Sydney, shrouded in darkness, with flashes of light moving across the black sea. Then the lights took shape, filling with color and taking on the form of the Serpent, and suddenly—in the pub, on the screen, in the arena—it was the first day of Dreamtime. A young woman sitting on a chair beside him exclaimed, clearly shocking herself, "My God, it's beautiful!" She was dressed in black, except for a purple beret. Her boyfriend, with a goatee and shaved head, nodded in agreement. They had probably been whining a week ago, thought Dan, about how much it was costing, and how all the blackfellas had been moved off the streets of Sydney, but now they thought it was beautiful. Stupid pricks.

From beneath the drone of the didgeridoo a new music emerged, and a European clown in top hat and tails rode into the arena on a bicycle, on the back of which was a rabbit in a cage. A woman near the bar said, "That's good, that's us bringing our serpent into the

Garden of Eden, that's great," and a man's voice boomed, "Fuck me, I think it's going to be good. I think they're going to pull it off." There were explosions of light on the screen and Dan was sickened, thought for a moment he couldn't support his own weight. He felt he was sinking into earth. But then he heard his name being called.

Demet and Luke were in a booth around the corner from the bar. Demet was there with Leanne, her girlfriend. When she'd told him about Leanne, he was not at all surprised; but he was still unnerved by the fact that she had someone else to share a life with. He worried that Leanne didn't approve of Demet's friendship with him, that she didn't think he was worth it. She hardly acknowledged him now, she was tilting her chair back, trying to get a view of the TV. Luke was standing up, beckoning him over. There was a woman with them who he didn't recognize, smiling shyly up at him.

The first thing Luke did was to hug him. They'd never touched, never embraced at school, but since starting university the year before Luke had begun hugging him. Dan accepted it but stood there stiffly, not sure how to respond, not knowing how to hold another body. Luke let go quickly, as if sensing his friend's discomfort, but not before whispering, "Mate, sorry, they've never had a TV in this pub before—that's why I chose it."

Dan forced a smile onto his face, widening his mouth and squaring his jaw. "It's all right," he answered, turning to the screen. "Fuck me, eh? I think they're going to pull it off."

And then Demet was hugging him and Leanne was blowing him a kiss, and Luke was gesturing to the other woman and beaming as he said, "Danny—sorry, *Dan*—this is Katie."

Katie rose, kissed him on both cheeks, and said excitedly, "I'm so glad to meet you, I've been so wanting to meet you."

And Dan knew at once that Katie and Luke were together.

"Dan, what do you want?" asked Luke. "It's my shout."

His first bourbon, that was the taste of sugar and sulfur, the sting to the nose of toffee burning.

"A bourbon and Coke," he said.

There were no chairs and Katie indicated that he should squeeze in beside her on the bench facing the wall. He was glad to—from there he couldn't see the screen. He could hear the music, could sense the celebration behind him, could even imagine the lights and the colors. But not being able to see it was good, he couldn't stand for it to be in his face.

"How did you get here?"

"Mum and Dad dropped me off," he told Demet.

"They're off dancing?"

He nodded and felt Katie's hand on his wrist.

"Luke's told me how your folks are rock 'n' rollers. I think that's so cool."

"Neal and Stephanie *are* cool," Demet agreed. "They're the coolest parents in the world." She had her body tilted away from the table, she too was looking at the screen. Even bloody Demet couldn't look away. And he *knew* that she had protested about the huge expense of it, had written articles for her uni newspaper on the racism of the cleanup of the Sydney streets. Even bloody Demet was being taken in by it.

Luke came back with the round and Dan had to tell himself not to scull the drink in one go, though the sickly sweet heat of the alcohol was exactly what he needed.

He sat and listened to Leanne and Demet and Katie and Luke talk about uni, about people he didn't know, ideas he didn't quite comprehend, futures he couldn't share. Demet and Luke didn't even attend the same uni, but it was as if just by being students they had a life in common.

Dan kept stealing glances at Katie; he thought she was so beautiful. Her skin was translucent, her features elfin, delicate. He wondered what her skin would feel like, how smooth it would be. He imagined his friend's hands touching Katie's breasts, touching her all over. Dan had never touched a woman. Would it be warm and dry down there, or would it be moist? Would the muscles there clamp tight on your fingers, squeeze deliciously on your prick? Dan downed the dregs from his glass, shattered the melting ice with his teeth. He stretched out his legs, and his thigh softly nudged Katie's leg. She subtly shifted away from him.

She was so good, and he was so disgusting; he was an animal.

Dan looked up from his drink. Demet was now observing him keenly—was she going to keep a close watch on him all night? He was both touched and resentful. If she wanted to mother him, the least she could do was buy him a fucking drink.

She reached over and tilted his empty glass. "Do you need another, mate?" She knew him, she *was* going to look after him all night. He nodded gratefully.

The pub was packed, filled with shouts and cheering. Dan could hardly hear Katie, but all that din was also drowning out the music and commentary from the television. Demet was making her way through the throng, carefully balancing a tray of drinks. Dan got up to help her and as he did so the bodies around him surged as if they were a current sucking them toward the television. Dan used his elbows to ease through the crowd. He took two of the drinks off the tray.

Demet inclined her head toward the mob in front of the television. "The teams are marching into the arena!" she shouted.

They both squeezed back into the booth. Sitting in the far corner again, he couldn't see the television at all.

"Will it be the Australians first?"

Dan couldn't look at Demet or Luke. He knew their eyes would be on him.

"No." He growled out the word. Then, apologetically, his tone softened; he was aware he had startled Katie. "The Greek team always comes out first, and the host nation comes out last. That's how it works."

"Fuck me," Leanne exclaimed as she reached for her tobacco pouch. "This circus is going to go all night."

Dan adored Leanne at that moment, her surliness, that she wasn't impressed. He'd have to make more of an effort with her, be more friendly and agreeable.

He held his drink in both hands. He took a gulp, knowing he should be sipping, taking it slow, but he couldn't. The syrupy drink warmed him, made him feel calm.

He drank and listened to the others talk. University was still at the center of their conversation, but Dan didn't understand how it could be that there was no mention of study, of classes or of books. It was the world around university that animated them, and he didn't know anything about that world. So he concentrated on what they were saying; not its meaning, just its sound. That way he didn't have to listen to the cheers, the euphoria in the pub and the delirium on the screen, he didn't have to be conscious of that world at all. So he took in sound: that Leanne's voice was nasal, that she breathed through her mouth as if she had a cold. And Katie's tones were hushed, fragile; her words fell like feathers and Dan had to lean in to hear her. As for Luke, he spoke confidently, with no trace of the old stutter; he had a pleasing low register marred only by a propensity to monotony: You've always had a pompous side, thought Dan wickedly. You like the sound of your own voice. And Demet, she was still strident in delivery and pitch; what had changed was that she didn't swallow the ends of sentences as she used to. University had trained her out of that.

Dan reached for his empty glass. "Another round?"

Leanne was the only one with an empty glass; the others all shook their heads. Dan walked to the bar, looking straight ahead but above the line of the television. The bartender smiled as she took his order but didn't move her attention from the screen, even as she poured the beer and mixed Dan's drink.

"Fuck me," said Dan, "this circus is going to go all night."

The woman was no longer smiling. "Fifteen dollars," she snapped, her eyes still fixed on the television.

When he got back to the table, Katie was talking about living overseas. "I'd love to do my master's in the UK. But I'd have to get a scholarship to do that and that's pretty hard."

"You're pretty smart," Luke interjected, and then added, reaching for her hand under the table, "and pretty, period."

"Fuck pretty," said Demet. "Katie is beautiful."

Leanne was rolling cigarettes, one for herself and one for Demet. "Europe is Disneyland," she said. "I only want to travel in Asia. I want to take Demet to Thailand, don't I?"

"Please, take me, let me be your kept woman."

"So you've been to Europe?" Katie asked.

Leanne nodded, licking the edge of her cigarette paper. "I took a year off after school, went through Europe, west and east, but then I came back through Vietnam and Thailand and I loved that. That was real." She handed the rolled cigarette to Demet. "Have you been to Asia?"

Katie shook her head. "Nah. I mean, my background is Chinese but, you know, three generations back now. I'm pretty much bog Aussie Chinese." She made a self-deprecating face, and Dan thought she *was* pretty, it was the right word for her. She was light, delicate, fragile as a sparrow.

"Luke wants to take me to Vietnam," she went on. "And to Greece."

"Why not?" Luke shot out. "We've got places to stay in both countries. You'll love them both." He tapped Leanne's tobacco pouch. "May I?"

"Help yourself."

Dan was reeling. He'd never known Luke to smoke. Luke *hated* smoking. Dan sipped from his glass, looked down at the ice in the tawny liquid. He was lost in this conversation about traveling, the ease with which the four of them could imagine flight and passage, the matter-of-fact way they had of claiming the world.

The other three had gone outside to smoke and he was conscious of the silence that had fallen between himself and Katie. He wanted her to talk, to drown out the television, the joy and pride of the crowd.

"Do you want to travel, Danny?"

She had slipped into calling him Danny. He wished he could tell her: "That name doesn't belong to me, it belongs to someone else." But that would mean explaining. And he couldn't bear that, he wasn't brave enough for that.

She was smiling, waiting patiently for his reply.

"Yeah, I guess." He shuddered, wanting to kick himself for the inanity of his answer. Once, not so long ago, he had assumed travel, he had felt entitled to it, in the same way the others had been talking about it only a few minutes before. But it was supposed to come from his talent. Water and swimming were going to take him there—he would see every city in the world, roam the five continents. His talent was going to be his wings. Except it had failed him. He hadn't been good enough.

And now, where would he go? What could he offer? Who would want him?

She was waiting for more. He could tell her that he'd been to Japan. But to tell her that would be to let her know about the other Danny and he didn't know how to do that, to recover that youth. He couldn't conceive of where that boy had gone.

Maybe she knew already. Luke's hands all over her body, her hands on Luke, maybe he'd told her everything—all was nakedness and all was revealed; it was only perverted virgin creeps like himself who lived in subterranean worlds. She must have known, she must have known every pathetic shameful thing there was to know about him.

For the first time Dan looked her straight in the eyes, looking for signs of condolence. He was sure he could see it, in the velvety softness of her dark eyes, the tinge of sadness there. He could see the pity.

Behind him a cheer had gone up. A masculine voice yelled out, "Go Spain!" The applause for the Spanish team was loud, but then another masculine voice cut through with "Aussie Aussie Aussie, Oi Oi Oi." It was followed by derisive laughter, but the chant went up: "Aussie Aussie Aussie, Oi Oi Oi."

Katie's hand was lying on his wrist again and he snatched his arm away.

"Danny, what's wrong?"

"Nothing's wrong," he said. "God, I hate that chant."

She nodded, agreeing. His abrupt movement had unsettled her, she was nervously scratching her elbow. "That's why I want to leave and go overseas for a period. I hate all this nationalistic bullshit—it's so disingenuous, just a cover for rank racism." She let out a forced, weary sigh.

The confection of her outrage, the smugness of her righteousness, Dan found pretentious.

"Sometimes this country makes me sick," she continued. "It literally sickens me."

Demet said that, Luke had said that: *This country, it makes me sick.* As if they knew there was somewhere else they could go where there wouldn't be nausea, somewhere else they could find home.

She was talking nonstop now, complaining the way Demet did all the time, about how small Australia was—a big country with a small soul—and she was deriding racism, cursing the government. Dan's glass was empty and he wondered how he could interrupt her to ask if she'd like another. Dan knew he should make his next a beer; the bourbon had seeped through every part of him; his thoughts and his body were woozy, warm. Katie couldn't shut up now, never-ending complaints fell from her lips and he was thinking, when you put a finger up a woman's cunt, was it hot there?, it had to be wet and sticky there, and he was nodding as she spoke, the way he nodded when his father ranted about the ills of the world or when Demet went on about how everything was fucked here, and so he just nodded, thinking, I could put my hand up her skirt and slide my finger inside her panties and that would wipe the look of pity off her face.

"Here, mate." Luke was smiling as he handed Dan another bourbon and Coke. Demet and Leanne fell back into the booth, and Dan
slurped greedily from the glass, letting the liquid soothe his tongue
and his throat, letting the liquid soak through him.

Demet was smiling at him across the table, Luke had his arm
stretched across the bench, folding in Katie, reaching out to Dan.
They were thinking he was that other Danny, they didn't know how
sick he was, what evil he had become.

A roar of celebration rang from the television and it was answered
in the pub by good-natured jeering. All of them in the booth stopped
talking, aware of the motion of a current once more, this one with an
elemental tidal force drawing everyone toward the screen. All those
bodies were pushing forward, and it was as if their table had been
cast adrift, quarantined from the rest of the crowd. Luke was down-
cast, examining his beer closely, Leanne was playing with the tobacco
pouch, Katie had her hands between her knees, and Demet was fix-
ated on Dan. Dan knew that they were caught up in the current and
they wanted to be experiencing what everyone else was—they wanted
to be celebrating, having fun. But they couldn't, they mustn't, because Dan was there, the loser was with them, and Leanne knew it,
and even Katie who had only just met him tonight, she knew it, that
Dan was so lacking in courage, so weak, so pathetic, so *pitiful* that
they had to protect him from that tide.

He emptied his glass in one swill, wiped his mouth. He stood up.
"Come on, let's go and watch."

He used his elbows, his shoulders, the weight of his whole body
to battle through the throng. He shoved a man aside, and the man
turned back ready to fight but one look at Dan's face told him to shut
his mouth.

Dan stopped behind a short young woman. Luke's head was bobbing over Dan's shoulder.

It was the Yugoslavians marching now, the athletes in white
shirts and shiny blue suits. "They look pretty hot, even I'd go for

some of those guys." Dan recognized Leanne's nasal voice and saw that the three women were behind him. He moved aside and Demet, Katie, and Leanne gratefully squeezed in between him and Luke.

He watched the screen but he didn't see bodies and he didn't see a crowd; he translated form into shadow and movement, the flicker and sparkle of thousands of flashbulbs were waves that shimmered and diffused the light. When Dan was a child his father had read him the stories of Aladdin and the Thousand and One Nights, and he recalled the stories now, those tales of unimaginable treasure hidden in caves, how the revelation of such magnificence and beauty would strike the beholder blind. Watching the lights spray out and splinter, he didn't see electricity, he saw shining diamonds, rubies, sapphires and emeralds, saw amber and opal, all the colors of the world splitting night into day. The people on the screen weren't human forms but jeweled shapes gliding across it. He wouldn't make them human, wouldn't delineate faces, for to see faces was to see joy, to see triumph. Demet had grabbed his hand, was squeezing it tight. He couldn't let it go, but he didn't want her touch.

The last of the guest teams was marching behind the IOC flag, four dancing youths from East Timor, who didn't have a country yet, and the bodies around him jostled and united in one joyous roar. Even Leanne was cheering, even she had a fist raised in the air. The noise from the television and the noise from all around him, writhing around him, through him, pulling him in so tight that he was struggling for air—they were cheering, one body one voice, and the noise was one ecstatic release. The basketballer was proudly holding the Australian flag and it was *Aussie Aussie Aussie, Oi Oi Oi* and his ears couldn't hear and his eyes couldn't see and he had let go of Demet's hand and had his hands cupped over his ears and was gulping for air, because all of his work and all of his training and his youth and his dreaming, his entire self; he should have been there. By not being there, by not fulfilling that simple stipulation, Dan realized he was nothingness itself, he had failed to exist, and though he had his eyes shut and though he was trying to shut out the sound, the world had rushed in, he couldn't stop it, it seeped into him and through him and around him: darting specks of red and yellow light were crisscrossing the darkness behind his shut eyelids, they made the bodies whole and they conjured up the athletes. He opened his eyes and there, in close-up, was Kieren Perkins, waving to the fevered crowd, and as the camera began to pan across the Australian team, that group of golden boys and golden girls, he knew that he had to inhale, he had to open his lungs, and so he turned and was fighting for breath, pushing and shoving and kicking and elbowing until he had broken through the deafening mass, and was on the footpath, in the open air. There wasn't a car in sight, there was no one on the street—not one other being to share his humiliation. He was alone and wretched in the world.

He was alone. He sucked in gulps of air.

He put out a hand, steadied himself on the wall. It sickened him how much hate he had inside him. All I am, thought Dan, is hate.

"Danny—you okay, mate?"

Dan spun around, facing Luke. "How many times have I got to tell you, *cunt*? It's Dan, not Danny. I'm *Dan*!"

Luke stepped back, his face drained of color, aghast. He looked so miserable Dan wondered whether he was going to cry. Dan told himself that was how he could do it, how he could snatch the pity from their eyes, rip it away from them. Luke no longer looked like a man; he was again the callow schoolboy who would do anything for Danny, who worshipped Danny.

Except that he wasn't that Danny. That Danny didn't exist anymore.

Demet had also come out and she wrapped an arm around Dan, brought his head near to hers, so they were touching. He started to pull away, but relented. There were no words and she knew that.

But Luke, of course, the reader, the swot, the prefect and straight-A student, he had to use words, he had to talk. "Let's all go back to

Katie's place, it's just around the corner." He offered Dan a hesitant smile. "I promise, no telly."

Dan shrugged, he didn't care. Just as long as there was more alcohol. He wondered how he could have denied himself it for so long. It deadened thought and anesthetized sensation—it gave you the most delectable numbness. He would drink till he passed out. On Katie's floor, on the street—he didn't care.

"Katie got grog?"

He noticed the look exchanged between his two friends.

Demet squashed the butt of her cigarette on the tiled wall of the pub. "I'll grab the others. There's a bottle-o down the road."

The two men were left alone. Just don't speak, Luke, just don't say a word.

But Luke spoke. "I'm really glad you chose to be with us, mate." He placed a hand on Dan's shoulder. "I was sure you'd be at Taylor's party tonight. It means a lot to me that you're here instead."

At first Dan didn't quite hear the words. Or he heard them but they didn't quite make sense, were just more sounds in the night. Was Luke slurring, was he drunk? But the words began to shift into a pattern and the pattern began to form a sentence and the sentence stunned him. "What are you talking about?"

Once again, Luke looked like that frightened schoolboy.

Dan repeated, "What the fuck are you talking about?"

"Sorry, Danny—Dan, I'm sorry, I thought you knew about Taylor's big party tonight. I saw him at uni this week, he told me about it and I just assumed you would know."

And Dan said, quietly, smiling now, "Yeah, of course, the party. Shit, yeah, I'd forgotten about that." He made sure to grin, to hold his body straight, to breathe in and breathe out as if everything were normal, as if night wasn't day and the rending of the vault of the sky had not happened. Luke and Martin, at university together, in their world together, the world he didn't belong to.

He smiled, he stood straight, he breathed normally. But inside, deep inside him, he understood what the songs meant, that the songs told the truth when they referred to a heart breaking.

He scooped Luke up in a wrestling tackle, held him from behind, whispered hoarsely in his ear, "Of course I was going to choose to be with you and Demet tonight. Of course I was." He let go of Luke. He thought, I could just tell him, I could just reach out to my friend and I could just say sorry.

He thought of Taylor and Luke at uni together, in that other world together.

Mustering all his will, all his strength, he faked a long, bored yawn. He forced cheer into his voice. "Mate, I'm pretty zonked, I think I'll just go home. I really think it's time I headed home."

He ignored Luke's protests, backed away, then turned and broke into a run. He could hear Luke calling after him, he knew that his friend had given chase. But Dan was running so hard that his feet were pounding the earth.

He ran. There were no cars, no taxis, no people on the streets. He ran like an automaton, without thinking, without being. He turned sharply up a street full of neon signs, barred shop windows. He stopped, he bent over to get back his breath. He used the sleeve of his jumper to wipe the sweat from his brow, his neck. Thought and memory were a king tide breaking through once more. The opening ceremony had been a hydrogen bomb; it had emptied the world of people. He was the only creature left alive. And he had no idea where he was, he couldn't see a street sign.

Across the road an electrical goods store had three televisions on display, all on, all showing the opening ceremony.

Dan crossed the street and looked through the iron bars at the biggest screen. The ceremony was still unfolding but there was no sound, and everything on the screen—the crowd and the athletes, everyone and everything—seemed puny. It was no longer the overwhelming spectacle it had seemed to be in the pub. It is nothing to be afraid of, he told himself. It was just sound and light and movement.

The stadium was in darkness and a woman in a wheelchair held the Olympic torch aloft. Dan knew that the old lady was Betty Cuthbert and the woman pushing her wheelchair was Raelene Boyle. "Cuthbert," whispered Dan, "you were at Melbourne and Rome; and Boyle, you won silver in Mexico City." He stretched out a finger, as if to touch the screen. "I know how you were cheated in Montreal," he continued whispering. "I think I can imagine what it cost you not to go to Moscow."

He watched the play of shadow and light.

When Shane Gould was passed the torch Dan crossed his arms so tightly across his chest that his lungs contracted. The woman was jogging around the track, between two tiers of mutely cheering volunteers and officials, but she was staring ahead, her pace constant, the torch held high. Dan was mouthing silently, to the beat of her feet hitting the track: Munich, two hundred meter individual medley—gold; two hundred meter freestyle—gold; four hundred meter freestyle—gold; eight hundred meter freestyle—silver; one hundred meter freestyle—bronze. He watched Shane Gould hand the torch to another athlete, and for a moment he didn't know who it was. Then he recalled the face, Debbie Flintoff-King, the athlete who won the four hundred meter hurdles in Seoul, the 1988 Olympics, the first Olympics he remembered seeing as a kid.

"*Cath-ee, Cath-ee!*"

Dan jumped back from the shop window, startled by the sudden return of sound. But it wasn't coming from the televisions. He looked up; the light from a screen flicked silver and gray and white on the walls and windows of an apartment above the shop. There was a party on up there, and he could hear muted cheering. He looked at the television again and saw the torch being passed to Cathy Freeman, the young Aboriginal runner. Dan gripped the bars, unable to look away from the screen. As the athlete was handed the torch, the cameras in the arena exploded and lit up the stadium. She began her proud jog up an illuminated staircase of brilliant white, smoke

wreathing and spilling like water down the pearl steps—*Cath-ee!*
Cath-ee!—and he was sure now that it was not only from the apartment above that he could hear the chant; he thought it was an echo
of the madness of an entire country, the whole of the world. "Go,
Cathy," Dan called softly through the bars. "Go, Cathy. You're not
one of those golden girls."

A shudder racked Dan's body.

The young athlete walked into the middle of a wide pool of water
in front of a wall of water. She leaned over and touched the torch to
the pool, and around her sprang up a circle of fire, which rose and
started up an incline. There was a hesitation, a malfunction, and the
machine stalled. From the apartment upstairs he heard a woman say
despondently, "I knew we'd fuck it up."

"Please," said Dan, "let it be a disaster."

The machine jerked and began to move again. The circle of flame
rose and kissed the towering torch.

The world burst into flame, into light. Music thundered from
upstairs, so abruptly it was as if a CD had been taken off pause.

Dan would never forget that moment. It was impossible to him
just then to conceive of a way to mitigate such loss. He should have
been there. He had been holding his future in his clasped hands.
Dust. It was all dust.

〜〜〜

His first vodka, that was licorice.

The bar was packed, a wall of sound, everyone crowded in front
of a giant screen against the back wall. The replay of the opening
ceremony had started. "This will go on for an eternity," he whispered
over the rim of his glass.

But at least he could sit at the bar, there were empty stools there,
and he could turn away from the screen. He drank his vodka and
lime. All those years of training, when he'd been the other Danny,
they had taught him to listen to his body. He'd only had vodka twice

before, on the night of his eighteenth, and once out pub-crawling with Bennie and Omar and Herc. It was clean-tasting, fast, it cleared the head, it offered speed. Vodka would straighten him out, vodka was what he needed.

He pulled his flip phone from his pocket and scrolled through the address book. He kept clicking onto Martin Taylor's number, then pressing the back button. Finding Taylor's number, returning to the home screen: he couldn't stop going back and forth.

Dan told himself that Martin was busy, studying law at uni, he'd just forgotten to tell Dan about the party. He rarely returned calls, he just didn't have the time, he'd claimed: "It isn't like school, Kelly—uni's tough, you have to work hard. It's not a piece of piss like working in a servo or a supermarket." Martin could hardly bring himself to say the word, it was as if he had never had to say the word *supermarket* in his life.

What are you going to do, Kelly? What are you doing with your life?

"A white wine, thank you. A Riesling if you have it."

His first wine, fruit juice left out too long in the sun.

He looked up from his phone. The young woman asking for the drink was leaning on the bar next to him. She was short and slight and her skin was the citrine hue of olive oil. It would be such lovely soft skin to touch, thought Dan, and he had to stop himself reaching out to stroke it. He must be high, this was what getting high must be like. He could sense the alcohol coursing playfully through his body. Vodka made you high.

The woman noticed him staring at her and offered up a confused, shy grin. Then, embarrassed, she looked away.

Say something, dickhead. Martin would have had some witticism at hand, Bennie would have made a joke, Omar would have flexed a muscle, and Herc would've asked for a light. Luke wouldn't have had to say anything. The girls always approached Luke first these days.

Say *something*. She was blond, straw-yellow hair to her shoulders, silken and smooth as a sheet of pressed metal. He wanted his first time to be with a blonde. The most beautiful people he knew, Emma, Martin, they were all blond.

Say something. The bartender had given the woman her glass of wine, she was searching for money in her bag.

"Hi." That was all he had, all he could think to say. But the young woman turned, smiled, and said hello in response. He didn't know what to say next. But she had stayed at the bar.

Dan quickly slipped off his stool and offered it to the woman. "Would you like to sit down?"

She hesitated, looked around, blushing, then took the seat. "Thanks."

"My name is Dan."

"I'm Mila."

Mila sounded exactly right, a sweet word. He silently repeated the name to himself; and then came a flash of memory.

"Mila means apples in Greek."

The girl, sipping her wine, looked confused.

"Mila," he continued, embarrassed now. "The word means apples in Greek."

"Are you Greek?"

"No. Well, my mum is, but I'm not."

She didn't respond to that, kept sipping at her drink, looking up at him from time to time—her mien now cautious but confident, as she sized him up—but mostly she was glancing over his shoulder, to the screen where the eternal now of the opening ceremony was unfolding. He wouldn't look.

Mila motioned to the screen. "Wasn't it fantastic? I didn't expect it." She was flushed, searching for words. "I guess I was so proud," she finally gushed.

"I didn't watch it."

She had no response to that. There was chatter and music and shouting in the bar, a tram rumbling down Smith Street, but between Mila and himself, thought Dan, the air was lifeless.

"Are you meeting friends here, Dan?"

He shook his head.

"Oh." Mila seemed suspicious of his answer.

"Are you?"

"Yes, I'm meeting a couple of girlfriends here."

He had to stop himself from saying, "Can I stay with you, can I just hang out with you? I don't want to go home. Can I please stay with you?" He didn't dare say that.

"Are you a student?"

He was going to lie. He wasn't going to tell her what he did; she looked smart and poised. He nodded.

"Me too. Whereabouts?"

"La Trobe Uni," he lied.

"Oh really? Me too." She was excited, but then her eyes narrowed. He didn't like that, it reminded him of a mouse.

"I haven't seen you there."

And her teeth were too big, Dan thought, she had to know it because she kept her mouth closed when she wasn't speaking. Her teeth were too big for her small round face.

"I haven't seen you around either." He liked how easy it was to lie. He could be anything he wanted to be with her. He remembered what Demet had told him about her classes.

"I'm doing sociology," he said, "and also cinema and gender studies." He finished his vodka and lime, tried to catch the bartender's eye. The vodka made lying easy, the vodka was telling the story. "Would you like another?"

Her glass was still nearly full and she shook her head.

He tried to check his money without her noticing. When his drink arrived, she raised her glass and clinked it with his.

"Happy Sydney Olympics," she said.

Dan smiled but said nothing.

"I'm doing health sciences," Mila continued. "I'm in second year."

"Same here."

Then Mila mentioned some people she thought he might know, and he had to keep saying sorry, he didn't know them. Her eyes narrowed. She looked like a mouse again.

The air had gone dead between them once more. Mila's skirt, ruby red, was riding up her thigh and her skin there was pale. Would Bennie touch her now, would Omar? Dan dropped his hand and the back of it slid off her leg.

It was the wrong thing to do. She was startled and shifted her body away from him, her eyes not leaving the screen.

Someone called her name and Dan could sense her relief. She jumped off the stool, turned to him hurriedly, and said, "Thanks, Dan, my friends are here now." And like that, she was gone.

Dan wouldn't turn around, he wouldn't look at her greeting her friends, at them whispering about him, laughing at him. The loser. The freak. He finished his vodka and lime, the full glass, it burned his throat as it went down. He put it on the counter and walked calmly out of the bar and into the street. He wouldn't look back to where they were laughing at him.

~~~~

He told himself that he didn't know what he was doing, that he had not yet made up his mind where he was going as he stood there in the street, his hand outstretched, hailing the taxi. He told himself that he was heading into the night by chance, that he had no destination in mind, even as he told the driver that he wanted to head to Toorak, across the river, where he hadn't been since school. It wasn't choice, it was fate. All he knew, he told himself, was that it was too early to go home, that he couldn't bear facing Theo, who would still be up waiting for him, ready to discuss every moment of it with him, even though they

would be watching it together tomorrow. No, he couldn't bear that—
better to just jump in a cab and take off into the night. So convinced
was Dan that he had made no decision about where he was going that
it came as a shock when the driver stopped outside the Taylors' house.
The street was dark, the brooding, massive elm trees denuded of foliage. He handed the driver the fare and got out of the cab.

Dan pressed the buzzer at the gate and after a few moments, a
voice answered. "Yes, who is it?"

He recognized the brusque tone of Mrs. Taylor. She repeated the
question, now impatiently.

He was so shaken at finding himself at the gate that he didn't
even say the right name. He'd become the other Danny again.

"It's Danny, Danny Kelly."

The wind was chopping through the naked branches and he realized he was cold. For a moment he knew that she wouldn't let him in,
that she would tell him that he couldn't turn up uninvited, that you
just didn't do such things.

But there was a buzz, a whirr of machinery, and the gates slowly
pulled apart.

Dazed, still not quite believing it, it had to be the high of vodka,
that had to be it, Dan found himself walking up the long driveway of
Martin Taylor's home.

～～～

His first rum, all he could taste was the Coke in it.

It was Mrs. Taylor who offered him the drink, who said that it was
so lovely to see him, but she didn't ask what he was doing, where he
was working, how his family were. Her lips on both his cheeks felt cold.

She said, "I'm having a rum and Coke. Would you like one?"

He nodded.

He remembered the long hallway with the tiled floor, the square
canvas with the bulky gold-leaf frame on one wall, a portrait of Mrs.
Taylor in swirls of thick oil pastel; and on the other wall a huge

photograph of the family, Emma and her mother sitting on a couch, the daughter in a ballooning saffron-colored dress and the mother in cream satin, the men standing behind them, Mr. Taylor in a suit, and Martin, grim-faced, in his school uniform. He recalled that there were steps off the corridor that led down into a sunken den. He could see Mr. Taylor's bald pate down there; he was sitting on a white leather couch. Mr. Taylor didn't turn around to say hello.

Mrs. Taylor ushered Dan through to the kitchen, fixed him the drink, and almost pushed him out to the backyard where a marquee had been set up, white sheets of gossamer material that curved and billowed with the wind.

"Martin," Mrs. Taylor called out, and the young men and women chatting on the lawn turned to stare. Some of the faces of the men were familiar. One of them, a tall young man in a blue-and-white-striped shirt, was walking toward him, his hand outstretched.

"My God, Kelly," he exclaimed. "Is that you?"

Mrs. Taylor pushed Dan gently out into the night. "Have a good time, Danny," she said, and then she slid shut the kitchen door.

It was like his first day at school.

It was Sullivan who'd recognized him, it was Sullivan, with a trim goatee, who'd come up to him and slapped him on the back, introducing him to this man and this woman, "We're at uni together," "This is Danny Kelly, we were at school together," "What are you doing, Danny?," but he didn't have time to answer, he was being introduced to Verena and Scott, to Marcus and Benjamin, Callista and Chloe, names he would forget, faces he wouldn't recall in the morning. A good-looking strong-jawed waiter brought over a tray of pies, but he didn't have time to reach out for one because there were more people to meet, a Seb and a Cameron, a Jacinta and a Melinda, and "What do you do, Danny?" and "Oh, you are a friend of Martin's, are you, Danny?" and "Wasn't the opening ceremony wonderful, Danny? Aren't you proud, Danny? I'm so proud of Australia tonight, aren't you, Danny?"

He was nodding, like a good dog, and found himself saying, "Yes, wasn't it wonderful?" and he had to stop himself barking out, *Aussie Aussie Aussie, Oi Oi Oi*, like a good dog. He nodded his head and it felt as though he was wagging his tail.

And then a familiar voice cut through the noise under the marquee, it called out to him, straight to him, only to him: "Danny Kelly, what are you doing here?"

Martin Taylor was coming toward him, wearing a white dress shirt and loose black trousers sitting on his hips, his hand extended. Dan grabbed it, held it, the palm cool and dry, and they shook until Martin pulled away. He had not put on weight; he was, if it were possible, even more handsome now. Dan sucked in his gut, straightened his shoulders. They did not embrace. Unsmiling, their eyes dared one another.

Dan answered, "I heard some faggot was throwing a party."

And Martin was laughing and pumping his hand, and sliding an arm across Dan's shoulders, and Martin was saying, "Have you eaten? There's plenty of food left. Do you need another drink? What are you drinking, we'll get you another rum," but all Dan could think of was that Martin's initial question hadn't been a query and there had been no delight in it. There had been ice in that question, the same chill that Dan had heard in Mrs. Taylor's voice.

Danny Kelly, what are you doing here?

A young woman had come up to stand at Martin's side. She was petite, with fine, white wispy hair that gave her an almost ethereal appearance; it was hair that belonged to the very old or to creatures from other worlds. Her strapless blue dress, of fine silk, evoked a timeless classical past: Dan's mother would have approved of such an elegant garment. The woman was touching Martin's elbow, not holding it, just touching it, just the glance of her fingertip against Taylor's elbow, but it was proprietorial, confident. Dan was astonished by the stab of jealousy that he felt; he was bloated with that emotion, it threatened to choke him. Taylor had had girlfriends before, Taylor had been with women. But none of them had claimed him with the authority and entitlement of that simple touch.

"Lauren, let me introduce you," Taylor said, now loosening his arm from around Dan, pulling in the woman and holding her close. "This is an old friend of mine, this is Danny."

The woman held out her small hand, a slender gold bracelet clasped tight around her wrist. "Hello, Danny, it is very nice to meet you."

And he knew, from the question lurking just beneath her polite greeting, that she hadn't a clue who he was, that she had never heard his name before.

Martin leaned down and kissed Lauren on the lips. They lingered on the kiss. Then Martin pulled away, laughing, and said proudly, "We've just announced our engagement."

Martin's gray eyes, his long blond lashes, his fine smooth cheeks. Dan wanted to reach out and stroke his friend's cheek. No, Dan wanted to rip the lips off Martin Taylor's face. Instead he told himself, Keep your voice steady. Instead, he said, "Mate, I'm so happy for you." And Martin had stepped forward, to accept a hug, to embrace Dan, but Dan stepped back and instead extended his right hand. The two men shook, Dan kissed the woman on both cheeks. "I'm so very happy for you." He couldn't hug Taylor. If he hugged Taylor, he'd squeeze the life out of him.

Lauren was holding Martin's hand. "Did you see the opening ceremony, Danny?" she gushed. "Wasn't it wonderful? We weren't going to tell anyone yet but it just seemed the perfect night to announce it to the world."

He hadn't answered.

"Did you see it?"

Dan wouldn't look at Martin, he kept his eyes on Lauren. "No," he answered, "I didn't see it. I couldn't be bothered."

Lauren's face fell; it was exactly that: her eyes drooped, her jaw slackened. As if he'd assaulted her, as if his answer was an affront. "Why ever not?" As if she couldn't understand why anyone would deny themselves such pleasure, as if she couldn't see why anyone wouldn't want to be part of that mindless celebration. *Aussie Aussie Aussie, Oi Oi Oi.*

Dan glanced around the marquee, over the top of Lauren's head, everywhere, anywhere, except at Martin. He couldn't bring himself to look at Martin. "I'm not interested in the Olympics," he said finally. "I don't care much for sport."

Taylor stooped down, his chin almost resting on Lauren's naked shoulder; he was whispering something to her. And then it happened. Her countenance softened. Her eyes were moist and kind when she turned to him again, he could see the pity there.

He wanted to reach out and grab her pretty face, reach out and rip *her* skin off. He *hated* her that much. Dan drained the last of the rum, crunching loudly on the ice, then held the empty glass up to Martin. "Fetch, Taylor," he said brightly. "You'll get me another, won't you?"

Taylor bristled at the insult. Good, fetch me another, *dog.*

Then Martin's face settled back into a smile. He took the empty glass. "Yeah, mate. I guess if I were you, I'd be feeling the need to get smashed tonight too."

Dan was buried, he had sunk wingless into the earth. Taylor had won and he had lost.

～～～～

So Dan drinks. He finishes one rum and Coke and then another. Dan drinks and he dances, savage ugly movements, his arms rip through the air, he makes up words to the loud booming techno that pounds through the backyard. And he doesn't just dance, he leaps and jumps, banging down on the lawn with the soles of his shoes. Sweat flies off him, people move away from him, but he doesn't care. He dances wildly, twisting and flailing and breaking the night. *Your name I remember, like a fever or a flame.* He calls out the words again and again, screaming them now so a young woman dancing beside him moves away, her face puckers in disgust. He doesn't care, he loves the song, bellows out those words: *Your name I remember, like a fever or a flame.* And as the song fades, a kinetic stuttering beat rushes up from behind it, overwhelming and drowning the song, the song that he believes will be forever his song. He stops abruptly, focuses, his throat parched, all these strangers looking at him. Looking at him as if he is filth, as if he is shit, as if he doesn't belong.

It is his first day at Cunts College and he doesn't belong.

He stands still. Couples around him dancing with a polite shuffle of feet, blond girls with handbags hanging over their shoulders, sandy-haired boys gyrating carefully next to them. Neatness and cleanliness, order and beauty. Dan can smell his own stink, he is lathered in sweat. Slowly, deliberately, he unbuttons his shirt, then tears it off, wipes under his arms with it, dabs his face, his neck, his shoulders. Let them see the full hairy ugliness of who he is, the paunch of his belly, the thick coarse hair matted and wet against his skin. Let them look at him, let them take him in. One of the women giggles, one of the men calls out sarcastically, "Strip, strip, strip," and someone starts a slow clap. Dan thinks, Why not, I'll strip, I'll strip, and I'll piss all over this lawn, I'll strip and piss and maybe even take a dump right in the middle of their fucking lawn, that's what they expect from me. *Aussie Aussie Aussie, Oi Oi Oi.*

A hand is on his shoulder, a quiet voice says, "Danny, come with me."

Dazed, he lets Emma lead him out of the marquee, past the faces turning away from him, past the whispers and the jeers. She takes him into the kitchen; she is holding his hand, tight, as she walks him up the stairs and into a bedroom. She gently pushes him onto the mattress and leaves him sitting there while she goes out and closes the door behind her.

Is he meant to stay here? Does she mean him to be locked in here? He looks around the room; it is exactly as he remembers it— the Wilderness Society posters, the school photographs, the chunky mahogany desk, the three walls of bookcases—except that now most of the books that filled those shelves have gone, only a handful of children's books and school textbooks remain.

Emma comes back and tosses a T-shirt at him. "It's one of Martin's old ones," she explains. "I think it will fit."

Dan puts on the shirt, sniffs at it. He can't smell Martin, only detergent and fabric softener.

Emma sits down next to him. She looks around her old bedroom. "Jesus," she says, shaking her head, "how I hate this room. It reminds me of a poor little rich girl's room." She groans. "I wish they'd change it, I wish they would make it a spare room—anything as long as it doesn't remind me of once living here."

Unlike the other women at the party, Emma is not in evening wear. She wears a rainbow-colored smock, which hangs limply over her shoulders. Her skin is as dark and honeyed as the wood of the desk. Without thinking, Dan reaches out and touches the small bump on her shoulder. "You're very tanned." Everything he says, everything he does in this house, it seems idiotic.

Emma wears no makeup, her hair is cut short, he can smell cigarettes on her breath. "I've been working in Asia for a year, Danny. Didn't Martin tell you?"

Dan shakes his head.

Emma snorts loudly. "No surprises there."

The collar of the smock hangs loose around her breasts, the skin is tanned dark there as well. Dan's finger slowly traces a line from the bump on her shoulder, across the smooth skin of her neck, down to the cleft of her breasts. He can sense her breath underneath his touch. But gently, Emma moves his hand away. It falls, dead, hitting the mattress with a thud.

Her next words shock him. "I know he's my brother, Danny, but he's not worth it. Martin Taylor is a shit. He's a shit from a long, long line of shits."

He doesn't understand why she is telling him this, he is suspicious of her words. He peeks at a necklace that sits skewed on the plump rise of her left breast.

Emma notices, holds up the pendant for him to look at. It is a swirl of fine silver lines. "This is from Laos, it's the symbol for charity." She drops the pendant. "I got it in a hospice where I was working, helping children whose parents had died from AIDS." She has dropped the pendant but her finger is tracing the swirls. "I used to be skeptical of the word *charity,* I thought it was some middle-class Christian hang-up. But I've learned that it's a universal quality. I've learned to appreciate it."

He is conscious of how sad she is. He tries to form words in his head, words that will banish the melancholy. Every word this beautiful woman utters, every word floats on sadness.

"I wish there was more charity here," she says bitterly. "In this house, in this city, in this country."

Dan blurts out, "Aussie Aussie Aussie, Oi Oi Oi."

And that makes her laugh, that chases away the sadness. "Absolutely right, Danny. You're absolutely right." She starts shouting. "Aussie Aussie Aussie, Fucking Oi Oi Oi!"

They are on their backs on the bed, shaking with laughter. Emma clutches his hand. "It must have been a tough night for you. I know how much you wanted to be there at these Olympics. I know what it meant to you."

He is rigid. His skin, his heart, his lungs, his whole being, it has gone cold, he is frozen. Her too—all they feel for him is pity. His lips are cracked, his tongue feels heavy. "I need a drink."

Emma stretches over and opens a drawer in the bureau beside the bed. She pulls out a bottle of dark ocher liquid. She points to the cupboard. "You're taller than I am. Up there, at the back, there's an old toy kitchen set, I think you'll find two cups in there."

Dan leaps up off the bed and is on his tiptoes: his searching hand unsettles dust and he shifts an old teddy bear, worn patches of faded hessian showing through; he feels an old Walkman, then a small flat disk. He slides it forward. The plate is covered with a film of grime and dust, he can hardly make out the design of the blue finch etched on the white china surface. He pushes it back, far back, and finds the two plastic toy cups.

He hands Emma the cups and she wipes them clean with the hem of her smock, then pours a generous slug of the liquid into each one. "It's Mum's bottle," she explains. "She keeps a bottle of whiskey in here, one in the bathroom, and a couple in the kitchen. That way she's never at a loose end." The words are hollow, there is no expression in her voice. Emma raises the toy cup. "Here's to the two fucking thousand fucking Olympic fucking Games."

And his first whiskey, that was fire. That was certainly fire.

The heat of the whiskey cuts the ice. He drinks a cupful, then another. And another. He reaches to refill the cup but Emma places her hand around his wrist.

"That's enough, Dan," she says. "I'm going to call you a taxi. You should go home."

But he doesn't. Walking down the stairs, the steps loom large and he has to think, I'm putting my left foot on that one, my right foot on that one; he is trying not to fall, Emma giggling behind him, they are in the kitchen and the bottle of rum is by the sink, it is nearly empty and he says, "Maybe I'll have another," and Emma shrugs. Dan rinses a glass and pours the drink into it and at that moment Martin slides open the door. Dan is by the sink, he has tilted his head back, he has had the last of the drink, his mouth is wide open and he is shaking the glass for the last drops to fall onto his tongue. Martin has slid open the door and is staring at him. He hears the exasperated click of Taylor's tongue.

"Mate," Taylor's voice is firm, "I think it's time you were off."

Dan can recognize a riff and a chug of chords from out in the backyard, from under the billowing clouds of the marquee. He takes Emma's hand. "Come and dance," he says. "It's Nirvana."

But Taylor has shut the door. Through the glass Dan can see Lauren, her skin a reddish hue from the light of the Chinese lanterns studded through the yard, standing at the entrance of the marquee, looking anxious, her hand to her mouth.

Taylor has shut the door and is standing there, arms crossed, shaking his head. "Kelly, you're going home."

And Emma has pulled her hand away from his. "Danny, Martin's right, I'm going to call a taxi."

But he can still hear the relentless riff of the guitar, the hypnotic bass, the simple propulsive drum pattern. It is calling him. "I just want to dance to this one, I'll dance to this and then I'll go."

"For fuck's sake, Kelly, you're a bloody loser. So you didn't make it to the Olympics. So you weren't good enough. Get over it."

Dan has to touch his own face. Those words, he saw them fly through the air and cut at his face. He has walked up to Taylor, he can see the sheen of sweat on the man's upper lip. No, not a man—they are boys, together, competing. Who will be the strongest, the fastest, the best? "You wanted it too," says Dan, and as the words are said, he feels the blessed release. They have both failed. They will always be together, he and Martin, for both of them have failed.

But Taylor is shaking his head. "No, mate. I never wanted it like you. Not like you and Wilco." Taylor has moved forward, his breath is caressing Dan's face. "You didn't see it tonight, did you, the opening ceremony? You didn't see Wilco there, his head high, proud because he's in the swim team? You didn't see it, did you?"

The music has disappeared, Emma isn't there, Lauren isn't peering anxiously out from the darkness. It is just Kelly and Taylor. And Taylor knows, Taylor knows that Dan was stronger, faster, better than Wilco. Taylor *knows*.

"Of course, he won't make it past the heats but the bastard was smiling like he couldn't believe his luck. And too right, I reckon. He shouldn't be there." Taylor's voice was almost—not quite, but so close to—disgusted. And like they were still kids in the change rooms,

Taylor is poking a sharp stabbing finger into Dan's chest. "You should have been there. Not him."

Dan smacks Martin's hand away, so hard that Emma starts. Through the glass, he can see Lauren walking toward them. "And you. How about you? You wanted it just as much."

Martin is scowling, rubbing his wrist; Dan's blow had hurt. "No, I was never hungry for it. I liked beating you but once I knew you were better than me I just didn't care. You can't get anywhere if you don't care, can you? You're the one who really wanted it." Taylor drops his hand to his side in distaste. "Why am I bothering? You know what you didn't do. You know exactly what I'm talking about."

If he could just close his eyes, if he could shut out Taylor's taunts and the noise and light and the crowd.

"Martin, stop!" Emma's voice cuts through the night, and for one moment she alleviates the harshness of the light. But Dan can't bear the way she is looking at him. His mother looks at him like that, it is the way Demet and Luke look at him, as if all they can muster for him is pity and compassion.

Lauren is sliding open the door, asking, in a frightened high-pitched voice, "Is everything all right?"

He hates her, he hates *her* most of all.

He responds to Emma, ignoring Lauren, "Nah—let him say what he's got to say." He faces Martin. "What didn't I do, Taylor? Tell me." Stare him out, give it back to him, give it right back to him. "Come on, cunt, what didn't I do?"

It feels so good to say that word, to hear Lauren gasp, to see Emma shrink back.

Taylor looks away, Taylor can't look at him. Then he says it all with a limp tilt of his shoulders—that says it all, that he can't be bothered. It says that Dan isn't worth it.

Lauren has squeezed in between the two men, faces Dan. "Can you please go? You're upsetting Martin."

Like she owns the house.

Dan is shaking his head. The song is ending, he's going to dance, he's going to dance and leap and fly. He darts toward the door but Martin grabs his sleeve, pulls him back. And as he does, Dan pulls his arm away from Martin's grasp and the back of his hand hits Lauren in the face. There is the shock of silence, and then she is crying, a thin trail of blood coming from her left nostril.

That's when Taylor shouts it to the night and to the world. "You fucking loser!"

Martin is holding Lauren, Dan is repeating over and over, I'm sorry I'm sorry I didn't mean to, but Martin is pushing him away.

Emma has wet a dish towel and Martin lets her clean up Lauren's bleeding nose. He faces Dan, the two men so close that their chests, their noses, are nearly touching.

"You always wanted to know what people thought of you, Kelly." Martin's voice is low, unemotional and cool. "You know what we thought? We thought you were a loser. You didn't have the balls then and you don't have the balls now. That's why you're not there tonight, that's why you'll always be a fucking loser."

The truth. He hears Martin tell the world the truth.

And Martin is now pushing at him, saying coldly, repeating, "Get out, get out of my house," and Dan shoves back, so hard that Martin slams against the glass door, it trembles, it bends, there is a loud crack, and Martin scrambles to his feet, he comes rushing at him, and Emma is between them and Dan can hear Mrs. Taylor's outraged voice screaming from somewhere and everyone is running up the lawn toward the kitchen and Lauren is still crying and Martin is pushing him back and the music is screaming out that one word, loser, again and again, all denial, loser, again and again and Dan's hand tightens around the empty glass in his hand and he thinks, I can crush it, it will shatter into a million pieces and it will cut my hand and then Martin pushes him again and Mrs. Taylor is screaming and Emma is crying but he doesn't care, she's one of *them*, he remembers the discarded plate, his forsaken gift. All of them are the same, just pity and mockery, how they must have laughed at him through the years, how they must have made jokes about what a clumsy, awkward, ugly, ill-mannered buffoon he was; so Emma is crying, let her cry, and Lauren is howling, let her howl, and to make it all stop to make it all go away to make himself disappear he raises his arm and as he lifts it he thinks for a moment that he has been lifted himself, that he is towering over the bodies coming to claim him and he can see straight over their heads through the windows to the night outside except that it is not night but a screen and in the screen he can see that a woman with white skin is relinquishing the torch to a woman with black skin and he thinks I'm somewhere there in between, I am in the in-between of my father's paleness and my mother's darkness, and as the woman holds the Olympic torch aloft ready to light the flame and as Martin is pushing him back and those behind Martin are grabbing at him, reaching for him, he knows that they are both there, he and Martin, that they are both there in the stadium that had been bronze with desert and silver with sea and gold with dreaming and that the glass in his hand is the torch in her hand and as he brings it down on Martin's face he hears the veil of the screen rip and through that tear the same woman's voice is now pleading and they fight and struggle as if the woman is guiding Dan's hand, she is guiding his fate, and the blood falls like hot rain on his cheeks and as he slices the man's face Dan raises the glass again and again and brings it down again and again and as his punches fall across the man's head and face and neck and throat and chest and belly and arms and legs and the man doubles over and falls, Dan sighs with relief because he has fallen with him through the crack of the sliding door and through the crack of the house and through the crack of the city into the nothingness in which he belongs. Martin Taylor's blood is on his lips, he can taste him. He falls into the darkness, and just before a boot crashes into his skull, he savors the moment in which his and Martin's blood and sweat are joined together: he and Martin, once again together, they are as one.

PART TWO

BREATHING OUT

I have to learn how to breathe again.

I am standing under the towering pin oak that shadows Frank Torma's house. I force my body to banish fear. The stone on my palm is as smooth as glass. My grip on it is strong. It is as smooth as glass but ancient and indestructible.

I have to learn how to breathe again because Frank watches me—I know he is watching me all the time. He watches me as I swim, but he also watches the way I walk toward the change rooms, how I undress, how I carry my sports bag over my shoulder. He takes note of everything I do—and everything I do, I do wrong.

"Stop slouching," he bellows, coming up behind me, resting one hand at the bottom of my spine, the other pushing my stomach so my back straightens. "When did you start slouching?" he roars. "When, tell me when?"

I don't answer. He must know, he must know the burden I carry. I push back my shoulders, I force one foot in front of the other. I inhale, try not to be conscious of the workings of my lungs, the forward thrust of my body. But I breathe too soon, I lose rhythm. Even something as simple as walking causes me fear. I don't trust the machine that is my body.

〜〜〜

I have to learn how to breathe again.

〜〜〜

There is a fog floating on the river, the city over the ridge is ghostly through the blue-and-gray mist. Through the glass doors I can see the staff at the front desk, a cleaner carrying a bucket and a mop. I am the first at the pool, I am outside, hopping on one foot, then the other, blowing into my hands, rubbing them together to keep warm. One of the women inside takes pity on me and though it is not yet six o'clock she comes over and releases a switch. The doors slide open.

"Thanks, Sonia."

She nods curtly, makes sure I've noticed that she's annoyed, but then she relents and calls over her shoulder, "The heating has just gone on in the change rooms, mate. It's freezing in there."

It is, it's like walking into an icy vapor straight off the South Pole. But I strip, slip on my Speedos, wrap my goggles around my neck, and run to the pool. I dive into the water.

That's not quite true: there is a moment, a pause. I hesitate, and then dive into the water.

That hesitation is constant, it is the load on my back. It stays with me as I complete one lap, and then another. The water senses it and does not yield for me. I have worked my muscles, I have sculpted them, they are supple and they are strong. Everything is in order, everything is in shape. But the water does not bend, the water resists me, pushes against me. I complete one hundred meters and I have to gulp for breath.

When the rest of the squad arrives, Wilco among them, I am treading water at the east end of the pool. They don't glance my way, don't greet me. Only Coach nods, then calls me over. I swim the

length, I swim the fifty meters and there is the load on my back. It is
the weight of all their eyes on me, it is their clocking of my pace, my
time, my stroke. I break the surface of the water and there is a din in
my head. I can hear their thoughts: That used to be Barracuda.

I look up. The squad are not paying me any attention. They are
doing stretches, waiting for a signal from Coach. A squad from another
of the private schools marches into the pool area, and we all warily eye
those boys. I have raced against some of them, I have beaten, thrashed,
some of those boys. The Australian Championships are in a fortnight,
and I must smash those boys again. I slip under the surface of the
water to cool my cheeks, my face. I must beat those boys again.

When I resurface, Coach is beckoning me and I hoist myself onto
the pool deck.

Wilco says, finally, "Hi, Kelly," and I am pathetically grateful for
his acknowledgment. I breathe in.

Wilco and I are the seniors in the squad now. There is no Taylor, no Fraser, no Scooter. Sullivan has gone and Morello dropped
out long ago. The younger ones keep their distance from me, as if
I could contaminate them. One of them, Lensman, is old enough to
have seen me win. The others, they only know about my failure. I
stand at the side as Coach speaks, I am at the edge of the half circle
formed around him. Coach pairs us off; I am matched with a Year
Eight, Costello. I see the glance he exchanges with Lensman, a smirk
at the corner of his mouth.

I dive cleanly, I do not hesitate. I plow through the water like
a threshing machine, I do not think of my breathing, my kick, my
stroke. And as if repaying my loyalty, the water carries me and the
water bends and shifts for me. I am not consciousness, I am drive
and I am body and I am force. My arms hammer down on the water,
and effortlessly separate the water. I have no thoughts but I dare
myself, the words are inseparable from the water and my body, they
are one: I am the strongest, the fastest, the best. I am the strongest,
the fastest, the best.

Waves of exhilaration flood through me. I beat Costello, I flog him. The boy is about to say something to me, to accept my victory, but I cut him off and raise my arms, my biceps flexed, my fists clenched triumphantly. I make a sound, somewhere between a grunt and a bray, and I repeat it. So he knows I have beaten him. Costello slips back under the water, he says nothing at all.

〰〰

I *will* learn how to breathe again.

As I am about to climb into the minibus with the others to head to school, Coach taps me on the shoulder, pulls me away from the squad. I can see the others looking back at us as they board.

Coach waits until all the boys are on, then he gives the driver a thumbs-up. "Come on, Danny," he says. "You come with me."

All the way out from the city we don't speak. It isn't until he turns his car onto the freeway that forms the spine through the southeastern suburbs that he turns to me. "Danny, do you trust me?"

I have to trust you, no one else will take a chance on me now. But I don't say that. I just nod obediently.

"Good. You have to trust me, son. You have to trust me if you want to be a swimmer again."

Two thoughts rebound against one another: that he has called me *son*; and that he knows I am not the strongest, not the fastest, not the best. I have to learn I can't reconcile the two notions—they confuse me and render me silent.

I pull my bag onto my lap, search for my water bottle, and drink from it hungrily. "I think I did good back there," I say meekly, not looking across at him, looking at the steady flow of cars in front of and around us. "It felt good to beat Costello."

Coach makes an ugly derisive sound. He is gripping the wheel so hard his knuckles are white. "Costello is fourteen, he's nearly three years younger than you—he has some talent, but he's no champion." His left hand slips off the wheel and his forefinger drums hard at my chest. "Is that who you want to compare yourself to? Is that the best you expect from yourself?"

I can't speak. I want his fingers to be a fist, I want him to punch me, bash me. Anything but his contemptuous words. They are no worse than the things I say to myself since I came back from Japan—in fact, they are much milder. He hasn't called me a loser, he hasn't called me a coward; he hasn't uttered that one word that is the load on my back, he hasn't called me a failure.

But he and I, we both know what I am.

"Answer me, boy. What is it you want?"

I am too frightened to speak. I don't dare say the words.

Coach again takes one hand off the wheel, and says, "I can train you, boy, I can build your muscles *here*"—and as he spits the words he punches, hard, his own chest—"I can make you strong *here*"—and he smacks the palm of his hand to his bicep—"I can work you so hard that every part of your body will be perfect. *Here*," he yells, and slams his fist into his chest again, "*Here*," punching his bicep, and "*Here*," he delivers a blow to his thigh. "But what I can't do, Danny," and his finger is pointing at my head, "I can't do anything about *here*."

He indicates to veer off the freeway, we are nearly at school. I know that I have to say something, that he has taken me aside to give me an ultimatum, he is asking whether swimming is over for me. And I can't believe it, my body is betraying me again, I can sense the shudders going through me, the tears about to flow from my eyes. I shut them tight, I inhale, I rein myself in. I can't break that promise, that promise that I have made to myself: that I will never ever *ever* cry again.

〰〰〰

I have to learn how to breathe again.

I open my eyes: the world in my vision is dry. I turn to Coach. "I want to be an Olympic swimmer."

We are in the school car park. Coach turns off the car and looks at me.

And I look at him. I don't see the drooping jowls, the fat face, the bulldog neck. I see large and dark and limpid eyes, a sheen of moisture there in the blackness.

"You are at a crossroads, son, but I have faith you can be a great swimmer. Do you have that faith?"

All I can think of is that he has called me son again. He is about to say something else. But he swallows the words.

I have to stop myself saying, Tell me, tell me what to do, what to think. Tell me. I have to trust you.

He orders me out of the car.

I don't walk toward the school buildings, I sling my bag over my shoulder, cross the ovals, slip under the wire. I head to the river. I can smell tobacco from somewhere, probably the copse, some boys are smoking. I make a path through the long grass and reach the bank. I sling off my bag, I drop to my haunches. I look out over the water.

Something about the word Coach used, something about that word, *crossroads,* it will not leave me, it scratches weakly at my memory. I watch a branch twist in the water and be carried away by the current; birds are singing all around me.

It comes to me, it is a story my father used to tell me when I was a child in my flannelette pajamas. Sometimes he would read to me but more often than not he enjoyed telling me stories. Of how a young Presley was taken up to Memphis or how a son of slaves called Lead Belly grew up in a whorehouse and discovered his genius for singing in prison chain gangs.

"Music's the best education, Danny," I remember him saying. "A true education, not like the manufactured crap on the radio these days."

And he told me about Robert Johnson at the crossroads. That night he showed me the sleeve of a record, Johnson smoking a cigarette, clutching the neck of a guitar. He didn't look old enough to be called a man.

Robert Johnson met the Devil at the crossroads, my father told me, and he wanted to play the blues so bad that he made a deal with the Devil. He sold his soul. That was how much the music meant to him, that was what it cost him to play.

The water rushes past me, a flock of yellow-tailed cockatoos fling from the trees and their squawks fill the day.

You are at a crossroads, son.

I didn't get raised with God so I am not acquainted with the Devil. But looking out across the river, I am sure that I have felt them both in the water. Poseidon was the god of the ocean and Poseidon carried a trident. I remember that.

Mum didn't want me to learn about God—she said God is just goodness. And evil? I never asked her about evil.

How much do I want it?

I look around me; the bush is empty, there isn't anyone else around. So I whisper, "I'll sell my soul."

The river, the birds, they are the only ones who hear me.

And I don't know God and I don't know the Devil. What would He want in return? What would be a sacrifice?

The thought rushes through me; and now I feel the cold, now there is only cold.

I'd give up my father. I'd give up my mother.

I see it, I see it clearly, a truck crashing off a highway.

I will give up my father and I will give up my mother.

And I'd give up Luke, I'd give up Martin.

And it feels right, it is right. Martin remains young and handsome and beautiful for eternity.

I will give up my mates.

And Demet?

I will give up my best friend.

And the cold is my blood and my blood is ice.

Now I understand evil. The shaft that is light between us, from her heart to my heart. I will break that light. That's how much I want *it*.

And Regan?

That shy little girl, hiding behind her long sandy hair, waiting patiently for my training to finish, who can't bear my father yelling at me, who can't bear anyone hurting me. Who adores me.

I will give up my sister.

And Theo?

Who is there in the morning and who is there in the evening, trusting me, believing in me. What would anything mean without Theo? I can't give up Theo.

What is it you want?

I have been holding in my breath and now I exhale.

The birds have stopped their song. Even the river is silent.

I will give up Theo.

The trilling returns, the rush of the water.

I get to my feet, but a thought is pounding, it is current and wave, it is coursing through me: Is it worth it? All I am is shame.

~~~~~

But there isn't a God and there isn't a Devil because in the pool that afternoon my legs are leaden, my arms are dead weights, my lungs gasp for air; I swallow water. Coach doesn't have to say a word, I don't have to look at him. I know the disappointment that will be there in his eyes.

I have to learn how to breathe again.

~~~~~

And after training, when we are all showered and dressed, Coach calls us aside and says he has decided who he will select for the Melbourne heats of the national championships. It is Wilco, of course, and it is even Costello. And then he says, for the two hundred meters butterfly, he says he wants Lensman to swim.

They are studying me, waiting for me to break. I stare straight ahead, not moving, not saying a word. Thankfully, my eyes are dry. I walk over to Wilco, to Costello, to Lensman, and I shake their hands. I don't dare look at Coach.

Do you trust me, Danny?

Give it back to him. But is there retribution huge enough to avenge such a betrayal?

〜〜〜

The following morning I begin to breathe again.

I awake before my alarm, I stretch out my legs, I raise my arms, I flex and I punch the air. But I don't rise. I turn off the alarm, turn over, and pretend to be asleep.

I hear Mum knock on the door. "You'll be late, Danny. What's wrong, mate?"

"I'm sick," I grunt.

Not long after I can hear Theo in the hall, incredulous. "Why isn't Danny up? Why isn't he at training?"

I can't hear my mother's hushed reply.

At seven o'clock I rise, I eat breakfast. Theo and Mum watch me warily; Regan keeps asking if I am all right. I scoff down my breakfast.

"I'm fine," I grin through a mouthful of cereal. "Never felt better. I'm good."

On the train, on the walk to school, I am cheerful, I have to stop myself whistling. I tell myself I am already changing—I am a chrysalis, I am becoming a completely new entity. The light seems different, sharper and alive, as if I can distinguish the very atoms within it. I have to stop myself whistling.

After prayers at the chapel, Coach finds me. "Why weren't you at training?"

"Sick, I guess."

"You guess?" He scratches at his head. His disappointment reeks, I can smell it, how foul he thinks I am. "I told you, Danny, you are at a crossroads."

I wait, I am eager, so fired up and ready: Go on, call me *son*, come on, just call me *son*. Use that word and I'll go you, use that word and I don't care what I do to you, what that will cost me. Come on, cunt, just say it.

"If you don't turn up this afternoon, you are dropped from the squad."

I am walking to my locker, first period is about to start, and I see Lensman coming toward me. The little squirt, the little faggot, he has that sly arrogant smirk on his face. He is walking straight toward me; it is a contest, who will move aside first, who will break first. We have both been trained to be fearful of injury—a sprain, a bruise, a graze—that could affect our swimming.

I use my body, my sculpted, molded, and perfect body, to slam into him so hard that he is lifted off his feet and slams headfirst into the lockers. I can feel the throb in my shoulder blade but I will not rub it, I will not show that I am hurt.

Lensman is holding his ribs, he is sprawled on the floor, all outrage and fear. I can see the outrage, I can smell the fear.

"Sorry, Lensman," I sneer down at him. "Next time watch where you're fucking going."

I am whistling as I walk out into the quadrangle.

I have to learn how to breathe again.

I am standing under the towering pin oak that shadows Coach's house. There is the broken gate, the heavy blue door, the cracked concrete steps, the ornate bay window, behind which used to be *my* room. The squad will be halfway through training by now. Oh, how Coach will be screaming at them, how he will be riding them, how he will be ridiculing them.

Do you trust me, Danny?

The stone in my hand is as smooth as glass.

I look up and down the street: there is no one around. I glance around quickly once more and then I walk up to the fence and I throw the rock with the strength and power and precision of my sculpted, perfect body. The crack is so loud I cower; a pane has shattered, shards of glass spray all over the veranda.

I'm running as fast as I can, because someone will have heard, someone will be calling the police, but that doesn't matter because I can outrun them all. My body is trained, my body is fearless.

I run all the way to the Studley Park bridge, but I am not out of breath. I have learned how to breathe again. I reach the main road and I keep on running. I am gleeful but I know what is on my tail, I can hear it, I can even smell it, the rank aroma of a body that will not listen, a body that betrays, a body that will give up everything and still prove to be useless. It is failure I can smell.

And I understand, I *know,* it is failure that is evil.

So I run, my strides enormous, not caring who I crash into, who I hurt. I run so fast that I am hurting the ground as I pound it, I run so fast that I am fire. But no matter how fast I run, the Devil is there beside me. The Devil is in me. I am a larva and that which is emerging is something vile, something uglier than what existed before.

He slid the plane across the wood, wisps of shavings falling softly to the ground. Dan enjoyed the steady motion, the tool gliding under his hand, the paint peeling off, the thread-like veins of grain appearing in the surface of the timber. A fine dust settled over his hands and arms, and on his clothes.

His granddad Bill was sitting on a decrepit folding beach chair, its aluminum frame so old that the tarnish on it had weathered to a bronze tint. An ancient transistor radio was perched on the chair's armrest, tuned to a station that played songs from when his grandparents were young: Elvis Presley and Frank Sinatra, Dusty Springfield and Helen Reddy. His granddad Bill called all pop songs *Yeah Yeah Yeah* music, as in the Beatles, and he meant it disparagingly, but now he was humming along to one of the songs. *I ain't mama's little girl no more, Baby you're the first to know.* It made Dan want to laugh, the old man with his shock of white hair, both hands clasped over the top of his walking cane, watching his grandson and singing, "*I ain't mama's little girl no more.*"

Dan brushed perspiration away from his brow. The morning clouds had dispersed and the sun was right over the backyard. Dan stripped off his sweatshirt; his blue singlet was damp with sweat. He used the old gray top to wipe his face, under his arms, across his chest. He turned the wood over and started sanding down the other side.

"Dearie, you'll catch a cold." His grandmother was carrying a tray on which were two cold beers, a jug of water, a glass, and some Monte Carlo biscuits on a white plate. She put the tray on the small garden table.

"It's all right, Nan, the sun's out."

She snorted softly. "Summer's gone, Danny. The weather will change any moment."

"Irene, leave our kid be. He said he's fine." His granddad wouldn't hear a word against Dan, not one word.

Taking a sip of her beer, his grandmother came over and ran her hand over the plank of timber he had been working on.

"I'll have the shelves up by tea," announced Dan. "Promise." His nan smiled at him.

Dan downed his water and poured himself another glass. He could feel the muscles in his chest, in his forearms, taut and strong, thick and ropy beneath his skin. He gulped down the water and got to his feet. "Righto, smoko's over."

What he liked most about being with the olds was that there didn't need to be talk. He could work, listen to the radio, stretch his muscles, toil. He often went days without speaking to anyone, days and nights of quiet. Sometimes Dan thought all words were useless. For him there was no emptiness in silence—quite the opposite, there was peace and calm; it was only in conversation that trouble lurked.

That was why he liked working the night shift at the supermarket. Sure, he had to talk to the customers, but it was never more than a *hello, how you doing, do you want a bag?, have a good night*. He greeted the delivery guys in the morning, called out *have a good one* to Vikram when he arrived for the morning shift. But that was it, not millions of useless words. There was no loneliness in silence. Loneliness could be found in conversation, it lurked in words.

His nan had cleared the kitchen, the table and chairs were stacked up against the fridge. Dan was happy to do all the work himself, to hammer in the nails, to build in the shelves, but he knew his grand-dad wanted to help, to be useful. So they worked in silence together, and in an hour the job was done and the table and chairs were back in place. His nan came in from the garden with a bunch of flowers, blue snapdragons, a cluster of honeysuckle; from the laundry she fetched the jade vase that had been their one wedding present. Dan knew the story: it had been given to them by Jenny, a woman who'd sailed with them on the ship from Glasgow, who then became his grandpar-ents' best friend. Now his nan arranged the flowers, and put them on the middle shelf next to their one wedding photograph. It was black and white, his granddad in a light-colored suit, his grandmother in a smart jacket and skirt. Jenny was standing next to his nan, and next to his granddad was his best friend, Bruno, who was the only one smiling in the photograph. His nan looked stern, his granddad had half turned away from the lens, as if he resented the presence of the camera. It was the men who were splendid, who looked handsome. The women seemed apprehensive, as if unused to the fine clothes, as if they knew they were playing parts that didn't belong to them, as if they feared they were overdressed for the unadorned walls of the registry office.

Dan glanced across at his granddad, trying to see a resemblance between the youth in the photo and the old man in the kitchen. Only a few years before he had seen it; as a teenager he had been able to match the mature, lined face of his grandfather with the smooth-skinned lad in the photograph. But in the last few years age and time had accelerated. His grandfather had shrunk, and his clothes hung from his thinning body.

Dan wrapped an arm around his granddad's bony shoulders. "They look all right, don't they?"

"Aye. You've done a good job, mate. Thank you."

"You sure you don't want me to finish them?"

"Ach, I'm not in the grave yet, kid, I can still stain a bloody shelf."

"Well, call me if you want some help." Dan hugged his granddad lightly for a moment. His nan had started placing plates and cups on the shelves, and other photographs: of Dan's family, of his uncle Pat and aunt Diana, of his cousins. She sat a small cuckoo clock, trays and bowls, on the new shelves. Soon the wedding photograph was jostled behind a stainless-steel water jug, and Bruno's smiling face disappeared behind the smoky opaque glass of a rose-colored decanter. "How is Uncle Bruno?"

His granddad had carefully sat himself down on a kitchen chair, using his cane for balance. He and his wife made furtive eye contact, as if Dan's question had somehow shamed them.

"Bruno's gone, dear," his nan said quietly. "He died over a year ago."

Dan knew why they felt ashamed. Bruno must have died when Dan was in prison. They didn't have to say it, he knew it by how the silence had changed, how it was no longer comfortable between them, no longer safe. Sensing it as well, his nan started chattering, going on about shopping and the Easter holidays, reminding her husband that the car registration was due.

Dan wasn't listening, he was blocking out the words, wishing he knew how to say to his grandparents that they didn't have to fear the eight months he'd been away, those months he'd been out of the world. He wished he knew how to express to his grandparents that he was reconciled to those lost months—indeed, that he was grateful for them.

But this was why words always tripped him up. In gaol he had rediscovered routine, it had been prison that had helped him recognize how precious habit was for him, how he needed order and repetition. He'd discovered again the joy of waking up at the exact same time every morning, of eating at the same time every morning, lunch and evening, of working the same hours and the same shift. Then there had been his gym workout every afternoon, and his daily visits to the library. That had been his favorite activity; he would rush there as soon as he'd finished in the kitchen or the workshop: work, gym, the library, and then reading till lights out at the exact same time every night.

Dan got up from the table, checking his pockets for his wallet and keys.

"Danny, you're not leaving? Aren't you going to stay for tea?"

He wanted to be on the move, to feel motion. He shook his head. "Got some stuff I need to do before work this arvo." He turned to his granddad. "You sure you're going to be all right staining the wood? I can come back on the weekend."

"You've done enough, kid. It'll give me something to do."

They were both watching him, both anxious. He could see the words forming on his nan's lips; she wanted him to stay, was scared every time he went out into the world. He wished he could have told her: I'm safe out there, when I don't have to talk to anyone, when I'm on my own. That is much safer.

He was about to lean in and kiss his grandmother's cheek when she said to him, "Danny, love, why haven't you called your mum?"

Words. They ensnared you, they unsettled you. They reminded you that you were no good.

"I will." And he did intend to—he wasn't making false promises. Every day he thought, I should call them, I should go around. Every day passed and it hadn't happened.

"Your *giagia* is sick."

He hadn't heard that word in years; it had always sounded odd coming from his nan, like it should have been the name of some toy. *Ya-ya.* It only sounded natural when his mother said it, and she hadn't done that for a long time.

Dan stood immobile in the small kitchen, looking down at his nan. She was the only grandmother he had, he really believed that. His other grandmother was just a few flashes of memory, none of them solid.

"Oh," was all he said.

"I know Stephanie needs you, would like you to go to Adelaide with her. Dan, she really does. I think you should." She only called him Dan when things were serious, sometimes Daniel when she was pissed off with him.

He looked across to his grandfather, who could only offer a wry smile. But that was answer enough; if his granddad said nothing, it meant he agreed with his wife.

"Can't Dad go with her?"

His nan's snort was so scornful, it made him blush. "You know our Neal can't go with her, Danny—he went across when Stephanie's father was dying and it was a disaster." She shook her head violently. "No, Dan, it has to be you."

It was an order. It made Dan want to run.

"Regan's up in New South Wales and your father can't go with her." His nan's tone had mellowed but her words were still determined.

"She could take Theo."

This occasioned another snort. "His grandmother's never laid eyes on him."

This time his granddad spoke. "And whose fault is that?"

His nan looked worn and weary. "Oh, Bill, don't I know it? That old bitch has three wonderful grandchildren she doesn't even know, wouldn't recognize them if they were right in front of her. But she's our Stephanie's mother, and Stephanie wants to see her before she dies." She clasped her hand tightly over Dan's wrist. "You have to go with her, dearie."

"But I've got to work."

"This weekend is Easter—surely you can get some time off?"

Dan knew he probably could. He hadn't had a day off since he started at the supermarket after prison, he hadn't asked for one and hadn't needed one. A day off was a break in the routine—it was no good to him. His grandmother was still holding on to him, her fingers pressing into his flesh.

"Okay, Nan, okay. I'll ring her. I promise."

She patted his arm gently and his granddad gave a relieved sigh.

〜〜〜

The railway station was at the end of his grandparents' street, but Dan went past it, walking so fast his backpack was thumping and slapping his shoulder blades. He dashed down the street, as if by rushing he could lift the burden of the promise he had made to his grandparents—as if he could outrun it, shrug it off. He crossed the railway line, walked parallel to it until he reached the next station, but then decided to keep moving, to make his way to the next one along. A city-bound train cannoned past and he wondered if he could walk all the way into town.

The sun was just dropping into the west and its blinding rays were in his eyes. He came to a small park and sat on a bench under a giant maple, whose golden leaves were just about to fall. He sat down on the bench and took out his phone, scrolling down to MUM & DAD, his finger poised over the call button. He didn't press it.

School was out and two girls were walking across the park, swinging their bags, giggling as they passed him. A little farther behind them a boy was coming up the path, slouching, walking slowly, his overloaded schoolbag hanging precariously from his shoulder. The boy was tall, lanky, his shirt untucked, the white flaps falling from beneath his gray school jumper. He had a mess of oily black hair, a down of black hair on his top lip, and his cheeks were crimson, spotty. Dan watched him shuffle past, keeping a measured distance behind the girls, who were still giggling. One of them let out a peal of laughter. The schoolboy slowed his gait even more. Dan knew exactly what he would be thinking, he would be thinking that they were laughing at him, that they thought he was ugly, a loser.

Dan wanted to run up to the boy, to tell him, You're wrong, you don't know how beautiful you are. He forced himself to stop looking at the boy. He turned to look back at his phone, slid his fingers

against the numbered buttons and the light came back on the screen:
MUM & DAD.

Dan had an erection; his cock was thick and straining against the tight cotton of his jocks. Two young mothers wheeling prams were coming up the path. Resentfully, almost savagely, he picked up his bag and set it on his lap. The two women were in the middle of an animated conversation but one of them, blond, her hair swept back over one shoulder, looked across at him as they walked past and offered the faintest glimmer of a smile. He smiled back, thinking, You don't know what I am, you would be disgusted if you knew that I am sitting here, thinking what it would feel like to have that schoolboy's cock up my arse.

His erection had gone. The sun had disappeared completely behind white cloud. The wind was blowing stronger and it was cold in the shade. He stretched his arms and hooked them over the back of the bench. He looked down at MUM & DAD and made the call.

His mother answered immediately, as if she had been waiting for it, as if she knew he'd be ringing. He could hear women's voices in the background and beneath them the numb monotone beats of a commercial radio station, the music his mother hated.

He didn't offer excuses about why he hadn't rung, he didn't apologize or ask how she was, if they'd heard from Regan; he didn't ask after his dad or Theo. He just said, "Nan told me *giagia* is sick. I'll come with you to Adelaide."

His mother was crying as they organized to leave on the Saturday morning, she was still crying when he said goodbye. Her weeping, her repeated *thank you thank you thank you* were the last things he heard as he clicked shut his phone.

∿∿∿

There was no television in Dan's flat, no radio, no stereo. He walked through the door and fell back onto the sofa, his palms flat on each thigh, staring straight ahead, through the window where the view dropped down to the railway bridge, the expanse of train tracks and the curved black arcs of the telephone wires, to the ashen cloud-filled sky. He was watching without seeing, wasn't even conscious of the trains roaring in and out of Footscray station.

He was listening without hearing; to his breathing, calm now that he was home, now that he was still.

He didn't want a television, he had no need of a radio. He didn't want the world to come in. He detested the news, couldn't believe it: the bombs and the terror and the wailing boatpeople; the oil and the money and the price of land and real estate. He couldn't stand the false hysteria of soap operas, the forced hilarity of sitcoms, the feigned outrage of commentators and the hosts of current-affairs shows. He didn't own a computer. He didn't need its temptations. He preferred the silence, the loneliness that was comfort; he didn't want uproar and infinite noise. Only books, books were all he wanted, and they were strewn across his flat. Books from the local library, books scavenged from boxes and crates at the Sunday markets. In reading he found solitude. In reading he could dispel the blare of the world.

Dan sat on his sofa looking out of the window to where leaden cumulus clouds slowly passed over the telephone lines. He could see the railway bridge, and a train shuffling out of the station. He was looking at the low dark clouds, listening to his breath going in and out of his lungs. Slowly a symphony began. He could hear the old woman next door turning on a tap, the sound of a clunking washing machine from the laundry below. He could hear the rapid footsteps of the student next door, the sound of his key in the lock; there was the faint sizzling from the kitchen downstairs, where the woman came home and immediately started opening cupboards and cooking, always the sting of garlic, the sour rich smells of her Tamil cooking; the faint hum of the television in the background. All the sounds converged, melting into his breathing, forming shape; and from shape they formed music and from music they returned to tranquillity, and thus receded. All that was left was the in and the out of his breathing. Lost to the world around him, he was still watching the heavy rolling clouds as the horizon darkened. Dan jolted back; he had almost fallen asleep. He realized he was happy.

He read two chapters of Graham Greene, *The Heart of the Matter,* and had to force himself to put the book down. He'd discovered Greene inside and had read him hungrily, and continued to do so on his release. He understood the writer's characters, sympathized with their weakness and cowardice, responded most to their refusal to find excuses for their failures. Alec, the earnest volunteer who worked in the prison library, would always say, "Dan, my man, don't you wanna read some modern stuff? Why are you always buried in those old farts?" Dan would accept the teasing good-naturedly for he knew it was apt. Contemporary writers annoyed him, he found their worlds insular, their style too self-conscious and ironic. Theirs was not a literature that belonged to him.

He could read Greene for hours but he needed to get ready for work.

Dan showered, brushed his teeth, and put on his work gear. It took him an hour to walk to work, an hour during which he felt and enjoyed the stretch of his calves, the pull on his muscles, the ache in his tendons. Night came as he walked. He stopped at Hadji's kebab caravan to grab a falafel and he munched on it standing on the bridge overlooking the dark flow of the Maribyrnong River.

At work, with a nod to Seeav behind the counter, he went into the storeroom to unpack cartons of biscuits and chocolates, boxes of liquid soap and shampoo. He liked the sensation of his biceps tightening as he lifted the boxes, his triceps flexing as he ripped away the tape, his abdomen stretching and muscles clenching as he placed the goods on the shelves. The night was quiet, except for the usual rush of famished taxi drivers at four o'clock in the morning. Dawn had just broken as he started his walk home, stopping only for an orange juice and a bacon-and-cheese roll at the Bakers Delight in Union Road.

He got home and sat himself on the sofa, looking out to the

lightening azure sky. The sun was partly hidden by clouds but its light was already stabbing; he forced himself not to blink, to look without seeing. His palms were flat on his thighs, and he listened to his breathing. It went in, it went out, and slowly he heard the world around him stir and awaken, as pipes throughout the building began to throb and rumble, televisions came to life, cars clicked open and engines started. He listened without hearing; he looked without seeing. It occurred to him that in two days' time he would be seeing his parents, his brother; he would be driving with his mother to Adelaide. He could sense the weight of that thought, slung heavy over his shoulder. With a groan he got up and headed to his bedroom, not bothering to brush his teeth, not wanting to shower. He dropped onto his mattress—there was no bed, just a mattress on the floor, a crate of books and a reading lamp bought secondhand from Forges. He kicked off his shoes, pulled off his socks, undid his belt but did not get undressed. He read twenty more pages of *The Heart of the Matter,* then laid the book open on the carpet and pulled the sheet and blanket over him. He could hear more pipes banging, more clamor from radios and televisions. This was what he enjoyed about living in a flat, he acknowledged: being hidden behind his walls but conscious of sound and movement and energy all around him. Life was all around him but he was protected from it. It was that moment when they shut his cell door, when he could breathe freely, when he did not have to think about how to behave or how to protect himself. He listened without hearing. He closed his eyes. In the smallest of moments Dan was sound asleep.

⌇

Theo opened the door. He looked sullenly at Dan, then turned and shouted down the hall, "Mum! Dad! Danny's here." Without another word he went into his bedroom and slammed the door. The brothers had not talked, not really talked, since the night over two years before when Dan had called from the Prahran copshop. It had been Theo who'd answered the phone. Dan did not blame Theo for despising him or being ashamed of him, but he couldn't think about it, so instead he reflected on how the cracks in the hallway walls had widened since he'd lived there, how the house smelled more of damp and soil, and how the earthiness of that smell was softened by the aroma of cooking and lived-in spaces.

His mother was rushing up the hall toward him. She wasn't wearing makeup and he realized how rare a sight that was. She was wearing an old black T-shirt, the lurid gothic script reading *The Beasts of Bourbon* now faded; she was hugging him, kissing him, on his face, his cheeks, even his lips. She released him from her grasp and he breathed out, but she wouldn't let go of his hand. He breathed in, she was dragging him past Theo's bedroom, past his old room; he breathed out, he was being pulled into the lounge, the television was on mute, *The Age* was open over the coffee table. She led him into the kitchen where his father was standing in a brown polyester top and cream pajama bottoms, standing rigid. Dan breathed in. His mother let go of his hand and the two men took a step toward one another, went into a hasty embrace, their bodies just touching, but long enough for him to hear his father whisper, "Good to see you, son."

Dan breathed out.

His father's hair was now completely gray. He still had his Elvis quiff, his rockabilly sideburns, but his hair was a grimy silver, there were deep furrows at the sides of his mouth, and his paunch was now definitely a belly. He was getting old, thought Dan.

"Will you two sit down? Anyone looking at you would think you were strangers."

Dan's mother was busy in the kitchen but her words brought a wry smile to his father's face, and the men were put at ease. They sat opposite each other, while his mother scurried around them, putting cheese and olives on the table, slicing bread. There was a plate of freshly made meatballs on the stove. She drizzled oil into a pan.

"I hope you're hungry, Danny," she said brightly. "I'm making *keftethes*. Your favorite."

He almost blurted out, Are they? Are they still my favorite? But he swallowed the words, knowing they would only hurt her. As the meatballs started spitting in the pan and the aroma of the meat, parsley, and onion filled the kitchen, he was reminded of how much he loved her food. He remembered how he would come home from training, ravenous, having flown through the pool, having dominated the water. She'd often have made two batches of *keftethes,* one for him and one for the rest of the family. He could eat all of his, a half kilo of meat, he could have even eaten double that. She'd have salad for him as well and some roasted vegetables and bread. And then, maybe, his hunger would be satisfied. But it seemed years since he had eaten her meatballs. It could *not* have been as long as that. But that would have been before prison, and in there, time had become elongated and space had changed him, hemmed him in, made him burrow deep inside himself. He was no longer of the sky, of water; he was now in the earth. He did not know whether her *keftethes* were his favorite anymore. It was as if he had to discover his taste and his desire anew.

His mother noticed the backpack at his feet. "Is that all you're bringing with you to Adelaide? You're just like your dad."

Father and son exchanged a glance, then quickly dropped their eyes.

His father's nervousness around him was new. There had been awkwardness before, there had certainly been that when he was young. They'd given each other the shits, they would argue endlessly. Dan understood all of it now, or thought he was beginning to: that his father resented the family's time and energy and expectations all being focused on the eldest child. Swimming and practice and competition and heats—they'd been all Dan ever thought about. And not just him; for many years it had been all Theo and his mother and Regan thought about too. Only his father had been cautious, only his father, Dan now knew, had thought ahead to what might happen if Dan couldn't swim. Dan winced; his father had thought ahead to what it would mean if Dan failed. Only his father had seen ahead to failure.

The act of violence that had resulted in Dan going to prison had terrified and confused his father. The one time he had visited Dan in gaol, he had hardly been able to talk, had had not a clue what to say. He had sat there, straight-backed and silent, unable to speak a word. Throughout the visit, his father's eyes had been watery, as if all his rigidity, all his discomfort had arisen from the effort of fighting back tears. When the visit had ended, all Dan felt was relief—and exhaustion, as if he had swum for hours.

It's my fault, thought Dan. It is my failure that has aged him.

"I don't need much, Mum. We're only going for a few days, aren't we?"

His father blurted out, "I'm really glad you're going with your mum, Dan. This means so much to her." Behind him, at the stove, his mother reached back and squeezed Dan's shoulder.

When the *keftethes* were ready, his mother asked Dan to get his brother. Dan walked down the hallway and knocked on Theo's door. There was no answer, so he knocked again, then opened the door.

The curtains were drawn and Theo was sprawled on the bed. Dan could smell the marijuana, the accumulated fetid stink of sweat and adolescent boy, strong, overpowering, straight down his lungs. Theo's shirt had ridden up and Dan was shocked at the flush of tight wiry curls on his brother's flat stomach.

Theo scowled. "What do you want?"

"Lunch is ready."

"I'm not hungry."

There were no swimming posters on his brother's wall, no more Kieren Perkins or Susie O'Neill. There were no athletes, nothing to do with sport except a Magpies pendant: all of Dan's old trophies and championship ribbons had gone. Instead there were two enormous band posters, ghoulish exaggerated faces, a man's face painted white, bloodred lipstick, his mouth opened wide in an expressionist scream. There was a smaller poster of a supermodel in a bikini, there was an A4 black-and-white leaflet for a rally against the war in Iraq, a poster of a thick-necked, preposterously muscled black rapper wearing a baseball cap with a dollar sign on it, gold chains decorating his oversized glistening chest. Dan didn't know any of them, what they were, what they sang, what they meant.

Theo had closed his eyes.

Dan tried again. "Come on, mate, do it for Mum."

The boy sat up abruptly. "As if you've ever given a shit about Mum!" His reply dripped with disbelief and scorn, the outrage rising to a juvenile screech. He couldn't steady the trembling in his voice. "As if you have ever given a stuff about anyone but yourself. When did you last call Regan? Do you have her address, do you even have her fucking number?"

Dan couldn't answer.

"Thought so. And she still defends you, she still thinks you care about us." Theo lay back on the bed and turned to the wall. His next words were muffled. "Just get the fuck out of my room."

Dan heard him clearly. He stood there, clenching and unclenching his fist. I could fucking kill you, I could take you by the fucking neck and wring it till you choked. He told himself to breathe, to remember the lessons he'd learned in prison: to count down from ten, slowly, not to rush through the numbers, to mouth them, to visualize them, to breathe in and out between the numbers as he counted. It was a simple trick and he always felt a little foolish doing it, but it worked. By seven his hands had relaxed and by three there was no anger.

"Okay, mate, I'll get Mum to save you some for later."

He shut the door, but not before he heard the mumbled words: "Fucking loser."

The *keftethes* tasted good, the *keftethes* tasted as he remembered them. But he didn't know if they were still his favorites, he had yet to rediscover that.

After lunch they hit the road. His mother had delayed their departure searching for CDs to take along for the drive. She had finally
got rid of her old Datsun—by the end the chassis was more rust
than steel, Dan remembered—and had bought herself a five-year-old
Hyundai.

"It doesn't have much grunt," his father explained, grinning,
leaning against the lounge doorframe with his arms folded, watching
his wife search frantically through cases of CDs, "but it has a shit-
hot stereo and that's all your mother cares about."

She had chosen good music for their long drive across the border.
There were the strong-lunged, honey-voiced singers that she adored,
Etta James and Mavis Staples. There were the growlers, Cash and
Jennings, Joplin and Cave. And then there were those she called the
angels, the ones who healed as they sang: Aretha Franklin, Nina
Simone, Presley. She sang along to all of them. Dan's father was the
singer in the family; Neal's voice was strong, it had character and
he could hold and tame a note. Dan's mother's voice was reedy, and
both high and low registers defeated her. She could butcher a melody,
could go badly off-key. But Dan didn't mind. As the city ended and
they sliced through the low plains of farm and scrub, he took pleasure in her joy at the music, in being on the open road, in the fact
that the space between them was being filled with music rather than
conversation. He was safe in the music, he felt at home in it.

After they'd reached the end of a George Jones CD his mother
said, "I've packed some Soundgarden, I've got *Nevermind*."

He knew she'd brought them along for him, but his heart was
sinking as she pushed in the Nirvana CD. The chords thrashed and
boomed through the car, lashing at his ears. He ejected it immediately. His mother said nothing as he chose another disk from the
pile, an Everly Brothers compilation. She sang along to "Unchained

Melody," her voice cracked on the final chorus of "Bye Bye Love" but stayed true on "Cathy's Clown." All the words came back to him. He could take comfort in the familiarity of all these words and notes and melodies.

In Ararat they stopped for a break. All the shops were open for the Easter Saturday trade. They went past a secondhand bookshop. "Do you mind if we go in?" his mother asked and he agreed gladly. They spent twenty minutes looking through rows of dusty books. Dan picked up worn copies of Faulkner's *The Sound and the Fury* and David Malouf's *Remembering Babylon*.

His mother chuckled as she stood beside him at the counter, and paid for the books. "That looks like pretty heavy reading there, mate," she said as they headed back to the car. She threw him a quizzical look. "I don't remember you reading much at all when you were at school."

Dan hesitated. He wanted to say that he'd learned to read in gaol, to really read. He wanted to tell her that the library had been his favorite place inside, that when he read *As I Lay Dying* he'd found a voice that made sense of time and space as he was experiencing it in gaol, that it had spoken to him more clearly and more profoundly than any voice he'd ever encountered before: of how the past could not be separated from memory, of how it was not only time that changed people, it was memory as well. He wished he could tell her how he'd read *Johnno* in one sitting at the library table and that he'd started it again before lights out that night. He wished he could tell her about discovering words and how words could become song, something he had never understood at school. Not that he had ever scoffed at books; his parents would never have tolerated that—even his father's suspicion of the learned had never extended to learning itself; he loved stories too much. But the young Danny had never worked out how to make time for books; he had believed that the dedication required would pull him away from routine and from his body, from his goal of success. In prison, however, where everything was ordered by time, but time itself was always elusive, out of reach, he realized that he had been wrong about books.

Sitting at a desk in the library, reading in his cell, losing himself in a dog-eared copy of *1984*, his whole being had been immersed in the ferocious lust for escape that drove Winston Smith. The novel had so shaken him that he'd had to gasp for air, as if he had swum an ocean. Desire and betrayal: George Orwell had chronicled Dan's soul. Soon after, he had picked up a slim volume from a donated crate of books, a collection of Chekhov's short stories, the spine broken, some of the pages falling loose. Dan had never read a short story before in his life. One particular story he had returned to again and again, reading it obsessively: "A Day in the Country," the story of an innocent Russian peasant world that could not possibly be part of the same universe that had created the brutal shaming world of prison. Dan couldn't understand how he had become the peasant boy Danilka, how he knew how the boy moved and breathed, how he could feel the soreness of Danilka's wrist when the old cobbler had freed it from the hole in the tree, how as he read of the journey through the fields and back to the village he could smell the scent of bird cherry, meadowsweet, and lilies-of-the-valley after the storm. He had reread it immediately, and realized that he had been wrong; that as the old man had crept into the deserted barn to make the sign of the cross over the sleeping orphans, Chekhov had indeed captured some of the brutality as well as the tenderness of the world. Dan had furtively torn the pages of the story out of the book—no one would know that they had ever been there; the book was old and that torn, no one would ever know—and he had guarded that story through his last few months in prison, kept it folded inside a tear in his mattress. That story had returned him to childhood, had made him shudder with a joy so intense it seemed almost erotic. Had he ever known such joy?

Dan had discovered that he had been mistaken, that books did not exist outside of the body and only in mind, but that words were breath, that they were experienced and understood through the inseparability of mind and body, that words were the water and reading was swimming. Just as he had in water, he could lose himself in reading: mind and body became one. He had taken the Chekhov story with him on release, and the pages remained folded in a tight square in the one gift Carlo had ever given him, an old vinyl pouch in which the older man had kept his tobacco and his drugs. The pouch now sat on a makeshift shelf Dan had constructed next to the mattress in his bedroom. That story was a song: in reading it he believed he was opening his lungs and singing.

He didn't know how to explain all of this to his mother, but at that moment, with the books tucked under his arm, he decided that when they were back in Melbourne he would show her his home, in which there was no television or radio, no stereo or computer, just books. And he would tell her that prison had taught him that books were all he needed, books were enough. They were music and light and sound to him—they were the world.

"I like reading," he answered simply, and held out his hand for the keys. "My turn to drive."

They hadn't driven far, listening to a live recording of Aretha Franklin backed by a gospel choir, when his mother lowered the volume. "It was Regan who was always the reader," she announced, suddenly. Her tone shifted. "Have you heard from her?" There was pleading in her voice.

"No," he said, and remembered with mortification his brother's scoffing words. "Have you?"

His mother didn't answer straightaway. She had her eyes closed, was swaying to the music. "She speaks to your father. He's visited her when he's been up north. We want her to go back to school, finish her VCE, but she won't hear of it."

The call and response of singer and congregation tumbled and rolled under his mother's words.

Her voice trembled on the edge of tears. "I feel like I failed her, Danny. I did what my mother did to me. I took my daughter for granted. I don't know why I did that."

His gaze didn't waver from the open road, the parched wheat-colored farmland. His mother turned up the volume. Franklin's ecstasy filled the car and Dan found that he could breathe out. It was safe again.

~~~

It was pitch-black night as they descended from the hills into Adelaide, only the weaving headlights breaking through the obstinate darkness. The descent had come abruptly, the drop sheer and frightening, the city's canopy of sparkling lights suddenly glimmering below. Dan was tired and had to snap to attention, fearful with every turn that he could lose control and send the car flying out into the night. Part of him wanted that flight, that release.

His mother had turned off the stereo; they were descending into silence.

"I'm scared, Danny," she said.

"Sorry, I'll slow down."

"No, not of your driving. I'm scared of going home."

Home. It surprised him that she would still use that word for this city. "Maybe Dad should have come with you instead?"

She shook her head vehemently. Dan was concentrating on the precarious twists and turns of the road but he sneaked a look across at her. No makeup, streaks of ash now in her once coal-black hair, which was tied back in a severe roll. She was wearing a corn-yellow cardigan over a white top, loose dark linen pants. No intricately embroidered stockings, no heels on her shoes. This was not the mother he knew, the woman who delighted in artifice, in elaborate dress, in exhilarating aromas. She had stripped herself down to a woman on the other side of middle age.

"Your dad came last time," she finally explained. "It was a disaster. Your *papou* was dying, he was so sick but he still found it in himself to rise from his deathbed and order your father and me out of the house." Again, she was shaking her head ferociously, as if by doing so she could shake her memories loose, untether them and toss them away. "He called me the most terrible names—it was awful. I thought your father was going to punch him."

She touched her son's wrist, the lightest touch, then put her hand back in her lap. "I really appreciate this, Danny. I need you here but I'm sorry to put you through this."

His neck hurt, he felt bone-weary from the driving and her words. A dull pain was thumping at the back of his head. He couldn't fail her, he must not fail her.

"You don't have to thank me, Mum. I'm glad I came."

〜〜〜

He had no sense of the city as they drove into it, his mother giving directions, but she ended up getting them lost, and they had to stop at a late-night service station to ask the way. At last they turned into a dark cul-de-sac and his mum told him to park outside a box-like dark-brick house with a tiny neat lawn. There was no fence; the yellowing grass came down to the footpath. Dan grabbed his backpack and his mother's suitcase from the boot and they walked up the drive and rang the doorbell. As they waited he was conscious of his mother's agitation, then there were footsteps approaching. The door was flung open by a plump young woman with lively, thickly lashed eyes, dyed-blond hair, and enormous gold-hooped earrings.

The woman peered crossly at Dan and his mother and then her face softened. "Hello, Aunt Stephanie," she said warmly. The soft purr of her voice, the self-conscious way she ushered them in, the quick kisses she gave his mother reminded Dan of a shy pet. "Hello," she added, turning to him and kissing him on both cheeks. "You must be Daniel. I'm your cousin Joanna."

The first few minutes were a rush as he followed his mother and cousin through the house, all plush carpets and richly patterned rugs, showy furnishings and endless photos on the walls. An enormous television dominated the lounge room. Two young boys were sitting on a white leather sofa, fighting over a gaming console. They stopped struggling as the adults entered, and looked up sheepishly; the youngest tried to hide the console behind his back. On the white leather armchair across from them sat a man in a black T-shirt, AC/DC printed on it in synthetic white Gothic lettering. He was wearing gray track pants; his feet were bare. He didn't get up to greet them, didn't meet their eyes.

"This is my brother, your cousin Dennis," said Joanna, and then pointed to the boys. "My eldest, Michael, and my baby, Paul."

Dan couldn't take in the names, forgot them as soon as he heard them. The two young boys couldn't hide their openmouthed astonishment at being introduced to him. The intensity of their examination of him disturbed him; it felt as if he were an animal on display, as if he and his mum were strange and alien beasts. But his mother didn't seem to notice or care as she swooped down on the boys, wrapped them in a tight embrace, and kissed them. They turned anxious eyes to their mother, and Dan caught Joanna's covert nod of permission. They returned their great-aunt's embrace. Dan's mother then turned to hug the large-framed man, who still hadn't risen from the armchair or looked their way. This disrespect made Dan want to lift him up by his shirtfront, this big-muscled wog jerk, all balloon biceps and puffed-up jock chest. But his mother didn't mind at all—she was affectionate with Dennis, caressing his face and messing his short spiky hair. The man relented a little, looking her way but not smiling, not really returning the hug.

"Do you remember me?" asked Dan's mother. "Do you remember your *thea* Steph?" Dan couldn't fathom why she was talking to the man as she would to a child.

They left the boys in the living room with Dennis, and went with Joanna into a small kitchen. The walls there were also plastered with photographs, but there were none of his mother, none of her as an adult or as a child, and none of Dan's family. Joanna asked if they would like coffee, and Dan's eyes didn't waver from his mum. He could sense how nervous she was, how unsettled she seemed being back in Adelaide. He wouldn't answer until she did. He had never felt such a strong urge to protect her. He stayed close to her, got her a chair to sit on, but stayed standing behind her, as though guarding her.

A car door slammed outside and his mother froze. Then there was the sound of a key in a lock and Joanna looked nervously to the hallway.

"Jo, the boys should be in bed." The voice was loud and throaty, so deep that for a moment Dan thought it was a man's voice, but then a woman appeared in the kitchen doorway. She was dressed simply in an oversized Crows footy jumper and navy pants. Her hair was damp, her skin flushed, as though she had just showered.

"Hello, Bettina, how are you?"

The woman ignored his mother. She stepped into the doorway of the living room and called out to the two young boys. They rushed to their grandmother and hugged her, shyly waved goodnight to Dan and his mother, and went to get ready for bed.

Her arms still crossed, Bettina came back into the kitchen and pointed to the digital clock on the wall. The bright scarlet letters read 10:43. "What kind of time is this to arrive?"

Dan's mother's voice was surprisingly calm. "I phoned Joanna and explained that we took off after lunch." She turned to smile at her niece. "I'm sorry, Jo, we didn't mean to put you out."

Jo shook her head, busy tamping down ground coffee into the

base of an espresso maker. "You're not putting me out at all. It's lovely to see you." Joanna turned to her mother. "Mum, don't make a scene, all right?"

Bettina said something in Greek and Dan could see that it had winded his mother, that her face had reddened and her hands were shaking. Dan wanted to punch the bitch, to feel his fist go through her teeth, through bone and meat. He wasn't going to count down to ten, he didn't want to let go of his rage.

"Of course," Bettina continued in English, "what else do we expect from Stephanie? It's always been about her. No one else matters to Stephanie."

"Don't you fucking dare speak about my mother like that."

Joanna's jaw dropped open, her eyes widened. Dan's mother recoiled as though his words had stung her. But not Bettina. Her hands now were on her large hips and she was nodding.

His mother said wearily, "Danny, please, be polite, this is your aunt Bettina."

The woman walked up to him, looked straight at him. He didn't want to be polite but he couldn't help respecting the fact that she didn't try to kiss him, pretend affection or familial feeling. This was his mother's oldest sister, only by a year or so, he remembered from his mother's stories, but he was pleased to see that she looked so much older than his mother. She was overweight, her body shapeless and unattractive, her face hard and unforgiving.

"Do you remember me?"

He shook his head. He recalled little from his first visit to Adelaide, except for a vivid memory of the wrathful old man who'd made his mother cry and who'd told him, "You are no grandchild of mine." He knew there had been other people there that day, but they were shades, ghosts in his memory.

"You look a bit like your cousin Dennis. You can tell you two are related."

It was the first softening in her, the first extension of warmth.

But Dan would not budge, would not smile. He remained standing guard for his mother.

Bettina turned to her daughter. "Are you just serving coffee? How about some food?"

"Mum," grizzled Joanna, rolling her eyes, "I've got some food warming up in the oven, I'm on to it."

Bettina finally took a seat and Dan sat down as well, making sure he stayed next to his mother.

The coffee came, and then the food. They'd only shared a packet of chips since Ararat, and he was hungry. Joanna's lemon-flavored potatoes and the grilled lamb straps marinated in rosemary and garlic were delicious. There was little conversation as Bettina and Joanna watched them eat, and Dan finished within minutes, wiping his plate clean with some pita bread.

This occasioned another smile from his aunt. "You even eat like your cousin Dennis."

Once Dan's mother had finished eating, Joanna asked after Dan's father, after Regan and Theo. It shocked him how quickly the talk switched to another language; he marveled at how easily Greek flowed from his mother's lips. He excused himself and went into the lounge room.

His cousin Dennis was still slouched in the leather armchair, watching the television, the volume low. Dennis didn't take his eyes off the television, but he shifted his weight and straightened himself up.

"What are you watching?" asked Dan.

He couldn't quite make out his cousin's reply. It was almost as if he were coughing out the words. They seemed disconnected from one another, as if each syllable took an effort to articulate. Was he retarded? wondered Dan.

"*Big . . . Big . . . Broth . . . Brother* is starting," Dennis finally managed to stutter.

There was a sudden clamor of shouting from the kitchen. Bettina was yelling and Dan's mother was screaming back at her. Dan leapt up from the sofa.

His aunt stormed into the room, tears streaming down her face. "Get up, Dennis," she shouted to her son. "Get up! We're going home."

The man's head was turned away from her. He hadn't budged.

"Come on, Dennis," she roared. "We're leaving!"

The man slowly rose from the armchair, eyes down.

Shaking, Bettina turned to Dan. Her eyes were red and she rubbed a hand across her nose. She tried to keep her voice steady but didn't quite manage it as she said, "I'm sorry, Daniel, but you shouldn't have come. Take your mother home, take her home tomorrow."

He brushed past her into the kitchen where his mother was weeping, her body racked with sobs. Joanna was bent down behind her, rubbing her arms, her neck.

"Is she ever going to forgive me, Jo? Is she ever going to let it all go?" His mother forced out the words between her sobs and gulps for air.

"Mum, what can I do? Do you want to go?"

His mother looked up at the sound of Dan's voice, grateful for his presence. She reached for his hand, and held it to her cheek, kissing it, and drenching it in her tears.

"Oh Christ, mate," she said, "I need a drink."

"Shh." Joanna put a finger to her lips. But the front door slammed; they heard the sound of a car's ignition. Bettina and Dennis had gone.

"Okay," said Joanna, no longer whispering, "now we can have a fucking drink."

～～～

His mother and cousin drank but Dan stayed sober. The peaty, heady aroma of the whiskey was enticing but he wanted his senses clear; he was tired from driving, from meeting these new people, he couldn't trust himself to drink. His mother was on her second glass when Joanna's husband, Spiro, arrived. He had round dimpled cheeks, an unkempt salt-and-pepper beard, gentle, shining eyes, and silver-streaked hair that fell around his collar. He and Dan's mother embraced warmly.

"How's work?" she asked him. "How is the restaurant doing?"

"It's okay, it's okay," Spiro answered nonchalantly, welcoming Dan with a tight, unembarrassed hug.

Dan responded to him immediately, as he had done to his cousin Joanna, but he couldn't wait for them to go to bed so it could be just him and his mother, just the two of them. He begrudged the man the whiskey he poured himself, the cigarette he rolled. Go to bed, go to fucking bed, repeated in Dan's head like a mantra.

"How was your mum tonight?" Spiro asked Joanna.

"She was Mum. She was everything you said she'd be."

Spiro winked. "Sorry, Steph, sorry, Dan. Was it awful?"

"It was no worse than it has ever been." Crestfallen, his mother turned to Dan. "I'm sorry, mate, that you had to see all that."

He shrugged. "It's all right." And it was. Now that Bettina had gone, his mother's anxiety had disappeared.

Spiro winked at him next. "Bloody Joeys, eh, Danny?"

Dan hated that they thought that was an excuse. "I don't get it," he snarled. "Why does she have to be so mean? What's her problem with Mum being christened once?"

The outburst of laughter that greeted his question surprised him. Joanna had to wipe the tears from her eyes. "Oh Danny," she finally managed to say, "don't ever use that word around my mum. Jehovahs don't get christened—that's what filthy heathens do. Your mum got *baptized,* she didn't get christened."

"Same difference, isn't it? So she got baptized." He spat out the word as if it were an obscenity. "So fucking what?"

The swearword worked. The laughter stopped.

Spiro threw back the last of his whiskey. "Come on, you," he said to his wife. "It's bedtime."

Then it was Dan and his mother alone. She poured herself another glass. This time Dan indicated that he wanted one as well.

He sat patiently, every now and then taking sips from his glass. His mother was quiet for the longest time. He didn't mind. He knew silence, he understood it. He waited, listening to the sounds of his cousin and her husband preparing for bed.

His mother had knocked back her drink and poured herself another. She sighed and took his hand across the table. "I know it's hard to understand all this, baby, but I kept it from the three of you because I wanted to protect my children from all this poisonous shit."

"I don't get it. Isn't Joanna a Jehovah's Witness? Isn't Spiro?"

"Your cousin Joanna is no longer a Joey—she left it a long time ago. But she never got baptized. That was my sin, Danny: I accepted God and then I renounced Him. Your aunt Bettina is making a great sacrifice even talking to me—even being in the same house as me." His mother tilted back her head and swallowed the last of her whiskey. "I'm damned, mate. I broke my promise to God. She couldn't forgive me even if she wanted to. For her, for my parents, I am exiled from them forever."

She indicated for him to refill her glass. He should have stopped her, he should have got her to bed. Her hand was still clasped tight around his, it was clammy, uncomfortable. He could feel her shame burning through her skin.

He wanted to tell her so much. About Carlo and prison, about what he knew of disgrace and shame, about what it took to emerge from out of the earth and be able to look up to the sky again. There was so much he wanted to tell her, but he was scared that he did not yet know how to. He needed the silence, he needed to learn how to use words, how to have faith in words again, so he could tell his truth without fumbling and without failing. But he couldn't, not yet. He had to trust the silence between them and trust her patience.

"I forgave my father," she said flatly, her face half in shadow, her profile severe and stark and old in the lamplight. "I forgave him before he died. But I can't find it in me to forgive my mother. I can't forgive her for staying silent, for never defending me, for being weak, for being so fucking weak. For never stopping him."

So Dan was not the first to fail her, to betray her.

"Don't ever trust the righteous, Dan, no matter how convincing their words may seem. You'll never be good enough, no matter how much you try. You'll never be perfect and they'll never forgive you for that."

She was looking down the well of her glass, then she took another long draw from it, spilling some liquid down her chin, onto her white top. Her next words were lost, she spoke them into the whiskey, the sounds unintelligible.

"What did you say, Mum?"

She held the glass away from her lip, and whispered like a child, "He scares me. Sometimes he scares me."

"Who?"

Her eyes were searching his. "Neal. Your father can be righteous—he frightens me when he's like that." She dropped his hand, put her hand over her mouth. "Oh, Danny, I'm sorry. I'm sorry."

"It's okay."

He rubbed his cold hand on his trouser leg, stretching his fingers to get the blood flowing again. He took the glass from her, ignoring the reproach in her eyes. "No more, Mum, you're exhausted and upset. You need to get some sleep."

She had closed her eyes. Had she fallen asleep?

He first mouthed, then whispered the words: "I understand."

Her eyes flashed open. The look she gave him was pure gratitude.

He put his mother to bed, then located the room in which he

was to sleep. There was a *Finding Nemo* mobile hanging from the ceiling, there were posters of Port Adelaide footballers on the wall. He stripped off and slid into the single bed. For a long time he lay there, his ears straining, trying to decipher the sounds of the unfamiliar house. There was a low rumble of traffic somewhere beyond the suburb, the scratching of branches against windows and beams. The house didn't breathe, it didn't welcome him—it evaded him. He switched on the bedside light, a toy model of Hogwarts, and grabbed the Graham Greene from his backpack. The first light was peeking through the slats of the blinds when he finished the novel, the first light touched his face as he fell asleep.

Spiro drove them to the hospital. Dan sat in the front passenger seat, the window slightly lowered. The air was crisp; the colors of Adelaide were the cyan of the clear sky, the steely bark on the eucalyptus trees, the weathered sandstone of the buildings. He had no memory of the city, yet the suburbs all seemed familiar, as did the roads, the parks, the office buildings; they all reminded him of the estates and neighborhoods and malls of Melbourne. Maybe all cities were kin, he mused, maybe all cities shared the same DNA.

They parked and Spiro led them through reception, to the lifts and up to the second floor where they walked past a common room, the blinds raised to let in the sunlight. In the room there sat a circle of old people, a few of them in wheelchairs, a few slumped over in their seats. Past the nurses' station, they walked through an empty dining room in which a small radio innocuously bleated out olden-days cheap disco music. They turned down a corridor and Joanna knocked on the door numbered eighteen.

"Yes?" It was Bettina's voice, gravelly, commanding.

Spiro opened the door and the family filed in. Dan and his mother were the last to enter, his hand on her shoulder.

Bettina was sitting by the head of the old woman's bed; she didn't acknowledge any of them, not even her daughter. His *giagia* was lying there, her mouth and eyes open in her skull-like head, but her eyes were unseeing—she was close to being a corpse. It nauseated him to look at her.

Two men in the room were introduced to him as his uncles; their wives were visiting as well. They were his mother's brothers, his mother's sisters-in-law, but they would not look at her. They nodded to Dan, said hello, but he made no attempt to be friendly. He shook the men's hands because he knew that to do otherwise would have distressed his mother, but he held each hand limply, as they did his.

Dennis was sitting in a chair in the opposite corner, still wearing his AC/DC T-shirt, his head down as he picked at the fabric on the chair's arm. Dan moved closer to his cousin, noticing the thick brush of hair covering the back of his neck, so dense it was like a coat of fur, disappearing into the T-shirt.

As if they were an audience at a play awaiting the opening scene, everyone had formed a half circle around the end of the bed. His mother took a place on the opposite side of the bed to her unsmiling sister. She bent down and kissed the old woman's sunken cheek. "Hi, Mum, how are you?"

The old woman stared blankly. A catheter was in the raised blue vein above her wrist, clear fluid dripping into her from the bag above the bed.

"She doesn't know who you are."

Dan's mother ignored Bettina and spoke quietly in Greek to the old woman, who didn't show even a flicker of recognition. "Come here, Danny," said his mother, beckoning, "come and say hello to your *giagia*."

There was a slow steady clicking from the heater; the room was overheated and smelled overpoweringly of antiseptic. He walked over to the bed and stood beside his mother.

"Mamá, this is Danny. This is your grandson."

Now that he was looking down at her, Dan could see that the old woman's eyes were glazed over, a murky film of silver veiling each pupil. Her breathing was erratic, terribly shallow. He couldn't believe how delicate her skin was, as if it were made of the flimsiest tissue; it looked as though it would tear at the slightest touch. The old woman's hair had fallen away, she had no eyebrows. There was no muscle on her, no flesh; just the insubstantial skin and the contours of the bones beneath. He was acutely aware of both the lightness of her body and the dead weight of the fear in the room. His mother was sobbing. Dan looked down at the extinguishing life and felt perhaps a little pity, nothing more.

Bettina's gruff voice said something in Greek. Then she shrugged and looked across at Dan. "Don't be offended. She doesn't recognize any of us anymore."

"I'm *not* offended." It made him feel more warmly toward his aunt, even though she'd been horrible to his mother, despite her lack of forgiveness. They must have thought that he was part of them, must have even *wanted* him to be part of who they were. But surrounded by his cousins and aunts and uncles, standing by his grandmother's bed, he knew he would never be part of what they were. He thought of his granddad's musical Glasgow accent, his nan's fierce, protective love. He was them: they were alive, they were flesh and muscle and blood, they were real memory and history. They were love. He felt as much for this old Greek woman as he did for the sad circle of old people in the common room: useless pity, nothing more.

Dennis got out of his chair and Bettina snapped her head around. "Where are you going?"

Dan could just make out the word, the three syllables of *cigarette* extended and twisted into one tortuous moan.

"Make sure you come straight back here," Bettina said. "You know how to get back here? Room eighteen?"

Dennis seemed to be looking past all of them to something high on the wall above Dan's head, invisible to everyone else but obvious and fascinating to him.

Dan saw his opportunity to flee. He nodded over to his cousin. "Hey, mate, I'll come out with you."

~~~~~

"*Sm-smoke?*"

Dan had left his jacket behind in the room, and the wind was brisk, glacial, but he didn't care. It felt so good to be outside, away from the artificial heat of the hospital room, the disapproving strangers.

His cousin was a full foot taller than he was, and was all muscle, thick-necked and broad-backed. Dennis didn't seem to feel the cold as the rising wind whipped around them, though Dan could see a spray of goose pimples on his forearm. Dennis spoke again.

"Pardon? Could you say that again, please?" Dan asked.

It was the longest sentence he had yet heard Dennis utter but he had understood none of it. Dennis finished his cigarette and put the butt out under the sole of his sneaker. He still seemed to be looking at something invisible playing out above Dan's head.

"*Sho, sho. Yar. Ma Ma Ma. Cuz. Een?*"

So you're my cousin? "Yeah, that's right."

"*And and yar yar fru fru frumma Mel Mel Mel. Burn?*"

Dan wanted to finish the sentence for him. He had to stop himself. "Yeah, you ever been there?"

For the first time, his cousin looked at him. The man's eyes were limpid and deep-set, the gray of wet granite; his nose had been broken in the past and there was a small scar on his left temple that disappeared into the dark wave of his hair.

"*Ya.*" Dennis breathed wetly, preparing for the struggle to form the next words. "*I dad ant like. Mel Ba Barn. It waz. It. It waz too big-ah!*"

"I guess it is a big city."

"*Ya.*"

"Should we go back in? It's freezing out here."

Dennis didn't respond. He was looking away again, as if he hadn't heard Dan, as if Dan wasn't even there. "*Ya ya. She—she is. Is. Dha-dha-dha-dha-ng.*" His words were a blur of hard consonants and slithering sibilants that made no sense to Dan.

"Sorry, mate, I didn't get that."

Dennis angrily wiped spit from the sides of his mouth. He looked flushed, embarrassed, as though he were furious at Dan. "*I-I wi-wish sh-sh-she wouwad. Wad. Wad. Wad dj dj djusshtd die.*"

Dan was shocked at the cruelty of his words but then he saw that his cousin's eyes had watered, he was trying hard not to cry. He wondered how long he had been coming to the hospital, watching the old woman slowly disappear. Watching her death. He hadn't thought of his *giagia* as anything but a stranger. But for Dennis she would have been a real grandmother, she would have looked after him, changed his nappies, watched him grow, told him her stories: she would have loved him. And he would have loved her.

"I'm really sorry, mate."

"*I-I-I hate hate this ho ho hos pi. Tal.*" It was said so vehemently that a spray of spit struck Dan's cheek. "*I-I fuck fucken hate. It.*"

I'd fucking hate it too, thought Dan. I'd hate to be here every day, having to watch this old woman whose soul has already left, who's nothing but skin and bone. What was happening to her wasn't life. All of that had finished.

"Dennis," Dan said, "why don't you and I just go and hang out? Why don't we just get the fuck out of here?"

〰〰〰

His mother and his aunt had not moved from their positions on either side of the dying woman. They were both visibly surprised at Dan's suggestion that he should drive his cousin home. For a moment Dan hesitated. His mother looked lost and fragile and he knew he was abandoning her, but the heat and the smell and the whisperings in a language he didn't understand, all of it was overwhelming, and when his aunt Bettina handed him her keys he felt nothing but relief.

"Come on, Dennis," he said brightly, then blushed at his transparency. But his mother winked at him and he knew it would be all right. He kissed her goodbye, and then looked down at the old woman on the bed, at her vacant eyes, and he knew his cousins and uncles and aunts would be expecting him to kiss his grandmother. But he couldn't bring himself to touch her, he thought it would be like kissing death.

As he and Dennis were leaving, his aunt said, "Don't let Dennis drive."

So Dennis could drive. Or he must have known how to at some stage.

In the car his cousin was cheerful; not that he said much, just pointed to which streets Dan should turn into, but he had a big grin on his face as he looked out to the clear blue sky above them. They skirted the border of a giant park on the edge of the city. The trees had started to shed their leaves, their mottled blue-gray branches spiking and twisting high into the sky.

Bettina's house was a small weatherboard cottage, with an overgrown front yard and a sleek gray cat asleep on the porch. The cat opened one eye as the men walked past it, then stretched out on its back purring as Dennis tickled its belly.

The front part of the house was dark, the corridor tiny, but at the other end a renovation had opened up the kitchen to make room for a long dining table; large windows looked out to a small, immaculately neat courtyard. Dennis headed straight for the fridge and took out a bottle of Diet Coke and poured a glass for both of them. There were photographs everywhere of the family, of Dennis and his mother, of Dennis with his grandmother and grandfather, and Dan recognized a young, slim Joanna. As in Jo's house, there were no photographs of Dan's mother, nor any of their family. There also seemed to be none

of Dennis's father, whoever he might have been. There was so much
Dan didn't know about his cousin. Dennis was twisting his solid body
on the revolving seat of a high stool, still grinning, still looking up,
through the tiny skylight in the ceiling up to the sky. He suddenly
stopped twirling.

"*Do-do-do ya wanna wanna see. Do do ya wanna see ma ma
rumm?*"

〰〰〰

Dan's cousin slept on a single bed tucked into the far corner of his
room. It looked like a gym: there were barbells and weights scattered
around, an expensive-looking steel rowing machine, a lifting bench
placed perpendicular to a full-length mirror. Posters of bodybuilders,
male and female, adorned the wall. There were only two photographs,
in simple black frames, both hanging above the bed. In one a teenage Dennis, dressed in a dark suit, had one arm around his mother
and the other around his sister. In the second photograph, Dennis
was older, wearing leathers and holding a helmet, standing next to a
motorcycle. A young dark-skinned woman held his hand, and in the
other she gripped a motorbike helmet. Dan maneuvered himself carefully over the barbells to look more closely at the photograph of Dennis and the girl next to the motorcycle.

Dennis had sat himself on the rower, idly shifting his weight back
and forth. "*Ma Ma Mama. She ha ha hate hates. Ha hates tha tha pho
pho phot. To. Pho. To. Graph.*" Dennis was looking high up above
himself, at the world beyond the ceiling, a grin on his face. His syllables still struggled to escape but he no longer seemed encumbered
or frustrated by them. "*Tha tha that. That was me. Be be four. Be.
Four that ha. Tha. Ax. Ax. Axi. Dent.*"

Dan turned back to the photograph, to the attractive young couple at the end of their teens.

"Handsome, wasn't I?"

Dan realized he was starting to hear between the spaces of his cousin's words, that he could separate the sounds from the spit that pooled in Dennis's mouth as he strained to enunciate.

"You were all right," Dan teased, and pointed to the young woman in the photo. "But she's the really pretty one. What's her name?"

Dennis's only response was to throw himself furiously into working the rowing machine. Dan sat on the bed and watched the man row. Within minutes Dennis was dripping with sweat; it ran down his brow and the back of his neck and plastered his hair to his skin. Dan waited for him to finish but Dennis kept pulling at the bar, pounding backward and forward, the gears of the rower clanking and spinning, the mechanism giving a low whistle with every stroke. Sweat had soaked through the T-shirt which clung to his powerful torso. And all the while Dennis looked up, as if urging his body to take flight, thought Dan, as if wishing it could burst through the plaster and beams and slate and break free into the sky. There was a clanking sound as Dennis's foot slipped off the pedal.

"Fucking bullshit!"

The wheel was still spinning manically. Dennis reached across and grabbed it, bringing it to a sudden halt.

"Her name is Christine. She was my girlfriend." There was a spitting and rumbling, a battle in his larynx before Dennis could get the sentence out.

"Did something happen to her in the accident?"

Dennis shuddered. "No, God no. She just left." And then he turned and faced his cousin. "I guess she got tired of hanging around a retard."

Dan blinked, at the force of the word, the way Dennis spat it out. "Do you miss her?"

Dennis's eyes were wandering again. "Not as much as I miss my fucking motorbike."

A choking sound came from Dennis's lips that at first alarmed Dan. He was choking and gurgling; there was a rivulet of dribble coming from one side of his mouth. But Dennis's eyes were dancing. He was laughing.

Dan leapt to his feet, grabbed the car keys, and flung them at Dennis, who caught them in a graceful swipe.

"Come on, cuz," said Dan. "Let's go for a drive."

Cuz. He liked the sound of the word as it fell from his lips.

~~~~

The two men were playing Mortal Kombat on the PlayStation when Bettina got home. Dan could see that she was unnerved to see the two men comfortably slouched on the sofa together, but she was also pleased. Dan handed his cousin the console and followed Bettina into the kitchen to give her the car keys.

"We went for a drive. Dennis showed me West Beach."

"It's his favorite place in Adelaide," she said. "He's always loved the water." She was standing in front of the open pantry, examining rows of cans. She pulled out a can of tuna and a packet of dry pasta. "You want some lunch?"

"No, thank you. I should eat with Mum."

Bettina grunted. He couldn't tell if she was disappointed or relieved by his response.

"I let Dennis drive part of the way to the beach."

She was scowling as she bore down on him and tossed the tin and pasta onto the bench. She's frightening, thought Dan. No wonder his mum was so scared of her, she was ferocious.

"What did I say to you? Do you know what could have happened? How dare you!"

Dan frantically searched for the words to explain that Dennis had only driven down a deserted dirt road behind the beach; that there were no other cars, that Dennis was a good driver. But the words eluded him, though he doubted they would have made any difference to this vengeful, angry woman. He was his mother's son—he could tell from the rage sparking from her eyes that she was prepared to loathe him as much as she hated her own sister.

"Mamá, I'm all right, it was safe. It was only for a few minutes on a quiet road. I had fun, I wanted to do it. Don't blame Danny for any of it."

In the time it took for Dennis to shape his words, both Dan's fear and his aunt's anger had dissipated. Dennis looked exhausted from the effort of making his speech.

His mother's tone softened. "I'm going to drive Danny to Jo's place. You want to come along for the drive?"

Dennis's gaze didn't shift from the ceiling. Dan had to fight the urge to look up.

"You want to hang out tomorrow?"

Dan didn't hesitate. "Yeah, yeah. That'd be good."

Dennis cocked his head in his mother's direction. "Nah, I'll stay and play some more on the PlayStation."

Dan patted his back pocket, took out his phone. "What's your number, mate?"

Dennis began to recite the number. As Dan started punching in the digits, Bettina was repeating each numeral.

"It's okay, Mamá, Danny understands me."

Bettina was silent as Dan saved his cousin's number. He typed a quick text and sent it. A tinny treble of techno rang from Dennis's pocket.

"All good."

All good.

Bettina didn't say much until they were nearly at Joanna and Spiro's house. It was then she blurted out, "Have you worked with disabled people, Danny?"

He shook his head.

"You're really good with your cousin. You know how to listen and you have patience. Thank you for spending time with him today. He really enjoyed it."

You don't have to thank me, he wished he could say. And stop treating him like a baby. He doesn't want that, he can't stand how you treat him like a child not a man. But he couldn't figure out how to say that without hurting her. And he was confused: his family loyalty meant he should see her as an enemy—he wouldn't and couldn't forgive the hurt she'd caused his mother—but he didn't want to be part of that enmity. *You're really good with your cousin.* He was grateful for those words. It was a long time since anyone had said that he was good at anything. That he was good *for* anything.

His mother was alone in the house, in the kitchen. Two bags of shopping were on the bench; she was slicing chicken breasts. She was still not wearing makeup, in a drab dark top and shapeless black slacks. She didn't look like his mother—Dan thought he could see Bettina in her, see the shape of Dennis's mouth in hers.

"I'm so glad to see you," she said. "I'm preparing something for dinner tonight, to thank Jo for having us. How did it go with Dennis?"

"Great. I really like him."

"He seems like a nice man."

Dan sat down. "What happened to him?"

"He had a motorbike accident when he was nineteen. He hadn't long had his bike. They thought he was going to die, he was in a coma for four months or so." His mother shook her head. "It was terrible—it must have been awful for Bettina."

"When did you find out about it?"

"Not till a few years ago." His mother's smile was wry and resigned. "In case you haven't noticed, your aunt and I don't talk very much."

"What about his dad?"

"He died a long time ago. Cancer—and from what I know, which is not much, it was a slow, horrible death. She's suffered a lot, your aunt."

"She doesn't have to be such a bitch to you."

His mother shrugged, wiped her hands on an apron, and started bashing a stem of lemongrass. It was clear she didn't want to talk about it, didn't want to think about Bettina.

Dan's phone vibrated. He had a new message, from Dennis: HOPE MY MUM DIDN'T BREAK YOUR BALLS. Dan texted back: ALL COOL, and returned the phone to his pocket.

"Do you want to come with me to the hospital this afternoon?"

Dan couldn't believe they had to return to the hospital. His grandmother was a vegetable. She'd never know if they were there or not. "If you want."

"Thank you so much for all of this, baby." His mother reached into a shopping bag and pulled out a small plastic bag of chilies, and started slicing one.

"I hope Jo and Spiro like Asian food," she said. "I can't find a bloody wok in the house."

〜〜〜

It wasn't that the food was Asian that was a problem for Joanna and Spiro, it was that it contained meat. They arrived back in the mid-afternoon, just as Dan and his mother were getting ready to go back to the hospital.

"Jo," Dan's mother said cheerfully, "I've cooked us a meal, it's in the saucepan. We can heat it up tonight."

Biting the corner of her bottom lip, Joanna said something in Greek.

Dan's mother's face fell. "Oh," she said simply, "I forgot."

"What's the problem?"

Joanna scratched her ear, obviously embarrassed. "It's our Easter next week and Spiro and I are fasting: we can't have meat."

Dan looked at his mother. "Is that some kind of weird Jehovah's Witness thing?"

Spiro burst out laughing. "No, mate, no! It's an Orthodox thing—
your cousin and I are both Orthodox and our Easter is next week,
not this one."

"Right." Dan marched to the stove, scooped the food onto two
plates, and sat at the table, beckoning his mother over. "We're eating," he announced. "I haven't had lunch, I'm famished."

He tore into the food, relishing every bite, every explosion of spice
in his mouth. He chewed slowly, extracting every possible flavor and
pleasure from it. He ate with a gusto and loyalty that declared him
his mother's son.

~~~

It was just Dan and his mum in the hospital room—himself and his
mother and his dying grandmother. His mother hadn't sat down; she
was standing at the head of the bed, holding the old woman's limp,
bird-boned hand.

Dan sat on the chair, flicking through a *Woman's Day*, faces he
didn't recognize, faces that didn't exist when there was no television. At one point a nurse came in, wheeling a steel trolley, all good
cheer. In a mellifluous Pacific accent she asked if Antonia was okay
as she stripped back the sheet and carefully disengaged and emptied
the catheter bag. "Does Antonia need anything?" she asked. Antonia
was a vegetable, Dan thought spitefully, Antonia was just a lump
of meat. But he smiled at the nurse, watching her buttocks swing
beneath the thick white fabric of her uniform as she wheeled the trolley back out of the room.

Sometimes his mother would say something in her first language.
It did sound like an old language, Dan thought, it sounded much
more ancient than English.

At eight o'clock he was roused by a cough. The nurse had popped
her head around the door to say apologetically that visiting hours
were over. Dan leapt to his feet but his mother wouldn't move,

wouldn't let go of his grandmother's hand. The nurse came up to her and gently patted her arm. "Time to go, sweetheart," she said softly. "You can see her tomorrow."

〜〜〜

"Oh, God, I don't want to go back to Jo and Spiro's. I don't want to see any of my frigging family, even the good ones. I just want to be with you." His mother had the key in the ignition, her hand was on the handbrake.

"We don't have to," he said.

Dan knew what his mother wanted. Her need was flowing through her blood, and her blood and her need were flowing through him. They both wanted the same thing.

"Do you want to go for a drink?"

It began as a small curl at the edge of her lips, then a crease, a wrinkle, that reached her shining eyes; the smile flooded across his mother's face and found its way to his.

〜〜〜

"I reckon Spiro really wanted some of that stir-fry."

His mother collapsed into giggles. "Poor guy, he's a bit of a doormat, isn't he? That's the problem—Greek men either have to go completely macho on their wives or they're pussy-whipped. Whatever you do, Danny, don't get involved with a Greek woman. They're bitches."

Dan was looking at an older man sitting at the bar, short spiky hair bleached by the sun, brown weathered skin, and a farmer's tan that finished at the neck and sleeves. He was scowling, but not at anyone or anything. He was drunk already, thought Dan, a few more drinks and he'd be looking for a fight. He was nothing like Dennis—he was short, unfit, with a paunch and flabby arms—but something about the way he was sitting, the way he was looking out into the distance, reminded Dan of his cousin.

His mother stirred her gin and tonic with the straw. "I can't bear another night in this city," she said. "It's so oppressive."

Dan was drinking a vodka and tonic. It was odorless, but also tasteless: a concentrate of lemon pulp had settled at the bottom of the glass. He'd hardly sipped from it. His mother had nearly finished hers.

"Driving here I was convinced that I was going to stay until she died, that I was going to show her, show them all, that I was a good daughter. I was going to tell you to take the car and drive back to Melbourne, leave me here to look after her. I was going to stay until she died." She made a gesture of frustration. "But I don't want to do that anymore. I want to go home, I want to be in my own house, I want to kiss and make love to your father, I want to hug Theo, I want to put on old records and put on makeup and dress up and dance to great music and I want to laugh. I want to dance and laugh and fuck."

She shook her head. "There was never music in my parents' house, there was no laughter. No wonder I wanted to run away first chance I got. No fucking wonder."

It was her third gin and tonic. She was getting morose, thought Dan.

But the next moment, she brightened. "I still remember the first night I ever danced. There was a girl at the salon where I was an apprentice, she was a dancer—every Friday night she'd take a dance class in a little studio on Rundle Mall. She kept inviting me and I kept declining, but then this one afternoon after work, I said I'd go." His mother was tapping the table. "Now what was her name?" She banged her glass hard on the table. "Renee! That's right, her name was Renee. Well, she took me dancing and it was the most wonderful thing I'd ever experienced. The music, the steps, the dresses, the joy on people's faces—I had never witnessed such joy. I danced there that Friday and I went the Friday after and the Friday after that. My father followed me that third Friday and dragged me home, literally pulling me by the hair all the way through the city and across the park to Mile End. And he hit me and we had the most massive fight and I told them then that I was never going back to a meeting, I was never ever going back witnessing. I told them that God wasn't in their stern bloody Kingdom Hall, I said that God was in music and in dancing. I told them I didn't believe in their God anymore. They threw me out that night. I left with one small suitcase and a pair of boots under my arms."

The memory made her falter, and melancholy returned to her face. "The funny thing is that it was what my father always used to say to me: 'You Aussie kids don't know how lucky you are. Look at what you have, all you have. Me, me, I came to this country with a suitcase and pair of shoes in my hands. That's all.'" Her eyes were wet as she turned her gaze to Dan. "Well, fuck him. I know what that's like. I learned exactly what that's like."

Dan rubbed at his face, almost scratching at it. He couldn't quite understand what his mother was saying, thought he must be missing something. "And they never wanted to see you again? Just because you didn't believe in God?"

His mother sighed. "Maybe that was an excuse, maybe they were already looking for a reason to chuck me out. Your dad thinks that was what happened, reckons I must have been too loudmouthed for them, too opinionated, too independent. I was already challenging their stupid rules. By the time I met your dad I was a couple of years out of home and working in that pub in Broken Hill. I had toughened up, mate, I had to."

His mum looked around the pub, as if she'd only just realized there were others around them, that other lives were being lived. "Your father doesn't get religious faith. He doesn't understand it. My old man, my mum, I can call them lots and lots of things, but hypocrites about their faith they weren't. Nah, they truly believed I was banished from them."

She finished her drink and looked wistfully at the empty glass. "One more? Is that okay?"

"Sure. I'll get it," he said. He went to the bar and ordered her another gin but also got her a big glass of water.

His mother unleashed a further torrent of words as soon as he sat down. "What I hate is, it's like I still want to prove to them all that I am a good person—that I'm not evil. That was what the fantasy of staying by her bedside till she died was all about. It wasn't about her, it was about proving something to Bettina and to my dickhead brothers. But what for? They can't forgive me, they have to be right with God. And why should I care? I know my kids are beautiful, I know my husband is wonderful, I know, I know my life is good. What do I want to prove?"

And Dan suddenly understood: They know I've been in gaol, they know what I did. That's why she wanted me here—not Regan or Theo—to prove to them that *I* am a good person, to show them that *I* am not evil.

"I don't give a fuck what they think. They're not my family."

His mother shrank away and he regretted the severity of his words. He hadn't meant to be that harsh, he just wanted her to know that, in this alien town, all that mattered was her and him, none of the others. Words, he thought, they betray you. Again, he thought about Dennis, how the mangled sounds, the agonized syllables, didn't matter. Dennis said what he meant, he had to—it took too much energy to talk in circles. Dennis was direct.

"Mum," he said, grabbing his mobile, "I'm just off to the loo."

He texted Dennis: MUM AND I ARE AT THE TORRENS ARMS. YOU WANT TO JOIN US? He sent it off, waited. Dan thought there was no way Dennis could join them: His mother treated him like a baby, she wouldn't let him out. How would he get there? Was he even allowed to drink? Just as he pushed open the toilet door he felt the phone throb in his pocket.

"Dennis is joining us," he said, as he slid into the booth.

"Really?" Then, suspiciously: "On his own?"

"I think so."

"Good, he's a nice kid."

He's a man. He's an adult. "He's my age, isn't he?"

"Two years older," his mother answered. She looked around the pub, at the despondent man at the bar, at the bored waitress tapping her cigarette packet in her apron pocket, at the three burly red-faced men shouting and joking in a corner, their table a forest of empty glasses. She screwed up her nose, as if she found it all distasteful. "I didn't even know he was born until much later. After I had you. I rang home to tell them that they had a grandchild. I got my old man. You know what he said? He said I already have a grandson, I don't want yours. I have Bettina's son, I have Dionysus."

Then she surprised him by throwing back her head and cackling and convulsing with laughter. "God, he was a tough old bastard," she said as she wiped the tears from her eyes. "You got to hand it to him—the last of the old patriarchs." She raised her glass. "Let's drink to that. Let's drink to the passing of the old guard. We'll never see the like of pricks like him again."

She sculled the drink, slammed the glass on the table, swaying as she rose from her chair. "If Dennis is coming, we should get another."

Dan grabbed her hand and pointed to the glass of water. "First, drink that," he ordered.

He could tell that she was surprised, but she sat back down and obediently drank from the glass.

"What did *giagia* say, when you told her about me?"

"I didn't speak to her, the old prick wouldn't let me. But a few weeks later I got this card, some stupid cheap Hallmark card of a stork with a blue balloon in its mouth. There wasn't even a note in it—she hardly had any schooling, I know that, but not even my name—just this dumb card with fifty dollars inside it." She cheekily pointed at him. "It kept you in nappies for a month. That's my mother, that's what she was like." Then she gently corrected herself, "What she *is* like."

The shriveled carcass, the mask-like face, the empty eyes. He had no sense of who this woman had been. Just the meat of her dying body and the shade of her in his memory, a ghost already, overshadowed by the untamed life force of her husband.

"What *was* she like, Mum?"

He didn't think she would answer. Time passed as though his mother had disappeared deep inside herself, had forgotten he was there.

"Frightened," she finally said. "She was scared, always scared. She was always running after us, telling us to be quiet, to not upset the old man. She didn't have any courage." Her tone was matter-of-fact. He was taken aback by how unaffected she sounded. "She was a scared mother hen, that's my image of her. I never saw her smile at home, only when we were witnessing. She used to love that, getting up on Sunday mornings, putting on our witnessing clothes, taking me along to speak for her. That's the only time I saw her happy."

Dan wanted more. None of this filled in the gaps, added blood and life and motion to the meat and bone and skin lying on that hospital bed.

"You know," he ventured, "maybe she was braver than you think. She migrated, didn't she? I mean, you know, she took that risk."

His mother had started shaking her head before he'd even finished. "No, Danny. Not even then. Her brother, my *theo* Arthur, sponsored her to come out. They had no money to marry her off in Greece so he brought her out here. Even that wasn't a choice." Her voice became animated. "It's that passivity I can't stand—it was her passivity that made me angrier at her than I ever was with Dad. Fuck!"

Her outburst startled Dan.

"Fuck fuck fuck fuck fuck. It was a wasted life, Danny. She just wasted her life in fear."

Forgive her, thought Dan, just go to her bed tomorrow and whisper it to her. He imagined forgiveness was like flying, that it made you soar. He imagined that it looked like an eagle, a silver bolt in the sky, that it was pure light.

"Mate, I've made a decision."

"You're drunk," he reminded her. "You might not be in the best state for decisions."

But his mother dismissed him with a wave of her hand. "No, I'm bloody well not. Listen. We're going to head off tomorrow, go back to Melbourne. And I'm going to drop you off at home—I really want to see your place, baby, it's not right that I don't know your place." She was slurring her words but her tone was calm, measured. "And then I'm going to go home, to be with your dad and with Theo. And after I tell them both how much I love them I am going to take my box of music and drive up the coast to see my daughter. I shouldn't be here, Danny, I should be with Regan, I should find out how she is, what she needs to say to me—the good and the bad. I don't know what she wants, what she wants to do with her life. I don't know who she is. I should know that, I should, I should."

What do I want to do with my life? He had been fleeing from that question. He hadn't gone up north, he hadn't left Melbourne, but he'd been running from that question nonetheless. *What could he do? What was he good for?*

He took his mother's hand. "Sounds like a fucking good plan."

His mother was looking over his shoulder; she slipped her hand out of his and waved.

Dennis was standing by the entrance. Dan had imagined he'd be in his usual Acca Dacca T-shirt, track pants, and sneakers. But his cousin was wearing an ironed black shirt, dark jeans, and shiny black loafers.

Dennis smiled at them both and sat next to Dan.

"My shout," said Dan's mother. "What are you having, Dennis?"

"A pot of beer."

Dan stopped himself from translating. His mother would work it out.

"How'd you get here?"

"My mum dropped me off."

Dan's mother put her hands to her mouth. "Oh, I'm sorry, Dennis, she wouldn't like you coming to a pub."

"It's okay, Thea Stephanie, I wanted to come, I told her I wanted to come."

〜〜〜

Dan's mother had only one more drink before he told her they were going to drive her home. Everything was dark at Joanna and Spiro's, everyone was asleep.

"I'll take Dennis home," Dan told his mother. "I won't be long."

In the car he turned to his cousin. "Let's go back to West Beach—you wanna do that?"

Dennis nodded enthusiastically. Then, just as Dan was about to turn on the ignition, his cousin said, "Tell me something. Do you prefer Danny or Dan?"

"Dan."

Dennis asking that question made him seem less like family and more like a friend.

〜〜〜

At West Beach, the waves thundered, the moon had disappeared behind dense cloud; the sea was all black and gray heaving shadow. They sat side by side, listening to the boom of the surf.

"I miss girls," Dennis said suddenly, the words tumbling out to the rhythm of the waves crashing on the sand. "It's been so long, so long since I had a fuck. I miss girls. I miss their kisses, their tits, the taste of their pussies." Dennis was looking up at the dome of the nocturnal sky, his thoughts seemingly far away, but Dan could sense the closeness between them; the communication felt like the warmest touch. "Do you know what I mean?"

And Dan, thinking his heart would stop, announced to the ocean the way that Dennis called to the sky: "Yeah, mate, I do know. It's been too long since I had a fuck too. But I miss guys, Dennis, I miss their balls, I miss their arms around me, I miss the feel of their cocks pressing against mine."

Even with the pounding of the sea, all was silence. They sat side by side, watching the surf recede and return.

"Come on," said Dennis. "Let's go for a swim."

Dan didn't tell him that he couldn't, that he wouldn't swim. "No, I'll watch you," and he watched Dennis strip to his jocks and go splashing into the waves.

When Dennis came back up the beach, he used his singlet to dry his legs.

"Come on," said Dan, "let's get going."

Dennis was looking up at the stars, shaking his head. "I know a place in Richmond, I reckon it's still there. Mostly girls but I hear they've always got a couple of guys working there if you're into that."

And then Dennis was looking straight at him, his eyes gleaming, a sardonic trembling on his lips. Dan, uncomprehending, stared back.

"Get up, you dumb poofter. We're going to get laid."

〜〜〜

As Dan dropped Dennis at home, he said quietly, "Mate, I have to go home. We're heading back to Melbourne in the morning."

Dennis made no answer. But before getting out he leaned over and embraced Dan, folding him in tight, squeezing him. It was a forceful hold; it was all the words they needed. When they finally pulled apart, Dan's face was damp with his cousin's sweat.

〜〜〜

Dan and his mother stopped at the hospital before they headed home. The Samoan nurse was there. Dan noticed the tag on her uniform: her name was Naomi. She was washing his grandmother's arms.

"Can I do that?"

Naomi gave him the sponge. Dan took the old woman's hand, hardly believing how light it was, like a twig that had fallen from a tree. Carefully he washed her right arm, cleaning around her armpits and shoulders; he squeezed the sponge, and returned to gently wiping his grandmother's neck.

"He's got good hands," the nurse said to Dan's mother, who was weeping. Dan squeezed the sponge again over the kidney dish and looked expectantly at Naomi.

"It's okay, honey," she said softly, taking the sponge. "I can do the rest."

It had felt good to wash his grandmother, it had somehow felt right. But when he kissed the papery skin for the last time he still felt nothing. For there was nothing there.

His phone buzzed as he and his mother were leaving the hospital. It was a message from Dennis. DRIVE SAFE. YOU KNOW I MEAN IT! D. It made him smile.

〜〜〜

In Dimboola they stopped for coffee and sandwiches. His mother ran across the road to the newsagent to get the paper. Dan could see that she was crying as she came out of the shop.

"What is it?" he asked, thinking it had to be something about Iraq, something to do with what the Yanks and the Poms had done in Iraq. But it wasn't.

"Nina Simone has died," his mother said shakily. "I know it's silly, but I just burst out crying in the shop when I read it. You know how much I adore Nina Simone."

Back in the car, his mother searched through the glove box, CDs and pens and paper tumbling out and around her feet. She found the CD, she turned the volume up loud. All the way to Melbourne they sang along to "Mississippi Goddam," "Feeling Good," "Obeah Woman," "Put a Little Sugar in My Bowl." They sang Nina Simone all the way to Melbourne.

〜〜〜

He was aching to be alone in his flat, to sit on the sofa, to look out the window, to watch the world outside without seeing it. But when his mother asked to come in, he couldn't say no.

"It's a nice place," his mum said. She opened the kitchen cupboards, looked into the fridge. "I'm getting you some pots and pans," she told him, and wouldn't allow him to protest. "When I come back from up north, I'll come over with your dad. We owe you a house-warming present."

She looked around one last time. "The walls are too bare, Danny. You need something for these walls. There," she pointed above a makeshift bookshelf he had constructed from discarded red bricks and timber palings, "I've a poster of Irma Thomas that will be perfect there." She swung around. "And I have a Matisse print that will do very nicely over there."

She hugged him for so long before leaving, held him so tight that he had to stoop, that his shoulders started to hurt. "Thank you, thank you, thank you, Danny," she said. Eventually she had to let him go.

He couldn't help it: he sighed in relief when she had gone.

〜〜〜

The sun was setting, the sky was slivers of indigo and gold, scarlet and blood. He sat, his back straight, his palms resting on his thighs, looking without seeing, listening to his breathing, as slowly the sounds of the other flats became distinct. The old woman turning on her taps, the children watching television. He sat for a long time, enjoying the bliss of being alone, until he was in darkness and he started to shiver from the cold. He grabbed a jumper from his bedroom and turned on the light. He listened again to his breathing, waiting to feel the warm rush, the salve that came from being alone.

He was breathing in, he was breathing out.

What was he going to do?

Dan picked up his phone. There were only a few numbers in his contact list—his granddad and nan, his parents, Leon the parole officer, the numbers for work. He found Dennis's number and sent a message: ARRIVED SAFE. He hesitated, then quickly typed again. AND MATE, ANYTIME YOU NEED YOU GOT A PLACE TO STAY IN MELBOURNE. MY CASA IS YOUR CASA.

I smashed it. I absolutely *killed* it. The others didn't even come close, I was three, four, maybe even five lengths ahead of the guy behind me. Go Kelly, Taylor is hooting—I can hear his voice ringing clear above the cheers and the chants across the pool. The whole school is standing up on the benches, they are stamping their feet, I can't see it but hearing it is better than seeing it, hearing makes me feel like I am seeing it from on high. I can look down and see all the other schools sitting down, they are silent and sullen, but my school, all of them, from the little pissers in Year Seven to the won't-deign-to-look-at-you-scum Year Twelves, they have their hands out of their pockets, they are stomping their feet, banging the benches, singing our school song out at the top of their lungs. I have dominated the carnival, I have thrashed swimmers three years older than me. I have broken the Schools Swimming Competition record in two events.

I feel it at this moment, just as the cold tremors begin, just as the shivers start, as the slog of the last few minutes starts to bubble in my blood and in my gut, I feel it, I know it. I can be the best. I killed it. I can be the *best*.

I can hear Martin Taylor. He's calling out, again and again and again, Go Kelly, Go. I hear his voice, it rises higher and higher to reach me. I am in the sun, I am higher, farther—beyond the sun.

The acid is starting to eat at my body, starting to twist and strangle my muscles. I am back in the water, the cheers and the stomping are dying out. I push back into the water, I stretch my arms, push out, feel the muscles tighten; the cramps start pinching into my flesh and my teeth are chattering so hard I think they will shatter.

"Warm down," orders Coach. He is at the side of the pool, his fat gut bulging but tight as skin stretched across a drum. He is unsmiling, his arms are crossed.

"I did good, Coach." I can hardly get the words out, my teeth are shards of ice. I can hardly speak.

"Kelly, warm down, now!" He won't smile, he won't congratulate me, he won't say well done. But he doesn't have to, he knows how good I was. All he does, all he has to do, is wrap a towel around my shoulders as I get out of the water. My legs wobble, like they aren't attached to my torso, aren't connected to me. He wraps the towel around me, supports me, just for a second, just a hand placed at the small of my back.

That's all he needs to do. He's proud of me, he's so fucking proud of me. But his only thought is to stop the acid that my body has just spewed out, that is filling my veins and my blood and my belly and my head, so it won't make me sick.

"Now, now," he insists, "straight to the warm-down pool. Now!"

It hurts, it is fever—the swim has put poison in my body. But it is also how I know how hard I have worked. This is how I know it is worth it.

On the bus back to school, I'm at the back, in between Taylor and Wilco. I don't say much, I just look ahead; all the Year Sevens are turning their heads, looking at me, whispering about me. I am silently telling myself, Don't look conceited, this will be what it is like when you win at the Commonwealth Games, when you get a medal at the Olympics in 2000. I'm going to be there, I know it now, I know it after today, I am going to be *there*. You don't get overexcited, you keep it cool. *Everyone* will be whispering then, *everyone* will be looking at my picture in the paper, at my swim on the television, everyone, every single person in the country will be looking at me, talking about me. This is the future, I know it, I see it. It has been given to me.

A few seats in front of us two of the Year Eights are arguing. One of them, with a mop of maple-syrup hair that explodes from his head, is nudging the other one, smaller, blond and pale, who is holding on to the competition program and keeps turning back to look at us, then quickly looking away. I can hear him saying, "No, I can't." Shaggy Mop elbows him. "Do it," I hear him say. "Do it."

The small blond kid gets up from his seat and comes up to us, clutching the program, trying not to stumble from the sway and roll of the bus. He is blushing so hard that his face is all tints of pink and red. He's so scared he squeaks: "Excuse me, Kelly, can you sign my program?"

He's so scared he's shaking. The kids around us start to laugh. But not me, not Taylor or Wilco. The kid blushes even harder. He holds out his program and I take it.

"Got a pen?"

He can't even speak. He's so in awe he can't even speak to me. He just shakes his head stupidly, looking dazed, as if the question is too big for him, as if he can't make sense of it.

"I've got one," Shaggy Mop calls out, as though getting my autograph is the most important thing in the world.

They want *my* autograph, *my autograph*.

"I've got one!" he calls again and rushes up to his friend, just as the bus makes a hard right turn and sends him sprawling across the laps of two kids in the seat in front of us. He's gone red too, and his mouth is like a fish's, open shut open shut.

The skinny blond kid snatches the pen and hands it and the program to me.

"What's your name?"

His squeak is so high that I can't make it out.

"What?"

"Byron!" He yells it now.

And I write on the top of the program, *To Byron,* and then I hesitate and I think, How big do you make your signature?, and I know that Taylor and Wilco are looking over my shoulder, waiting to see what I'm going to do. I'm thinking it can't be too big because that will be showing off and it can't be too small because that will look stupid, so I just scrawl across the page—and it is big, I can't help it, it looks enormous—I sign it *Daniel Kelly.* That's what I will be, how I am going to sign my name—that's how they are going to know me. Not Danny, not Danny the Greek, not Dino. I am going to be Daniel, Daniel Kelly.

"Give it here." Taylor grabs it out of my hands and I think, You can't sign it, they don't want yours, you came fourth, mate, a piddly fourth, but he doesn't sign his name, he just writes in very neat capitals under where I have signed my surname: AKA BARRACUDA. Taylor hands the program back to the kid.

The kid's face is still flushed but he is pleased, this is gold, my signature means something. He squeaks, "Thank you," and goes back to his seat but he and Shaggy Mop keep turning around and whispering.

Taylor leans into me, and whispers, "You're a hero, Kelly."

"Shut up!" I say, punching his arm. I can't stop grinning.

〰〰

That night Theo wants to ride on my shoulders as soon as I get home. I give him the ribbon and the trophy—he's building a shelf of my trophies and ribbons in his room. I run through the house with my little brother on my shoulders and he's chanting, "Danny's a champion, Danny's a champion."

Mum says, "Congratulations, son," and hugs me, can't stop hugging me. Regan chokes up and can't speak, but the pride in her eyes is almost as good as a medal, as good as any trophy, her eyes are shining brighter than when sun strikes metal.

And even Dad, who has been home for three days, who hasn't got out of his pajamas in all that time he's that tired, all he's been doing is playing rock and roll and reading on the couch, he too says, "Good on you, Dan, I'm proud of you." He says it. He's proud of me.

I'm a fucking champion.

Or I'm a fucking champion till dinner. I shovel in the food, can't stop speaking, I'm telling them that Coach is having me and Taylor, Scooter and Wilco over for dinner at his place, we're going to eat the best pizzas in the world and Coach will tell us all about what competitions are coming up next and who we have to beat and what Swimming Australia is doing and who is putting in the money and who we have to watch and who we have to impress. I have signed my first autograph and tomorrow night we're going to be celebrating at Coach's place for dinner. I'm so excited that I eat and talk at the same time, food sprays from my mouth as I rush the words out. And then I realize that no one is saying anything.

Dad pushes away his plate. "Tomorrow night is Theo's birthday."

It sinks in. I forgot: tomorrow is Theo's birthday and we're taking him bowling. He's already organized the teams: Mum and Dad and Regan on one team, Theo and me on the other.

I look across at my little brother. He's sliding his fork around the plate, not looking at me. I feel like shit but I know I'm not going. I know I am going to Coach's house, I have to be at Coach's house. I deserve to be there. Don't spoil it for me, Theo, I am thinking, please don't spoil it for me.

"You're coming with us." It isn't even Dad, it's Mum. I can't believe it's *Mum*.

"I'm sorry," I begin. "I know I should have remembered—"

"Danny *has* to go to pizza with Coach, he *has* to." It is Theo who's blurted it out, Theo who is glaring at Mum and Dad.

"No, Theo, he's going bowling and then to dinner with us for your birthday."

"No!" Theo bawls it out so loud that we are all shocked. Theo's never been a brat, he never loses it. But now he's smashing his fist on the table; plates jump, his water spills. "I don't want to go fucking bowling, I don't want to." And my little brother is crying, real weeping, the kind that makes you think his insides are tearing. It is a storm that wraps all of us inside of it: the kind of crying that hurts to listen to. Mum has rushed over to him, she's trying to hold him and he won't be held, he won't stop. "I don't want to go, I won't go!"

"Theo," says Dad sharply. "Theo, stop. We'll go Sunday night—how's that? Dan can go to pizza tomorrow night and we'll go bowling on Sunday. As a family." Those last three words are for me, they slam into me as hard as a thumping.

Theo tries but he can't stop his sobbing, he can't stop it now that he's started, but he lets Mum hold him and he is nodding, snot running down his face.

And I think, My first gold medal will be his, I promise, the first gold medal is Theo's.

"Don't you have to do a drive to Sydney on Monday morning?" Mum cautions Dad.

He shrugs. "I'll be okay."

"Okay, then that's settled," says Mum. "We'll all go Sunday."

〜〜〜

That night I look into Theo's room before going to bed. His bedside light is on but he is asleep, holding something tight in his left hand. It's the ribbon, it's my championship ribbon.

"I promise you, mate," I whisper to him, "that first gold medal is yours." It feels good to make that vow. "Theo," I repeat softly, "that first gold medal is yours."

It had been a mistake to go to the beach, to go away with Demet and Margarita. Dan stepped out of the shower, grabbed the clammy towel, and rubbed his body vigorously, as if the scalding under the hot shower hadn't been enough to rid his skin of the sand that had got in between his toes, stuck in his leg hair, in his arse crack. He dried himself off, put on his underwear, and shook his T-shirt; fine grains of sand fell from the fabric onto the wet tiles. Fucking sand, fucking sand everywhere. Dan breathed in and held his breath.

Clyde was smoking a cigarette on the balcony. He didn't look up as Dan slid open the glass door and took a seat next to him. The sun was a fireball of flaring light melting into the inky dark water.

"It's amazing, isn't it?"

Dan released his breath. He could hear the concession in Clyde's words.

"Yeah, it's beautiful."

"When I'm by the ocean I know why I'm living in this country." Clyde stubbed out the cigarette and smiled at Dan. "Just a pity the place is full of fucken Australians."

Should he laugh? He should laugh.

But Clyde was solemn, his eyes were searching. Dan had to look away.

"Mate, I don't understand. Why can't you swim?"

~~~~~

They had awoken to a glorious day. The sun's rays through the slatted blinds were tassels of light gently breaking into their slumber. Dan had risen first. Clyde stirred, then rolled over and went back to sleep. The night before had been chilly, but the morning had banished the cold. It was not yet eight o'clock but a soft warmth already bathed the apartment. Dan had just poured the boiling water into the coffee plunger when Clyde stumbled out of the bedroom, yawning. The russet spray of hair over his torso, the thick thatch of copper bush wreathing his cock and balls, brushed gold by the light. Lust, as fierce and insistent as hunger, made Dan shudder.

It was what bound him to this man. The brewed coffee went cold as Clyde fucked him, his body splayed over Dan's as they screwed savagely, relentlessly, on the floor. Afterward, as Dan came back from the toilet, he could see Clyde, still naked, standing out on the balcony, looking down over the ocean and the township of Lorne. Dan resisted the instinct to scold, to tell Clyde to put on some bloody pants. Instead he threw the plunger of cold coffee into the sink, and refilled the kettle. He heard Clyde greeting Margarita or Demet; one of them was on the balcony next door. And then he heard: "Put some fucking pants on, will ya." It was Demet. Through clenched teeth Dan whispered, "Thank you."

~~~~~

"Come on, pal. Come into the water."

He had been reading his book, looking up occasionally to watch his lover and his friends swimming. They had driven out of town and found a cove that could only be accessed by a steep descent down a narrow cliff path that cut through a gully. People had already staked claim to the beach on the other side of the rocks, at an estuary. But the hidden cove was blessedly theirs. Dan had given himself over to the glory of the day, the sun beating down on his skin, the words in the book rolling in and out of consciousness. It was Rushdie's *Midnight's Children,* and the halcyon ease of the morning meant that the language of partition and exile and displacement had trouble penetrating, and he had to reread sentences and paragraphs. The lazy hedonistic joy of being on an Australian beach in summer negated the words. So the book had been laid over his face, shielding his eyes from the fierce sun, when Clyde's shadow fell on him.

"Come on, mate, come into the water."

Dan peeked, squinted, from under his book.

"Nah, I'm enjoying myself. I'm happy just sitting here."

"Don't be a dick, man, it's fantastic out there, come on." Clyde was holding out his hand, waiting.

"Nah, I'm fine."

"Come on." The pleading in Clyde's voice had been replaced by irritation.

"I said I'm fine."

"Come. On."

"I. Don't. Fucking. Want. To."

"Just leave him, Clyde. You know he doesn't like to swim."

Even with the sun in his eyes Dan could see Clyde's face change, see how his body stiffened at Demet's words. It had been the wrong thing for her to say—it claimed an ownership that Clyde would not be able to forgive. They'd been the wrong words, but then any words of Demet's would have been the wrong words for Clyde.

Clyde walked back into the surf.

Demet spread her towel next to Dan and plonked herself down on it. "You okay?" she asked, teasingly flicking water on his bare arm.

"Yeah, course I am."

"Things all right between you and Clyde?" She asked it lazily but he was immediately wary. He was cautious when talking about Clyde to Demet, and also when Clyde asked him about her. "I'm okay, Clyde and I are okay." He picked up his book and started reading over the same damn paragraph, the words refusing to settle.

"Cool." Demet was looking out to the water, where Margarita and Clyde were splashing and dunking each other. "She's having such a good time. She really likes Clyde—they have fun together."

There was affection and warmth in the way Demet spoke of her girlfriend. That lightness wasn't there between him and Clyde, only the ferocious rush of desire. The lightness and warmth only came to them just after their bodies were spent, the glow of their orgasms depleted. Only then, maybe, was there light between them.

Dan told himself to be kind. He'd promised himself that he would be kind that weekend, that he would be tender with Clyde.

That afternoon, at the café on the esplanade, Clyde had laughed and joked and camped it up with Margarita, and was even teasing and gentle with Demet. The surly adolescent waitress with the nose ring and pink streaks in her hair brightened visibly on hearing Clyde's accent; afterward, when Clyde went up to pay, Dan looked through to where his lover was charming the cashier. But to Dan, from that moment back on the beach, Clyde hadn't spoken a word.

〜〜〜

He didn't know how to answer that question: "Why can't you swim?" To answer it honestly would be akin to telling Clyde that he didn't know Dan at all. To answer would be to reveal himself completely to his lover. The risk of it was unimaginable.

He breathed out and made sure his words were offhand. "I've told you, I spent most of my teenage years training for four hours a day in the bloody pool. I've had enough of swimming to last me a lifetime."

Clyde's fingers were wavering over his tobacco pouch, itching to roll another. But he pushed it away. "And you really don't miss it?"

"I fucking hated it, do you understand? I fucking hated swimming!"

Clyde sighed loudly.

Dan looked down at the slow roll of traffic on the esplanade, he was watching the sun spill into the mouth of the ocean. All the vehicles were BMWs, Volvos, massive SUVs. He and Clyde shouldn't have come here, shouldn't have accepted the invitation. The ocean was splendid here, the coldest blue in the world, the sea rising to kiss the undulating green hills was spectacular—but he had no right to be here. This was the world that belonged to the boys from school—they owned that stretch of the coast. It was a world the other Danny could visit, the Danny that Clyde had never met, must never know. They should never have come.

The thought of seeing someone from that world transformed into something solid that filled his throat, threatening to choke him. They're not here, he told himself desperately. They'd be in Europe or in expensive Asian resorts. Tourist season would be too crowded for them, too plebeian.

He swallowed, and could breathe again.

"Are you okay?" Clyde was looking concerned.

His words came out as a plea: "Fuck me."

The men fucked like animals, Dan's face squashed against the harsh acrylic of the cheap carpet. He forced himself to mentally outline the green-and-yellow floret patterns on the rug, he needed to fixate on that, but the lines blurred because his teeth were grinding together so hard he was sure they would crack, but he couldn't open his mouth; to open his mouth would be to let out a howl from the lacerating pain, the buckling and tearing of his bowels, he was convinced he was tearing. Look at the pattern on the carpet, concentrate on that, only on that, he thought, clamping down on his teeth, telling himself, Don't shit, don't shit, as Clyde plunged into him with ferocity and fury. It was violent and savage, and within minutes Clyde was bellowing, with such force and exhilaration that Dan could finally relax. Clyde was spasming, grunting as he came, falling on top of him; the room was a furnace from the heat of the day so when their wet skin slid together it sounded like farting. Dan pushed Clyde off him onto his back on the carpet, then straddled him, jerking his cock violently for only a couple of seconds, feverishly chasing that brief moment of light, and three spurts of semen landed on Clyde's chest and neck.

The men lay next to each other on the floor. Dan's skin was stinging from carpet burn. He slid his hand over the wet clumps of hair on Clyde's chest and belly, flicking off a glob of drying ejaculate from Clyde's crucifix. Their combined breathing slowed and separated. The sound of crashing waves and the slow rumble of the traffic re-entered his consciousness. Dan peeled the condom off Clyde's prick and got up to go to the bathroom. He chucked the mess of plastic and semen into the toilet bowl, then sat down and immediately allowed himself the relief he had craved from the moment Clyde's cock had pierced him: his shit, wet and putrid, slid seamlessly out of his bowel. He could smell the previous night's dinner in it, lamb, garlic, and wine. He flushed the toilet and went back into the living room.

Clyde was still spread naked on the floor. He raised his hand, examining his fingers, pursing his lips in distaste. "I need a shower, I'm like a mangy dog." He wiped his hand disdainfully on the carpet, his nose wrinkling in revulsion. "Your cum," he blurted out jokingly.

Dan could relax. It had worked. Clyde had forgotten all about the water and why Dan didn't want to swim.

〜〜〜

Dan checked his phone again. It was seven twenty-five and Clyde was still in the bathroom. They were meeting the girls next door at seven-thirty—they were going to be late. Dan couldn't fathom how Clyde was not capable of managing time. It was simple, time was allotted in discrete units, it was logical—the day was measured by it. How could Clyde not get it? He looked again. Seven twenty-six. He couldn't stop himself; he opened the bathroom door, about to say they were going to be late, but then stopped in amazement.

Clyde was smiling at him in the bathroom mirror. He was standing there naked, a razor in one hand, his chest, belly, the skin of his pubis blotchy and red. Dan was transfixed.

Clyde frowned. "Don't you like it?" He rubbed at his shaved chest. "I know it's going to itch like hell, but I've always wanted to try it. I was sick of all that sand scratching at me all day. Don't you like it?"

A memory he had to stifle, a joke from that other world: You look like a skinned rabbit.

Dan didn't know what to say. It was Clyde's face but it wasn't his body. It was the body of a youth, a glimpse of the past, the change rooms after a meet. It was pale white smooth skin. It was Clyde's face, but it was Martin's body.

And for the first time, looking at his lover, it wasn't just lust that was a bolt of radiance through his body. It was falling through the earth, and at the same time it was flight. It was swooning. Was it love?

Clyde watched quietly as Dan found a tube of sorbolene cream in his toilet bag. The men were silent as Dan carefully, lovingly applied the cream all over Clyde's freshly shaven body.

"It's going to be itchy for days," he counseled softly, his hands cupping Clyde's balls. "You'll have to stop yourself scratching."

He continued soothing his partner's skin. He had forgotten that Demet and Margarita were waiting. Time had been stalled, it had been vanquished.

Margarita had booked a table at a Greek restaurant by the jetty. Their table was at the far end of the deck, overlooking the water. A young waitress briskly handed them their menus, took their drinks order, and was about to launch into a recital of the night's specials when Clyde held up his hand. "We'll settle on food after our drink." But there was charm in his smile and he'd put an extra lilt into his accent, softening the brogue. It worked, as it usually did. The girl returned his smile and poured out water for each of them.

When she left them, Clyde grabbed a menu and started fanning himself with it. "Oh my God," his voice an exaggerated mince, "it is *so* furcken hot."

Demet poked out her tongue. "It's perfect weather. Just shut the fuck up, you whining Scottish poofter."

At the next table, an elderly woman scowled and said something to the old man across from her. He looked over, caught Dan's eye, and quickly looked away.

Just don't be so loud, don't swear so much, he silently begged of his friends.

The drinks arrived and Clyde raised his glass. "Well, happy Australia Day."

"Happy Invasion Day, you mean," Demet said loudly, making sure that the couple at the next table had heard. Dan knew that she wanted everyone around them to hear.

"Happy Invasion Day," repeated Clyde as they clinked their glasses, but he couldn't help adding, "I see that you aren't too outraged to accept the public holiday?"

Demet's eyes flashed but then she shrugged and chuckled. "Well spotted, Scotsman," she said as she took a sip from her champagne. "I am a hypocrite."

Dan saw Clyde's brief bristle of irritation. It was the inflection she gave the word, Scots*man*, the stress on the second syllable. *I don't know how she does it,* Clyde had complained to him, *how she makes it sound like an insult every time.*

"Hypocrisy is inevitable."

They all looked at Margarita. She was holding her cool glass to her cheek.

"What do you mean by that?"

Margarita touched her lover's forearm. "I don't mean to be heavy about it, mate, I just meant that it is hard not to be conscious of how hypocritical we all are. You know, we all believe in reconciliation, we all believe in Aboriginal statehood, we all believe in social justice, but here we are on the day that should be about acknowledging how this land was stolen from its original owners and we're living it up on one of the most expensive coastal strips in Australia. That's all." She wasn't like Demet—she didn't have to announce it to the world. She'd said it softly, a statement just for them to hear.

"I mean," she added even more quietly, as if ashamed of what she was about to say, "is there even one Aboriginal person in this whole fucking town?"

Clyde patted her hand. "Don't worry too much about it, sweetheart. You're the darkest person here." He made a gesture that took in the whole restaurant. "I mean, they all probably think you *are* Aboriginal."

Demet's laugh was a roar, a crack of thunder that made the couple next to them flinch. But Dan didn't mind. He just felt relief every time Clyde said something that got a laugh out of Demet. I can relax, thought Dan, as Clyde lit a cigarette. It's going to be all right.

The waitress rushed over, exclaiming, "Sorry, sir, but it's no smoking here."

Demet jumped in. "But we're outside."

The young woman looked serious. "Yes, but we serve food in this area and so there is a no-smoking policy till eleven o'clock." She pointed across to a boat landing a few meters from the restaurant. "If you like you can smoke out there. As long as you're at least nine meters from the eating area."

Dan felt that they were all being given a reprimand.

Demet had pulled out her pack of cigarettes. "Come on, Clyde, I'll come with you." But as she left the table, she called back over her shoulder, "I mean, for fuck's sake, it *is* a Greek restaurant."

The waitress looked mortified. "Right," she declared, turning on her heel, "I'll come back with the specials when they return, shall I?"

~~~~~

Dan watched Clyde get drunk. There was the first gin and tonic, and then the second when Clyde and Demet had returned from their smoke. Not that Dan was counting; he was just glad that Demet and Clyde had found common ground and bonhomie in their shared outrage at the pettiness of Australians. He could tell that Margarita was also relieved that the night hadn't turned into another sparring match between their respective partners. Dan had heard the mantras before; Clyde's dissection of Australia had become both more bitter and more resigned the more his frustration with the country grew.

So Dan sat and listened while Clyde listed all the things he found perplexing and annoying about Australia. "You all think you're so egalitarian, but you're the most status-seeking people I've met. You call yourselves laid-back but you're angry and resentful all the time. You say there is no class system here, but you're terrified of the poor, and you say you're anti-authoritarian but all there is here are rules, from the moment I fucken landed here, rules about doing this and not doing that, don't climb there, don't go here, don't smoke and don't drink here and don't play there and don't drink and drive and don't go over the speed limit and don't do anything fucken human. You're all so scared of dying you can't let yourselves live—fuck that: we're human, we die, that's part of life. That's just life."

And Demet was his chorus; Demet answered every insult, every jibe with her own litany of complaints that Dan knew of by heart—he could have recited it along with her. We are parochial and narrow-minded and we are racist and ungenerous and we occupy this land illegitimately and we're toadies to the Poms and servile to the Yanks; it was an antiphony between Demet and Clyde.

The elderly couple at the next table had fallen silent and Dan wanted to say sorry to them, to explain that Demet and Clyde didn't know they were insulting them, they just didn't see them, and the young waitress wasn't smiling anymore; she refilled their water glasses and brought out more drinks without glancing at any of them; she no longer found Clyde's accent charming. As both of them finished with a flourish, Clyde saying, "It's soulless here," and Demet instantly echoing him: "You're right, mate, it is soulless here," Dan kept his mouth shut because he knew he could say to his lover that that was because it wasn't home for him—that was what people meant when they said a place was soulless, it meant it wasn't home to them and they didn't know it—but what could he say to his friend? Where are you going to go? Where are you going to find peace? Where will you have to go to find soul? This is the only home we have.

〰〰

It was just after the plates had been cleared away, after the waitress had asked if they wanted dessert. Margarita had smiled, shaken her head, and asked her to bring the bill. Dan was looking up at the moon straining to reach its full brilliance, and listening to the waves slapping against the posts of the jetty. The tables around them had been cleared and on the foreshore a group of teenagers were playing loud thumping dance music. That was when it all started to go wrong.

The bill arrived at the table and Demet leaned forward to say, "This is on us."

"No, you don't have to do that," said Clyde, shaking his head in protest.

Margarita took Demet's hand and held it to her chest, as if the two women were about to make a vow. "No, it's our shout because we wanted this weekend together to ask you both a favor."

Demet was nodding, encouraging Margarita to continue; and stumbling at first, then gaining courage, she blurted out the words: "Demet and I want to have a baby, we want to become parents, and we can't think of two men we'd rather have as fathers to our child. Are you interested? Will you think about it?"

Dan barely had time to absorb the meaning of the words when Demet added, "Of course, it would be totally up to you how much or how little responsibility you want to have in raising the child."

That made the words break through and Dan thought, No, I want to know her, I want to know my daughter, because his very first thought was of Regan and how a child of his and Demet's might look like Regan. His next thought was that Clyde, next to him, had stiffened. And that made Dan unable to answer. That made him unable to speak.

"So, what do you think?" Margarita was searching Dan's face, clearly shaken and dismayed by Clyde's resolute silence.

Clyde was also looking at him and Dan couldn't speak or look in his direction. The moon was reflected brilliantly and solidly on the surface of the calm water. The spears of light were paths to a future. Demet and Margarita were offering him a future. But he couldn't speak, he couldn't bridge the in-between of Clyde and Demet.

Margarita turned to Clyde. "What do you think?"

Clyde cleared his throat. He no longer sounded drunk. "I don't think that is for me to answer," he said, chillingly polite. "You're not asking me to be the father, you're asking Dan."

And it was true. It was confirmed by the women's shared awkward silence that it was Dan's future being woven and crafted, *his* future.

Clyde turned to him. "Do you want to be a father, Dan?"

Demet confirmed it again by using his old name. She reached for his hand and said, "Danny, please say yes. We'd so love you to be the father."

He could see her, his young daughter, he could conjure her up: Regan's placid good nature, her desire to please. She would have Demet's almond-shaped dark caramel eyes, with a sparkle in them that would come from Dan's mother. But he couldn't answer Clyde because he didn't know what Clyde wanted and he couldn't say anything if he didn't know what Clyde wanted.

It was then Margarita said, "We've talked about it so much, we're ready to be parents." She couldn't mask her delight, her pride: she too was seeing their future, it was spread out in front of her, as vivid and clear and compelling as the moon above. He wanted to say yes. But there was Clyde, stiff and unbending and forbidding beside him.

There was the longest silence, behind which was thumping music from the shore, the breaking waves, the clanking of plates and cutlery being collected by the waiters, the good cheer and murmured conversation from the remaining customers: there was noise everywhere but over it was their cheerless silence. The three of them were waiting for Dan to speak.

Clyde finally clicked his tongue in exasperation. He refilled his glass and, deliberately avoiding Dan's gaze, said, "I'm not sure I will even stay in Australia. I can't be part of this."

A convulsion snapped at Dan's spine, a disquieting surge of dizziness flooded through him. Was it fear? Was it relief?

Margarita shook her head. "We don't expect either of you to put any of your plans on hold. Please believe us, this won't stop you and Dan heading off to Europe to live if that is what you want to do."

The men couldn't look at each other. Clyde unfolded his arms and dropped them to his sides. "I appreciate being asked, I really do, thank you, but being a father has never been part of my plans."

Dan was looking down at the soiled tablecloth, at the streaks of lurid pink taramasalata smeared on the cloth. He sensed that Margarita had blanched at Clyde's words; he looked up to see that Demet's face had darkened. "That's bullshit, Clyde. I don't believe you've never thought of being a father."

Clyde was tapping his pouch of tobacco. When he replied his tone was mockingly effete. "Aye, I did once, sweetheart, you're right. It was back in 1999, peaking on a pill. I think it lasted all of ten minutes."

Demet snapped, "That's right, make a joke of everything. Why

don't you just say exactly what you mean? Why don't you just be
upfront and say that you're not interested in having a baby with *us*?"

"Baby, please." Margarita placed a warning hand on her lover's
arm.

But Demet wouldn't be pacified. This was the old Dem, thought
Dan, the furious wild Demet from his past, the Demet who was convinced she was right about everything. He wished he could tell her
that in this case she was wrong. Clyde had no fear of saying what
he thought—Clyde had never talked to him about having children.
It wasn't Clyde's future. But it could have been Dan's, it could have
been *his*.

Clyde was taking deep, frustrated breaths. Dan sneaked a look at
his partner. Could it be that Clyde was lost for words?

"It's okay, guys. The last thing Demet and I wanted was to put
any pressure on you. We don't have to talk about it anymore." Margarita's tone was measured. She was making peace. She turned to
Demet. "It's okay, mate, we said that there was no need for anyone to
make a decision tonight."

But Demet couldn't let it go. "Exactly what is your problem with
having children?"

"Jesus Christ!" Clyde started rolling a cigarette. "I'm not interested in the middle-class fantasy of being superpoof. I don't want to
get married, I don't want the responsibility that comes with being a
father. It's fine if that's what you and Margarita want—no bother.
Good luck to you. It's just not for me."

The drying pink crusts of dip were fascinating and repulsive to
Dan. There was a pressure in his belly, in his bladder. He wanted to
say yes to the women, but he didn't want to say the wrong thing to
Clyde. He wouldn't look up. He was sure they would be glaring at him:
his lover, his best friend, her girlfriend. They wanted him to speak.

"We have to grow up, Clyde." Demet's tone was bruising, callous
in its disdain. "Being queer doesn't mean being bloody Peter Pan forever. Wanting to have some responsibility is not middle class."

"No? Moralism isn't middle class?" Clyde's tone was equally scornful. "Who the fuck do you think you are preaching to me about responsibility and growing up? Don't think you're excused because you are some self-declared working-class hero. Having parents who are immigrants doesn't make you working class, not where I come from. I should take you to Glasgow—I should drop you in the middle of fucken Easterhouse and see how much working-class solidarity they extend to you there."

He paused to lick the cigarette closed. The slide of his tongue across the paper conveyed his disgust. "How long are you going to be dining out on your folks' experience, appropriating it as your own? You went to university, pal, you're an academic. What the fuck are you if you're not middle class?"

Dan shut his eyes. She would fly at Clyde now, she would fling herself at him and strip away his flesh. She would retaliate with all that she was, all of her pride in who she was. She would tear him apart.

Nothing. Dan opened his eyes. Demet's features had slumped; she was staring at Clyde, slack-jawed, red-faced, punch-drunk. He recognized the shame, he read her confusion. And for the first time he got it, how university had shaped and molded her, how for Demet, university was her own Cunts College.

Clyde couldn't understand what that loss, that realization, would have meant to her. Everything he'd said had been true, he had laid her bare: Demet had confidence, vocabulary, manners—she had all that came from opportunity and knowledge. She now lived in a different world: Shelley and Boz and Mia and Yianni, those friendships, that past, that world had gone. She *was* middle class, and so was Dan. But what Clyde didn't understand was what Dan and Demet both knew in their bones. Clyde was the son of a pharmacist and a teacher, he'd excelled at a selective comprehensive school, he'd grown up in a part of Glasgow that Dan's granddad had never visited—"They didn't allow our kind there," Bill had teased Clyde when the two had first been introduced—he was a cosmopolitan with the freedom of an EU passport, but what Clyde could never understand, because he could never conceive of such a thing, never concede the thought, was that for all Dan and Demet had gained, they both shared the same fear: that middle class wasn't worth it.

Couldn't she just look at him? He was desperate for her to look at him. He knew that there would be light between them, a light that they shared. A past from before university and Cunts College.

But Demet was cowed, her bottom lip was quivering. Margarita was about to speak, to allay the tension, to bring their table back to equilibrium. Dan couldn't let her; Margarita didn't understand that for all her talk of social justice and human rights—she was still the child of a successful lawyer and a father who was a top public servant—it couldn't be Margarita who defended Demet, it had to be Dan. It had always been Dan.

He straightened his back, ignored the searing discomfort from his full bladder. Margarita had begun talking but he cut her off, interrupted her without apology, addressing Clyde. "That world you're describing, that world in Glasgow you keep banging on about, you know, that world of council estates and drugs and three generations of unemployment? The one you want to drop me and Dem in? That's not fucking working class, Clyde. I don't know what it is but it isn't working class."

It worked. It was a sucker punch and it was now Clyde who was deflated. Margarita appeared uncertain and confused, as if Dan's words were another language. But Demet looked up, he'd made Demet look up. He couldn't read her expression.

Dan was exhausted. He *had* to piss.

Clyde quickly recovered, incredulous and incensed. "What the fuck are you talking about, pal? If *they* aren't working class, who the fuck is?"

Dan understood that it was because he'd defended Demet. It was the school yard again and he'd defended Demet. He groped for words that would pacify his lover but would also be loyal to his friend. But words remained dangerous, elusive; he couldn't move them in the direction of his ideas and notions. He saw himself slicing open boxes and stacking supermarket shelves, smelled how sour and tart his sweat was at the end of an all-night shift; saw his father driving back and forth across the sea of the Nullarbor; saw his mother cutting hair. *Someone's got to cut hair.* He thought of Mr. Celikoglu's long years at the Ford plant in Campbellfield, and Mrs. Celikoglu's lifetime as a seamstress and his granddad Bill's skill as a bricklayer and his nan being a typist: all that labor and exertion and sweat, how the body was molded and transformed by that work.

He struggled for the words. "I don't know, mate, I don't know what those people you talk about are, I don't know them. But they are not my class."

Clyde and Margarita were still unsatisfied; for them the words were certainly not enough. But Demet was nodding, was mouthing something covertly to him: he catches it, can almost hear it. "Thank you."

His and Demet's daughter. There was no Clyde, no Margarita—they didn't belong to his future.

The sounds came rushing back: the sea, the music, the restaurant.

Clyde flicked the rolled cigarette to his mouth. "Enough. This was meant to be a holiday." But his tone was conciliatory, his ire had vanished. One of his fingers was beating a double-stroke at the small of Dan's back. "I'm going to have a smoke." He nodded shyly at Demet. "You coming out, mate?"

She didn't quite let him off the hook; she waited for a tense few seconds to pass. They were all holding their breath. Then she reached for her cigarettes and followed Clyde out to the landing.

Margarita and Dan sat in an uneasy silence, watching their partners outside. Clyde said something to Demet and her response was a raucous laugh.

Margarita visibly relaxed. "God, they're alike, aren't they?"

Quick to anger, opinionated and loud but also generous.

"Yes, they are," Dan answered.

The pressure from his distended bladder was now acute, he was desperate for the toilet, but he knew it wasn't the moment to leave Margarita alone. He twisted and shifted in his chair.

The smokers returned and Clyde looped an arm around Dan. "So what do you say, Kelly? You up to being a dad? I was just telling Dem that a son of yours would be one handsome lad."

Dan buckled, the pain in his bladder overwhelming, a flame torching at his heart, his lungs, as if some beast had landed on him, its weight crushing him. A *son*. To love, to raise, and to teach. To fail.

In a fury, he twisted away from Clyde's arm, pushing him away, clumsily rising and upsetting the table. He almost ran from the table, needing to piss, but also to get away from Clyde.

Inside the restaurant, he saw a group of people, an extended family—there were grandparents and there were children, a little girl had fallen asleep in her high chair.

He is at the head of the table, he is pudgy now, carrying a weight he never had at school, he is thick-bellied and his hair is thinning. And it is then he recognizes him. He is calling out to a little boy at the end of the table, he is saying, "There's ice cream, Michael, you can have ice cream," and it is Tsitsas; he recognizes the boy's voice in the man, and Dan spins on his heel, knowing he daren't walk past them, and goes back to the table and takes his seat and Demet and Margarita are talking but their words make no sense. Clyde is examining him anxiously and saying, "You all right, pal? You okay?" but his words fall like blows and Dan can't breathe, he can't manage his lungs, his lungs won't work and he is going to turn blue and he thinks what a mistake it was to come here, to their world. He could never take a son here, he could never bring a child here because they know who he is and they know what he did and he can't breathe, why can't he fucking breathe, and now the others are frightened and Demet is half out of her chair and there it comes, it comes, the blessed relief. He hungrily devours the air, sucking it in in heaving gulps.

I'm sorry, he says quietly as the warm stinging fluid fills his crotch, slides down the back of his legs and starts a terrible slow *drip drip* onto the wooden decking of the jetty. All he can see is the soiled, screwed-up white napkin on the table, filthy and stained from their meal.

He bolts from the table, knocking his chair flying, off the deck and across the boat landing, through the adjoining grassland, his shoes pounding, staggering on the unstable sand, making for the waves, ignoring the puzzled looks and cries of the teenagers on the beach, lurching and splashing into the water until it has reached his waist, until the unexpectedly icy water has covered the humiliating warmth and wet and stink of his drenched trousers. This is me, he thinks, and the shame is almost comic, it reveals exactly what he is and who he is. A life lived in and only through shame, it clings to him, it rises like the sun within him every morning, and it is there waiting when he sleeps. He lives in the shame, he reeks of it. And then, the next thought: I am in water.

But the water doesn't want him, the water is repelled by him. He hears his name called, can make out Demet's urgent, frightened plea, the shock in Clyde's voice. He turns from the unwelcoming sea to meet his friend, his lover, who are rushing to him. Margarita is hiding back in the shadows, fearful, disbelieving. He smiles weakly at her. She's finally seen who he is.

"Dan, what happened?" It is Clyde who has spoken but it is Demet who has got to him first. She takes him in her arms, holding him, ignoring the wet, not caring that he is dripping the ocean on her. She smoothes back his hair, she caresses his cheek. Without words; she knows to not use words.

"Dan, what the fuck happened?" Clyde snaps it out. He wants words, he wants explanations.

"I'm sorry." Dan's teeth begin to chatter. Even in the mild

warmth of the summer night, all he feels is the cold. "I'm sorry, mate. I pissed myself."

A young girl nearby on the beach begins to giggle, and one of the boys with her lets out a loud hoot.

Dan doesn't care. *That's what I am.*

They lead him back to the apartments, Demet on one arm and Clyde on the other, Margarita treading warily behind them. He is aware of people stopping, turning, couples and families sitting at the footpath tables, all turning to look. Back in the apartment, Clyde says briskly but gently—with fear, there's fear in his voice now— "You have to get in the shower, warm yourself up, babe." The whole time he's in the shower, Clyde stays in the bathroom, won't leave him alone.

He comes out in a robe and Demet doesn't want to leave, she's insisting that Dan wants her to stay and he is relieved that Margarita says firmly, "No, Dem, let's leave the guys alone." And Demet is kissing him, on his brow, the top of his head, on cheeks, his lips, she keeps saying, "I love you, Danny, I love you, and I'm sorry we put you on the spot, you don't have to make a decision, Danny, and whatever decision you make is the right one," and Clyde has his arms crossed and Margarita is pulling at her girlfriend, saying, "Dem, he knows that, let's just go," and even at the door, even on leaving, Demet turns around and says, "I'm sorry, Danny," and then says, "I love you, Danny," and he just wants her to go, just go. Because he knows she loves him and it isn't enough. There's not enough love in the world to cleanse, to eradicate, to scour away the dishonor of who he is.

And you wanted me to father your *child?*

~~~~

"You know you can cry, Dan, there's no shame in that."

They were sitting next to each other on the sofa. Yes there is, he wanted to say, there is shame in that. And his body had lost the language of tears, it had been too long.

"I think I need a drink."

They had bought a bottle of whiskey at the local bottle-o, and Clyde poured a long tumblerful for himself and another for Dan.

Clyde took a long swig from his glass. "Why is it so hard for you to speak? Why can't you have your say? What is it that stops you?"

Words. The words inside are not the words that come out into the world.

The men were sitting together but they were also sitting apart. Their skin was not touching.

"I was watching you all night, mate, all night. You don't want to offend Demet and you don't want to offend me. You can't live life like that—that's not living." Clyde shoved him hard against the armrest of the sofa. He pointed a finger at Dan's head, pointed it exactly as if it were a gun. "What's in there, man? What's going on?"

The waves were pounding in the world outside; there was a grunt of an ignition coughing to life; the beam of light from the car flashed through the window, and then was gone.

"Are you going to fucken answer?" His finger was still there, drilling into Dan's head, like the barrel of a gun.

"What do you want me to say?"

Clyde dropped his hand, gave an empty laugh. "Yeah, answer a question with a question. That's your form, isn't it, Dan Kelly, that's exactly your fucken form." He gulped from his drink again. "I want you—I've made that clear. I want *you*: the man who knows how to sit in silence, who is not mean, who is like he is from another planet. I mean, you've never been to a dance party, you can't tell bitchiness or cynicism when it is being aimed right at you, right fucken at you."

Clyde was pointing that finger again, but not violently—almost indulgently this time. "I like you, Dan, I like that you are so into me that fucking with you is like having sex for the first time. Every. Time. I like you so much, Dan, that I am scared I'm falling in love with you. And why it is so terrifying, why I haven't said the words before, is because I really don't have a clue what you think, what you feel. I don't have a fucking clue."

Clyde's breathing was heavy, measured; Dan could hear the faint wheeze in it, the whistle from a smoker's lungs.

"And I'll tell you what I don't want, mate. I don't want to be a father and I don't want to be a co-parent and I don't want any of that shit. I want to be forty-five and be able to travel and not have to think about little Bobbie's school fees or little Jacqueline's bloody dancing lessons. I like being a faggot, mate, I like it a lot and I think being free in our middle age is what we deserve for straights making our childhood and our teenage years so cuntish." He spat on the word, made fire of it.

"And even if I wanted to be a dad, I wouldn't do it with Demet and Margarita. They'll want to control their kid, she or he will always be *their* kid and they'll resent it every time I disagree on what food the brat should eat and what school the brat should go to and who his friends are and who our friends are."

He finished the whiskey and poured another. "I don't want that life, pal, but that's me. What is it you want?"

There was the rolling of the ocean, the breaking of the waves. Dan knew he had to answer. He had to concentrate, he had to find that space beyond the sounds and sights and motion of the world. He had to say something—*The first fucking thing in your head, mate, just answer him, answer him, the first thing in your head, what the fuck is it?*

What was it?

"I want you to hold me."

And Clyde did, Clyde held him tight.

An age passed. Clyde was still holding him, had carefully twisted his hand around and over Dan to pour himself yet another whiskey. Dan's face was buried in his lover's chest and as Clyde lifted his glass off the table the first two buttons of his shirt came open and Dan found his lips, his mouth were resting on that pale shaven chest, smooth as a boy's. That skin was not Clyde's; it reminded him of another man, of another boy. Clyde still smelled of the sea, it was the smell of a day long ago when he and Martin were by the sea in that big house and that night they'd shared a room. Dan knew that for all of Clyde's insistent urging that he wanted to know Dan's thoughts and to hear Dan's words, there were things about Dan that he would not be able to hear, that he couldn't have stood knowing. So he whispered into that chest, he made the decision. He would fasten his future to this man. He would make Clyde his future because there were no other futures left.

"I want to be with you."

Clyde pulled away from him. Words, Dan was right not to trust in words.

But Clyde wasn't angry. He was grave and cautious but not angry. "I want to be in Scotland this European summer, Dan. When we get back to Melbourne, I'm going to book my ticket." He was gently stroking Dan's back. "I want to see Mum and Dad, see my family. I miss them. God help me, I never thought I'd say this but I want to see Glasga again, I want to see home. I want to see rainy streets and people getting sodden drunk in pubs and I want to hear people laughing, really laughing, because they know it is all fucked up and they'll tell you that, but they are also happy, they are not asking for the world. I want to be somewhere where people aren't perpetually banging on about mortgage rates and refugees and blackfellas and how fucking great this country is, how lucky I am to be here in the luckiest country on earth. I don't want to be told how lucky I am, I want to *feel* lucky. I just want to be home."

Clyde's hold was so tight that it was starting to be painful, but Dan let it hurt. He didn't want to say anything that would make Clyde move away.

"But I promise you, man, I give you my word: if you really want to be with me, I will come back. Will you trust me?"

"Yes. I trust you."

Relief flooded through him, and with it a shudder, a small tremor that came from the realization that a future was being made.

The only future he had.

Clyde fell asleep, snoring loudly on the sofa. Dan woke him, lifted him gently to his feet, and guided the drunk man to their bed. But he lay next to Clyde, unable to sleep. Dreams wouldn't come. Dan quietly got out of bed and returned to the living room. There was a small shelf next to the stereo, filled with maps of Otway walks, books about the Great Ocean Road. But there were also books left behind by guests, spy stories and romances, crime fiction and kids' books. Dan found a dog-eared copy of Dickens's *David Copperfield* and sat down to read.

Whether I shall turn out to be the hero of my own life, or whether that station will be held by anybody else, these pages must show. It was a book he had read before, but he found that his mind kept returning to that opening sentence, that the words always struck him with a visceral force. He turned the pages, making sense of the sentences and paragraphs and chapters but at a distance, as if his reading were like the disconnected passive act of watching the television screen: words flowed past, sense briefly attached to them, but they disappeared from memory as soon as they'd been read. The only sustenance came from that opening sentence. He read to the point of exhaustion, and with the arrival of the soft light of dawn he was still deliberating on the challenge the question posed for him. He couldn't think how anyone but himself could be the hero of his own life, but he knew that he wasn't a hero.

∼∼∼

The following weekend, Dan went to his parents' place to pick up Dennis. His cousin had been staying there, in Regan's old room, since he'd moved to Melbourne in the summer. Dennis was working with Dan's father. Neal Kelly had kept his promise to his wife and given up long-haul driving when Theo had left school, starting a small business as a removalist.

Dan knew that his father respected Dennis, respected his strength and determination. He admired that the man knew work. Watching his cousin getting ready to go out, the bulge of his muscles but also the slight limp that would only worsen with years of heavy lifting, Dan understood why he had not been able to express himself in words at that disastrous Australia Day dinner. Being working class wasn't *about* words, it could only be expressed through the body.

They had lunch at a pub on Sydney Road and then, wobbly from three pots of beer, they strolled into Brunswick. Dan popped into a bookshop, Dennis following him.

"I won't be a moment, mate," Dan said, searching the shelves for that book, that title that would excite his curiosity and draw him in. Dennis just stood there as the customers walked carefully around him; as always he was looking up to that canvas that only he could see painted across the sky. Dan stopped in front of the travel section, a part of the bookshop he'd never been interested in before. A young woman wearing a loose black singlet and a red embroidered bra was apologizing for bumping into Dennis. He responded, "It's okay. It's my fault, I'm too big," and the way he spoke didn't intimidate her— she asked him to repeat his words, and listened and understood. Her back was facing Dan; he looked straight down the aisle to Dennis and raised his thumb in encouragement before going back to the books.

His finger traced the spines, and landed on the word *Scotland*. He opened the book. The photographs showed water everywhere: islands and rivers and lakes. He searched for the section on Glasgow and began to read: *Over the last thirty years Glasgow has enjoyed a remarkable renaissance, thanks to some serious investment in cultural venues and blue ribbon events.* Dan couldn't help chuckling. How Clyde would hate that.

"What are you reading?"

"A book about Scotland."

Dennis was looking over Dan's shoulder, examining photos of bird's-eye views of a city: redbrick terraces, the smoky gray spires and domes of cathedrals, a few lean lonely office towers in the distance, dwarfed by masses of white-and-violet clouds.

"It looks a lot like Melbourne."

"It does, doesn't it? But it's not Melbourne, it's Glasgow and I'm going there."

The flat planes of Dennis's broad dark face creased in suspicion, and his brow furrowed. "When are you going?"

"Not now. One day, I'll be there one day."

"That's all right." Dennis's features relaxed. He let out a loud contented burp.

"Charming."

My cousin is a lot like me, thought Dan. *Not now* is enough, *not now* is all he needs. One day at a time.

He snapped the book shut. "Come on," he said, playfully shoving Dennis down the aisle. "It's time to go home."

Mum is nattering away as we cross the bridge over the river. She's pointing out the Skipping Girl, the neon outline of the young girl with the skipping rope, and she's reminiscing about how when she first moved to Melbourne, when she first got with Dad, he would take her down to the Yarra, past the Skipping Girl, past the firefighters' training center, and they'd walk hand in hand over the suspension bridge and into the woodlands and she thought it was the most romantic place she had ever seen.

"All that parkland in the middle of the city," she's saying. "Adelaide has parkland, but it isn't such a gorgeous green. And back there!"

She turns to point behind us, and I panic, reach for the dashboard, yell, "Mum, watch where you're going!" but she is still blathering on about a little pub, back there, behind the factories in Burnley Street, where they would go dancing every Thursday night.

"They played the best soul music, Danny, old rock and roll and rhythm and blues—I thought it was so wonderful. We'd get there on the dot of eight and we'd still be dancing when the lights were turned on at one a.m. Oh," she shivers, grabbing my knee, squeezing it tight,

"I just danced and danced, and Adelaide and the Jehovahs and all that, I just imagined I was dancing away from it all. And I was!"

"Uh-huh," I sigh. She's told me this story so many times. About falling in love, with Dad, with Melbourne, with old R&B and soul. I look out the window, grab my sports bag. It's got all my swimming gear in there and my toiletries and three changes of jocks and socks.

A few hundred meters past the bridge, we turn right and now the streets are wider and lined with huge trees. Their branches stretch out over the road, as though the branches are fingers reaching out to touch each other. The gray and the concrete and the towers of the city have disappeared, and as Mum negotiates a bend I can see the muddy river; beyond that, the office buildings and the skyscrapers look like toy models from here.

"This is a pretty part of town," Mum says. She slows the car down, peering at the house numbers until she says, "That must be Mr. Torma's place."

It seems weird to think of Coach having a life outside school, outside of us, the squad and our training. Until now I haven't really considered that he would need a place to sleep, somewhere to live. I haven't thought about him having a family or friends. I don't reckon any of us have given a thought to him having a life outside the school, the pool, outside *us*.

It is a single-fronted redbrick terrace house, with green gables, a white picket gate with peeling paint and one missing slat. Concrete steps lead up to a solid door painted a metallic blue, and the paint there has also weathered; streaks of undercoat show through. There are a couple of rosebushes along the fence, wilted and untended, and a large crack that zigzags down the front of the house to the top of a large bay window. It's not a grand house, but I like it immediately— it's got old-fashioned elegance, and looks solid and permanent.

I go to kiss Mum quickly on the cheek.

"Do you want me to come in, Danny?" she asks.

I don't want her to come in. I want to get into the house, to be with Coach and the boys, to focus on the competition in two days' time. "Nah, Mum, I'll be fine." I have one foot on the footpath, the other is still in the car. I am eager to get going.

But she's clutching my hand. "Mate, I should be taking you to Adelaide, but you know it's hard for me to go there?"

She holds my chin in her other hand, forcing me to look at her. I'm so impatient that I could just jerk my hand away from hers and wrench my head aside, but her eyes are so sad that I have to make myself not look away. I bring my foot back into the car and close my door.

"By rights, you should be staying with your grandmother or my sister or my brothers, but it just isn't meant to be, kid—I hope one day you'll understand. I'm so sorry you don't know your *giagia*, Danny, I'm so sorry about that."

Is this what is making her so sad? I don't mean to, but I have a big grin on my face. "I don't mind, Mum. It's okay."

And it is okay. I don't want to think about her family, that mad old bastard screaming in Greek at Mum, that scared old woman who wouldn't let herself touch me. They aren't family—they're strangers I never want to see again.

But nothing I can say will take her sadness away. I just want to get out of the car. I want to be in the house, with Coach and my squad. "Can I go?"

"Of course, Danny." She wraps me in one of those enormous hugs, where all I can do is let my body go floppy, just give in to it. I wait, and eventually she lets me go.

I wave goodbye to her, standing on the path. It is a relief when the car turns the corner and she is gone.

The ringer for the doorbell is a small white cube, and it hangs a little askew from the wiring. I press it. There is no sound so I press it again, and then I knock. There are lumbering sounds and then the door opens, and there is Coach. I have to take a step back. He is smiling, and just for an instant, a wrinkle in time, I don't recognize

him. It is the same heavy body, the same Bonds shirt and baggy
shorts, but the smile has changed his face. I forget to say hello. But
it doesn't matter. He says, "Good to see you, Danny, come in, boy,"
and ushers me inside.

I am in Coach's house.

I never notice houses, I realize now that I've never paid much
attention to them. I know that our house is cramped and funny-
looking, the sleep-out that Dad added when Theo was born is just
tacked on to the laundry, and every room in our house is dark because
all the windows are too small. Of course I've noticed the houses of
my friends from school—their places are ginormous. I know that
Luke's house is modern, that his architect uncle designed it; I know
that the Taylors' house is a mansion and that Wilco's is nearly a hundred years old. I know every part of Demet's house; it has the same
ill-begotten shape as ours. But wandering through Coach's house,
I have a dumb and childish thought and I stifle a giggle. It reminds
me of Goldilocks: not too big, not too small—just right. I feel right in
it. I feel at home.

The first thing I notice inside is the beauty of the ceilings. The
Taylors' houses have ceilings higher than this house, but they aren't
beautiful; I can't remember anything about the ceilings of Martin's
houses at all, apart from their height. But the ceilings in Coach's are
sheets of rectangular reliefs, a sea of stuccoed ingots.

The front room, with the large window that looks out over the
street, that window has a sill as deep as a seat, you could sit on it
and watch the world go by. I can tell immediately that the front room
is Coach's bedroom. There is hardly anything in it, it's really neat.
There is a high bed with a double mattress, with shoes and slippers
on the floor underneath it. There is a wardrobe with double doors; on
one of them is a full-length mirror. There is a white chest of drawers
next to the bed, and on it sits a digital clock and a photograph. It is
of an old man and woman, their faces stern as they stare straight
into the camera. The photograph is black and white but there is a

faint copper wash through it. The woman is wearing a black scarf around her hair and the man wears a peculiar hat, like a cap without a visor. It is an olden-time photograph, the oldest photograph I have ever seen.

Coach sees me examining the photograph and clears his throat. "They are my parents," he announces. "That is my father and mother."

I can't help it, I say, "But it looks really really old."

And he surprises me again, he tilts back his head and roars. A real laugh, a genuine and generous laugh. "Back then in Hungary, boy, everything looked really really old." He takes my bag from me and points to the bed. "You will sleep here."

It is both statement and question, and I just nod my head; I can't stop nodding.

Above the bed there is a painting, of a courtyard high on a mountain, there is a pond and fountain and below stretches a calm and tranquil sea. It looks like a fantasy, like the mansion you'd imagine if a genie were to appear and grant you three wishes. I can't wait for morning, I'm already thinking of waking and having breakfast sitting on that wide sill, looking at the street and beyond it to the world; then turning around and gazing at the painting, imagining that Coach's house will be my house when I am famous and rich enough to live anywhere I want to in the world. I would never feel cramped in this house, I would never feel lost.

I put my bag on the bed and Coach takes me through the rest of the house. There is a second bedroom, with a single bed in it, one small, lopsided bureau and a bank of gym equipment piled up against one wall: a treadmill, a rowing machine, barbells, and a bench. A fold-out has been put next to the equipment, like a bed in the army or a camping bed. It is made up with clean sheets and a duvet. I feel pleased with myself as I look at it—it won't be me camping out tonight.

In the shadow by the door, I suddenly spy a cluster of photographs on the wall. They are all of swimmers. Two of the photographs are ancient, in black and white, and the bathers on the guys look more like underpants. Then there are three other photos, more recent, in color. I don't take in the other boys: in the center is a photo of myself, grinning like a dickhead, but proudly, clutching my shivering body at the edge of the pool.

"That was when I won the Interschool Championships last year, isn't it?" I say excitedly to the Coach.

"Yes," nods Coach. "That's you, Danny." He is pointing out the other swimmers but I'm not really listening to him. He's got *me* on his wall, I am smack bang in the center. I must be the one he considers the strongest, the fastest, the best.

There is wallpaper in the hallway and a dank smell. But I ignore it as Coach rushes me through the lounge room, into the small kitchen, and out into the backyard; not really a yard, not like home with all the grass and flowers and veggie garden, more like a courtyard with a set of weatherworn garden chairs. There are no flowers, no vegetables, there is only a yellow patch of grass and a path made of concrete. But it doesn't matter, because when I look down from the slope of the courtyard I can see the lights flickering in the city below.

"Wow," I say to the Coach. "Wow, the city is *so* close."

Coach points to the back fence, to a bolted gate made of cast-off wood paneling, and he says, "You can walk through that door, Danny, and turn left into the alley, and if you follow it all the way then you are at the river."

"This place is amazing!"

I didn't think I'd said the words out loud, but Coach is beaming, Coach is nodding his head and beaming.

We sit inside at the kitchen table and Coach slices some salami, putting it on crackers and handing them to me.

"Wait till you have the pizzas tonight, wait till you boys taste them. Marika's pizzas are not like that shit you eat, full of that cheap cheese and those bland vegetables." Coach clicks his fingers, he is almost swaying. "Marika's pizzas are the best in the world. You'll eat them, you'll see—you'll say, 'Coach, these pizzas are the best in the world.'"

∼∼∼

There are just three of us from the squad going across to Adelaide: Taylor, Wilco, and me. Coach will drive us there tomorrow. It is not the national championships, nothing as important as that—I can't wait till I get a chance to shine at *that* event—but it is an under-sixteens meet and Coach wants us to compete. He says he wants Swimming Australia to sit up and take notice, he says he wants those stuck-up pricks to see what real talent is. It is under-sixteens, which is why there is no Fraser and no Scooter, and Wilco has just scraped in. If he'd been born a month earlier, it would have been just me and Taylor. How brilliant would that have been?

Coach asks, "Are you hungry?" and the three of us bellow, "Of course we are." He rings and he orders, and afterward he clicks his fingers again and again, saying how Marika's pizzas are the best in the world.

When he's driven off to get the food, Taylor says, "Can you believe how he's going on about those fucking pizzas? And what's with his being so cheerful? What's got into him, what the fuck is going on?"

I bite my lip. Coach is happy, can't Martin see that? Coach is just happy.

Wilco says, "He's always like this when he's got the squad over, always in an up mood. Fraser reckons it's 'cause no one else ever visits, says he's just a fat lonely bastard."

I can't answer, I can't look at him. I don't dare open my mouth. If I did, I'd say, "Coach isn't lonely, Coach has us." But that's not what really gets me, that's not what is causing the churning in my gut. It's that Wilco has been here before, Wilco knows this house. Wilco has known it before me.

~~~~

Coach is right, it is the best pizza I have ever had. At first, the crust seems too thin, the toppings weird, there doesn't seem to be *any* cheese. There is capsicum and pumpkin, there are thin slices of potato, eggplant, even *mince* on one of them. But as soon as I taste them, I can't stop wolfing them down. I take a slice, I take two, I have to stop myself from having more than my share. Not that Taylor or Wilco would allow me to—they are also stuffing them in, they seem to be guzzling them down whole. When we're finished we've got grease around our mouths. I burp, and Martin grins and says, "Good one, Dino," but I know now that it isn't an insult, that he means nothing by it. I burp again and now I am the one grinning.

"Coach," I say, "they *are* the best pizzas in the world."

Coach takes the boxes outside and as I wash the plates and Wilco dries, Taylor wipes down the kitchen table. Not one of us has said a word but it is clear that we have come to an unspoken agreement, that to show our gratitude to Coach we're cleaning up for him. When we're finished he herds us into the lounge room, reaches under the coffee table, and pulls out a pack of cards.

We play gin rummy, then Coach introduces Taylor and me to poker, teaching us about straights and royal flushes, about bluffing. He tells us that gambling is nothing like swimming, that it is about luck. We three boys steal looks at each other whenever Coach is dealing or shuffling the cards. None of us has ever seen him so talkative or so animated. I can't believe how much he is talking. Of course, it's all about swimming, and it's all about the competition in Adelaide. But he's enthusiastic and laughing, and I wonder whether I have ever heard Coach laugh before. He teases us, he scolds us, and then he teases us again. And when he wins a hand, he's loud and gloating, like Theo gets when I let him win at Snap. It's not like he's the Coach—it's like he's one of us.

He wins another round and then he says, "That's it, boys, it is a long drive tomorrow. Let's get ready for bed."

And Wilco, of course Wilco has to say, "So who's sleeping where?"

I look at my cards, the red and black numbers, the sharp diagonals of the kings and queens. I hear Coach say, "I am sleeping here," and look up to see him pointing at the sofa. "Danny has the front room; you and Taylor are in the spare bedroom." And before Wilco can say anything, Coach adds, "It is fair. Danny got here first."

Wilco isn't going to argue; even when he is in this odd lively mood, no one is going to argue with Coach.

And then Martin says, "Anyway, Kelly deserves it because he's the best—he's the best swimmer of any of us."

Wilco sneers, "Says who?"

There is a beat; then Coach orders, "Come on, off to bed!"

But bloody Wilco isn't going to let it go. He's still sneering at Martin. "What's going on between you and Kelly, Taylor? You bum pals—is that what's going on?"

"Nah," replies Martin coolly, and winks at me. "Nah, we're just best friends."

I can't think about Demet and I can't think about Luke. I wink back at Taylor. "Yeah, we're best friends."

After brushing my teeth and going to the toilet, I walk back through the lounge. Coach has a sheet folded over the sofa and is laying a blanket across it.

"Thanks for tonight," I blurt out. "Thanks so much, Coach, it was fantastic."

"You had a good time?"

"Yeah, yeah," I keep saying. "Yeah, it was a brilliant night."

Coach is eyeing me keenly. He comes over and pats my chest. "You are strong here, Kelly, you can feel it, no?"

I'm not sure what he means, I know my pectorals are getting more developed, more powerful. I can feel that.

"Next competition, I want you to compete in the butterfly. I think you will do well at it."

I'm confused, I don't know why he's saying this. The butterfly is effort and skill and sheer bloody hard work. My body doesn't know the butterfly, my body knows freestyle—my body knows that is my stroke.

"Trust me," says Coach, as if he has read my thoughts, as if he is far ahead of me. "Listen to your body. I think the butterfly may be your stroke."

~~~~

The sheets are flannelette and far too hot. But the mattress is firm and comfortable and I know sleep will come easily. It's not like being in a strange room—it is like I have always slept here, it is as if I am home in this room. I'm not thinking about the trip to Adelaide, I'm not thinking about the competition, I'm not thinking about swimming, or my strokes. I'm not thinking about Demet or Luke. Martin said we are best friends. All I can think of is that Martin said we are best friends; and that it feels as if I'm home.

"Are you really sure you want to go home?"

Luke had a smartphone in his hand and another device that Dan didn't recognize clipped to his belt. They were sitting in the Qantas lounge of the Hong Kong International Airport, on their second beer each. Luke apologized every time he had to check his phone. Dan told him not to worry, waved his okay as Luke grimaced and said he had to take the call.

Dan didn't mind. He slowly sipped his beer, enjoying the thought of being in Asia, being one continent closer to home. He knew he wasn't really in Asia, he was in the limbo of international transit. But the waiters and bar staff were all Chinese, and there were woody, spicy flavors coming from the Cantonese buffet. It wasn't Scotland, it wasn't Europe. It was one step closer to home.

He had been shocked by the tears stinging his eyes when the plane broke through the slate-colored clouds and the islands of Hong Kong had appeared below. He had drawn in his breath: at the luminous sheen on the greens of the forest, the deep shadows of the water, the vivid clarity of the light. The European skies, seas, and land were all muted beauty; these dazzling stepping-stone islands seemed of another world, one much closer to his home.

Luke had suggested they meet in Hong Kong. I CAN CHANGE MY FLIGHT, he had e-mailed. I DON'T NEED TO BE IN SEATTLE TILL THURSDAY MORNING. Dan had four hours to kill before his connecting flight to Melbourne. He had hardly dared hope that he could meet up with his old friend, but when he checked his mail at a computer terminal at Heathrow, Luke had confirmed that he'd managed to change his flight. WE CAN GET DRUNK IN HONKERS, Luke had written. I MISS YOU, KELLY, I CAN'T WAIT TO SEE YOU.

But their first minutes together had been awkward. Dan was conscious that he smelled of the flight, and that his clothes were awful—a frayed mixed-blend hoodie and ugly baggy track pants. Luke was dressed in a well-cut charcoal suit; he had the physique of a gym fanatic, and was sporting a neatly trimmed beard, which suited him and gave him gravity and solidity. Luke had wrapped Dan in a wrestler's embrace, and feeling the silken beard against his cheek, and the strength of his friend's muscular arms encircling him, Dan had marveled at how they were no longer boys, that they were finally men.

Luke returned from his call and fell back into the club chair opposite. It was then that he had asked, unable to disguise his incredulity, "Are you really sure you want to go home?"

The question had brought back those last awful weeks in Glasgow; he could feel shame flame his cheeks. Clyde's fury, all his regret and disappointment had been channeled in snide, bitter attacks on Australia. *Go back to that fucken arse end of the world.* Dan had worn the vitriol stoically and that had only enraged Clyde further. It had been a relief for Dan to get to London, to disappear into that vast, unknowable metropolis. He had rented a room at a hostel in Shepherds Bush, and apart from the most cursory of exchanges with his fellow plasterers and laborers on the cash-in-hand jobs he managed to find advertised on Gumtree or pub toilet walls he had not spoken a word to anyone. He'd had enough of words. No words had been able to appease Clyde.

He didn't know how to answer Luke. He was trying to form an explanation, not sure that he could convince his friend, but Luke had already launched into a torrent of conversation, and didn't wait for Dan to answer—it was clear that he was also feeling the unfamiliar and unnerving distance between them. "Katie and I can't imagine going back to Australia. China has spoiled us, mate, every time we go back to Melbourne it's like we've stepped back in time. The complacency, the inwardness, the self-satisfaction, it gets on your nerves."

Dan nodded and feigned agreement; he had no defense and in the pit of his belly that familiar feeling of humiliation started to bite. He had no retort to Luke's argument: the return had to be a retreat, the future was China and the EU and Luke's world of trade and exchange and frequent flyer points. It was a cosmopolitan future that balked at return, for return would always be a backward step. The future was change—how could Dan even admit his longing for things to stay the same?

"I'm looking forward to the summer," he said, giving an embarrassed smile. But that was also the wrong thing to say.

"What's so great about an Australian summer?" Luke countered. "I'm so sick of all the Aussie ex-pats banging on about how great our beaches are, how good our weather is. That's what vacations are for, to get to a great beach, to experience the great weather. That's not the real world," he ended accusingly.

The word is *holidays,* Dan wanted to spit out, *we* say holidays, not *vacation.* But he kept sipping at his beer, wishing they would call his flight, wanting to be in the plane, next to a silent stranger.

"Of course, I'm not sure how much longer we're going to stay in Beijing—Katie really wants the kids educated in Europe or the States." Luke squinted out to the long horizon of planes outside the windows. And then it was all about how the school system was too rigid in China, it was all rote learning, with no space for imagination, how they should have been in London or DC by now, except for the damn economic crisis that had stuffed everything up. All the jobs were in China, it looked as though they were going to have to stay put in the Middle Kingdom for the moment, but he didn't want to raise the kids there, where everyone called them bananas: yellow on the outside, white on the inside. They didn't want the ex-pat life for their kids, it wasn't the real world. If they ever returned to Australia, it would be for their kids' education, but they'd prefer Europe or the States. How long could the frigging economic crisis last, anyway?

And then, coyly, as if he couldn't quite believe he was doing it, he slid the phone across to Dan to show him a slideshow of photographs: Luke in a short-sleeved shirt, a toddler on one knee, a little girl in a smock beaming at the camera (that's Costa, that's Lissa); an unsmiling Katie clutching a giggling Lissa, a craggy hillock of rock jutting out of a jade sea behind them (we went to Vietnam last Christmas); Lissa standing in front of a thin gray-haired man, a petite harried woman holding the little boy (that's Mum and Dad, back on Samos—we took them there for their thirtieth anniversary). The final image was of an elderly Asian woman, much older than Luke's mother, unsmiling, looking straight at the camera. Lissa had her arms wrapped tight around the woman, Costa was hugging her neck—that was their nanny, that was the apartment at home.

"They're gorgeous," said Dan. "What beautiful kids."

And suddenly it was as though no years had passed and sculpted and changed them, and Luke's grateful smile was that of the little boy who'd always looked up to Danny Kelly. The awkwardness started to dissipate. Luke reached out and softly grazed knuckles with Dan. "It's so good to see you, mate." He slumped back in his seat. "They *are* gorgeous kids, Katie and I are really proud of them. And I'm glad we raised them here—I'm glad we can offer them the world."

And that was when Dan realized that Luke wasn't really challenging Dan about going home—that he wasn't thinking about his friend but was justifying his own actions, to himself, convincing himself that he and Katie were doing the right thing. Changing or retreating, both were futures taken on trust.

Dan now knew how to answer his friend, he knew exactly what he had to say. "I have to go home. I miss my family, I want to return to them. I want to see my new niece."

It was the right answer. Luke's quietness and warm smile said that he understood.

Dan talked about Scotland, Luke explained China. They had another beer each and then delicately, ever so carefully, Luke asked about the breakup with Clyde. Dan thought Clyde would have e-mailed Katie, maybe even spoken to her about it. How much did Luke know? The digital departure screen clock above them was counting down and there wasn't time enough for that conversation. Dan did want to tell Luke about Clyde, and maybe one day he would. But he and Luke needed more time, they had to draw maps for each other, to mark the borders of their experiences, to show the roads they had traveled, to shade in the frontiers they had reached, and to plot their cities of work and love and desire. A terrible sadness over-whelmed him, at how far they had traveled from one another, how much time it would take to sift and reconcile their shared past to their individual presents. He wished there was time to explore the kingdom his friend had created.

He would make sure there would be.

Luke walked him to the departure gate. His hug was crushing. Dan couldn't believe the strength in his friend's arms, the power of the embrace. The man and their history was in that embrace.

〜〜〜

"I was going to visit you in Scotland, mate, I really was. It's just that time got away from me. I'm sorry."

Theo and Dan were in the backyard of their parents' house. Theo was rolling a joint; even though the night was cool, he was wearing a blue cotton singlet. It was almost scandalous how Dan couldn't stop looking at his brother. The younger man's body was slim, athletic; his skin was tanned and burnished from his days working in the sun. Theo had allowed his hair to grow long; his curls fell to his shoulders, and he had to keep brushing them away from his eyes. He held the joint out to his brother but Dan declined.

"Still saying no to drugs, eh?"

"It's not a moral issue," Dan said. "They just don't do me any good. They make me feel like I'm drowning."

Theo sucked hard on the spliff, then expelled the smoke in one long thick plume. "Bro, it's the only thing keeping me together at the moment."

Their parents had finally gone to bed. His mother hadn't been able to stop hugging and kissing Dan from the moment he'd stepped through the security doors at Melbourne Airport. His father's reaction was more reserved, but he too grabbed hold of his son, brought him close, and said how good it was to have him back.

No one asked about Clyde, and Dan was relieved. Instead they listened as he talked about Scotland, about Glasgow and Partick, about the southside and the westside, described the uncanny colors of the Argyle coast and forests and bens; blues and greens he'd never seen before, a softness to the light that he'd never known in Australia.

Then he'd asked them about Regan and his father said, "I just want her here, son, she should be home." His mother was crying, and Scotland and Europe and that world was stripped from him and soon forgotten. He was back home.

Now, for the first time in years it was just him and Theo alone together and talking.

"What's been happening?"

"Same as you, mate. I broke up with Annalise. It's been nearly two months and it still kills me, it still fucking does." Theo was peering through a tangle of golden curls. "Is it the same with you?"

Dan then noticed the heavy shadows under the younger man's

eyes, the sharp, gaunt lines of his jaw and his cheekbones. He wasn't
sleeping, Dan thought, and he wasn't eating. Dan went and sat on the
concrete step just below Theo. He wanted to put a hand on his brother's knee, just to touch him—he knew that more than words, touch
could speak. But he didn't know if his brother wanted it; he feared
that Theo would recoil from it.

He didn't know Annalise, had never met her.

"How about you?" Theo's question was an appeal. "Does it still hurt
not being with Clyde?" Theo needed to not feel alone with his hurt.

"I wasn't in love with Clyde," Dan said. "I realized I wasn't because
of how relieved I was when it ended." He didn't touch Theo; he leaned
down and ran his fingers through the unmown grass. "I think meeting
Clyde brought me back into the world." Dan could feel his cheeks burning, his heart racing. "You know, after fucking up so badly, ending
up in prison." The next words were the hardest, they labored to come
forth from deep in his belly, from within the very cells of his blood.
"You know," he continued, his voice husky, "after failing at swimming,
after failing at everything." He was shivering, but not from cold. He
couldn't look at his brother, couldn't bear what he might see there.
"I mean, failing all of you." He stopped, drank some beer to cool his
mouth and tongue and throat. His whole body was burning.

On the other side of the fence a sensor light switched on, a yellow
glow, and an old man was calling out, "Pssh psssh, Caruso, where
are you?" Both brothers laughed as a slim tabby cat jumped out from
the bottom of the garden and scaled the fence.

"So the Rizzos are still next door?" Dan's voice was back to normal.

Theo nodded, scraping the butt of the joint on the sole of his
sneaker and flinging it into the garden. "Well, I fucking loved Annalise and I still do. And you didn't fail me, you dumb fuck—not when
you didn't make it as a swimmer. You failed me when you left us,
when you wanted nothing to do with us. That's what fucking hurt."

I want to run away, Dan thought. I can't bear this, the crush
of it, the shame of it. But he just sat there. He would not get up,

he would not leave. He was alert to it now, how the shame began in the belly, how bile flooded his insides, seeped into his blood. He was aware that the anger, the poison inside him needed to escape, as if his shame could transform into wrath and he could spew it all out, turn on his brother, wring his brother's bloody neck: It wasn't about you, I couldn't think about you, I was drowning and I was falling, I was plunging down to earth and I couldn't think of you, or of Mum, or of Dad, or of Regan, or of anyone. He could spring up from the cold stone of the step, smash his brother's face, wring his neck: It wasn't about you, you little cunt, I was falling. I was drowning. The excuses and the defenses came to his lips—he was ready, to strike, to run; his muscles tensed, his jaw clenched. Dan turned to his brother.

Theo was a young man now, an adult; his hands were callused and large, his skin was the darkest shade of honey from the sun. He was scratching the inside of his arm, something he had always done whenever he was nervous or afraid.

Dan could smell the eucalyptus, the old tree at the back of the garden, its bark shining silver in the light of the moon, its canopy gleaming golden from the light of the street lamps. He released his breath. "Mate, I'm really sorry for what I did. I'm really sorry for hurting you."

The two brothers sat in silence on the steps. Finally, Theo put his hand on Dan's shoulder, then flicked a finger hard at the back of his head, so hard it hurt. The younger man cackled and slapped his knee, enjoying Dan's outrage. "Evens?"

Dan couldn't help laughing at the infantile term, the word that brought back childish skirmishes and teasing. "Yeah, okay, we're even."

He got up from the step, stretched his arms out into the night sky; he breathed in the air. "It smells wonderful," he marveled, "the eucalyptus and the pure night air." He was being reminded that it wasn't just the horizon, not just the light, but even the sounds and smells in Australia that stretched to the infinite.

Theo snorted. "You're an idiot. All I can smell are the fumes off the bloody highway. What the fuck is so wonderful about that?"

Dan then said, "Tell me about Annalise."

"What do you want to know?" Theo's tone was hesitant, sulky.

"What does she look like?"

Theo went into the house and came out holding a laptop. He sat back down on the step and Dan came to sit beside him again as his brother turned on the computer. The screen was white, then blue, and then an image washed across it: Theo and a young woman. She had smooth pale skin, her mouth was serious and unsmiling, her eyes were solemn and gently hooded—they dominated her face. Theo was smiling, his hair much shorter. Dan could see the adoration in his brother's eyes, the limpid submission in them as he pulled her into him. Her eyes gave nothing away, but he could tell exactly what his brother was feeling at the moment the photograph had been snapped. Annalise had not allowed the camera to glimpse anything of her.

"She's beautiful."

"Yeah, tell me about it." Theo's voice broke, and then he slammed down the top of the computer. "So now you've seen her." His voice was distant.

"Are you seeing each other at all?"

"She's visiting family in Townsville. She'll be back next week."

Dan could hear the choke in his brother's voice.

"But she doesn't want to see me, she reckons it's best that we don't see each other for a while."

Dan didn't think there was anything to say. Words wouldn't do Theo, couldn't do Dan himself any good.

Theo pulled out a pouch of tobacco and began rolling another joint. Dan stared up at the dark sky, the distant tremor of the stars. It felt like looking at the ceiling of the world, he thought to himself, it was so much higher here than it was in Europe. Here the stars had to exert themselves, had to struggle harder to shine their light.

Only after the first puff of the joint did Theo speak again; the nicotine and marijuana steadied his voice, pushed back the tears of rage and longing. "How did you realize you weren't in love with Clyde? How did you know?"

Because I can't see him. Because I can't recall his eyes, his mouth, his skin, his cock, his balls, I can't picture his stride, I can't hear his voice, I can't bring back the smell or even the taste of him. Because of how quickly he has gone from me.

"Because I don't miss him."

"But that's now." Theo's tone was insistent, as though Dan could tell him something that could make his pain bearable. "Did you realize you didn't love him when you were with him? Do you think you *ever* loved him?"

Martin Taylor's voice was a deep vibrato from the back of his throat, a man's voice even in youth; he had a pronounced cleft in the middle of his chin—Dan could remember that clearly, how he wanted to place his finger exactly there. He could see the splash of sandy-colored hair under Martin's arms, wet and splayed across his fine, pale skin, skin that was flushed and pink after a swim. The stone-gray transparency of his eyes, the fixed assurance of that gaze. And Martin's smell, a drug composed of all the boy's emissions, heady, almost hallucinatory, the smell of his body and the smell of chlorine. In the night, Dan could smell him, he could smell Martin Taylor. He could remember everything about Martin Taylor.

"No, I don't think I ever loved him."

"Then why the fuck did you stay with him? Why the fuck would you go all the way to Scotland for him?" Theo's tone was unsteady again, the languid pull of the drug fighting the rage inside.

It came to Dan: she had never told him that she loved him, she'd never given him that.

"I didn't go to Scotland for him," Dan answered, as he saw it all with clarity, shocked at the severity in his voice, the ruthless calm of the truth. "I went for myself."

Theo shook his head, not comprehending.

Dan sighed. Would he only ever feel the burden of words? He had spent the previous six months in virtual silence, alone in London, knowing no one, having no one. All he'd had was silence and he'd been content with that. Now he was back to the treachery of words— what to say and what to withhold, what to create and what to destroy.

What to create.

"I had a future," Dan found himself saying, and he was astonished as the words began to flow: the sounds were coming out first— that was what shocked him—and then words were forming from the sounds, the words and the sentences and the meanings were originally sounds, originally breath. "I had a future, and I was going to be one of the greatest swimmers that ever was and I wasn't good enough and it had nothing to do with talent or skill or my body—it had to do with who I was. I just wasn't good enough. All I had was that future and when that future was stripped from me, there just wasn't anything else there—and I'm sorry that even you, even all of you, all my family, you weren't enough. There was nothing but this hole and all I was was just this hole. All I knew how to do was swim and all I wanted to do was swim and I couldn't ever swim again, so I was just this hole where a man should be, and I hated myself for not being strong enough and not being good enough. I don't give a fuck what everyone says about how all I could do was give it my best shot, and how not everyone can be a winner, and not everyone can achieve their dreams. That's bullshit—without my dream, I was just a hole, an absence, that's all I was. I failed; the failure was within me and all I knew was that I wasn't strong enough so I was just floating. My whole life was floating and that's what I never could bear about the water, just floating on it—what I loved about swimming was that I could fly in it; it wasn't liquid for me, it was air. So Clyde came along and he kept me afloat and he wanted to go back to Scotland and that too kept me afloat, and Glasgow was all right, Glasgow could even be home, but I was still empty and only floating, and Clyde knew it, Clyde could see it and he began to hate me for it, because how can you love an emptiness? And then one day we were in this place called Luss, this fucking freezing loch in the Trossachs, and it was summer and the place was full of holidaying Scots having a great old time. I looked out at the water and it was calm and still and I knew it was deep enough to kill me if I wanted it to and I just stripped off my clothes and I dived in there and I swam for the first time in years, as fast as I have ever swum, and even though the water was so cold it was squeezing my lungs and my heart, I kept on swimming because I wanted to fly and because I was sick of being nothing. And then I just stopped, I just stopped swimming and the people on the shore were calling out to me and I could hear Clyde shouting for me and I just lay on my back in this icy, Arctic water, thinking, Let it fill me up, let me not be a hole, and nothing happened, nothing changed. I realized then that there was nothing left of my dream to lose, so I just turned around and headed back to the shore. People were staring at me and Clyde was drying me, going, 'What were you doing, man? What the fuck were you doing?' and I was just standing there and I thought, Well, I've swum, and I've been so terrified of swimming and I'm still here and I am still empty and swimming won't take me back to my future and my future begins now. Clyde was asking if I was all right, calling me a mad bastard, and I said to him, 'I don't want to stay here, mate, I can't. I want to go back home,' and he said, 'I cannae go back with you, Danny,' and that's how it happens, Theo, that's sometimes what just happens. You can't dream the same future. I didn't know what the future was going to be but I knew it wasn't going to be in Glasgow and Clyde knew his wasn't going to be here and realizing that, understanding that, was more important than the question of whether I was or was not in love."

Dan breathed in the eucalypt, the scent of wattle.

Theo was silent; he had let the joint burn down to the end, and now he flicked it across the yard.

Dan opened his mouth, but now that he had let the words loose, let them run, he could feel the old caution return. This is a story,

Theo, he could have said. I've just told you a story. The truth he knew abounded with sound, a pulse beating to infinity, an ocean of only waves; there was too much sound to be trapped in words. Dan shut his mouth.

"Maybe you're searching too hard, mate." Theo's voice was also wary; he too was trying to catch sound and trap it into words. "Maybe Clyde is enough? Maybe if you just gave it time, you'd find that being with Clyde would fill that hole? Isn't that possible?"

Dan knew he could break his brother now, the way you squashed ants, breaking backs and souls with the press of a finger. Annalise doesn't want you, bro, you're not enough for her. He could crush him if he wanted to.

"It's not going to happen, Theo. It's over."

"You sure?"

"I'm a thirty-year-old man and I'm not sure about anything. That's the only thing I know—that I'm still not sure of anything."

With a shudder—from the winter chill? from Dan's words?— Theo got up. The laptop was sitting on the step. "You can check your e-mails if you like. The connection's stuffed out here but you can log on in the kitchen."

"I don't need to, thanks though."

"Yeah." Theo rolled his eyes. "You know you never answered *one* of my e-mails?"

Was this another thing to be sorry about, another reprimand to bear?

"Not that it matters, mate, truly." Theo's tone was conciliatory, tender. "It was kind of nicer to get the postcards. I really looked forward to your postcards."

"I liked writing them."

"See you in the morning, bro."

"See you."

Theo was still standing nervously in the doorway. He then stepped down and offered Dan the most blundering but earnest of hugs, from behind, his arms tight around his brother's chest. Dan could smell him, the sweat and the tobacco, the dope and the soap on his skin. Theo let go of him and went back up the steps and opened the screen door. But he still didn't go in, he kept the door ajar with his foot.

"Are you still planning to drive up to see Regan on Saturday?"

Dan nodded. He'd come home to see Regan.

"I've been working like a dog, mate, everyone in this city is building an extension or renovating or building apartments." Theo was hesitant, shy. "If you want, I can drive up with you. Nowra's a long drive—we could share it."

Dan had been dreaming of being alone on the open road, where the expanse of sky and the earth reached to the end of the universe. He had been looking forward to driving it alone, heading for that sky on his own.

But he heard the question and the plea in his brother's voice and he said, "Yeah, of course, that would be great."

∼∼∼

Dan took his brother's laptop into the kitchen. He sat at the table with his finger hovering over the keyboard, over the mouse, to enter Safari or Firefox, to answer that siren call, that infernal music, the spinning electrons, the percussion of information. His finger hovered over the mouse and then he decided, banging on the keyboard, entering a portal, the spinning letters on the screen forming the word *google*. For the first time in his life he was going to put in his name, he was going to search for his name. He had never let himself do that before, knowing what he would find, that the record of his shame would be there for all to see: the details of his failure, of his fall—what he did, how he was punished. It would all be there, the tantrum in the pool in Japan, the howling selfish boy, the degradation, the awful failure. He would type in the words "Daniel Kelly, swimmer," and then would be shame and infamy and revulsion. He held his breath. He typed: DANIEL KELLY, SWIMMER. The electrons sparked and the screen transformed; he was astounded by the speed of the machine. He read down the list with dread; there was a Dan Kelly in the US and there was a musician and an architect and he read about a family reunion of a woman called Margaret Kelly somewhere in Canada. Though he scrolled and scrolled, though he tapped the keys again and again, there was no record of him, no evidence. There was nothing about him at all.

At that moment he realized that it hadn't all been about being better and faster and stronger; that hadn't been all he'd wanted. It had also been to make a mark, to be a photograph and an image, to be a record and a name. *To be a name.* There was no mark and there never would be. No one knew his name.

Dan could feel the blood rushing violently to his cheeks. With a savage strike he hit quit and the electrons danced. The photograph of his brother and Annalise glimmered there, the colors sharper than life, the intensity of a child's painting, and this time softly he tapped buttons and the photograph briefly shimmered before the colors washed away. The screen was blue and then it was white and then it was black. All that remained was his face reflected in the glass.

~~~~

When Dan awoke, his brother had already left for work, and so had his mother. It was just him and his father in the house. His dad was sitting at the kitchen table reading the paper, wearing a Collingwood sweatshirt and his pajama bottoms. Dan could see his granddad Bill in his father's features. A record was playing in the lounge room, an old song that Dan recognized from his earliest days. *Help me, information, get in touch with my Marie.* His father looked up, nodded at him, abruptly folding the paper and pushing it aside.

"Do you want a coffee, son?" he asked, then added, "This country's fucked, mate. I don't know why you came back."

Dan watched his father rinsing the espresso pot at the sink. The years of long-haul driving were starting to show: there was a stoop to the man's shoulders, and though his limbs were still thin and sinewy, his middle and his buttocks had ballooned. It was this disparity in the man's shape, the body parts that somehow didn't quite fit, that made Neal Kelly finally an old man.

Dan picked up the paper, glancing at the front page, something about the mining industry, something about tax. His father had settled the pot on the flame and sat down opposite Dan, pointing to the paper. "Can you believe it? Do you know what's happening?"

Dan shook his head.

"Guess what happens here isn't really of much interest to the folk back in Scotland, is it?"

And there wouldn't be anything about Scotland in the papers here, thought Dan, that was the way of the world. Behind his father he could see leaflets and photographs curling under fridge magnets: a rainbow-colored stencil of Barack Obama; the green triangular masthead of the Greens; the photographs of himself, of Theo, of Regan, of Layla, the new baby; a sticker from the TWU that read, CARRYING AUSTRALIA; a black-and-white postcard of a young Keith Richards collapsed on a chair, his eyes shut, a cigarette between his lips. There was the Aboriginal flag, the beginnings of a shopping list, and a card he'd sent from Scotland, the brilliant, still stretch of the Great Glen.

His father was still ranting, about how the resources of the country belonged to everyone, how the mega-rich mining companies had been flooding the media with their propaganda and fear, how the country was selling all its ore and minerals and wealth to the Chinese and how there would be nothing left for his grandchild.

Dan watched the espresso maker start to tremble, steam spurting from its spout; it began to whistle but his father was still heatedly outlining the country's ills, so Dan got up and turned off the flame. He poured a coffee for his father and one for himself.

"And the worst thing, mate, the worst thing is that Australians just sit and take it, we just let the mining companies dictate policy and we take it." His father was shaking his head. "How can that be, Danny, what the fuck is wrong with us?"

Clyde would say, "You're spoiled." Luke would say, "You're all ignorant and parochial and too far away." And later that day Dan would catch up with Demet and she would be raving on like his father, repeating his words verbatim, the same well-rehearsed script.

His father was staring hard at his son, his eyes narrowed, his lip curled. "Danny, do you care about any of this at all?"

He should have said, Of course I do. That was what his father wanted to hear and if his granddad Bill had been sitting there, Dan would have agreed with alacrity, Yes, of course I agree. The face of his father was the face of his grandfather and it would have been the easiest and wisest thing to do. *Of course I do.*

Dan breathed in the bitter aroma of the coffee. "No," he said. "Sorry, Dad, I don't think I do."

His father's face twitched—as if he'd kicked him, thought Dan, as if he'd punched him in the guts.

Then his father's chin jolted upward, his eyes were steel, fierce and remorseless. "I wish we'd never said yes to sending you to that school. That fucking school did this to you."

Dan wanted to throw his head back and explode into laughter— that would upset the bastard, that would make him hate him even more. Dan was tapping the table, wishing he could slide under his father's steel-cold gaze—like a cobra's, he thought; the old bastard was ready to strike, with hatred in those icy blue eyes. The two men stared at each other, across the table, neither moving, except for the tapping of Dan's fingers on the table. His father gave way first, with a sneer; then he blinked and looked away.

He shook his head. "Are you going to say anything?"

There were words and sentences, arguments and explanations, justifications and resentments, they were all building inside him, in his belly, deep in his gut, syllables forming words forming sentences, and seeping into blood. But he sat still, looking straight at his father. He would not let the words betray him. Keep it in, Dan, he silently counseled himself. Don't say a word.

His father exploded, "What the fuck do you mean you don't care?"

The words were fighting to get out, they were shooting into his lungs, waiting to pitch from his throat. Keep it in, Dan, don't say a word.

"You were always a selfish little prick, always bloody Danny Kelly having to come first. It didn't matter how tired your mother was from working all day, no, she had to drive you back and forth, wherever you wanted, whenever you wanted." His father had risen now, and was pacing around the small kitchen, the words tumbling out so fast that they collided into each other. "Did you ever ask about your brother, or your sister? No, you didn't give a damn about anyone but your bloody self, all of us tiptoeing around the great Danny Kelly, all of us, me included."

He kept returning to the same phrase, he couldn't get the words out of his head, repeating them in anger, folding them into a question. *What the fuck do you mean you don't care?*

Dan wouldn't give him the satisfaction of a response. He just raised an eyebrow and shrugged.

Dan's father grabbed a shiny apple out of the fruit bowl and aimed it straight at Dan's head, throwing it with such force that it ricocheted with the violence of a gunshot when it hit Dan's temple, the apple cracking apart, the flesh exploding over the table, the floor. The juice splashed into Dan's left eye, stinging, forcing tears.

Stricken by the ferocity of his own violence, his mouth opening and shutting, searching frantically in the sink for a dishcloth, his father, this pear-shaped, aging man, his father was fumbling, dropping the cloth, picking it up and dropping it again. "I'm sorry, son, I'm so sorry." His father's hair had gone white, Dan could see liver spots flecking the rough skin on the back of his hands.

Dan sat still as his father wiped his face, his hair, his neck, wiping the bits of fruit from around his shirt collar. He could have taken his father's hands and bent them back so far that they broke.

His father was on his knees, scrubbing the floor, chasing bits of apple across the lino. Dan could have kicked him, Dan could have aimed his foot and brought it back into a kick that would have made the old man's head and face and skull displode as completely and as messily as the fruit he'd just thrown at Dan. It would have been so easy to do, to walk away and never be forgiven. The thought of it, the simplicity of it, was like a bolt to his cock, like being famished for sex. His father was bent over, trying to scrub away the evidence. His pajamas were falling around his buttocks; Dan could see the thin gray hairs disappearing into his arse crack, and had to look away in disgust. He sat still, smelling the juice of the fruit, he made himself stay there, not letting his body rise, because of what it could have done, what it was capable of executing.

Dan took in a deep breath. He could have killed his old man, the way he felt then he could have got up, unzipped, taken out his cock, and *raped* his old man—that was how much he hated him. He breathed out. His father had clumped the sodden cloth in his hands and was wiping down the table. The basket of fruit shook. Dan breathed in but his body wouldn't settle, the gaping ravenous hole inside of him would not retreat. Dan breathed out, grabbing at the sounds and syllables and fragments of words colliding inside him. He breathed in and let the words out.

"You're the ignorant one, Dad," he began, jerking his head at the refrigerator, at the multicolored face of the US president, the blood-red earth and the night sky and the golden sun of the Aboriginal flag. "I don't care about your fucking windbag American president, he isn't saving the world, and I don't care about the fucking Aborigines and they don't fucking care about me and I don't care about your fucking Labor Party and your fucking Greens—let the world burn and choke itself in greenhouse gases: no one wants to give up anything, no one wants to sacrifice anything for anyone else.

"I've been to where you're from, Dad, and the working class have gone, they've left the fucking building. The best of them got out long ago, they've moved on, and the worst of them are getting pissed and getting high and having babies for welfare checks, and they're exactly like everyone here, blaming immigrants and blaming refugees and blaming everyone else but themselves. There's no difference, Dad—this is what the world is like now and you think you are so much better than the other truck drivers you know because you and Mum protest against the war in Iraq and the war in Afghanistan, and you sign petitions protesting about refugees being kept in detention centers and you think that makes you special, you think that means your shit doesn't stink, but really the refugees and the poor and the desperate, the blackfellas here and the blackfellas in the rest of the world, they don't give a shit for any of that. They're just trying to get ahead the best they can, and you've wasted all your years on caring about that shit and what have you given Regan? What have you given Theo? What have you given any of us? All I wanted was for you to support me. All I wanted was to be the greatest swimmer there ever was and you never once carried me, honored me, supported me, did you? You didn't, because you didn't want me to get too big-headed, didn't want me to succeed, didn't want me to be anything but what you are, an old man with a chip on your shoulder about being working class and poor, banging on about your Irish roots and your working-class Scottish heritage as if that meant anything. As if anyone in Scotland or Ireland gives a fuck about you and where you've been and what you've done—I've been there, Dad, I've lived there, and if they were here, they'd say, what the fuck is this cunt whinging about with his backyard and his four-bedroom house and his car and his truck and his family and his grandchild and all the fucking safety in the world? How dare you complain about anything, you fucking spoiled Aussie cunt, that's what they'd say, that's what they are saying, Dad."

Dan stopped, and wiped spit from the sides of his mouth. His father was sitting again, opposite him, and Dan could see in his father's swollen frightened eyes that he had succeeded, that the man was broken, that the man was split and torn. But Dan was not finished: one final blow had to be struck. "You failed me, Dad. You could have carried me, you could have supported me, you could have been there for me. I just wanted to be the strongest and the fastest—I wanted to be the best and you didn't let me, you didn't want that for me. I wanted to be a name, Dad, I didn't want to be an ordinary decent good Aussie bloke, I never wanted that. You wanted me to be humble and grateful and kind and considerate and socially conscious and just and honest and good and instead I am nothing."

Dan breathed out. "Do you understand now, Dad? That's why I really truly don't care. Do you understand, Dad, why I really don't give a fuck?"

A cloud passed across the sun; the kitchen fell into darkness. The shadow played across his father, moved across the table, and passed over Dan. Dan was conscious of his heart pounding, throbbing so hard it could have burst through his chest. He could feel the blood rushing through every vein in his body, as cold as ice; every hair on his body was upright, every single part of him was alive, as if he was flying, taking in the world, the scent of blood, of bone and victory. His old man was just that, an old man, his head lowered, his skinny wrists weak and brittle. Dan had won. He had beaten his father.

The wind rose outside, the branches from the silver gum drumming across the slate roof over the kitchen, and more clouds skated across the sky and the sun disappeared again. In a breath, his exhilaration had gone and all he saw was the older man across from him, too shattered to find the strength to raise his head and look at his son. Dan had won and he felt nothing at all.

His lips dry, his tongue thick and unyielding, this time Dan thought through the shape and volume and sense of words before he let them loose.

"Dad, it's not true that I don't care about those kinds of things, it's just that I have never known what to do about it all."

The glowing rendition of the US president on the fridge door; the ink as thick as blood on the Aboriginal flag.

"I was never that smart, you know, to figure all that sort of stuff out. All I was good at was swimming, that's all."

The words had been released and then they just melted away. They had meant nothing.

His father lifted his head, gave the weakest of smiles. The dark lavender half-moons under his eyes, the stubborn smoker's lines at the corners of his mouth. "We should have visited Scotland, I should have taken your mum to Greece. That's one thing I have to do; that's one thing I have to honor." Dan heard the regret, Dan heard the guilt.

"I didn't mean you don't know anything about the world." Dan pointed to the door of the fridge, where so much of the world had been pinned and stuck and posted. "You know so much more about the world than I do." He was scrambling for words that would soothe and offer peace. "This is the world too," he continued. "You've worked and raised a family and you've looked after us all. You've been a good man."

His father was a good man. It struck him with the force of revelation, exultation, light flooding through him. His father was a good man. His father was the hero of his own life.

"That's all I want." As he spoke, it was now his face that was lowered. Now he was the one stuck, nailed to the ground. "That's all I want for myself."

His father's intake of breath was sudden, followed by the wet crunch of words kept back. Dan looked up. He knew his father had been about to speak, about to reassure him—You are, son, you are a good man—but he'd held it back. Those were words that had to be earned. He was a good man and a hard man, thought Dan, recognizing his father as a man for the first time, knowing his father was seeing his son as a man for the first time.

The two men looked at each other across the table, not daring one another, nor goading. They looked at each other cleanly.

"Your granddad and nan are dying to see you. I know you're heading up north to see Regan and our kid tomorrow. Do you want me to drive you over to see Granddad and Nan today?"

"Sure."

"He can't wait to ask you about Scotland."

"I can't wait to tell him."

～～～

The two men stood silently next to each other, doing the dishes. The father at the sink washing, the son drying. Neither man had spoken, neither man had uttered the words *I'm sorry*. They were reaching toward it, finding a rhythm in their labor, the scrubbing, the stacking, the drying, and the putting away. The words loomed too large and both of them feared that they were far from enough. So they found a rhythm together, doing their task in unison, with calm and deliberate care. There was a bluish mark forming on Dan's temple where the apple had struck him; his father's hands occasionally shook as he worked at the sink.

～～～

His granddad Bill was waiting on the porch, sitting on an old kitchen chair. He was sitting upright, a tweed flat cap shading his eyes from the weak intermittent sun, his hands resting on the neck of his black cane. Even in the wind, even in the cold, he was sitting out on the porch, eager to see his grandson who'd been away for so long. As soon as the car turned into the street, his grandfather rose slowly, shakily, waving at them and calling, "Irene, Irene, they're here." And his grandfather hugged him—how bony he felt—and his grandmother couldn't stop kissing him and offering him tea and coffee and Monte

Carlos and shortbread. The three generations sat around the gas heater with the orange coils, and his granddad asked him about Scotland.

"Yes, I visited the Gorbals but they've knocked down your tenement a long time ago" and "I went running in Queen's Park" and he told his grandfather what the new Glasgow was like and how Rosemary had sent her brother and sister-in-law all her love, and he told them about the summer days on Loch Long and on the west coast and how the midges had buried themselves deep into his skin, and that made his granddad laugh, hard and loud.

Dan continued to answer the questions fired at him by his granddad, by his nan, his father too; he answered the questions asked by these people who knew him best, because no one else knew him; this was all he had. He was not the strongest, not the fastest, he was not the best—he was not anyone at all, but this son and this grandson. This was where he started, this was where he began.

"Go, Danny, go, Danny, go, Danny, go!"

All the kids I am competing against, all the other boys are gawking up at the benches and then they all look down the line at me. I squish shut my eyes and I can see swirls of thin red in black. I squish them real tight, my face is all hot, I reckon my skin is red all over. There is a draft coming through the pool, it is freezing and I am squishing my eyes and I am shaking. Shut up shut up shut up, I'm thinking, but of course they don't shut up, they just get even louder.

"Go, Danny, go, Danny, go, Danny, GO!"

I can hear her. It's Dem, she has the loudest voice.

I open my eyes and look up at them. Sava is leaning over, banging, thrashing the seat in front of him. Boz has his hands cupped around his mouth to make his yelling even louder. Mia and Shelley see me looking up and they start waving at me like idiots. Yianni too, he's flapping his wrists and his hands, jumping on one foot then the other, like a demented monkey. "Go, Danny, go, Danny, go, Danny, go!" I'm staring straight at Dem, she's got the biggest doofus smile on her face and she's screaming it out at the top of her voice: "Go, Danny, go, Danny, go, Danny, GO!" Only my dad is silent, he's the only one not calling out. But he's got a big smile on his face too. He's nodding at me. Go, Danny, go.

I give them all a thumbs-up and then I turn to face my lane. Don't think about them, forget about them, I tell myself. I look out at the still water. I can't wait to dive in.

The chant abruptly stops. Some parent or official, some adult, must have said something to them. The pool goes quiet.

I am looking at the water. I have to stop myself leaping in, I have to control myself. I can't wait. Not yet. Not yet.

The starter raises her whistle to her lips. But she doesn't blow it yet.

Wait, Danny, I tell myself. You just have to wait.

The boys either side of me, I can tell they're impatient too. One of them has the skinniest body I have ever seen, there doesn't seem to be anything between skin and skeleton. The other one is shuffling from side to side, as if the race has already started, as if his feet have already started to kick.

Look to the water, that's all that matters. Don't think about the other boys.

Will you blow that whistle, will you please blow that whistle.

The sound is screechy but thin. I am like a coiled spring. I don't know how it is I am on the starting block. It's like I moved through time. I am on the starting block, I am nearly there. I rein myself in. This is the moment I always have to watch it. In my second race, I slipped up and dived too early, and was disqualified. I didn't want to get back in the pool for weeks, I was such a sook. I just couldn't forget it, couldn't get it out of my head or my sleep or my daydreams— how could I have been so stupid, how could I have been so hopeless? I'm never going to be that stupid again.

On your marks.

She's called it. I put my right foot forward, I arch my arms. And then I stop thinking.

Don't think, just listen.

She's putting the whistle to her mouth, I can almost hear the slip of her spit over the metal. But it's some other sense, it's not hearing or seeing, I just *know* she's about to blow the whistle. I have my arms out in front of me. The sound this time is strong, she's blown with all the force of her lungs. And I'm ready. I leap and—just for a second, just a flash in time—I know that I am faster than the sound and I am entering the water before the sound has reached the other boys' ears. I am in the water. I'm away.

〰〰

It's easy. Not that I'm not working for it, not that I can't feel my muscles twisting and turning, turning and twisting, all up my arms, all down my legs. I can feel them working hard. But still it's easy. What I don't understand, what I can't work out, is how it can all be still. Not that I'm not racing down the lane, not that my strokes aren't splitting the water, not that my kicks aren't thrashing the water. But it's like I know the water doesn't mind, that the water is guiding me and so I am swimming in stillness. I see it as a tunnel that the water makes for me, but a tunnel filled with bright blue and white light, a light so bright I can't tell where the blue is white and where the white is blue. I sense, as though the water is explaining it to me, it is somehow whispering it to me without words, that other boys are not capable of calming the water, they don't know how to do that. In the lane to my right the boy is punching hard, water churns and erupts around him but it is defeating him. I'm at the turn and he's still struggling to reach it. I am away. All around me the water is in an agitated panic but where I am, there is the stillness.

It's over too soon. I don't want to stop but I slap the tile and I start to shiver. The cold has gone through me. I am trembling. I look up at the benches where they're jumping up and down, making noises like wolves and dogs, sounding like the big birds in the aviary at the zoo. But I look for Demet's face, I search for my father. Demet isn't going spaz, she's just got the biggest smile on her face

and she's swinging her Carlton scarf around and around. And next
to her, Dad's only half smiling, only a little smile, but that's all I
need. He winks at me.

I've won.

I wish I could stop time, I wish I could make life a movie where
you can stop time and be frozen forever. It feels so good, all the
warmth in the world is coming from the center of me, even though
my teeth are chattering, even though I'm shivering. I nod, shake my
head at all the other boys, at the boy who came second and the boy
who came third, but I don't even see them. I can't stop time. I have to
move. I have to get out of the water.

~~~

There's a lady with a camera who grabs me after I've changed, says
she's from the local paper, says can she take my picture. I look to
Dad, who nods. I hold up the trophy they've given me, I hold it up and
beam at her. Demet and Dad, Boz and Sava, Mia, Shelley and Yianni,
they're all waiting for me, Sava is pulling dumb faces trying to make
me laugh. But I just beam at the camera. I hold the trophy up high.

In the station wagon, heading home, Dad asks Yianni and Sava to
keep low until he can drop them off. He doesn't want to get in trouble
with the police. Mia and Shelley are buckled up in the backseat; Boz,
who is a shorty, is in the middle. Yianni and Sava are lying flat in
the back, I can imagine them, trying to lie as flat as they can. Arms
tight by their sides, loving it, loving that my dad is letting them ride
like this. That's why everyone adores my mum and my dad, because
of what Mum and Dad let them get away with. I am in the front
seat, with Dad, and Demet is in the middle. Dad has his weird music
on, old music from long ago, the music Dem calls skinny music, but
she is swinging her legs in time to it, making up words and singing
along. I am holding on to my trophy.

Dem turns to me. "Can I hold it?"

"Course." I give her the trophy. She doesn't even look at it, she just holds it clutched to her chest, smiling, banging her feet, making up words to a song she's never heard.

We drop off the others, pick up burgers and fish and chips, and we're heading home. But I'm so hungry that the smell of the food is making me dizzy. I rip open the bag containing the hamburger, and I stuff it in my mouth in four or five bites, the sauce dripping down onto my trackie daks, onto my shirt; I don't care, it feels so good to eat. Dem is laughing at my appetite but when we get home, she scowls. There is a new sign up in front of her house, her house next door to ours. It reads: AUCTION. There's going to be an auction in a month. She does something then she's been doing since she and I were kids: she wraps her Carlton scarf tight around her hands, like she's a prisoner. Except now my trophy is caught up in the middle of it; it kind of looks like she has three hands.

Everyone's in our backyard. Regan is playing in the small blue sandpit and little Theo is pushing his Thomas the Tank Engine around on the grass. Mrs. Celikoglu is sitting on a kitchen chair and Mum is behind her, scissors in one hand and a comb in the other, doing her hair. Mr. Celikoglu is sitting on the steps to the kitchen, drinking a beer and listening glumly to the radio. Carlton must be losing.

I grab the trophy from Demet but it's caught in her scarf and won't come loose. I start tugging harder and she yells at me, "Stop it, Danny, that hurts."

"I want to show Mum!" I don't mean to but it sounds like I'm whining.

Demet jerks her hands apart and the trophy falls, clang, on the concrete. I rush to pick it up but there's a scratch, a dull streak across the polished aluminum surface. Demet puts her hand up to her mouth, she's going to start crying, I know it, and I have to stop her doing it. I can't bear it when Demet cries. No one else's crying hurts. Only hers. When she cries it's like I want to cry too.

I'm shaking my head. "It's all right, Dem," I lie. "It's all right, it's okay, the trophy is okay."

"So how'd you go?" asks Mum.

Dad is standing behind me and he puts his hands on my shoulders. He kisses the top of my head and gently pushes me toward her. "Our son is the Under-Twelve Northern Region Freestyle Champion. How's that? How bloody good is that?"

And then Theo is holding fast to my legs and Regan is giving me a high five and Mum hugs me and Mrs. Celikoglu kisses me and Mr. Celikoglu lightly pinches my nose shut, his palm caresses my cheek. "You champion, Danny," he says kindly. "You champion."

But it all goes, it goes too quickly. The fish and the chips, the potato cakes and the burgers, they've all gone and Dad has put a record on, he and Mr. Celikoglu are discussing politics and Mum is back to doing Mrs. Celikoglu's hair and Theo is demanding Regan play with him. It always goes so quickly. I can't bend and shape time the way I can water. I want to be back in that moment just after I won the race, just when I knew that there is something I can do so well that I might one day be the best in the world at it. I want that feeling back.

Demet and her mother are arguing. Her mother snaps, says something sharp in Turkish.

"It's okay, Dem," I say. "You're just moving down the road. We'll still be able to see each other all the time."

"And it is closer to your new school, for next year," Mr. Celikoglu says. "It is just a short walk and you are at school. Danny can pick you up on the way."

Dem and I glance quickly at one another. I am excited and I am scared. High school. We'll be in high school next year and the Celikoglus are moving. Winning, the thrill of it, has all gone. I want to get back in the water.

"I hate the new house." Dem has folded her arms and looks mutinously at her mother.

"Oh, don't be silly, child. It is much bigger—you and your brother can have your own rooms. You'll like it very much."

"I won't."

"You will."

I hold my breath. Dem can lose it and when she does she screams and yells and says the worst things to her mother. But she doesn't go off, instead she turns to me.

"It's okay, Danny is going to buy us a big big house and we'll all live there together. There'll be . . . there'll be heaps of rooms and . . . and . . ." she's scrunching up her eyes, trying to think of something that will shock and impress her mother, " . . . there'll be three bathrooms. And you're not going to be allowed to live there." She grins, pleased with herself.

"Ah," her father is grinning too, "and how is Danny going to pay for such a mansion? Do you think it is fair that only Danny pays? You must pay your half as well."

"Nah." Dem's eyes are shining, she is looking at me and her eyes are sparkling like stars. "Danny is going to be a world champion swimmer. He's going to win massive amounts of gold medals and he's going to be really famous and really rich. Tell them, Danny, tell them!" She's looking at me, her eyes are stars in the night sky.

My father's been lying on his back on the blanket, and he now gets up on one elbow. "That right, Danny? Is that what you want?"

I want to be back in the water, in that quietness that is only in the water. I'm angry that Dem has let out our secret and I'm scared because I don't know what Dad is thinking behind his eyes. I know what Dem is thinking, and it's obvious there's delight in Mum's eyes. But I can't tell with Dad. It feels like a test and I don't know why.

He lies back down and puts his hands behind his head for a cushion. "Son, you've got plenty of time. You've got plenty of time to work out what you want to do with your life."

No, he's wrong. I've started, I'm panicking because I realize that he doesn't know I have started.

"But I know already, Dad," I insist. "I'm going to be a champion swimmer. That's what I'm going to be."

It's like my words have made the world stop. Except for the radio, the radio blaring out the scores at three-quarter time.

Mr. Celikoglu breaks the silence. "Good, that's good, son. You will be a champion and you will buy us all big big houses to live in." He gently kicks my dad's leg. "You should be proud of your son, Neal, he's a good boy."

I hold my breath. There is a tap-tap-tapping in the pit of my stomach; the source of me is not my heart, it is something else, something even more important than my heart. It is what makes me know I am going to win. I am sure of it, that in everything I do I will win.

"I am," answers my father, peering up at the blue sky, the golden sun, reading my future up there in that ocean of light. "I am very proud of him."

I breathe out.

"Not today, Victor, I'm not putting up with any nonsense today, you hear me?"

Victor wouldn't take off his clothes. He was standing in the change room with his arms crossed, a rebellious scowl on his face.

"Come on, mate." Dan tried one more time. "Get changed."

Victor shook his head and sat down on the bench, his arms still folded.

"Righto, then, you stay here. I'm going in."

Dan quickly kicked off his shoes and stripped off his clothes. As he stepped into his board shorts he noticed Victor slyly peeking across at him. Dan pushed his clothes into his backpack, slung it over his shoulder, his towel and goggles in his hand. "Okay, mate, I'm going out to the pool. I'll see you there."

Victor's response was to stamp his feet and start braying, his roars so outraged and desperate that the other man in the change room left with his shirt still unbuttoned, carrying his shoes and socks.

Dan didn't turn around, he continued walking purposefully to the door.

"Please, please!" Dan was sure the whole pool could hear Victor. "Wait for me, wait for me!"

Dan went back and put his backpack on the bench, and put an arm around Victor, who had tears rolling down his face. "Okay, mate, it's okay, I'm here."

Victor nodded, sniffing, and went to unbutton his shirt but his fingers kept slipping. He stopped, shrugged, and without a word let Dan do it for him.

"Hands up," said Dan, and Victor obeyed, raising his arms like a child. Dan pulled off the heavy cotton shirt. Victor's skin was chestnut-colored, smooth, except for the wiry black briars under his arms and the trickle of flattened hair around his plump belly. Victor stood up and crossed his arms again.

Dan wanted to order him to take off his own bloody track pants, to shout at him, Come on, mate, you can do this. But he didn't want more tears or games. In one motion he pulled down both Victor's track pants and his navy Y-fronts. Victor's shriveled cock, the skin almost indigo there, flip-flopped and Dan caught a whiff of something mustardy, soiled. "Up," he ordered, and Victor lifted one foot and then the other. Dan whipped the pants and jocks from under him, then searched through Victor's sports bag for his swimmers and almost threw them at him. "I'm not putting them on for you. You can do that yourself." Victor sniggered, as if suddenly aware of his nudity, and started carefully guiding one leg into the shorts. Dan pummeled Victor's gear into the bag, then hoisted it and his own across his shoulder.

"Finally," he muttered. "Finally we can get bloody started."

〜〜〜

It was Dan's favorite time in the pool, not yet ten in the morning, the office workers had done their laps and gone, the school buses had not yet arrived. All the lanes were empty except the fast lane where a solitary swimmer, a lithe long-limbed woman, was swimming determined, measured laps.

Dan walked behind Victor as the young man shuffled around the pool to the shallow end. Dan got in front of him and jumped into the water, then held out his hand. Victor was shaking from cold, even though the air in the pool area was humid and lines of condensation were seeping down the windows. Victor leaned over and warily took Dan's hand, then crouched and half fell into the water. Dan pulled him up, and Victor emerged, spluttering, and made straight for the steps out of the pool.

"No, no, mate," Dan whispered encouragingly, wrapping his arms tight around Victor's belly, saying *shhh* into his ear until he relaxed and his hands stopped thrashing. "It's okay, Victor," he said calmly. "You just slipped, but we're in the shallow end. There's nothing to worry about." Victor fell back onto Dan, no longer struggling.

Dan was teaching Victor how to swim again, reminding him how to breathe, when to hold his breath and when to expel it, showing him how to coordinate his arms and his legs, when to push back in the water, when to move forward, how to balance and feel safe in the water. Every time Victor forgot one of the instructions—and it happened often in the hour they had together: forgetting when to fill his lungs with air, misjudging when to kick and sinking under the water—Dan was there, to hold him, to reassure him, to repeat the instructions.

"One day," he'd insist, "one day, you're going to get into this pool and you won't have to think about any of this, you'll just jump in the water and it will be like walking, like breathing. It will all come naturally."

Except he knew that for Victor none of it *could* come naturally. He'd even had to learn how to walk again, had to be taught how to breathe properly. But Dan kept saying that to Victor because he knew that Victor understood that everything could be relearned— how to feel his muscles in his mind and get them to work again, how to remember to inhale and exhale without the assistance of a machine—it could be taught and it could be learned, how to navigate

the world again. What had once been so natural to him that he had
not had to think about it since he was an infant, all those instincts
had had to be relearned after the night he'd picked up two drunk
teenagers in his taxi in the city and drove them to Keilor Park. When
he'd asked them to pay the fare the one in the back punched him in
the head and the one in the front pulled him out of the cab and into
a dark suburban street, where they kicked and kicked and kicked at
Victor's head and chest and balls and cock and back and neck and
left him for dead. After that, Victor had had to learn how to breathe
and move and walk again.

And to swim again.

"He would swim all the time," Prasangi had told Dan the
first time he'd gone to their place to take Victor for a swim. She'd
explained that near their village in the north of Sri Lanka, the sea
was warm and gentle, and they'd loved swimming. Victor's wife spoke
shyly, so quietly that Dan had to lean close to hear her. She'd told
him how Victor had chosen his English name even before they had
emigrated to Australia, even before he'd saved for years to get them
there. "You will teach him to swim again, yes?" she had inquired.
Dan had wanted to tell her that he knew what it was to have to start
over. "Yes," he had replied instead, "I will teach him to swim again."

〰〰

It was the shortest day of the year and the wind was merciless, the
rain falling in diagonal slivers and blades. Dan ducked into Box Hill
Plaza, past the Vietnamese shops displaying their synthetic-looking
pink-and-scarlet slabs of pork belly, ribs and chops, past the Chinese
grocers, the Greek delis, the Asian bakeries, and the food court, and
out onto the street, flipping up the collar of his windbreaker to his
chin, and in the open-air mall he slipped into Russell's coffee shop.

Russell was slouched behind the coffee machine, speaking Mandarin to the new young waiter in his white shirt and black pants. His
face broke into a grin on seeing Dan. "How are you doing, man?" he

chortled. "How is Danny the Greek?" He unleashed a rush of words and the young waiter rushed to the coffee machine.

Russell had started calling him Danny the Greek very soon after Dan had started going to the café. They had fallen into conversation and he'd told the man that his father was Scots-Irish and his mother was Greek. That had made Russell cackle. "A Greek called Dan, a Greek called fucking Danny! Who could believe that?"

"What's so funny about that?" Dan had countered. "It's no more strange than a Chinese man called Russell."

"What do you *mean?*" Russell had seemed outraged. "I know many many Chinese called Russell, many—but Danny the Greek, that's funny!"

Dan sat in Russell's café, drinking his coffee, looking out to the mall, at the rush of people battling the rain and wind and sleet. It seemed to Dan that he had only looked away for one moment, forcing a laugh at some sick joke Russell was telling, but when he looked up and out again, the darkness had vanished and the streetscape was flooded by pale winter sunlight. The wet street outside glistened, and every surface seemed to sparkle.

Russell stepped outside, his hands clasped behind his back. He sniffed the air, peered up at the sky, and turned back to Dan. "It is going to be a very good day, no more cloud."

Yeah, thought Dan, swirling the last of his coffee in the cup, it was a great day to be going to a funeral.

〜〜〜

Until he'd applied for the job with Eastern District Health, Dan had never been to that part of town. Just back from Glasgow, bedding down in his old room at his parents' house, his first priority was to get a job, any job. That would be his chance to start his life again, and starting life again meant work and money, and that meant a place of his own. What had scared him most on coming home was the idea of being a man in his thirties who still lived at home with his parents. He was terrified of coasting, determined to resist the temptation to just lie back, take it easy. Life in Australia could be like treading water—no, even simpler than that, effortless and much more addictive: with arms outstretched and eyes closed to the sun, like endless floating. In time your thirties became your forties and then your forties became your fifties and you'd become nothing more than driftwood. He remembered how when they first got together, Clyde would always say, "That's what I miss about Glasga: at home you cannot float the way people here in Oz do—you gotta get into your boat and start fucken rowing, otherwise you're sunk."

The recollection brought forth an unexpected chuckle. "Ah, you Scots wanker, no one gets away with not rowing," he whispered tenderly to the day. "Everyone has to row, even here."

He had Regan to thank for getting him going. As soon as they had seen her in Nowra, he and Theo had wanted to rescue her, to bring her back home. Nowra definitely wasn't home. She had not long before given birth to Layla and was living in a dilapidated fibro house near the town's ugly industrial area, with the child's father, a bad-tempered twenty-three-year-old called Trent, with a twitching left eye, a Southern Cross tattoo on his right breast, and a terror of fatherhood. He was dealing with it by smoking methamphetamine. One afternoon he had come back from visiting mates, all jittery and aggressive, and had screamed at Regan for inviting Dan and Theo to stay. "But they're my brothers," she'd said, trying to reason with him, and he responded incredulously, "What's that got to do with anything?" Dan realized with dismay that the man was being genuine. He really didn't get it, didn't understand how she could be loyal to family.

Theo had been unable to contain his rage. "What are you doing with him, sis? That piece of shit already has one foot out the door!" Dan had kept his cool but he too was desperate to get her out of there and back to Melbourne.

Regan had shot back at her younger brother, "I know I can't

depend on him but I can't go back home, I can't live with Mum—it would drive me spare."

"But Mum can help you with the baby," started Theo. "You're gonna need her help."

God, thought Dan, now it was Theo who didn't get it. But Dan had understood—maybe as a result of the time he'd spent away from them all. It wasn't that their mother did not love Regan, or that Regan didn't love their mum. But somehow when they were all growing up, their mother's focus had been on the boys; she hadn't meant it to be but it had turned out that way: her sons had dominated her thoughts and attention. *Regan will be all right, I don't have to worry about Regan*: Dan had grown to adulthood hearing those phrases. Regan was no doubt scared that it would happen again, that it would be Layla who received all the attention and Regan would again be sidelined, in the corner, watching it all.

"Regan," Dan had said, interrupting his brother, "you and Layla can come move in with me, we'll find a place together. How does that sound? Would you like that?"

The worry and fear had been instantly erased from Regan's face. In their place had been relief. And for the first time in a long, long while, Dan had felt trusted again.

〜〜〜

Once again the three Kelly children had been living at home, and everyone doted on the baby. Dan had applied for a permanent job while working the night shift in the warehouse of a cannery in Broadmeadows. He'd been scouring the job classifieds in the newspapers and on the net. It felt as though he'd written hundreds of application letters—he'd been upfront about his past, had acknowledged the spottiness of his work history in Scotland, all that cash-in-hand work, the volunteering for disabilities services, and had written briefly but honestly about his criminal conviction and sentence. Few responded; only a couple of agencies even bothered to call him in for an interview. And then one morning he had come in from work to find his sister reading through yet another of his job applications as she fed Layla, the little creature sucking sturdily.

Regan placed the printout down on the table, watching him as he filled the kettle. "Dan," she said, "why don't you put in a mention about the swimming?"

"What would that have to do with getting a job?"

"It could be really useful. It certainly proves you can commit. And who knows, they might want you to take some swimming classes. You'd be great at aqua therapy." Regan was nodding purposefully, her voice peremptory and increasingly excited, so much so that her nipple dislodged from Layla's mouth. "Honestly, you should think about being a sports therapist."

Before Dan could answer, the baby had started to wail. Regan tried to put Layla back on the breast but she would not be appeased.

Dan tickled her tummy and stroked her hair, but the crying continued. There was the sound of the key in the door; their mother was home. She came rushing in and reached out for her grandchild, saying, "Let me show you." Regan passed the baby up to her mother, who cooed and cuddled and kissed and tickled Layla, and soon the baby's sobs had subsided and been replaced with gleeful gurgling. Over his mother's shoulder Dan had looked at his sister and searched her face: sleep-deprived, weary, inscrutable.

In the end, it *had* been his swimming experience that had got him the job. Noah, the earnest absentminded man who interviewed him, had asked whether Dan would be prepared to develop a swimming and aqua therapy program, and Dan had answered enthusiastically. The interview went for forty minutes, and at the end of it Dan had walked out, dazed, into the neighborhood he'd never visited until then; broad-trunked European trees lined the main avenue, the sky was clear, the sun was high in the sky, affording him an unimpeded view down a valley to the cobalt-and-silver silhouettes of the mountains on the horizon. Everywhere he looked, down the small streets, in the alleyways, the shop fronts were covered in Vietnamese writing, while other windows were painted with red-and-blue Chinese characters. He had walked into the first place he'd come to, and ordered three main dishes from a menu half written in English, half in Vietnamese, had eaten till he thought his belly would burst. As he finished his meal, he had come close to praying that he'd get the job and that he, Regan, and Layla could move here, where the worlds of Asia and Australia seemed to collide and merge and be transformed into something close to an idyll.

"Box Hill," his father had said that night, raising an eyebrow. "That's pretty middle class, isn't it?" and Dan had replied, simply, "Yeah, maybe, but I really like it."

Noah had called him the next day. Dan had got the job.

〜〜〜

He opened the squeaking gate and bent down to stroke the cat that was stretching out on the sunlit steps. Regan opened the front door, as if she'd been waiting for him. Layla was in her playpen, and music was softly calling from the small stereo on top of the fridge. It was old-school soul, Otis Redding plaintively, thrillingly crooning that he'd been loving her too long; old-school rhythm and blues, thought Dan, the music our parents loved, the music all of us have returned to.

Regan asked him if he wanted something to eat and he shook his head. He didn't think he could keep anything down today. He was nervous, shaky; his skin tingled. It was more than just nerves. It was real fear, it was anticipation and dread.

"I've got your suit ready." Regan held up the trousers and matching jacket that she'd found last week in the Savers store. She'd also ironed his white shirt. He thanked his sister, leaning down to kiss her cheek, then brushing a finger across his lips and gently grazing his niece's brow. He walked out the back to his bungalow, the air bruisingly crisp. He carefully laid the clothes on the bed and turned on the heater. He sat, placing his hands on his knees, staring straight ahead. The old soul music was still encircling his memory and it stayed with him as he took a moment of peace.

Dennis had found them the house. It belonged to an elderly couple who were retiring to Tathra, up on the New South Wales Far South Coast. Dan's father had agreed to serve as their removalist. Dan's father had always loved that part of the coast and it hadn't taken much for Dennis to convince him to make the long-haul trip. The woman had offered Dennis and Neal coffee before they started loading the truck, and it was then that the man had mentioned that they were looking for tenants.

"My cousin would be perfect," Dennis had replied, so eager to tell them about Dan that the words were jumbled in the mash of tongue, lip, and saliva. "He's got a job just down the road."

The old couple were none the wiser but Dan's father had understood and told them about Regan and Layla and Dan, and asked what the rent would be.

Having the bungalow attached, that small space apart, was what had made it perfect for Dan. Which was why Dennis had been so eager and so excited on seeing the house; he *knew*, he understood.

~~~~

Dan showered, shaved, and dressed quickly. He pulled out the full-length mirror nestled behind the desk, wiped the dust off with a rag. He couldn't quite recognize the man staring back at him in the unfamiliar dark suit, the slightly pudgy man with the furrows at the corners of his mouth, the man who was no longer the boy. He took off his jacket and stood side-on; his shirt seemed to billow above the belt, so he tucked it in again. He wished he had gone to the barber; his hair seemed too long and was uneven at the sides, making his head appear lopsided. He shrugged. It is who you are, he told the mirror, standing so close to the glass that a small mist formed then swiftly dissolved. He put his jacket back on and headed for the tram.

~~~~

Walking up the drive past the wrought-iron gates with their elaborate crest, he found himself automatically heading for the Great Hall, as if he were still the young boy in the striped blazer running up the drive. Only at the last moment did he veer back and make his way to the other side of the quadrangle: the service was of course going to be held in the college chapel. Heavy fat clouds hung low in the sky and there was a light drizzle falling. Dan walked up the steps to the chapel. A man holding a clipboard nodded as Dan approached. "Are you here for the service?" The man peeled off a four-page photocopied sheet and handed it to Dan. There was the date of birth, the date of death, and there was the picture of the Coach, not smiling, staring defiantly at the camera, as if challenging the world.

~~~~

When Dan had first moved to the bungalow in Box Hill, his father had driven over in the truck with the cluster of boxes packed with books, the crate of kitchen utensils, and his bag of clothes, along with furniture Dan and his mother had found at the Brotherhood of St. Laurence on Brunswick Road. Among his things had been a pile of magazines tied up with string. "What are these?" he had asked, and his mother had told him they were from his old school.

Dan had grimaced and untied the string, and his dad had grinned. "I always had a look at them when they came," he said, "just to see what the rich little fuckers were up to. See how they were ruining the world."

"Now, now, Neal," Dan's mother had said. "Some of them are doing good things, aren't they? Working for Médecins Sans Frontières, stuff like that. They're not all fat cats."

"Yeah, yeah," his father had snorted, "some of them are salt of the frigging earth, aren't they?" He had turned to his son. "Anyway, they're all yours, mate, do what you want with them."

What Dan had done with them was put them in the recycling bin, then ring up the college and ask for his name to be taken off the mailing list.

"Oh," squeaked the flustered woman who'd answered the phone, "I'm not sure how to do that, I'll have to talk to someone and get back to you."

Dan had replied, "It's okay. Maybe I'll just change the address you send them to, can you do that?" He was about to make up an address, some fake street, some nonexistent number, a suburb picked out of the air, but then he just recited his own address. They can come here, he thought, and when I move out of here they can be returned to sender or chucked out. They'll never find me again.

That was how he had found out that Coach had died and the school was planning a memorial service. On page five had appeared the same black-and-white image that was printed on the prayer card; the grim-faced man in the open-collared shirt, the man he had not seen for over fifteen years, the man who had wanted him to be better, faster, stronger. The man he had failed.

〰〰〰

Walking into the gloomy vestibule of the chapel, he recognized a few of his old teachers milling around, now elderly men. They all looked past him, over him, and through him. Then there were the younger men, his age—a few had brought partners, one or two had brought their children along—they too looked past him and through him. It wasn't because of his secondhand suit, it was because of who he was and what he had done. He saw Wilco, recognized him straightaway, and raised his hand in an anxious awkward wave, but his hand fell to his side as the tall man looked up, noticed him, and then refuted him.

Danny Kelly did not exist. Danny Kelly had never been there. Danny
Kelly should *never* have been there.

Dan held his breath as Wilco turned to greet someone, and there
was Martin Taylor, heftier now, his hair darker, and with dark shadows beneath his eyes, but it was Martin Taylor, lean and elegant and
confident, still perfect except for the two scars: the pink crescent tick
at his right temple and the long thin line that started just below
his left eyebrow and finished at the corner of his mouth. Dan felt
his hands shaking as the man looked across and there was just a
moment when their eyes locked, Martin Taylor's eyes still gray and
cold. Without missing a beat, Martin continued his conversation.
Martin Taylor also seemed to think that Danny Kelly did not exist
at all.

Dan took a deep, shuddering breath and then he was walking toward Martin, as a half circle swiftly formed around the man,
shielding him from Dan. He walked up to the crowd, he was facing
Martin Taylor and he knew that more than the memorial for Coach,
this was what he had come for, this was what he must do. Dan almost
had to shove aside two brick-backed men to get to Martin, to stand
before Martin; and Dan, words stones in his throat, Dan said, "I'm
sorry for what I did to you, I hope you can forgive me."

There was a piece of mournful classical music playing, in the cold
stone chapel, a harmony of strings, resonant and deep; the music
itself seemed to be weeping. And Martin Taylor finally looked at him,
and then Martin Taylor looked away again, continuing his conversation as if Dan Kelly were not there. As if Danny Kelly had never been
there, Danny Kelly had never existed.

Memories are knives at the throat of Danny Kelly. He turns
abruptly, forcing himself not to run as he hits the steps, as the freezing wind slices at his face. The oval and the school and the sky are
in darkness, the light has been extinguished from the shortest day
of the year as instantly as a candle flame could be snuffed out. He is
almost at the bottom of the steps when he hears a voice calling him,

cutting through the rain and the wind, and he knows it is not a voice from out there in the darkness, he knows he is not hearing things; it is a voice from memory, it is a voice from inside of himself. A gruff accented voice calls to him, so loudly that it cuts through the rain and the night, cuts through the tight ball of shame that is shriveling his gut and his scrotum. The voice says, *Always answer back when you receive an insult*. And Danny stops, Danny turns around, Danny begins walking back up the steps, his head held high. He *is* seething, alive with the fire of hatred, the recollection that he *is* the fastest, the strongest, the *best*. He *is* going to go roaring into that chapel, scattering those smug pricks, going to destroy the lot of them, the whole of Cunts College; I am Barracuda, I am Danny Kelly, and I am faster than you all and I am stronger than you all and I have survived you all—and it is this that stops him, makes him remember: he has indeed survived them all but he is not Barracuda. He is not the fastest, not the strongest, not the best.

So he did not tear up the stairs, he climbed them slowly, humbly, and took a seat in a pew at the back. He was there to pay his respects to the man he had failed. He was doing that. He was there to apologize, to the man and to the boy.

He did not hear the service; instead he spoke silently to the Coach, thanking his ghost, and laying his soul to rest.

You didn't always have to give it back. And in that cold, somber chapel, Dan Kelly discovered that there were some things that you could not be forgiven for, and those were the things that you carried into the next life, if there was such a place; and if there was no next life nor any God, the consequence was the same: if you were not forgiven, you would die with regret.

〰〰〰

As he crossed the quadrangle to take his last ever walk down the bluestone drive, he heard his name being called. Dan swung around. A man was descending the chapel steps.

There was something familiar about the man now standing before him, overweight and moon-faced, perspiring even in the cold, his head shaved close to hide his waning hairline. The man held out his hand, not looking through him, not refuting him.

Dan breathed out and examined the man more closely. "Morello?"

"Yeah. You remember me?"

Though the man was no longer a boy there was still something youthful in his gleaming dark eyes and the way his face crinkled as he smiled.

"John?"

"Yeah, that's right." John fell into step with him as they started down the drive. "I'm glad you came, Danny, I'm glad you came to pay respects to Torma. He was a good man, wasn't he?"

Dan wasn't sure how to answer that, not sure he knew anything about the Coach except that he'd wanted Dan to be a champion.

"Yeah, I guess he was." They were at the gates and Dan indicated the tram stop. "Good to see you, John," he said. "I better head home."

"You didn't drive here?"

"No."

"Where do you live?"

"Box Hill."

"Look, I'm heading off to Frank's house—there are some things I need to check there. Why don't you come with me? I'll drop you off afterward. I'm in Mont Albert, not far from you at all."

Dan was trying to remember something about Morello, something more than the fact that he'd been one of the group of boys who'd teased him when he first went to the new school. He remembered then that Morello had always been a follower, always sucking up to Taylor and Wilco, always a little arsewipe. He'd been an average swimmer with little talent or drive, and had only lasted in the squad for that first year. Then he just dropped away from Dan's memory.

He couldn't think why the Coach would have had any time for him, why Coach would have bothered with him at all.

"Nah, mate, thanks, but I should get home."

Morello's easy grin was widening, becoming a smirk. Dan wished he could wipe it off his face. He wanted to get away from him, from all of them; he'd come to farewell Frank Torma, that was enough. He didn't want anything to do with that life anymore.

"Mate, I think you should come with me and see the house." Morello's eyes were still bright, but his mouth was set in a thoughtful serious line. "After all," he added, "a third of it belongs to you."

Dan struggled to make sense of the words. "What are you talking about?"

"Come with me, I'll explain." Morello was holding tight to the upturned collar of his jacket, protecting himself from the wind now beginning to howl down the side street he was turning into. "Come on, my car's here. I'll tell you everything."

～～～

Morello's car was a brand-new Audi that smelled of leather. The roads were heavy with evening traffic, outside was dark and cold, but Morello had put the heater on and the car was soon warm. Morello could not stop talking. Dan let the words flow over him, let them run around the cabin of the car.

Morello was railing against the snobbishness of their old school, abusing Taylor and Wilco. He couldn't stand them, he kept repeating, he couldn't bear to be with them.

"You were a man back there," he said, glancing quickly at Dan, "going up to apologize to that prick—that was a brave thing to do. Those fucking people just live in their own world, they don't have time for people like us—wogs like us," he added with a laugh. "I tell you, Kelly, it's been years since we were at school but they still fall into using surnames, because that's what you did, the surnames mattered. I was so glad when I heard you'd punched out that prick, and I wasn't the only one. There were a few of us who high-fived when we heard what you did to Taylor."

For the first time since he'd got in the car Dan opened his mouth, found the words. "What I did to Martin was one of the biggest mistakes of my life—no, *the* biggest. I regret it every day." Dan wanted to escape from the clammy claustrophobic heat; he just wanted to be out in the clean night air. "You were a prick too, Morello, let's not forget."

"We were all pricks," said Morello, merging the car into the long queue of traffic waiting to turn right onto Barkers Road. "You too, Kelly, bloody Barracuda—you wouldn't even look at me at school. You'd just look right past me like I didn't exist."

The throbbing at his temple, the incessant sound of the heater, the sweat under his collar; Dan needed to be out of the car, to be in open space.

He was about to say that to Morello, but before he could speak, Morello said, "You and I were kids, Danny—we can't blame ourselves for all that. We were just trying to survive it, weren't we? You wanted to be the best swimmer in the world and I walked up that fucking drive for six years promising myself that today, today, I wasn't going to look like a poor wog, I wasn't going to smell like the poor wog whose mother worked in a fish-and-chip shop, whose father never had an education. I did that for six years, Danny: I lied about my father and I lied about my mum, I never let anyone come over to my place so they wouldn't have to meet my parents, so they wouldn't know who I really was. I'll never forgive myself for that."

The boyish charm had gone. The man was glaring out into the night, his teeth gritted, his knuckles white on the steering wheel.

"We were kids, mate, we were just kids." It was only when John breathed out that Dan let himself exhale as well.

~~~~

And there it was, Frank Torma's house, untouched, unchanged. There was the dark narrow passage, the small bedroom at the front, *his* bedroom, the one Danny had always slept in. The crammed tiny living room, the small kitchen out the back; the fridge was new but the bench tops were the same. One cupboard door was hanging off its hinges; the stovetop was black from the congealed ancient grease.

Dan went back to the first bedroom, his room. It was exactly as he remembered it, except the dusty photographs which had once hung next to the door had been placed on the bedside table, as though Coach needed to be closer to them, had wanted them to be the first images he awoke to and the last things he saw at night.

Dan was there, a young boy, fourteen, in brand-new Speedos with a towel around his shoulders and a smile a mile wide. The boy seemed about to leap out of the frame, having tasted victory. There he was, framed in the Coach's bedroom, forever unchanged. There was another photograph, of another young swimmer, fair-haired and smaller than Danny; and another, more recent photograph showed a boy wearing their school uniform, his dark, wet hair slicked back, holding up a small blue ribbon, a look almost of gratitude on his face as he stared proudly at the camera. Next to the three photographs was the one of the unsmiling old couple.

"That's his mum and dad, in Hungary somewhere." John had sat down on the bed.

"I know." Dan didn't need Morello to tell him *anything* about that house.

But John seemed oblivious to Dan's gruffness. "I've got a photograph of my grandparents that looks exactly like that one." He gave a quick self-deprecating laugh. "*Paisans* are *paisans* are *paisans,* eh, wherever they're from?"

Dan couldn't bear Morello's assumption of camaraderie. He looked around the room again. He'd used to think that room meant freedom—he once thought it offered him a possible future. There were the four photographs, the dresser, the bedside table, an old weathered cupboard, the bed, and the thick dusty curtains drawn across the window. There were no books, no papers; it could have been the room of a monk, thought Dan. It could have been a prison cell.

John picked up the photograph of Danny and examined it. "He always talked about you. He said you were the best swimmer he ever coached."

Dan silently begged John to put down the photo. He couldn't bear looking at that photograph. He knew it was of him but he couldn't find himself in it. "Well, he was wrong, wasn't he? I failed him."

John put the photograph back and said, "Funny—that's what he always said about himself when it came to you. He'd always say to me, after a few drinks, that he'd failed Danny Kelly."

As John said this, a sudden gust of savage wind whipped at the window. For a moment the curtains separated and Dan saw a panel of battered and gnarled plywood fastened with masking tape to a broken pane. The wind died away and the curtains fell back into place.

John Morello was a stranger; the distance from the shadowy boy to the man before him was equal to the distance between who Dan was now and the boy in the photograph. But in front of that stranger, Dan allowed his body to break and to finally breathe. Dan allowed himself to cry.

He sat huddled on the bed, his hands shaking, the force of the grief bursting through in waves. His body seemed relieved of all solidity, as if he had become a swimmer again at the end of a marathon, the outpouring coming from deep within himself, as if all that was inside him had been expunged, as if the inside were the outside. All he was conscious of was that he couldn't stop the tears, the bestial howling. He must have frightened John, or more likely disgusted him, as he'd fled the room. It was just Dan, alone, in a room that had reminded him of his boyhood glory but was now the prison cell of adult disgrace; and he knew that when he'd glimpsed the future all those years before, it was indeed such a room that fate was putting in store for him.

The breathing, in and out, one of the first things he'd learned as a swimmer; it helped.

Afterward, spent, sitting on the Coach's bed, it was as if there was nothing left inside him: no flesh and no muscle and no bone.

John had not disappeared, he came back into the room carrying a tea towel, which he handed to Dan. "Sorry, mate, this is all I could find." His voice was gentle.

Dan scrubbed at his face, at his shirtfront. He screwed the tea towel into a knot. John sat down beside him. The two men were breathing in unison.

"Do you own your own home, Danny?"

The question was so unexpected that it made Dan laugh. He shook his head.

"Well," Morello continued, "it will take a bit of time, of course—it'll be months before all the probate paperwork is finalized, and we'll want to get a good price for the house." John's voice was back to normal now that he was discussing property and the law, on safe ground; his tone of boyish jocularity returned. "It's a small place, Danny, but it is in Hawthorn, the river's just a few blocks back. These old cottages, especially when they're brick—fuck me, mate, I don't want to get your hopes up, but I reckon we can get just shy of a million for it. That's roughly three hundred k for you, mate. Of course, the bloody taxman will get his share, but still, that should at least give you a fifty percent deposit, eh? That's what I would advise, mate, property." It was as if Dan had never broken down, as if that had happened in another time, in another space, away from the world.

"You married, Danny, you got kids?"

Dan opened his mouth, then quickly shut it. He just shook his head.

John proudly flashed the thin gold ring on his left hand. "I am. My wife's name is Dora. We've got a beautiful little boy, Troy, and we're trying for another. Best thing that can happen to you, mate, having kids. That gives you perspective, shows you what really matters in this world."

"I'm not going to have kids." Dan straightened up, surprised how weight had returned to him, how he felt anchored to the ground once again. He turned to John. "Why me?"

"What do you mean?"

"Why did Coach leave me this house?"

John waggled a finger. "Hey, mate, don't get too greedy. He left *part* of his estate to you—a third. The estate is divided between three parties. Initially it was four, yourself, a man called Ronald Crane, another man, Joseph Hanna, and the fourth share to the descendants of his two sisters and brother back in Hungary. But Hanna is dead, and the will specifies that if one of the parties is deceased then their share is returned to the others." John shrugged. "There's some money, of course, some super, some stocks and bonds, but not much—the GFC took care of that—but whatever money there is goes to his family back in Europe. They probably deserve it, poor bastards."

He leaned over to tap the wooden bedhead three times. "We're lucky here, Danny, this country just sails on, impervious to the shit that the rest of the world is drowning in. Jesus, no wonder any bastard who gets on a boat wants to come here."

Dan didn't want to hear it. He wanted answers. "But why would he leave it to me?"

"Mate, I don't know, I can only guess. The only things you have in common with the other two are that you were all scholarship boys, and you were all trained by him. Crane was a student of his in the early eighties, Hanna was there after us." John sounded tired. "Hanna offed himself, got in a bad way, I think, from talking to his family—drugs maybe, who the fuck knows? They're a big Leb family, out in Westmeadows. I feel gutted for them, what they've been through. They didn't have much, and I think Joseph was their great white hope."

John was shaking his head. "Can you imagine being a Lebo

Mussie having to deal with the pricks at that place? You ever heard of him?"

"No."

"Thought you might have, he was a bit of a wunderkind for a while there in the pool and then he got into the Commonwealth Games and fucked it up—just didn't have what it takes." His voice trailed off and he lowered his head.

He thinks he's offended me, thought Dan, he thinks he's hurt me. But Dan was thinking about a Lebo kid, a Muslim at that school, what they would have thought of him, how he would have needed to be the strongest, the fastest, the best, just to survive, just to walk that corridor every morning, to hold his head high.

"I used to call it Cunts College."

John's head tilted up. "What?"

"Our school. I used to call it Cunts College."

John collapsed into hysterical laughter, then pulled out a handkerchief to wipe his eyes and blow his nose. He sat up straight. "Crane's got a family, he's doing sports medicine, he's all right. The money will be useful. He's up in Brisbane, wanted to be here for the service but one of his boys got sick."

John tentatively raised his hand, then placed it gently on Dan's shoulder. "Torma thinks he failed you all—for what it's worth, that's my theory. He wanted to train a world champion, but he never managed that." John's hand slipped off Dan's shoulder, and the two men were once again sitting apart.

"And you? Don't you get anything? I mean, it sounds like you were the closest to him of any of us."

John's smile was rueful. "Yeah, I ask myself that too. He always said that he hated lawyers, that we were scum—maybe that's why, maybe he thinks I've got enough." John's voice lightened; he threw up his hands in an exaggerated shrug. Like a boy, thought Dan, you could see the boy in him still.

"And he's right, we're doing okay, me and Dora, we don't need the money. It's because I wasn't a good enough swimmer, simple as that. That's what mattered to the old man, being good enough. I guess you and Crane and Hanna were golden boys." John's eyes were now teasing, his tone mocking. "You do know that, don't you, Kelly? You and Taylor and Wilco, you were fucking golden boys."

He rose, looked down at Dan. "I should get going. Come on, I'll drive you home."

"I think I want to stay."

But John was shaking his head. "I'm not sure if I can let you, mate. Officially I'm the executor of this estate and I don't feel comfortable giving you the keys yet. Sorry, it sounds officious, I know, but that's me with my legal hat on."

"That's all right, I understand."

John took one last lingering look around the room. He seemed to be about to speak, but his mouth stayed closed.

"What were you going to say?"

"I was going to say I'll miss the old bastard, but that's not exactly true. In the last few years I'd come by, every six months or so, more out of duty than anything. I owed him. He protected me from some of those bullies we went to school with. But he was a lonely old bugger, by the end all he wanted to talk about was being a boy in Hungary, even started talking to me in Hungarian from time to time. He was a sad old man. I wish I could say I'm going to miss him but it wouldn't be true. To be honest, mate, him being gone is a bit of a relief." John was drumming his fingers on the old bureau. "Men like that, they're not much use, are they?"

Dan couldn't remember anything about Morello—the boy's smile, his adolescent body, one word they had exchanged—even though they had been on the same team, had showered naked together every day, had swum together; he couldn't recall the boy's form or face or body at all.

"Okay, mate," said Dan, getting up and putting on his jacket. "Let's get going."

John dropped him off. The last thing Dan said to him, just as he was getting out of the car, after they'd shaken hands in farewell, was, "John, you're a good man."

John gave a short chuckle. "No, mate," he answered. "No, I'm not. I'm just a fat suburban lawyer. I'm just a soft bastard doing all the right things. I've even enrolled Troy at Cunts College—that's how much I go with the flow."

The night was so cold that Dan had to sit for ages in front of his small heater with his suit jacket on, with it buttoned to the collar. He sat in front of the heater, staring into the orange electric glow, the rain splattering and beating against the shingles of the roof. He sat and dreamed about what money could do. He imagined a house, two rooms, a short walk from the station and the shops. That was what money could do. He thought of going back to Japan, going to China, really reconnecting with Luke; he could travel anywhere, he could learn about different worlds. He imagined a brand-new car, and travel, and bricks and mortar. In the pit of his stomach was a glow, he could feel it, a tiny flame that began in the center of himself and spread and flickered and warmed his blood. Dan took off his clothes and put on track pants and a jumper, but even in that midwinter chill he didn't think he needed them. The glow he felt inside himself would keep him warm. This was what money could do, this was how it could protect you.

In the back pocket of his suit trousers he spied the folded pages. He took them out, unfolding them to stare at the face of the Coach, then turned the prayer card over and for the first time looked at the words printed on the back. They had been recited at the service but he hadn't listened then, he hadn't taken them in. All he was conscious of at the service were the looks that went through him, the eyes that did not see him at all. But now he read the words of a poem by Walt Whitman. *I see a beautiful gigantic swimmer swimming naked through the eddies of the sea.* At first the letters, the words, the stanzas, remained shapes and line and curvature; they didn't make sense—*His brown hair lies close and even to his head, he strikes out with courageous arms, he urges himself with his legs, I see his white body*—but he went back to the beginning and this time Dan's mouth was forming the shapes and sculpting the words: *I see his undaunted eyes, I hate the swift-running eddies that would dash him head-foremost on the rocks. What are you doing you ruffianly red-trickled waves? Will you kill the courageous giant? will you kill him in the prime of his middle-age?* The glow inside him receded and he saw a man battling the sea, saw him as if from above, as if Dan were a creature of the sky, gliding over the sea, bearing witness to this swimmer—*Steady and long he struggles, He is baffled, bang'd, bruis'd, he holds out while his strength holds out, The slapping eddies are spotted with his blood, they bear him away, they roll him, swing him, turn him*—and then the creature he'd become dived deep into the sea, and the creature was the swimmer and the swimmer was at the mercy of the uncaring monstrous ocean, *His beautiful body is borne in the circling eddies,* and the ocean was as beautiful and sublime as the possibility of the world could be: *it is continually bruis'd on rocks, Swiftly and out of sight is borne the brave corpse.*

Dan was in his room, looking at the photographs on his wall: of Theo, of his parents, of Regan with Layla, of Demet and Margarita at Uluru, Luke and Katie on the Great Wall, Dennis hugging Bettina, himself between his granddad Bill and his nan Irene. The last flickering light of the fire within him was extinguished.

He was alone in the small bare room, the prayer card had fallen from his hand. He was the swimmer, the old man, he was the Coach and he was Danny Kelly. The electric purr of the heater, the sonic whisper of the light globe above his head, they returned him to the room and to himself. There was a gnawing tightness in his stomach, there was a heaviness in his bladder, a pain in his left wrist, which he'd knocked against a cabinet at work a few days before. It was breathing, in and out, it was a return.

He whispered to the cold night air, "Thank you, Coach." Dan knew now what he had to do.

Dan rushed home the next day to pick up Regan and Layla; they crossed the river and headed toward his parents' house, and now he had not a spark but a fire in his belly, with purpose there. This was what the Coach had wanted from him, needed from him; this was what he had failed to deliver, but now he could because now he knew how to be what he needed to be.

When they arrived, everyone was seated at the kitchen table, having been summoned there by Dan. Dennis was there as well, having an after-work beer. They all looked startled as Dan impatiently shepherded Regan into a chair, and then he sat too, so he could address them all. He couldn't wait, he blurted it out, telling them about the inheritance, the money he would have and the future that could be built on it. His words jumped and danced and slipped and he had to go back and repeat them but he finally got it out, it finally made sense—he could see it in their stunned faces. Breathlessly he came to the end of his speech, his face red, his eyes shining: "And I want to give it to all of you, I don't want any of it. I am giving all the money to all of you."

His breathing was heavy, his face expectant.

His father, showing control in his voice, was the first to speak. "I can look after my family, Dan, I can do that and I have done that. You keep your money."

Dan's mum was looking down at the table, "You don't have to do this, mate," and Theo too then said, "Yeah, Danny, what the fuck are you doing this for?"

Regan was holding Layla; she stopped kissing her baby to say, "You don't have to look after us, Danny. We didn't ever expect you to look after us. You don't owe us anything—is that what you think, that you owe us?"

None of them could look at him, and Dan thought, I am ensnared in this earth, and I have never felt so distant from all of you.

Dennis cleared his throat. "You're not listening to him, this is what he wants to do for you." He took Layla off Regan's lap, held her tight. "That's all I'm saying. Listen to him. I'm gonna take the baby to the next room."

Once he'd gone, Regan exploded, "We're not taking your money! It's yours, not ours."

Dan was treading water, Dan could see the shore but he was caught in the rip and being taken farther out to sea and he knew this was how you disappeared, this was how the water could take you down. He slumped back in his chair. He was going under, he was disappearing.

Words formed, he could see them shift and unfurl just above the waves, he could see them dancing just where the sun touched the water.

He straightened, looking at his father. "I do owe you. And I am grateful and you are the only family I will have." As he clutched at the words he dropped under the rip and broke free. He was swimming toward the shore as he spoke. "I want to do this for what I owe you and for the love you have given me, and because if I do this, I feel I can begin again, I can start life again. So please, please, for me, please take this gift."

His mother reached across the table, took his hand. "We never wanted anything from you, baby, don't you understand?"

He breathed in and let the words out as he exhaled. "That's exactly why I want to do this." He was still looking at his father. "This is the one way I think I can be a man." He tightened his grip on his mother's hand. "I don't know if you can understand, but I want to be a man, I want to start living, I just want to grow up."

He had tried, but he could see that his family weren't convinced. He could feel the weariness seeping into his bones, an acid starting to consume him from inside. It was not finished.

"Don't you understand? I haven't earned this."

This time it was his mother who was furious. Her rage spat and flared from her eyes. "You have, Danny, you have. I was there, all those mornings, all those afternoons—all that effort you put in, I was so proud of you. Don't you dare say you haven't earned this."

"Not on my own, I didn't earn this on my own."

They were all looking at him now. And he realized they were seeing him for the first time.

And though other things were said, so many things were expressed, so many arguments and objections put forward that he had to counter, in the end it was agreed: they would consider the gift. They finally accepted that, for Dan, the gift was worthless if it couldn't be shared.

On the drive back home there was fog and drizzle, there was the thick blanket of night, but Dan thought that he could see far into the horizon and up through the cracks in the vault of the sky to the stars. He believed he had glimpsed the infinite. He was in the sky and it was as clean as being in water.

〰〰〰

Dan was in town, being buffeted by an uncompromising Antarctic wind racing up his sleeves, lashing at his neck and cheeks. He escaped by ducking into an arcade off Bourke Street. He was hunting for a birthday present for Omran, his godson, Demet and Margarita's son. The gust of hot air that flushed through him as he stepped into the narrow mall had, momentarily, the force of a furnace. But once he stepped off the vent the heat subsided and he was embraced by the soupy warmth of the artificial heating. He took off his windbreaker and hung it over his arm.

Margarita had been offered a scholarship to continue her PhD in a college in Southern California.

"I'm going to be a kept woman," Demet had laughed when she'd told Dan about it. "I can't believe my luck."

But he had heard the hint of guilt underlying her joy and had interrupted her. "You deserve it."

Demet and he would never assume good fortune for themselves.

Martin certainly had never understood that, but then neither had Clyde nor Luke. But Demet got it.

"You deserve it," he insisted.

He passed a small shop front in the overheated mall, its window filled with jewelry and trinkets. Among them he spied a cluster of small brooches, each of them with a face of shiny blue stone marked with the sharp black outline of an eye. He knew it would be perfect, absolutely right for Omran, and a gift that both parents would appreciate. An eye to ward off evil, an eye to *give it back*.

He bought the present, put on his jacket, and prepared himself for the jolt of returning to the freezing air outside.

〰〰〰

Darkness had enfolded the city, and he was shaken by a recollection of Glasgow as present and sharp in his mind as the final image retained when awakening from a vivid dream. He had to steady himself against the solid wall of an office tower to reassure himself that he was indeed in Melbourne. And within a beat of his heart, between breaths, the memory of the other city had gone and the ground beneath him was once again firm. He knew where he was. He walked to the end of the street, heading toward the underground station at Melbourne Central, but as he did so, he was thinking about Clyde. It had been a long time since they had been in touch; he would send an e-mail tomorrow, just a short note. It was through Clyde's city that he could bring forth memories of his former lover, as if the map of the city was a mirror that reflected the man. Clyde and his city belonged to one another, it was impossible to think of one without the other. That was true belonging, Dan acknowledged.

He decided against going underground. The wind swirled around him, bringing a chill but it was also bracing, exhilarating. He pushed against it, almost running into it to stop being pushed back by it. It had the power of an ocean current. It howled around him.

Dan stopped. A poster in the window of a travel agency had

caught his eye: a double-decker bus, a black cab, London Bridge, Buckingham Palace, and the Tube. And at the bottom of it, the five thin intersecting rings of the Olympic Games. That old unsettling spasm—he could sense its echo, but from a distance; all he needed to do was breathe out and it subsided. In a different history, he would be going there, he'd be a month away, all he'd be thinking and dreaming about would be the Games. He saw his reflection in the glass, his pale face, the thick stubble on his cheeks and chin, the messy hair in need of a cut, and it occurred to him that even if he had been the strongest and the fastest and the best, he would not be there, he could not be there, he would already be too old for *there*.

Dan stepped back from the window with a grin, dug his hands deep into the pockets of his windbreaker, and kept walking. At the lights on the corner of Little Collins Street he found himself next to a throng of students, all talking excitedly about the night ahead. They were so young that they could brave even the remorseless wind, the merciless cold. Except for one of the women, who wore a mini-skirt and the flimsiest of tops; she was hugging herself, her teeth chattering, her shoulders trembling. One of the boys grabbed her, nestled her into an embrace, and she gratefully fell into him. The lights flashed green and Dan was carried across the street with them all, the boy and the girl still huddled together. He found himself swept along by two currents, the ferocious dance of the wind and the steady pace of the group of students. He could hear their chatter about drinking and school and this nightclub and that bar, but he let their words fall without collecting them—he did not need them to make sense. The elfin shivering girl reminded him of Katie the first night he'd met her, in the pub. And the sinewy tall boy who was embracing her, protecting her from the bitter night, all finely muscled limbs, he could be Luke. And another of the boys, flaxen-haired, with freckles on the bridge of his nose, he could have been a shaggier version of Martin Taylor, and if the girl next to him had been wearing less makeup, she could be Demet. There was a boy on the edge of their group, who had let his hair grow long; he walked ahead of the others, diffidently but purposefully weaving through the oncoming crowd. Dan was tempted to reach out to him, to touch him lightly on the arm and say, I recognize you, I see myself in you.

He slowed his pace and the group of young people was carried away from him, merging into the crowds walking up and down Swanston Street, falling away into the shadows.

Climbing the stairs to Flinders Street station, Dan was jostled by the throngs coming the other way, emptying out into the city. There were the young and the very old, boys wearing makeup and girls with football scarves looped around their necks. The faces of the whole world were around him, people from every continent, and they were going into the treacherous primal night. He allowed himself to swim against the tide, not to challenge it or overcome it, not to conquer it. He inserted his travel card into the turnstile, passed through, headed toward the platform.

On the journey home, Dan sat huddled between a beefy council worker sleeping with his head slumped back and a sharply dressed young man talking loudly into his smartphone. Dan looked out into the darkness, to the reflection of his face in the grimy glass of the train window. He stared so intently at the ghostly specter of himself against the sea of darkness that everything else dropped away. He was alone in his world. Belonging: that was something he had once had and now it was gone. He turned away, sifting through the patterns of light and color till they formed shape; he became aware again of the phlegmy snores of the council worker, the inane posturing of the man on the phone. The air in the carriage was fetid and stuffy; he wanted to be back in the sharpness of the cold night. Everywhere he looked, people were playing with their screens. They didn't seem human. The humid air was suffocating.

He breathed in and he breathed out.

The faces all locked in concentration on their phones: Dan wondered why it had seemed so unsettling just a moment before. Belonging, he knew now, was the wrong question. The contest between country and nation, the tussle between home and roaming, here and elsewhere, all the relentless claiming and the ever-shifting mapping, none of it could settle the question that had mattered most to him since he'd found himself moored on dry land: was he—Danny Kelly, Psycho Kelly, Danny the Greek, Dino, Dan, Barracuda—was he a good man? He needed to answer that first, and then all would fall into place.

He perceived his shape, his self, emerge from the black of the shadows outside the speeding train.

He belonged to water. And water, he was now convinced, was made of the same substance as the sky. Dan rolled his shoulders; he missed the touch of Clyde's kisses on his tattoo. In the feel of his lover's lips on his inked skin, that too approached a sense of belonging. He had trouble recalling the man's face, but he knew how to revive that memory of touch. And the conviction that Clyde had been a good man.

The train moves forward and he is still, he allows the machine and its engines to carry him. He is listening without hearing, watching the world without seeing it. Dan closes his eyes. He imagines the ceaseless motion carrying him from one end to the other of this enormous island of infinite horizon. He draws the arc of the end of this world in his mind, sees the train hurtling off the tracks, leaping into the sun, diving and plummeting, into the depths of the ocean. But the train has grown wings, its arc is the pearl thread of moonlight banishing its shadows from the night. The train has sprouted wings and it is soaring.

The water goes on forever, I have my feet in the sand and I am sinking, the waves are coming in and going out and I am sinking and I laugh because I think that I am going to fall over and Dad says oops you go and he holds me and lifts me up and the sun is close and I put up my hands and I think I can reach it and then Dad swings me again and again and I am flying in the wind and I am scared that he is going to toss me in the water. No no Dad, I scream, don't chuck me in the water. He holds me tight and his skin is itchy rough where the sand covers his shoulders and he is patting my back saying, No no I'm not going to do anything to you little fellow. I'm looking back at the beach, Mum is lying on the big big red towel, Regan is next to her picking up sand in her hand, she is picking up sand and it is falling through her fingers picking up sand and it is falling through her fingers. Mum is sitting up and looking at me she is waving at me and I stop crying and I wave back. She has a big big belly a big round belly where my brother or my sister I want it to be my brother is growing, she lets me touch her big big belly says Can you feel your sister or your brother growing every day he is growing. I wave back, my chin is on my dad's shoulder he is standing up and I am taller

than anyone at the beach my dad is the tallest man on the beach he is
the giant on the beach and when he holds me up I can touch the sun
the sun is close to me when he holds me up and I look up at the big
big sky and look out to the big big sea and the sun and the sky and
the sea they are going to forever. Put me down, Dad, put me down
and he laughs, I slide down, my feet in the sand I can sink back in
the sand the water that comes in and goes out that water he says is
the tide and when the tide goes out it is going to sleep and when the
tide comes in it is hungry for little boys and it will EAT YOU ALL
UP! Come in, Danny, come into the water with me and I say No, no,
I don't want the water to eat me up and he laughs and says It won't
eat you up, the tide is out now. But what if it is waking up and the
water is hungry I can feel it around my feet it is grabbing at my feet
it could take me in and I will be in its mouth like the boy in the whale
and I say No, Dad, no I don't want to and he is holding my hand and
says Come on, I won't let go Danny and he is holding me and the
baby waves are coming around my feet and then the mummy waves
are coming around my middle and it's so cold so cold that I say No no
Dad I don't want to and he says It's okay Danny I won't let go, and
I am pulling and fighting him because when the daddy waves come
they will pull me into their mouth and they will eat me and I scream
No no no and Dad lifts me up again and his skin is cold and wet but
he holds me closer and I am higher than the daddy waves and they
can't get me and he is walking into the water and we are walking
into the tide but I am being held by my dad and he is bigger than the
tide he is stronger than the tide and the tide must know this because
when the tide reaches my father's middle it stops and is still and the
water is calm and Dad says Just lie there, lie on the water, I'll have
my arms beneath you, I won't let you go, Danny, I promise, and I lie
on the bed of the water like I learned how to lie on the bed of the pool
and the sun is nip nip nipping at my eyes but Dad is in front of it and
Dad is so big that he can make the sun disappear and Dad is smiling and his skin is wet so it shines like metal and the pictures on his

arms and the picture over his heart they are lines as blue as the sky
and I close my eyes and the water carries me and Dad's hands are my
pillow and they are my mattress and he says I'm going to just let go,
for a second, just for a second, Danny, but I'll catch you, I promise
I'll catch you and I take a deep breath and his arms are gone but I
am still lying on the water and he is laughing and smiling down at
me bigger than the sun and he says See, Danny, you don't have to be
afraid of the water, do you, do you want to try and swim, and those
words make me scared again and I fall into the tide and the tide gobbles me up and the tide is in my eyes and my nose and my mouth and
I am fighting the tide as it gobbles me up and Dad has lifted me, Dad
has lifted me to the sun. He drops me again and my feet thrash and
my hands hit and hit and I know that I have to hit the tide if I can
just keep hitting the tide it won't get me so I thrash and I bash and
I punch and I am moving on the bed of water, and I am flying, it is
flying, this is what it is, it is leaping and gliding and rushing and
the tide can't get me and Dad is calling out Not so fast, mate, not so
fast, but I'm not scared anymore and the tide can't get me, I am in
between the tide and the sun, if I keep thrashing I could reach the
sun and I want to be as high as the sun I want to be as high as my
dad and he is behind me he is next to me he is flying past me and he
calls back Can't reach me, can you, mate, and I try so hard oh I try
so hard to beat the tide to win against the tide and I'm hitting and
thrashing and my legs are tired and my arms are sore and my eyes
are stinging from the water but I won't stop and I have reached him
and Dad grabs me, he holds me tight, my face is against the picture
on his chest and my cheek is lying on the hairs and the skin of his
chest and I am breathing so hard that my heart is my breathing and
Dad holds me and says This all belongs to you, son, all this belongs
to you, he is holding me with one arm and the other arm is stretching
out over the sea and stretching up to the sky and it touches the sun
because when I look up I can see the flame burst through his finger
where it has touched the sun and he says All this, Danny, all this

belongs to you. I breathe in and out till my breath and my heart separate and Dad holds me and carries me back to the beach where Mum
is sitting up and her giant belly is so big it looks like it will pop just
like a balloon when it gets too big, and Regan squeals because Dad
is still holding me and I am dripping from the sea and the drops fall
on her and she squeals again and she looks up, she looks up but she
can't see me because Dad is holding me and he is the tallest man on
the planet and he is so tall that I am above the sun. He is a giant and
I am his son and we are both, together, stronger than the tide and we
are both, together, bigger than the sun and higher than the sky. He
is holding me tight, so tight that I am sinking into him and we are
standing still but standing still we are flying. He is standing between
the sun and the sea against the sky and though we are standing we
are flying. Together, we are flying.

ACKNOWLEDGMENTS

The writing of this novel began when I was fortunate to have been a recipient of a residency at Cove Park, Scotland. I would like to thank Cove Park, all the staff, and all my fellow residents for their support and encouragement.

Many thanks to Lisa Forrest, Dean Ayton, Sophia Pappas, Rick Halsam, Andrew Nette, Marilen Tabacco, Bill Sultan, and Tim Sultan for sharing their stories and experiences.

I am fortunate as well to have the support and encouragement of everyone at Curtis Brown Australia; at Rogers, Coleridge and White; at Smartartists; and at Allen & Unwin.

As ever, I am so very grateful for the support of my family, of Jane Palfreyman, and of Wayne van der Stelt. *Muchas muchas gracias*. And much much love.

This book is dedicated to Angela Savage, a fellow-traveler in this literary life. Thank you, Ange, for giving me that most gentle but most purposeful of shoves in the right direction.